AUNTIES OF VASANT KUNJ

Anuradha Marwah is a professor, playwright and novelist. Her wide-ranging publications also include poems, essays, articles and reviews. She and her partner live peacefully in Vasant Kunj, Delhi, but they complicate their lives by saving trees and feeding community cats. *Aunties of Vasant Kunj* is Anuradha's fourth novel. You can reach out to her on:

Instagram: @author_anuradhamarwah
Website: anuradhamarwah.com

'Brilliant and incisive, Anuradha Marwah succeeds in hilariously bringing to life a whole cross-section of society, ranging from liberated single to conventional married, represented in the microcosm of Vasant Kunj.'
—**Manju Kapur**, author, *Difficult Daughters* and *The Immigrant*

'*Aunties of Vasant Kunj* is as much a mirror to the inner longings of women and the need for identity as it is a reflection of the wider universe it seeks to depict. Anuradha Marwah writes with profound empathy, a nuanced wit, and a sharp sense of observation that can only be the terra firma of a skilled and superior novelist.'
—**Murzban F. Shroff**, author, *Breathless in Bombay*, *Waiting for Jonathan Koshy* and *Third Eye Rising*

'Anuradha Marwah's greatest strength lies in depicting the hearts of women. By the end, they feel like old friends. We are deeply invested in their lives, empathizing with their struggles and cheering for their small victories.'
—**Shilpi Gulati**, filmmaker and academic

'Anuradha Marwah traverses the lives of middle-class India through *Aunties of Vasant Kunj*. Heart-warming and evocative, it leaves you smiling as you meet familiar characters confronted with challenging circumstances! A book that will make you smile, laugh, and pull at your heart strings!'
—**Sanjoy Roy**, entrepreneur of the arts

■

Praise for author's earlier books

Idol Love

'Anuradha Marwah is erudite, has a way with words and compels attention.'
—**Khushwant Singh**, *Hindustan Times*

'Anuradha Marwah's *Idol Love* presents a chilling picture of an Indian dystopia in the twenty-first century.'
—**Antonia Navarro-Tejero**,
The Essentials of Literature in English Post-1914

'This is an intricately crafted story, and marvelously innovative in the use of English to suggest Indian languages—the author indicates subtle differences between the Hindi spoken by the Dasas and the Urdu of the Drohis without using a single italicized desi word. A novel of ideas, *Idol Love* is an ambitious risk to take at this moment when fiction by Indian women seems largely to swirl gently around the vicissitudes of quotidian life.'
—**Nivedita Menon**, *The Book Review*

'To call *Idol Love* a novel of ideas is to overlook its more literary merits; to focus only on its artistic elements is to minimize its insightful examination of an important moment in contemporary Indian history that threatens to dominate all other notions of India. *Idol Love* is Anuradha Marwah's second novel and is a

sharp dystopia of the consequences of India's hard turn to Hindu fundamentalism in the 1990s.'
—**Uppinder Mehan,** *South Asian Review*

The Higher Education of Geetika Mehendiratta

'Anuradha Marwah's remarkable first novel, intelligently crafted, touchingly told. Free from stylistic affectations, her fluent prose is devoid of the subverting impact of pleonastic frills—a virtue few debutante-writers can claim to possess. Reflecting a bilingual sensibility, what emerges as a very obvious concern is her desire to be recognized as a natural storyteller.'
—**Bishwadeep Ghosh,** *The Sunday Times*

'What is not to be taken for granted are the clear flashes of insight into character, the incisive use of dialogue to pad out the even tone of the narrative style, so that Geetika becomes unforgettable not just for her polysyllabic name (which she hates) but because she has been so believably and recognizably put together—the new Indian woman coming to terms with herself in an Indian society from which she can expect no quarter and to which she will grant none.'
—**Carol Andrade,** *The Metropolis on Saturday*

'Not many Indian writers have dared to use the M-word and one appreciates the candid talk, especially because it is almost impossible for women writers in India to tear away the strait jacket of social-prudery and feminine grace imposed on them—more so when the narration is in the first person.'
—**Antara Dev Sen,** *The Indian Express*

'The book is wholly modern and yet Indian enough, is fluently written and easily read.'
—**Muriel Wasi,** *Hindustan Times*

Dirty Picture

'*Dirty Picture* by Anuradha Marwah deals earnestly with difficult realities. Set around the Ajmer sex scandal of the early nineties it goes beyond the news to discover reasons and processes. Having grown up in Ajmer, this professor of English Literature at Delhi University uses her immediate knowledge to write a moving and sensitive tale.'

—**Nandini Nair,** *The Hindu Metro Plus*

'Peeping out from every corner of India are the exploited stories of Reena and Bharti that come to us day after day in the form of news clippings and voyeuristic news cameras. The author's matter of fact approach to caste stereotypes that haunt India, i.e., the great Hindu–Muslim divide couples with the stories of the protagonists to create disastrous consequences.'

—**Preetika Mathew,** *And Persand*

'While most contemporary feminist writers see no reason to transcend their comfortable urban location to engage with poverty, male domination and issues that trap middle class women in small dusty towns, Anuradha Marwah presents an unflinching picture of two sisters who become victims of their of their own mind set in her third novel *Dirty Picture*.'

—**Richa Bhatia,** *The Indian Express*

'To weave in fact and fiction, biographical and imaginative elements and structure a story that will hold the readers' interest could not have been an easy task.'

—**Purabi Shridhar,** *Femina*

'There is ambition, desire, politics and much more in this novel about small town India. An interesting read.'

—**Ramya Sarma,** *DNA*

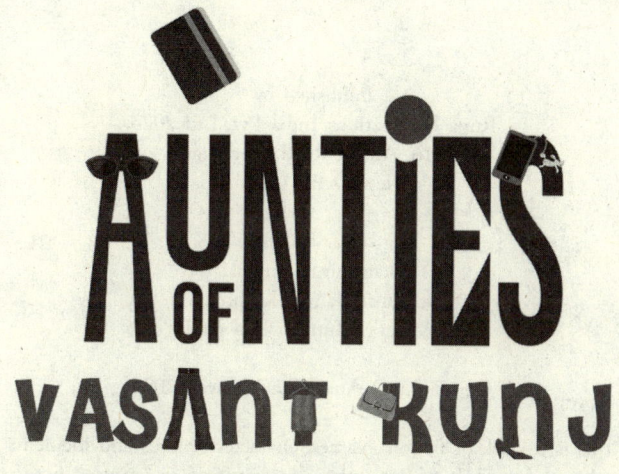

AUNTIES OF VASANT KUNJ

Anuradha Marwah

Published by
Rupa Publications India Pvt. Ltd 2024
7/16, Ansari Road, Daryaganj
New Delhi 110002

Sales centres:
Bengaluru Chennai
Hyderabad Jaipur Kathmandu
Kolkata Mumbai Prayagraj

Copyright © Anuradha Marwah 2024

This is a work of fiction. Names, characters, places and incidents are either the product of the author's imagination or are used fictitiously and any resemblance to any actual person, living or dead, events or locales is entirely coincidental.

All rights reserved.
No part of this publication may be reproduced, transmitted, or stored in a retrieval system, in any form or by any means, electronic, mechanical, photocopying, recording or otherwise, without the prior permission of the publisher.

P-ISBN: 978-93-6156-092-7
E-ISBN: 978-93-6156-332-4

First impression 2024

10 9 8 7 6 5 4 3 2 1

The moral right of the author has been asserted.

Printed in India

This book is sold subject to the condition that it shall not, by way of trade or otherwise, be lent, resold, hired out, or otherwise circulated, without the publisher's prior consent, in any form of binding or cover other than that in which it is published.

A Saturday in May

Three Women

SHAILAJA watched the undulating progress of her blue second-hand refrigerator astride two glistening shoulders. Perspiration was running down her face as well. The top floor was going to be a scorcher. Setting up home in a third-floor apartment of a building that didn't have a lift wasn't going to be easy.

Her 'pocket' had fifty blocks of four four-storeyed buildings each. These buildings were built around a small square. Each block, thus, had sixteen flats that diminished in area and price from bottom to top. Viewing the block the first time through the window of her newly rented top-floor flat, she had at once designated it as the dry step-well or *baoli*.

A small, fat boy riding a tricycle wheeled around her feet as she stood her ground at the bottom of the step-well. The boy sounded the hooter on his tricycle; Shailaja flinched. It was a loud report and a sputter, something suggesting cosmic diarrhoea. The boy was delighted. Every time he caused the upset, he grinned.

'You like children?' a woman asked. She was evidently the noise-polluter's mother and had emerged from the ground-floor flat of the building opposite hers.

'Ah, yes! How did you guess?'
'All women like children. You are moving to the top floor?'
'Yes.'
'What does your husband do?'
'I am not married.'
'Oh!' said the woman.
There was silence.
'Divorced?' she asked.
'No—yes,' hazarded Shailaja.
'You alone?'
'Yes.'

The woman tut-tutted. 'It's so sad! I could make out from the way you were looking at Ganesh.'

The tricycle came dangerously close to the two women and one of the rear wheels grazed Shailaja's big toe.

'Ouch!' she squealed, more in surprise than pain.

'Ganesh, come here, I will break your cycle,' roared the tricyclist's mother. 'Are you hurt?' she asked.

'Not much,' Shailaja insisted on replying, even though the woman was no longer looking at her.

Ganesh hooted from the other end of the square.

Shailaja rubbed her toe vigorously. The woman bent almost double to take a look at her feet.

'Nothing happened. Thank God. Boys of this age are devils, no? Come in and have a cup of tea. We are all like family here.'

'No, no, I should keep an eye on things,' Shailaja replied, somewhat disappointed that retribution was not going to strike. She had already started rehearsing for the role of the beloved 'aunty' of the neighbourhood children in her head: No, no, please don't hit him. One shouldn't hit children; it creates psychological complications. But the opportunity had been denied to her. The mother–son duo claimed centre stage again.

'Yes, that's right, you must. Just as well you don't have too much stuff. Now when we moved in, I told Ganesh's father to get his office staff to help, but we still lost so many things,' the woman was saying rather pointedly.

Shailaja had resolved that she would cultivate a pleasant working relationship with her neighbours in Vasant Kunj, but her unfamiliarity with the social codes of this colony was becoming obvious to her.

For thirteen years, she had shared a *barsati* with her boyfriend Ranjan in upmarket Defence Colony. Sitting atop a huge terrace, the two-room apartment gave a sense of transience. Usually, the residents of barsatis would be foreigners on short-term assignments, single people who travelled frequently, etc. Ranjan had told her that barsatis were afterthoughts in architectural conception, constructed years after the two- or three-storeyed main houses had been built. The word 'barsati' is intended to make one think of torrential rains. Indeed, they were built as temporary structures where the occupants of the main house could enjoy the showers and the cool breeze that followed. But economic considerations, born out of spiralling property prices, had made house-owners rent them out, and sometimes even sell them.

The concept of living in the temporary barsati had seemed very romantic at that time. In her imagination, it would always rain in Defence Colony. She had visualized herself on a merrily creaking wrought-iron swing, humming, while Ranjan made *adrak wali* chai in the makeshift kitchen. 'Our relationship is abiding, home can be anywhere,' she and Ranjan used to say whenever anyone asked them about the future and whether they intended setting up a permanent home. But when Ranjan fell in love with a starlet ('A whirlwind, Shailaja'), it was their relationship that had revealed itself to be ephemeral at the first gust.

So here she was, adrift in a Ranjan-less place, an alien place where this quintessential neighbourhood aunty dared to be uppity with her. It suddenly occurred to her that if she hadn't taken what her father had deemed the 'wildly unconventional step' of moving in with her boyfriend and instead agreed to an arranged marriage, this is the kind of place she would have been occupying for the last thirteen years. She could have even become this loud, plump woman, with her champion-tricyclist son, boasting about her microwave. In fact, didn't some of the other lecturers in her college go on about their homes in the same way? Shailaja regarded her unsolicited companion with something akin to fascinated horror.

'—and six dinner sets,' the woman was saying. 'I still have boxes that I haven't opened, and we've been here ten years. Teenu and Ganesh were born here; Neeru, my oldest, was born when we were still in our family home in Old Delhi. Divorce affects children the most. Grown-ups can always begin their lives again. It's good you don't have children. But you know, it is bad to let the childbearing years go fallow. This is why so many women need to go to hospitals in order to conceive.'

Shailaja bridled at the phrase 'childbearing years go fallow', spoken in Hindi with the certainty of self-evident truth.

'You know, there is another way of looking at it. All women don't want children,' Shailaja said.

'Ultra-modern women, must be! But ninety-nine out of hundred—'

'No, not only these days! Long ago—in the Mughal period, for instance—the concubines of the emperor practised a way of family planning. There are documents. It was also believed that having children ruined the woman's figure. Actually it does, doesn't it?' Shailaja hit back.

There was silence as the new adversaries took stock of each

other. 'Must be so for concubines, not for ordinary women. For wives, it is different. Men want women to be young and pretty forever. But ageing takes place, no? If there is a child to hold the men, they stay put. Otherwise they begin straying.'

The rapier-thrust was startling. The plump woman had unknowingly stabbed her where it hurt the most. Shailaja was knocked back.

This morning, while she was vacating her Defence Colony 'home' and the tempo was being loaded with her meagre belongings, Ranjan had appeared to give her a scrap of paper with names and numbers of a couple of his 'associates' in the neighbourhood who could be 'helpful in an emergency'. The perpetually bored-looking landlady also emerged just then from her palatial main-house dwelling, ostensibly to say goodbye, but in reality, Shailaja suspected, to see for herself the inevitable end of the bohemian live-in relationship. Destabilized by the landlady's sudden smirk, Shailaja, without thinking, put the paper with the phone numbers into her newly bought fridge. 'That's not cool,' an embarrassed Ranjan tried to joke. 'So that your generous gesture doesn't begin to stink—like other things,' she had retorted sharply, making the situation worse for both of them. Was the real reason for the split so transparently obvious in Vasant Kunj as well? Greying, thickening, middle-aged woman...

'I'll go in and send some tea for you. I have to finish cooking for the evening. It is our fifteenth wedding anniversary today,' said the victor of the joust, gathering her juvenile delinquent in a tight embrace and thankfully removing him from the scene. 'I am Mrs Nilima Gandhi,' she finally introduced herself.

'Shailaja Sharma. Congratulations, Mrs Gandhi,' she said.

Perhaps she too should start her new life here with this awful hair dye, Shailaja muttered in her mind. Mrs Gandhi's hair was raven black except at the roots, which shone silver. Such obviousness might help her blend better in Vasant Kunj, a space that seemed to have no truck with subtlety in either looks or conversations. 'You're so natural, Shailaja. The grey in your hair is beautiful like the rest of you,' was what Ranjan had said when the first strand of grey appeared in her hair. The whirlwind starlet who had swept Ranjan away had strawberry hair, flamboyantly coloured.

There was a shriek behind her that pulled her out from her musing. 'The entire weight of this corpse is on my shoulders,' one of the movers was complaining. Her sweaty workforce, now bearing the steel almirah, had managed to wedge itself into the second turn of the staircase. 'You are not lifting it high enough,' the mover on the lower level shouted. 'Am I a *pehelwan* or what?' the one at the higher level sneered. 'I'll ask the contractor to replace you with someone with muscle,' the underdog growled.'

'Do so. If I leave it now, you'll be buried under it, and I will then use it as your coffin,' threatened the guy at the top.

'Call the contractor,' they demanded, almost together. It seemed like a dire emergency, so Shailaja hollered in alarm. The contractor emerged from the van and took stock. In a calm and slightly amused tone, with the air of an expert negotiator of narrow staircases, he stood at the bottom of the stairs and ordered them to turn the almirah to the side. It hung precariously over the step-well momentarily. 'It is all about the correct angle,' he said. The ascent began again.

Five years ago, the coffin imagery would have set off Shailaja and Ranjan. They used to be like children at a circus. In fact, they had got together because of a fairly standard joke that she had narrated shyly at her first all-night party outside the university.

'Why is Jesus Christ considered to be a Bengali?'
'Because he lived with his parents till he was thirty; he thought his mother was a virgin; and his mother thought he was God.'

Unexpectedly, the entire gathering on the terrace responded with shouts of laughter at the young college girl's witticism. The spirits were high and the raconteur charming.

'Shailaja, don't you want to check out whether I'm Jesus Christ?' There had been rum on his breath, sweet as hell.

'Want a girl?'

A young woman with a tray bearing a solitary cup-and-saucer and a plate of Marie biscuits, arranged in a circle, had appeared at her side, her knowing eyes sizing her up, her hissing tone conspiratorial.

'No,' barked Shailaja, too shocked to keep her voice low. Wasn't this supposed to be a decent middle-class colony? Ranjan hadn't thought so. 'Wasn't Vasant Kunj in the news some time ago for a murder? Hope you've checked out security, Shailaja,' he had said to her just before the landlady appeared.

'Just too touching, Ranjan! Don't kill me with your solicitousness, please,' she had been dismissive.

Such propositions were made to Ranjan in places like Thailand. He would narrate anecdotes about being pursued by ladyboys with just the right hint of distaste. Did it mean that because the new stylist at Sunflower Salon had cut her hair too short, unscrupulous women-pimps of Vasant Kunj were identifying her as...?

'My mother is looking for a job,' observed the young woman shaking her head sadly. 'You already have a maid?'

'Yes—no,' replied Shailaja, things falling in place. Embarrassed, she picked up the cup of tea and took a big sip.

'My mother is a very good cook. And to be able to be

near me, she will charge very little—much lower than the rate.'

'Ssssend her tomorrow,' whispered Shailaja, her tongue scalded by the hot tea.

'Tomorrow is Sunday, she has to collect her salary from all the houses she works in. She'll leave one house and start your work on Monday.'

'Why does she want to leave that house?'

'Too much work. There are six people, and dirty utensils pile up like anything. She wants to work for a single woman.'

'Alright,' replied Shailaja.

The girl smiled and urged her to try the 'biskut'. Suddenly she seemed to remember something and rushed back into the flat she had emerged from.

'Come what may, Rajni will always try to find somebody to foist her mother on. The old woman can barely walk,' said a sharp voice. Shailaja turned and saw the disapproving face of a woman, her hair tied neatly into a bun.

'Mrs Gandhi has served you tea? You could have easily had it at my place. I am on the first floor, one floor below you,' the new lady complained.

'Oh yes, of course!' replied Shailaja, surprised at herself for sounding almost apologetic.

'I'm Mrs Jain. You are…?'

She told her.

'Are you working?'

'Yes, in a college,' Shailaja answered.

'Your workers have broken my pots, Shailaja,' Mrs Jain finally came to the point.

'Oh, I'm sorry, Mrs Jain.'

'They will have to be replaced. Such careless men, they walked right into my rubber plant and zinnias.'

'Oh! The staircase is rather narrow and they carried all that heavy stuff,' Shailaja felt her face stretching into an abject grin. This woman managed to have that effect on her.

'Shruti Mathur, who was in the flat before you, would always inform me before taking delivery of anything big. Such a nice, considerate girl! Had I known that you would be moving in, I would have removed the plants from the landing. The rubber plant is ruined. Rubber plants are so expensive these days.'

There was silence as she fixed Shailaja with an accusing look.

'Oh, of course, I am so sorry. May I compensate you?' Shailaja asked nervously.

'No, no. God has given me enough money. Our family has never needed to ask anything from anybody,' the lady's voice rose in indignation.

The supplier of girls reappeared like a genie and stood by morosely with her empty tray.

Shailaja's face burnt with embarrassment. How stupid of her to offer money and insult her neighbour the very first day!

'You settle down and replace the plant at your leisure,' Mrs Jain continued, thankfully at a lower pitch.

'I am very sorry that this accident happened,' Shailaja replied automatically, and wondered what replacing the plant meant. Was she to grow one on her terrace and nurture it to an ideal height?

Mrs Jain nodded, as though partially mollified. Her face still looked disapproving.

'Very careless men,' she repeated. 'Making such a racket all afternoon! I couldn't get a wink of sleep. Rajni, your mother will work for Madam?'

Rajni nodded while Shailaja wondered whether she should politely enquire why, when jolted out of slumber, did Mrs Jain not bother to rescue her invaluable rubber plant.

'Tell her she will have to work properly, not like you. Mrs

Gandhi says you come late every morning,' Jain admonished Rajni. 'Madam goes to work, so your mother will have to handle everything. Working women these days don't do anything at home.'

Mrs Jain reminded her of somebody. Shailaja racked her brains. Yes, the teacher-in-charge of the English department in her college. 'I'm sorry you'll have to pull your weight, Shailaja. I personally don't think so... but there is a feeling in the department that you're not really committed to the profession.' This was while she was handing her the new course, Popular Fiction, that apparently nobody else in the department was prepared to teach. 'It's full of light readings,' she had added, wrinkling her nose. 'But you had argued in favour of it at the department meeting, so you can teach it.'

'She—a big problem, always complaining about everything,' said Rajni as soon as Mrs Jain's back was turned. 'I will send my mother on Monday. Tonight and tomorrow, you order food from Chimney. Momos are seventy rupees a plate.'

In her ground floor flat, Mrs Gandhi was instructing Bahadur, the cook, to put finishing touches to the special anniversary dinner. He had come in only at half past six, having been sent to the market to get grapes by her mother-in-law when he should have been assisting her.

The kheer was ready; only water-soaked dry fruits were left to be added to it and also some powdered green cardamom seeds. 'Just a pinch,' she told him.

The mutton-mince koftas were fried and had to be added—very gently—to the tomato gravy that needed to simmer on the stove for at least fifteen minutes. 'Don't turn on the stove full flame,' she said. 'And remember not to sprinkle any coriander leaves on it.' Sunil disliked coriander in meat dishes and it had been a real challenge to find a substitute for it. The mint leaves she had found as replacement were not very fresh— Sunil might point out that they were yellowed; he could be quite critical.

'Onions have to be cut very fine and fried till brown and crisp. Take care that they don't burn. The peas pulao is already sitting in the rice cooker. Don't overcook it or the taste will spoil. Sprinkle the fried onions last of all,' she said as Bahadur began to chop the onions as if he had a train to catch.

'You have to make the children's dinner before this and then Mummy-ji's,' she reminded him. Bahadur knew that her older daughter didn't like koftas and the two younger children would find them too spicy. He also knew that her mother-in-law was vegetarian. But he had a way of looking put-upon and confused if there was any extra work to be done.

'I have soaked *rajma*, and you can do the usual potato chips as well for the children,' she added before beating a strategic retreat. Mummy-ji was staging an entry into the kitchen. Whenever the old woman found her instructing the cook who came in twice a day, in afternoons and evenings, or the full-time, all-purpose maid, she got very excited and began to interfere by giving contrary instructions of her own. Mrs Gandhi knew from years of experience that the evening cooking was far from over and that she would have to apply herself again at a more propitious time.

Her mind ran to the new arrival in the colony as she came out to the verandah that overlooked the step-well and provided a panoramic view of the flats around the square. Mrs Gandhi perched there for her evening surveillance of the block. It had a deserted air; all the women must be in their kitchens. Shailaja must have finished moving in hours ago. She could see her flat clearly from her verandah.

Poor, lonely woman! Nobody to speak to; nobody to cook for. Why had her husband divorced her? Must be because she hadn't had children. Suddenly, the lights in Shailaja's flat turned on.

What would she do alone in the flat all evening? pondered Mrs Gandhi.

She squinted her eyes, as if to peer into Shailaja's apartment. Was she unpacking those few cartons? It seemed she possessed very little by way of furniture, crockery and kitchen gadgets. She was dressed very simply too—black kurta and orange printed salwar—like Shruti Mathur, the journalist who lived there before her. These single and divorced women rented the top-floor flats because they were the cheapest. But then, the black wedge-heel sandals Shailaja was wearing were Italian. Mrs Gandhi recognized the distinctive design. Who even wears imported footwear while moving house?

And her hair was cut stylishly too... Although what was the point if one didn't take the trouble to dye the greys? Shailaja probably had more money than Shruti. Sunil was bound to ask many questions about her. Men were all alike, weren't they? A woman just had to be single to get their interest. 'Nilima, why don't you call Shruti also for the *kirtan*?' he would say. 'If Mrs Malhotra and all the other women from the building are coming, why leave her out?' He would insist on calling her every time they had a kirtan, even though Shruti invariably made an excuse for not being able to attend. Once, she had even made a face when Mrs Gandhi offered her *prasad*. She would have liked to point her rudeness out to Sunil, but he was always busy offering to carry something or the other up the stairs for her. As though Shruti was old or disabled! To top it all, the thankless woman didn't even have the courtesy to come and say goodbye to them when she left. Sunil had been surprised too: 'Has Shruti left already? I didn't realize she was going away this month. Didn't she leave a forwarding address? You should have taken it from her in case an important letter or something comes for her.'

Shailaja seemed different. For one, she had talked much more to her than Shruti ever had. Also, she looked affectionately at Ganesh. Should she take up some koftas for her? Mrs Gandhi regretted not asking whether she was vegetarian or non-vegetarian. It would have been a good idea to try the mutton-mince kofta on someone beforehand. For the first time, she had used raw papaya in it, like they did in Lucknow. Or she could just take up some kheer.

Just then, she saw a delivery boy from Chimney, the eating outlet, enter the courtyard on his moped. She stopped to see which flat had ordered Chinese. It was still early for dinner. The boy took the stairs in the building across hers and ran all the way up to Shailaja's. So, Shailaja had decided not to cook. The gas stove and a whole carton full of provisions were all there; Mrs Gandhi had seen the movers taking them up. Shailaja too was just like Shruti, who used to buy all sorts of fancy provisions and order in five evenings out of seven. Why were these single women so wasteful and lazy? How much time did it take to cook for one person? Mrs Gandhi tut-tutted her disapproval and made for the kitchen.

It was full of smoke. Bahadur had burnt the onions, just as she had feared. 'Mummy-ji told me to make a vegetable too; I got distracted,' he said by way of explanation. The next hour was spent in procuring more onions from the corner shop and getting them fried just right. 'I am not going to leave anything to you from now,' Mrs Gandhi said to Bahadur after the meal was ready at last. 'I am thinking, if I have to do everything, what's the point of employing a cook?' she threatened for good measure.

After he left, she sank into the sofa. She had tasted a spoonful from every dish to check the seasoning—everything was perfect. Sunil should be coming back any minute; she had asked him to come early. After all, it was a Saturday, and he had not refused, as he did almost always, by saying there was too much work.

It was a usual evening in all other aspects. Rajni had brought Teenu and Ganesh back from the park and was getting them changed. She would be giving them dinner soon. Neeru was about to return from her tuition. In fact, shouldn't she have come back by now? But if Mrs Gandhi called her, the headstrong girl would only get irritated, like her father. 'I am just next door. Why do you keep calling me!' Mrs Gandhi felt a little tense. There were simply too many pressures on her. What if she too started ordering food from Chimney, like Shailaja, to get some respite? It was a wild thought that, strangely enough, calmed her.

But then something happened just after eight in the evening that drove Shailaja, and everything else, completely out of Mrs Gandhi's mind. She got a call from her husband's office.

Mrs Gandhi sat down on the sofa after the two-minute conversation. With some effort at composing herself, she dialled a number. The few-second conversation only served to induce a panic attack. She felt weak; she couldn't breathe. She decided she needed to get out of the house. With a superhuman effort at pulling herself together, she took a bowl of the kheer that had come out exceptionally well—in spite of Bahadur chopping the dry fruits with the same knife he had used for the onions—and rushed out. All this, without seeing to Ganesh and Teenu's dinner or stopping to snap at her mother-in-law, who was mumbling something about modern women having one foot out of the house all the time without a care as to where their adolescent daughters were roaming around at night. No, she wasn't going to Shailaja's. She was going to seek that woman with the strange name who lived in the building across, also on the top floor. Di—Dinshee, she thought her name was. She worked for women's... em... empower or something. She must have returned from office by now. She had a daughter (so surely a husband somewhere). Her daughter was Teenu's age, and they often played together. She would ask her what it meant—the information that made her droop and almost faint on her wedding anniversary. Yes, Dinshee would know for sure.

'Controlling women and their sexuality has been the bedrock of patriarchal systems like arranged marriages.' In the Vasant Kunj step-well, where aunties congregate, the maker of such a statement would have been sniggered at for being 'cracked' in the head. While Mrs Gandhi was standing guard over home and hearth and Shailaja was moving in, Dinitia or D<small>INI</small>, as she preferred to be called, had travelled very far from this setting—literally 20 kilometres—into a world where such a perspective could be presented in relative safety. She was at the India Habitat Centre, building up her argument in a conference where the cognoscenti were discussing the track record and future scope of the Protection of Women from Domestic Violence Act, commonly called the PWDVA, which had come into force a decade or so ago.

Dini was quoting a scholar she admired greatly. She had first read Veena Talwar Oldenburg while doing a Master's in Social Work, and it had changed the way she thought of marriage. She was now of the firm belief that women needed the strongest legal fortification to be able to survive marriage.

Dini began to present her findings on domestic violence in a low measured voice. She described the world of the *basti* through the eyes of the women she had rallied into a group. She enumerated case studies of rampant alcoholism, routine rape, and systematic sadistic abuse by husbands and by other men in the home. With a lump in her throat, she described an instance of resistance that had especially moved her. There was a cough and a splutter at the word 'resistance' from the audience. It was terrible the way vocabulary was being sanitized in such a gathering as well, Dini thought to herself. It must be a disapproving bureaucrat. She went on nevertheless, 'To protect her pregnant daughter-in-law from drunken rape, the mother had started to give her son food laced with a local sedative whenever he came home drunk. Bonding between women can pose the most effective challenge to domestic violence. This women-friendly Act, even though it might have been diluted considerably in practice, continues to provide this opportunity.' Dini concluded with the recommendation that NGOs working with the PWDVA should especially encourage women to talk about sexual relationships. There was more coughing and some shuffling as well at that. Irritated, she decided to go all out. 'The hidden war on women's bodies should come out in the open,' she asserted. 'Men cannot keep going scot-free.' She walked back from the rostrum to her place in the large conference hall with the feeling that she had presented her case rather strongly.

Once the conference broke for lunch, she met responses she had expected: some commendations, but many more doubts and challenges.

'In the village where I work, it is the schoolmaster who first heard about the PWDVA and began to talk about it,' said

Radhey Shyam—RS, as he was called. He managed an NGO in Banswara, Rajasthan, and she held his work in high esteem. He had a PhD in rural communities and globalization from the esteemed Jawaharlal Nehru University.

'I'm sure he would prove useful in your work,' parried Dini.

'But don't you think it is important to include men in these discussions about sexual violence? I mean, if one consciously excludes men from such discussions, wouldn't it just alienate them?' he persisted.

'It is important to get the women to talk first,' replied Dini. Would women even come out with the kind of stories that had made her shiver if it was a mixed gathering?

'Frankly, I feel you are putting too much emphasis on sexual aggression. All Indian men, all these men in your basti—they are not rapists. There are also good sexual relationships there,' RS continued.

Why must he look like this at her and speak about good sexual relationships!

'I am saying that too much routine sexual aggression is going unaddressed in India,' said Dini a little weakly.

'Are you saying there is no sexual aggression in the so-called developed societies?' RS argued back, sensing his advantage.

'I don't know why this comparison is even called for. We can't be defending sexual aggressors of the Nizamuddin basti or Bhunswaar,' Dini fought back.

'Banswara, Dini,' he said, suppressing an inadvertent smile at the anglicized Tamil inflexion in her pronunciation of the name of his village. 'All I am saying is that there are other kinds of violent acts that are equally serious. I mean, like breaking a woman's nose. At last, there is a law that has created the forum to talk about such cases. Earlier, the police would say that it was a domestic matter. But last month, we took such a matter to the village elders. The schoolmaster reasoned with the husband, told him about the law and made him admit his mistake.'

Dini sighed. RS did some pretty amazing work with a small radical outfit. But his sensitivity to gender issues was sorely inadequate. She wondered why the man in RS's village had broken his wife's nose. Nothing to do with sexuality? Of course it was a deeply Freudian act. Does RS really think that such a couple's sexual relations were unproblematic?

'He hasn't touched her since then, you know. It has been three months,' he continued.

'Touched her?' interjected Dini, unable to stop herself.

'Beat her. Really, Dinitia!' he exclaimed exasperatedly. 'It can be a bit obsessive to look for sexual reasons everywhere.'

Dini felt her cheeks grow warm. It was so typically male to suggest that a woman was sex-obsessed if she dared to talk about sexuality. Even RS hadn't let go of the opportunity.

'Have you spoken to the victim?' she challenged him.

'Of course. She told me that she had no complaints now. You know, it is possible to bring about rapprochement if we deal with domestic violence upfront. All that is required sometimes is for other men to give the aggressor a good talking-to and a stern warning. You people want to read all sorts of meanings into what is basically a case of reactive behaviour arising out of an economic system that castrates the lower-class, lower-caste man.'

'Who are the "you people", RS?'

'Highly qualified feminist women working for international NGOs,' came his reply like a shot.

He got her; he knew she wasn't confident about the grassroots impact of her high-profile NGO. What he didn't realize was that his gaze on her while talking about good sexual relationships in the bastis was having an unusually strong impact on her.

'All I want to emphasize is that we shouldn't underplay sexual aggression, which has been overlooked for years and years,' she replied bravely.

'There's hardly any danger of that in such gatherings. But Dini, I'm not sure that the PWDVA can be used to create the kind of open forum for women you are recommending. Ultimately the complaints are dealt with by the policemen and the lower courts. Anyway, no point in my going on,' said RS. 'How's Maithili doing?'

'Growing up into a really stubborn little miss!'

'Why am I not surprised?' RS smiled and his eyes seemed to glow.

Dini said her goodbye hastily and moved on to talk to other delegates. RS had been asking her out for coffee rather obsessively, and she did not want to offend him by refusing yet again.

Soon after she got into her Uber, she began to feel sheepish. She had been acutely conscious of RS all afternoon. What was it with her? Why was she letting him get under her skin in this manner? She had even spluttered while introducing him to some new recruits of her NGO. Didn't she know rural partners with all sorts of strange, clunky names? But this was a fellow activist with a dark, glowing complexion and smouldering black eyes whom she had known for years. Why did she react so strongly and then left so precipitately that she did not even take the time to talk to the delegates she had corresponded with in advance? This was a conference she had been waiting for. She wanted to exchange notes with the Nari Shakti delegates from Uttarakhand. The organization had formed some women's groups that were experimenting with wedding songs. They remade traditional songs, rewrote some lines, making them naughtier, more provocative. She wanted to discuss the methodology of popularizing these radical songs within the community. But RS had driven all this out of her mind. Why did she let him destabilize her like this? With all her intellectual resources, she should have been able to handle a drop-dead handsome man with minimal gender sensitivity in a more effective manner.

Coming back to herself, Dini realized that she did not really need to get back to office. She changed the destination on her app to Vasant Kunj. Today, after months, she would have a couple of hours of free time as Maithili was going to return late from a birthday party.

■

Dini unlocked her flat with a feeling of anticipation. It was not often that she had the luxury of solitude in the evening. Perversely, she began to think how relaxing it would be to run a bubble bath, soak in it, and reread the second-hand copy of *M for Malice* she had picked up recently. Anyway, as there was no bathtub in her bathroom or, for that matter, in most flats of the parched Vasant Kunj neighbourhood, she decided to use this time to finish off some pending chores. This was just a fantasy persisting from her youth, she told herself sternly. She had always been a voracious reader of novels. As a child she had started with Enid Blyton's mysteries, Secret Seven and Five Find-Outers, but soon graduated to feminist crime fiction—Sue Grafton, Sara Paretsky, Linda Barnes, Josephine Tey and Kate Atkinson. Her alternate lives!

'Must you waste time on all this?' her father would protest instinctively, seeing her immersed in the latest paperback she had got issued from the library.

Dini hummed to herself as she began sorting out her

cupboard. She was singing Raga Hindolam. Like all good Tam-Brahm girls, she had learnt music as a child. With the flame-coloured *kanakambaram* flowers in her hair and a sandalwood mark on her forehead, she used to go to the music teacher in the colony thrice a week with other 'South Indian' girls in Matunga, Mumbai.

She looked like any of them, but a secret part of her had always recoiled from tradition. Her mother had given her a strange, exotic name, Dinitia; intuitively so, she liked to think, even as she kept trying to mainstream her into the community. 'Ma, you look like an Anglo,' she would remonstrate if Dini didn't put oil in her hair and plait it. 'Will anyone believe you are a Brahmin girl?'

Dini looked at the black-and-white portrait of her mother that graced her bedroom wall. Amma had been a typical traditional housewife on the surface. But Dini had, on multiple occasions, found Mills & Boon novels—with their embarrassing covers of garish lovemaking—hidden behind the drum of rice in the kitchen. They had never talked about the books or about the oppressiveness of a household that didn't allow a wife to enjoy reading romances in front of her husband. Dini, for her part, had grown up as an ideal daughter who topped all her courses and, to her parents' obvious relief, never went out with boys. Her refusal to marry in a time-tested manner had come as a huge shock to both of them: 'No, Appa, I will not meet the suitable *boy* who lives in San Jose and earns so many dollars!' By then, Amma, the secret reader of romances, had been wasting away, dying of cancer. 'Why are you doing this to me, Dini-ma?' she had implored weakly, wrenching at her heart.

Dini frowned, working swiftly and efficiently, bringing her light, summery clothes to the front and tucking away the thicker ones to the back of the wardrobe. She should have done this a couple of months ago. And why was she thinking of those old issues around marriage? She was strong, independent and self-sufficient. She and her daughter were a complete family. She had no cause to be dissatisfied. She believed in what she was doing; she loved her work even though the place she was affiliated with seemed elitist occasionally. RS was right about that.

Should she throw away the red-and-orange top now? It had started to look quite old. She had noticed her colleagues' eyes resting on the faded patch just above the pocket. But she was never going to spend as much time and money as some other people did on clothes. At times, she wondered about them. How could they bear to lead such wasteful lives in a poor country like India? How could they spend precious hours hunting for the latest designs, burning money on shopping expeditions? No, she would wear it a few more times and go shopping for tops next month.

This is when the doorbell rang and Dini espied Mrs Gandhi through the peephole.

Uff! Dini wondered how long it would take her to shake off the pesky neighbour. Mrs Gandhi must have seen her ascending the stairs to her third-floor house. The lady from one of the ground-floor flats in her block was a friend of Mrs Gandhi. Very often, in the evening, both women would sit on the bench that was strategically placed to provide a view of the comings and goings in all four buildings. Dini sorely missed the anonymity of lifts, especially when someone or the other struck up some inane conversation with her. Practically every building had lifts in Mumbai, but here, DDA had constructed these four-storeyed monstrosities without giving any thought to how the old, the very young, the pregnant or the differently-abled would negotiate the endless flights of stairs. Her father was having trouble with his knees, and when he visited next, he would need more support to climb three flights up. But as his visit wasn't due for at least six months, she could tackle the issue later. The immediate problem was Mrs Gandhi ringing her bell.

'I got you some kheer,' said Mrs Gandhi, her eyes alive with untold tales, as soon as she opened the door a crack.

'Oh, thank you so much,' replied Dini, taking the bowl and physically blocking the door.

'I thought Maithi would enjoy it. When she came to our house last time, I had offered her *rasgulle*. She enjoys Indian sweets, like my Teenu and Ganesh. Now, Neeru and Sunil will only have chocolate desserts…'

Mrs Gandhi's eyes seemed to beseech and appeal. Dini wondered for how long she could hold her off. She was being very rude by not even inviting her indoors. After all, the woman had taken the trouble to climb the stairs with a bowl of kheer in her hands; she was very obviously out of breath. She must be only slightly older than me and look at the level of her fitness, Dini thought irritably.

'Maithili will love it. Do come in, Mrs Gandhi. I am so tired that I'm quite unable to think straight. It's been a very long day—'

Mrs Gandhi settled down on the sofa.

'Does her father also like Indian sweets?' she asked.

'No,' said Dini, as short as she could make it.

'Is he thin?' she persisted, uncharacteristically brave. 'I have never met him.'

Dini stared at her without blinking. Mrs Gandhi quickly lowered her eyes.

'It is so important to relax after a day's work. You put your feet up and have some of this kheer… Do you want me to make you some tea?' Mrs Gandhi asked. As though I would allow her to mess around in my kitchen, Dini thought even more irritably. 'You will feel much better after having something to eat and drink,' Mrs Gandhi continued. 'I keep telling Sunil the same thing. But men—they are like children, aren't they?'

'Yes, some men refuse to grow up, and our social structures, families especially, ensure that they stay that way: infantile and dependent on women.'

'Absolutely, this is what I always say. Now, Sunil's mother, she refuses to accept that her son is forty-five. It is always "Nilima, do this for him, do that for him", "He works so hard in office"—as though Nilima's life is a luxury vacation! Today, the old woman wanted me to peel *grapes* for him. Have you ever heard of anyone peeling grapes?'

'Um...' Dini was feeling weary. This could go on for hours. 'I used to peel grapes for Maithili when she was two because she tended to spit out the peel, but then I stopped and she got used to eating grapes the normal way.'

'Well, here you are! And the old woman says that Sunil has never been able to have grapes unless they are peeled. I must leave all my work and sit for half an hour peeling grapes, while the man is out gallivanting—'

'Yes, the grapes were wonderful this season.'

'The season is over but the old woman still got 250 grams of the imported variety for her son. Rest of the household can subsist on bananas for all she cares...'

Dini ate a spoonful of the kheer in sheer desperation. There was no escape. Mrs Gandhi had retrieved the bowl from the table and was holding it out to her. 'This is so good, Mrs Gandhi. You are a great cook. What have you made for dinner today?'

To her shock, Mrs Gandhi's grin disappeared and, instead, there was a little sob.

Taken aback, Dinitia committed the ultimate solecism

against her well-earned evening of rest. She gasped, 'What happened, Mrs Gandhi?'

'Dini-shee, I spent the whole day making special dinner... I made mutton-mince koftas, peas pulao...' Mrs Gandhi's mountainous body heaved.

'Oh, Mrs Gandhi!' exclaimed Dini in alarm.

'This kheer,' continued the crying woman, while the bowl of kheer she had abandoned on the sofa trembled riskily. Dini rescued it holding it in one hand. To balance herself, she slid onto the same sofa that Mrs Gandhi was sitting on. Mistaking this as a gesture to comfort her, Mrs Gandhi plonked her head on Dini's shoulder and wept noisily.

'Come on, Mrs Gandhi. Let me get you a glass of water.'

'No, no, you are tired, I will get it...'

'I'm not that tired.'

Dini hated Mrs Gandhi's head on her shoulder. North Indians have no respect for personal spaces, she complained to herself, knowing well that in this direction of thinking lay parochialism and prejudice. She habitually flinched from the physicality that seemed so much a part of middle-class women's interactions in Delhi. It was one thing to have an uneducated, poor woman grab her hand—this was something Dini had made her business to understand and empathize with. But it was another thing altogether to be compelled to make her shoulder available to this fair-complexioned, thick-set woman who, in spite of her trauma, had found the time to spray herself with a perfume that was making her head reel. Dini disengaged herself and got up, carefully balancing the bowl of kheer. Mrs Gandhi had almost spilled it on her spotless sofa. But she couldn't help noticing that the woman was in considerable distress.

'Would you like to talk about it, Mrs Gandhi?' Dini asked.

She was a women's rights activist, wasn't she?

'What to say, Din-she-ji. It is the usual thing.'

'Dinitia—my name is Dinitia. Yes, mothers-in-law are difficult, but—'

'It is because of her that he gets the encouragement to treat me like this.'

'Oh, yes, perhaps—' Dini tried to make a point.

'Today is our wedding anniversary, and I have such a headache.'

'You really shouldn't have spent so much time in the kitchen,' soothed Dini.

'The old woman keeps both the servants busy. She sent off Bahadur to get grapes. He came back in half an hour saying he couldn't find any in the colony, so she sent him off to Central Market. Now who is going to do the work he is supposed to do?'

'This is definitely unthinking on her part.'

'She's only bothered about the fact that her son likes grapes; it is my wedding anniversary too. And then she put Rajni to work in her own room, folding her clothes, pressing her legs. So there I was alone in the kitchen—'

'You really should have done a simpler menu.' In spite of herself, Dini was exasperated.

'No, I like cooking. Now, you go out to work; you are so busy. What do I do? For me, there is only the kitchen.'

'Mrs Gandhi, it is really nice of you to make a special meal for your husband. You must tell him how hard you worked.'

Mrs Gandhi was sobbing again, 'No appreciation, I get no appreciation. I got a phone call from his secretary saying that he won't have dinner.'

'Oh. He must have forgotten…?'

'No, no, we went three days ago to buy my present. I took

a gold set. The old woman was complaining about the expense and I told her that when Neeru gets married—she's already fourteen—all of you will thank me for my foresight. All this is for my children, isn't it? How much gold can I wear? I hardly go out!'

'You should have worn the gold set today... I must get to the kitchen; Maithili is about to come home,' Dini tried to get her neighbour to leave.

'Rani hasn't come today?'

'She's taken Maithili to a birthday party. Besides, I like to do the cooking if I'm home.'

'You mustn't spoil the maid. It is her work, isn't it?'

There was silence as Dini mulled over the selfishness of the middle class.

'He must have gone with that bitch,' said Mrs Gandhi suddenly.

Dini was taken aback; it was the first time she was hearing Mrs Gandhi swear.

'When I called the office back, the receptionist told me he had gone to Surya Sofitel, and when I asked for the secretary-bitch, he said she had left with him.'

'But Mrs Gandhi, this doesn't mean—'

'He is not answering his mobile.'

'Mrs Gandhi, how do you know he has gone out with her?'

'I'm too fat, na. He doesn't want to be seen with me... This is why I cooked dinner at home,' said Mrs Gandhi, ignoring Dini's question.

'Come on, Mrs Gandhi. Why should you be so suspicious?'

'That bitch is twenty-five.'

'Yes, but is this the only reason for your suspicion?'

'I don't know what he does! I don't look into his phone and laptop,' replied Mrs Gandhi and just as Dini made to nod approvingly, she continued, 'He keeps everything locked anyway. But you tell me—is it alright to go for a business dinner in your boss's car?'

'Mrs Gandhi, you must have a talk with your husband. Tell him your fears. You cannot assume that he is having an affair with his secretary just because she is twenty-five and they travel in the same car.'

There was silence, only broken by Mrs Gandhi blowing her nose a couple of times.

'Dini-she-sha,' she said at last, 'I don't know how office works. Now you have told me this... I am feeling better.'

'I'm glad,' replied Dini, wondering why the dashed woman could never get her name correct. She got up before the woman could change her mind about feeling better.

'I got a packet this morning from Mehrasons, the jewellery shop,' said Mrs Gandhi, almost at the door.

'Your new set? You should wear it this evening,' exclaimed Dini distractedly.

'No, a diamond ring, and then the delivery boy came right back to take it away, saying that the order had got mixed up.'

'Why didn't you pick up the set when you went to buy it?'

'The clasp had to be re-done.'

'You are also going to get a diamond ring. Isn't it nice!' muttered Dini, thoroughly confused. She imagined what it would be like to push Mrs Gandhi with her perfume and her jewellery down the stairs.

'No, the delivery boy took it back.'

'Oh,' exclaimed Dini, none the wiser.

'I called and asked the shop whose order the diamond ring was, but they said they could not reveal.'

'Yes, yes, these things must be confidential,' she replied, quite aware that she knew nothing about buying jewellery. The only jewellery she knew of was family heirlooms. Her mother had left her a small jewellery case; it now lay in her bank locker. She would occasionally bring home the diamond studs it contained, though she never wore them. She just loved the way they caught the light and glinted.

'Then Sunil's office peon brought me my set and said it was delivered to the office by mistake,' said Mrs Gandhi. 'I thought he had ordered the diamond ring and meant to have it delivered to the office. I thought he would get it for me this evening as a surprise gift. But when I got the call this evening that he was not coming for dinner...'

At last, things clicked into place in Dini's mind. It seemed like a typical case of marital betrayal. Mr Gandhi must have bought two pieces of jewellery—one for the wife, the other for the girlfriend. To lock his phone and laptop but mix up the gift delivery orders... What did it say about the man? Was he plain stupid or subconsciously dealing a blow to his wife? However, Mrs Gandhi had wiped her tears and seemed to be in control at last.

'He will give it to me when he comes home tonight,' whispered Mrs Gandhi as if to reassure herself. 'Bye, Dinshee-ji.'

'Dinitia,' corrected Dini automatically as the door shut behind Mrs Gandhi.

The Following Monday in May

Home and Sunrise Elsewhere

A bell was ringing.
But Shailaja was dreaming of a pilgrimage to a mountain shrine. Mrs Jain was leading the pilgrims.

'Water's come,' somebody screamed. Shailaja turned on her side.

Mrs Jain turned to look disapprovingly at her, 'Your pot is only half-full,' she said.

Water was spouting from all sides. The rocks had opened up, fountains were springing.

'Fill it,' ordered Mrs Jain without a smile.

The sound of water rushing in an underground stream was like a buzz. It was all around her. Shailaja felt too tired. 'Not now,' she muttered. She turned to the other side.

Suddenly she found herself in a school play. She was playing a tree. She wore a mousey-brown dress right down to her ankles, and had leaves tied, stuck or sewn on various parts of her anatomy and costume. She drooped sadly as the curtain lifted, along with six or seven other trees that made up the forest in which St Francis of Assisi would perform miracles. She was waiting tensely for the crucial moment: the resounding *sama* after the climactic build-up of the tabla-beat, when she was to rejuvenate and move her arms like swaying branches to the hymn from backstage.

With a pang of anxiety, Shailaja sat up in bed and looked around. That was years ago. School days were mercifully over. She was a grown-up and not answerable to bad-tempered theatre directors. She had spent the entire Sunday getting her new home ready and felt she had made an impressive beginning. Due to her foresight and advance planning, both the TV and the Internet were functional. But the housework that she realized she was quite unaccustomed to had tired her out completely. She decided to take an off from college; she was entitled to a break. Shailaja quickly sent an email to college from her phone, pleading sick leave—'due to a bad attack of food poisoning', she typed with a flourish—and lay down again for just a brief nap.

Back drowsily to Assisi's forest. The girls in her class giggled and joked that the Catholic school had got it all wrong. Trees should have been depicted as impassive beings, neither drooping and pining, nor responding so enthusiastically to the saint's touch or to off-key paeans of praise. Nevertheless, it was the only performance in which she had ever excelled in spite of her bouts of anxiety. She was much too self-conscious otherwise.

Had the identity of the tree, so sincerely cultivated for the play, taken? She must have been twelve or thirteen and impressionable. And in class they had been reading Yeats's poem 'A Prayer for My Daughter', anti-feminist and reactionary, as she found out later. But it was taught as the great poet's vision for home and women by the English teacher she had a crush on.

May she become a flourishing hidden tree,

That all her thoughts may like the linnet be...
O may she live like some green laurel
Rooted in one dear perpetual place.

Would Vasant Kunj become a dear perpetual place for her? She would have to send her roots right down three floors, next to Mrs Gandhi's ground-floor flat. It was too late for her to transform into a bird and fly away; she was no longer hollow-boned and light. The movers as well as the men who had come to install the TV and Internet connections had called her 'aunty'. Aunty? But it was the plump Mrs Gandhi who was the Aunty-ji. In Shailaja's still half-asleep imagination, Mrs Gandhi appeared standing broad and solid with the promise of a million cups of tea and plates of biscuits. She was the true Yeatsian tree of Vasant Kunj, offering succour to so many.

Was it Mrs Gandhi's voice she could hear so early in the morning? Or Mrs Jain's? Aunties get up at the crack of dawn, thought Shailaja, almost drifting off again. Her phone pinged and she realized that it was past eight-thirty; Vasant Kunj had been awake for more than two hours.

Shailaja heaved herself out of bed at last and took herself to the kitchen. She tried to fill water in a saucepan to make tea but the tap only hissed and spluttered.

■

With still half-shut eyes, Shailaja took stock of her new home. The sink could do with some hard scrubbing, so could the patchy-grey floor. She closed the tap and opened it again: the hissing and spluttering repeated and not a drop emerged. But she had pumped up water from the storage to the overhead tank just last evening.

Vasant Kunj was infamous for water woes. In fact, hadn't a colleague advised her to cross-check whether her building got water at all from the official supply line? There were many flats in Vasant Kunj that were totally dependent on private tankers, she had informed Shailaja. There might be a problem just with the tap, Shailaja thought optimistically. She went into the bathroom and was irritated at once. Of course DDA flats were constructed for utility, but did that necessarily mean that the budget homes had to look like a child's drawing? The number of floor tiles on the supposedly rectangular bathroom floor were six at one end, five-and-a-half at the other. The wall tiles going halfway up also had an unequal distance between the ceiling and the floor. The entire construction seemed to be tilting. It made her feel like she was hungover. But of course she wasn't; she hadn't had a drink in ages. Why was she thinking of alcohol in that case? The bathroom tap replayed the hiss-and-splutter score. There was no water in her overhead tank. With some trepidation, Shailaja switched on the pump. It had worked quite well yesterday. The house agent had warned her that it was old and it would take a while for the water to go up four floors. 'You can get it changed after six or seven months if you like,' he had said.

She was craving a nice strong cup of tea, what she used to make first thing in the morning in Defence Colony to wake herself up properly. In the good old days, Ranjan and she would go to bed quite late. It had been a ritual for them to drink together every evening, even though she had never really taken to alcohol. She would nurse her half-peg or half-glass of 'whatever you are having' and feel deliciously sophisticated. Ranjan was particular: only smoky single malts would do—Ardbeg and Laphroig—and sometimes wine. *The grape called Malbec makes a dry red!* And at parties, if his preferences were not available, he would have rum. *Indian rum is much better than anything else we make.* He had unfolded a life of distinction and taste, and she had been a willing student. So much information was supplied enthusiastically in the beginning of the relationship, and then, towards the end of it, it came only if she could wrest it out of him, in dribs and drabs, his attention wandering. Or she sat waiting every evening with her heart wringing, tossing in her lonely bed most of the night.

But now she had no time anymore to think of her previous life, no time to wring that heart. There were pressing demands to meet. Most of her stuff was still lying where the movers had deposited it. She would deal with all this slowly over the week, but the primary need was water. She had to sort this problem out before doing anything else. There should be some water in the overhead tank by now. Shailaja tried the kitchen tap, and then again the bathroom. Nothing. What was the protocol when such things happened? Could she ring the Jains' bell and pretend she had dropped by at nine in the morning to ascertain the height of the ravaged rubber plant? Or should she go to the Gandhis' and ask after their son—express concern regarding the strain of tricycling? She could also offer to service the tricycle.

Shailaja sighed. She switched on the TV that sprang to life with a soulful rendition of a *bhajan*. She hurriedly changed channels. The doorbell rang.

'I am Rajni's mother,' said the old woman who stood at the entrance. 'You need a maid for cooking?'

'Yes, I do. Also for sweeping-mopping and washing utensils,' Shailaja replied. Indeed, she had told Rajni to send her mother. And here she was!

'I can do everything. Should I begin?'

'Yes, I suppose. What's your name?'

'Call me Rajni ki Ma; everybody does ever since Rajni was born.'

'I would rather call you by your real name,' Shailaja protested.

'How does it matter? Even I have forgotten my name,' she shot back. 'Should I begin?'

'There's no water, though…'

'You did not switch on the pump in the morning,' Rajni ki Ma said at once.

'I switched it on just now.'

The old woman cackled, 'As if you own a well.'

'What do you mean? Water must have come this morning. There must be some in my storage tank anyway. It just has to be pumped up.'

'So you think,' she said. 'Water doesn't come unless you switch on the pump at six. Give me a bucket, and I'll go across to the next door. They're about to leave for work. You don't work on Monday?'

'How did you know that I didn't switch on the pump in the morning?' she asked her all-knowing visitor who had by then brought the bucket out from the bathroom.

'I rang the bell earlier but Jain Madam said you must be asleep as your light was on till one in the morning. She said you were watching TV.'

'Did she tell you whether or not I had brushed my teeth?' The words were out before she could bite them back.

'No,' replied Rajni ki Ma with a deadpan expression. 'But how can you brush your teeth without water! I'll go and get some.'

'I will charge seven thousand per month with tea twice a day,' she said fifteen minutes later, banging the brimming bucket down on the kitchen floor.

Shailaja had again checked the taps without success and was feeling slightly tearful. 'Why is my storage tank empty?' she asked plaintively.

Rajni ki Ma shrugged, 'You must get up at six.'

'Water must go into the storage tank even if the pump is not on,' Shailaja insisted. After all, their barsati was also on the top floor in Defence Colony and she was used to pumping water up.

'I'll call the plumber,' Rajni ki Ma suggested.

'Make me tea, please,' she said to Rajni ki Ma, 'and then quickly call the plumber and the electrician. It seems my fridge isn't working either.'

'They come later, at ten or so. Let me finish the other work first.'

Rajni ki Ma was small and shrunken, with bright eyes set in a wizened face. Shailaja thought uncharitably of the monkey the *bandar-wallah* would dress in women's clothes. 'Look, look, Sita is now going to cry for Ram.' Surrounded by a group of shrieking children, the unfortunate rhesus would put its hands to its eyes and make its emaciated body heave up and down to depict emotion. That image was buried within layers of denial: the small-town mela of her childhood, the melee she hadn't acknowledged in years. Somehow, the appearance of Rajni ki Ma had tapped that forgotten seam, sending her back to her childhood in the hinterland of UP.

'You haven't started setting up the house,' she scolded. 'Everything is in a mess. When will the man come?'

'Which man?'

'Your man. You have a man or not?'

'No.'

'Good. Nobody to interfere. Go and wash up but don't finish the entire bucket.'

She took out a mug of water from the bucket before handing it to Shailaja. 'Give it back quickly. I will make tea and then get you a couple of buckets more.'

Rajni ki Ma scolded, cooked and cleaned. She exclaimed over the kitchen utensils: 'So many, what's the point? Single woman!' She opened the suitcases and took out Shailaja's clothes, 'Hardly any saris! What depressing colours! Dressing like a widow!' After two hours of watching her incessant activity in a hypnotized manner, Shailaja insisted that she should now go and call the plumber and the electrician.

The plumber came immediately and informed her that she would have to install another pump that would suck water directly and illegally from the main line. It was the standard practice. Everybody had two pumps—Gandhis, Jains, everybody. And as everybody had illegal main-line pumps, water wouldn't reach her storage tank unless she installed one too and switched it on when everybody else switched on theirs. 'People who were in the flat before you obviously had two pumps because the pipes are all laid already. You must get up at six, Madam,' he concluded. It seemed to be the theme song of Vasant Kunj.

Shailaja paid him for his visit and for installing a new pump, feeling highly indignant. Shouldn't her property agent have disclosed all this? And did Rajni ki Ma have to call a plumber who repeated every sentence four times, and that too indistinctly? It seemed to her that a good part of the day had gone by in receiving the wisdom of Vasant Kunj that ran thus: you get up at the crack of dawn to gratify your sneaky acquisitive instinct. It didn't matter if what you were doing was contrary to plain logic. If everybody was to get rid of the main-line pumps, all the storage tanks would fill up in the normal course. Nobody would have to get up at an unearthly hour to waste precious human hours and electricity. It was self-evident. But all that everybody said and did was get up at six.

Rajni ki Ma, who had returned with the plumber and was listening to the conversation, said, 'I said so.'

She reluctantly bid adieu, informing Shailaja that she would be back at five in the evening 'to finish the work, so don't go here and there at that time. Two boxes of *raddi* have to be still arranged on the shelves.'

The electrician came an hour later. The Gandhis ran five air conditioners, and somewhere an MCB had tripped because of overload. Five or six flats were affected and it was up to the main electricity office to send their electrician, he said. Some wires would have to be changed too.

'Why would they run five ACs together?' Shailaja wondered aloud.

They must have definitely switched on three, the electrician backtracked. He knew that they had an old AC that sucked a lot of electricity, like Madam's. It would cost two thousand rupees to install an AC, and the carpenter would charge extra, he continued, switching gears. New ACs were so much lighter. Now, whether or not they had switched it on, how should he know? But the line had tripped because of overload, he knew that. For the last two years, it had been tripping because of the Gandhis. She would have to go and talk to them, he emphasized, otherwise the electricity office won't do the repairs. He couldn't be expected to talk tough with Madams and Sahibs.

Shailaja could see that it was imperative to discuss the tripping electricity connection with her neighbour. The setting up of a home in Vasant Kunj was proving to be more challenging than she had imagined. She ate the surprisingly tasty lunch dished up by Rajni ki Ma and then took herself to the home with too many ACs.

■

Nilima Gandhi was likely to have one of those over-stuffed homes that she had always disliked, Shailaja thought. Ranjan used to call them catalogue homes. Too many cushions, too much furniture, curtains and tapestry matching thread for thread. Ringing the bell, she began to feel a little nervous.

A male servant opened the door. Shailaja stepped into a cool space. But it was so dark; not a ray of sunlight was filtering in from anywhere. There seemed to be no windows at all. Whatever renovation they carried out in the flat had served to take away the only redeeming feature of Vasant Kunj architecture. The servant switched on the lights and a red-and-gold vision was revealed suddenly. She hadn't expected such flamboyance. She sat down gingerly on a carved sofa and looked around her. The walls were papered. Shailaja stared—whoever uses wallpaper with a golden paisley-pattern these days! But it was peeling from the corners. She felt an almost uncontrollable urge to rip it off the walls. When she looked closely, she found that the furniture was heavily ornate: flowers, leaves and cherubs were carved into the sides of a huge side-board and the curved arms and legs of the sofa. The tapestry, however, was old and frayed. The room made her think of an abandoned film set.

The male servant entered with *nimbu-paani* and Mrs Gandhi followed. Even before Shailaja could complete her hesitant plaint about old wires and the overload because of too many ACs, she took off.

'It must be that fool Sanju who told you. All lies. Of course we have five ACs; so many people do. But we don't run them together. This has nothing to do with us.'

'Oh, but is your electric connection working fine?' asked Shailaja.

'No, where is it working fine? The power line is down in my bedroom. I have such a headache. It is migraine and I can't rest at all in the heat. Somebody needs to do something about the electricity.'

Mrs Gandhi seemed edgier and somewhat less complacent

than she had been on Saturday, Shailaja noted.

'I have made a complaint on phone,' she repeated patiently. 'But Sanju said I must speak to you.'

'Yes, the electricity company will say it is not their business. He knows that.'

'He said that some wiring would need to be changed by the residents and only then would they do the needful.'

'Last summer too, the same story. Everybody blames us just because we have an AC in every room. They feel we should get the repairs done.'

'Oh...' replied Shailaja. If they had an AC in every room, what was the problem in getting the old wires replaced? The expense probably wouldn't even come to the cost of one AC.

'I told Sunil he shouldn't put an AC in every room; everybody in the colony will talk. But he and my older daughter can't be without an AC for a minute also. His mother is so old. You know, old people don't feel the heat so much. She would have been comfortable with a cooler...'

'Yes,' Shailaja wondered where this line of argument would go.

'But he is so emotional, you know, and such a good son. How can we have an AC in our room and the girls' room and Mummy-ji sleep perspiring? But she is the one to blame... She could have refused, no?'

'Yes, I suppose.'

'It's not like her to think of others. Only thinks of herself... Old people are like this. You are lucky you don't have old people in the home. Of course all old people are not the same. My mother was so different. She was always thinking of my brother and his wife... Never of me, her own daughter. She always told me to sacrifice.'

'Yes, Nilima-ji. But what should we do about this problem?'

'Which problem?'
'The power problem.'
'Nobody does anything but blame us.'
'Oh, Nilima-ji, I am not blaming you,' she protested weakly. 'We can divide the expense. My fridge is on the power line and—'

'Nilima,' called out a voice from inside, 'Where is Rajni? Tell her to get my walker.'

'Mummy-ji, it is afternoon. You should do your puja now,' Mrs Gandhi answered her, distractedly. Then she turned to Shailaja with full attention, 'You want to divide the expense?'

Shailaja nodded, a little uncertain now. 'I suppose all the affected flats will pay?'

'They should; all run two–three ACs. You have only one but yours is a full flat, no? Actually you are alone! So lucky! You don't have to listen to so many people—I want this, I want that.'

'So, should I go to the electricity office and ask them to send somebody to start the process?'

'You will go?'

'Yes, I will have to go. I need the power line.'

'Yes, yes. Single women have to do everything themselves. This is why families are better.'

Shailaja wondered whether the distracted Mrs Gandhi was aware that she had, just minutes before, called her lucky because she was single.

'I want to go to the park now; I will do my puja later,' said the voice from inside. 'Call Rajni.'

Mrs Gandhi went on without paying any attention to it, 'Where did you say you were staying before your di– um, before Vasant Kunj?'

Shailaja was quite sure she had not divulged any such information. What the hell! 'Defence Colony,' she replied.

'Oh okay! Nice colony, no? We were also in South Extension before Vasant Kunj. You don't go. I will call my electrician and ask him to take a look. Last year he repaired the line without changing wires. Sanju is no good; only blames us and knows nothing,' said Mrs Gandhi.

Before Shailaja could thank her, she screamed suddenly to her invisible, hyper-voluble mother-in-law, 'Mummy-ji, it is so hot; you will fall ill if you walk in this weather. There's no one to take you out just now, anyway. Rajni is doing the cleaning-up and Bahadur has left.'

The startled Shailaja emerged out of the dilapidated grandeur. The litany of complaints from the old woman had continued making it difficult for her to take her leave: 'Nobody thinks of me; I come last. Two servants but nobody to take me out...'

Was the old woman the reason for Mrs Gandhi to neglect her furniture and walls? And was she actually jealous of a 'divorced' woman who did not have a single dinner set to her name? Shailaja would never have behaved in this manner had she been in her place... She would have peeled off that paper from the wall at the first opportunity and got it painted. There were so many options available in paints these days.

Mrs Gandhi was indeed a strange character, but if she was ready to call her electrician and save her the bother of running around, Shailaja wasn't going to complain, especially if this electrician managed to repair the line without changing the wires.

Mrs Gandhi put a call through to her electrician as soon as Shailaja left. She knew well that they were using electricity much beyond the permissible limit. They needed to apply for a higher wattage meter and there was no escaping that considerable expense and hassle this summer. Additionally, the main meter would also need to be repaired and wires tightened privately as the official electricians had refused to continue doing it, in spite of handsome tips. Mrs Jain and Mrs Malhotra would probably descend on her to fight about it in the next couple of hours. Both of them, and even that Shruti, for whom they had done so much, had been so rude to her last summer. If they too had kept to three ACs like most other flats, or at most put just one extra, she wouldn't have been singled out. At least now there was one good neighbour who was ready to share the expense of repairs. She would quote Shailaja's example to Mrs Jain and Mrs Malhotra and ask them also to pitch in for the repairs. Shailaja was so much better than Shruti! But due to her selfish mother-in-law's shouting, she must be thinking Vasant Kunj residents had no manners. Did she realize that electric work was an expensive proposition? She hadn't even asked how much it would cost. Divorcing-husband from Defence Colony must be paying good maintenance.

Sunil too wasn't miserly, but she was reluctant to broach the topic of the meter with him. They had had words just last evening.

'Don't be silly, Nilima,' he had said impatiently when she asked him about the reason for the ruined anniversary dinner. He had returned home only after midnight and left again early morning, even though it was a Sunday. She was able to confront him only in the evening. His voice had kept rising and she felt so embarrassed because the children were in the next room and both the servants were in the house too: 'Can't you see I have been working day and night—even on a Sunday? I am not a housewife with all the time in the world for special dinners.'

And then: 'Reeta went with me to the shop because she had to finish some official work nearby. She must have bought the ring and asked for it to be delivered to office.' 'How would I know how much it cost? Call up the shop and ask!' 'Obviously, the delivery boy had made a mistake! He's not a delivery boy anyway but their clerk. Must have got confused! I spent a lakh-and-a-half on buying an anniversary gift for you. How much money should I spend? Is nothing enough for you?'

The explanation would have been enough if her husband hadn't yelled at her like this. Of course it was her mother-in-law who was responsible for his behaviour, whatever Dini or anybody might say. She had always put her down.

She was twenty-two when they got married. In the beginning, in their overcrowded home in Sadar Bazaar, she battled the entire extended family for her husband's attention. There were seven people in the tiny flat. Her mother said that this was usual in traditional structures and she was lucky to have her husband on her side; her father was more understanding. Together, they kept pressing Sunil to get an independent home for his new family.

When they at last moved to a flat in South Extension provided by his office, Mrs Gandhi felt ecstatic. Finally, her dream of creating a modern nuclear family in an upmarket neighbourhood was coming true. She had already had her first baby; she did up the 'nursery' all in pink. She aimed to achieve a tight circle of mother–father–baby surrounded by every domestic happiness. But this ideal state was not destined to continue. Neeru was barely eight months old when Sunil's family besieged them. Her father-in-law died suddenly in an accident, and a family feud ensued. Sunil's brother, they found, had surreptitiously transferred the family property—the Sadar Bazaar shop and three flats in different parts of the city—to his own name. When Sunil confronted him and demanded his share, he was told in no uncertain terms that he had lost his moral right over the property. Allegedly, Sunil, at his wife's behest, had betrayed his parental family and humiliated them. He was left with no choice but to file a case against his brother in court.

It turned out to be a four-year-long protracted battle that eroded their relationship. Sunil blamed her. 'If you had not fought with everyone, I would not have lost my claim to the property.' 'After all, this is my family. Why couldn't you just realize this simple thing? Women are supposed to adjust in their marital homes.' 'What kind of wife blackmails her husband in the manner you did?' In an out-of-court settlement, they got the Vasant Kunj flat and some money. But this meant that they had to abandon the office residence with the pink nursery and move to the flat immediately. 'Possession is nine-tenths of the law,' the lawyer had explained. 'I would advise you to move into the Vasant Kunj flat even if it remains in your mother's name. Courts take a lifetime to resolve most cases; property disputes take several lifetimes.'

Along with the flat came the responsibility of taking care of the mother-in-law. The old woman resumed the deferred task of putting the daughter-in-law in her place. Sunil became increasingly irritable when she complained to him. 'What can I do about it? It is your duty to adjust with my mother. It is only because of her that we have got this flat!'

She had been stuck with the old woman, managing the home and children for the last ten years. Of course, it was the duty of housewives to do the housework; she didn't mind that. Whatever her in-laws might say, her parents had brought her up well! But husbands should be nice to their wives too. Especially these days, when everything was fifty–fifty between women and men. This morning when Neeru said that the Math teacher believed that boys had a more scientific mind because they opted in a much larger number for Physics–Chemistry–Math in Class XI, Sunil had at once said that nowadays it wasn't like that in India; there were many, many women scientists. To prove how modern he was, he went on to give Neeru permission to go for a party over the weekend without even talking to his wife about it.

How would he like it if she turned ultra-modern like Dini? Nobody knew anything about Dini's husband! Speak to your husband, she had said! What use had that been? It only led to a fight. Whatever anyone might say, traditional ways are important in India—this is what her mother always said. She was so pious and had such a happy life with Mrs Gandhi's forward-looking father. She wondered whether she should go to the colony temple and make an offering.

Mrs Gandhi suddenly remembered the new kind of worship that Mrs Malhotra had told her about when she went to invite her for a kirtan: 'It is Buddhism, Nilima. And very easy! You don't have to arrange for a priest or anything. You just have to chant a mantra for ten minutes in the morning and ten minutes in the evening. You won't believe the kind of benefits one can get from this.'

Mrs Malhotra had told her she had been chanting the Buddhist mantra 'Nam-myoho-renge-kyo' for her son to get a job.

'I chanted for a month, and he got three excellent offers. And you know, these offers were from companies that had rejected his application earlier. He was so surprised. I told him it was because of my faith, and now he chants too.'

'It is a proven scientific way,' she had said. 'It is based on the karma theory. Chanting increases good karma and reverses bad karma. It will transform your life, Nilima.'

She could chant for Sunil to transform! She remembered how she used to playfully cover his eyes. 'Sunil, you can't look at anybody else but me.' 'But I don't need to look at any other woman,' he would protest, laughing and kissing her. Would chanting bring him back in spite of her mother-in-law? It couldn't be as difficult as getting a job for a young man who only had an undergraduate degree. No harm in trying it out. Mrs Malhotra had told her Buddhism was just like Hinduism. One didn't have to convert to start chanting, and kirtan and pujas were also allowed. She decided to visit Mrs Malhotra in the evening. It would also be a good opportunity to bring up the matter of the electric meter repairs.

Dini usually took the minutiae of domesticity, the uncertain water supply, the power breakdowns, the hostile neighbours in her stride. She managed such things in a distracted manner, with great competence and minimal fuss.

Monday was the beginning of her hectic working week. She got up at five-thirty. But her recurrent sinus headache was threatening to strike, so she only did a couple of Surya Namaskars and skipped the rest of her yoga routine. Then she brewed her coffee and was having it sitting in her favourite chair from where she could watch the brilliant-green treetops. But today the greenery that surrounded the ugly Vasant Kunj flats did not have the usual uplifting effect. She wanted to creep into bed again and think of RS, who was fast becoming her new obsession, she scolded herself.

She had chosen to live in Vasant Kunj because she was delighted to see the ashoka, gulmohar, neem, jamun, tamarind and silk cotton trees nodding their heads the first time she visited the flat. Vasant Kunj was possibly the greenest colony out of the ones she could afford. Most of the trees were still here after nine years because when the government workers had come with their obsolete implements, the pickaxes, the clippers, the ropes to chop off branches in the name of pruning, and the contractors brought their trucks to carry away the valuable logs of wood surreptitiously, she, along with a handful of environment activists, demanded to see the permission letter from the 'competent authority'. They took photographs of illegal activities and sent them to the forest department; wrote articles in newspapers and appeared on news channels; organized human chains and demonstrations; followed the trucks to the wood mart where the logs were being sold and took more photographs. They even filed a case against unknown persons who were felling trees and destroying the environment.

There had been a price to pay. The people she had to fight included not only the greedy contractors but also a sizeable number of neighbours like Mrs and Mr Gandhi. 'It is a residential colony, not a forest,' Mr Gandhi said. But what else could one expect from this petit bourgeois lot! They had paved the area surrounding their ground-floor flat with shiny granite. Mrs Gandhi had actually remarked that trees should be of a particular quality in order to be allowed into Vasant Kunj, now that property prices were so high. Dini found Mrs Gandhi, Casanova Gandhi and their ilk utterly stupid. Indeed, she was articulate, intellectual and egalitarian; they were wannabe elite, nouveau riche, casteist. They were with neoliberal globalization; she was left-leaning. They were selfish Indian yuppies with big families and too many cars; she was a single mother who used public transport. Her activist credentials had been quickly established soon after she took up residence here. She got the environmental organization, Delhi Tree Champions, to take up the issue of the merciless cutting of trees in the name of pruning in Vasant Kunj. A couple of MNC-type young men had sniggered, calling her Aunty Acid to her face. Not that she cared a jot for what they said!

Interrupting her musing, her daughter Maithili came pouting into the room, having woken up earlier than usual. 'I want stuffed okra for tiffin, Mumma,' she intoned sleepily.

She had just learnt the word 'okra' and wanted the 'American' vegetable for her lunch every other day. Potatoes and peas would take half the time and effort. Dini took herself reluctantly to the kitchen. After handing the pink strawberry milk to her daughter, her latest fad, she began slitting the okra, implanting in each finger the mix of spices Maithili liked. Her daughter's obstinacy was getting more and more pronounced. She's growing to be just like you, Dini's father had pointed out when he visited last month. You're spoiling her silly like your mother spoilt you, he added.

'Mumma, you forgot to hem my new skirt,' said Maithili, entering the kitchen.

'Sweetie, I will do it this evening. Or you can tell Rani-di to do it for you when you return from school.'

'But I want to wear the new skirt today.'

'Maithili, there isn't time. I still have to make the parathas for your tiffin. Look, the okra smells so good.'

Maithili was beginning to pout again. It was going to be a difficult morning.

'Let the parathas be. I will eat in the canteen.'

'You know what, today you wear the new skirt as it is, and tomorrow I will shorten it, and it will look new again. You will end up getting two new skirts instead of one,' Dini knew she was sounding desperate.

'I hate this skirt,' Maithili screamed.

Dini sighed inwardly. She knew she needed to be firm but the hammering in her head wasn't helping in thinking straight. She took the skirt and began to put safety pins to put it up to the right trendy length.

'The pins will show.'

'Just a little!'

'Why can't you hem it up?'

'I have a headache, Maithili, and there isn't time.'

Maithili snatched the skirt away and flung it across the room.

'Maithili, this is—'

'I hate you.'

'Maithili, really! This is very bad behaviour.'

The young girl stomped off to her room.

Dini finished her cooking and put the tiffin box in Maithili's school bag. Her daughter needed discipline, like her head needed some tender, loving care.

•

After Rani managed to drag her tantrum-throwing daughter away to the bus stop, Dini rubbed tiger balm on her forehead, popped seven globules of arnica, the homeopathic medicine that always worked for her, put a few drops of lemongrass essential oil in the diffuser for aromatherapy, and lay down.

Maithili was a difficult child all right, thought Dini, willing the headache to go away. Of course, her father had been hinting at the crucial absence of a father to lay down the law. He was one to talk! He had been so absent, so ineffectual all through her growing years. Things hadn't changed much, had they? Most men—Mr Gandhi, for instance—continued to act neglectfully towards their families.

But of course, there were men like RS too. Her mind glided to the first time they had met.

It was at an office meeting with some community NGOs to discuss the outreach of her international organization. Dini was new to Delhi and to Empower. She had been compelled to bring the six-month-old Maithili along to office due to a situation at home. She joined the meeting late and threw herself into suggesting women's group programmes with gusto, even though she was having a tough time pacifying the baby while making her impassioned points. Maithili was attracting the kind of attention that only served to excite her further. RS was the only one who managed to offer effective help, silently volunteering to take the baby from her at coffee time.

'She's getting very irritable; she might puke or something,' she had cautioned him, not wanting to hurt the feelings of this 'community-level worker' by refusing his help outright.

'Don't worry, babies like me. Have your coffee,' he replied comfortably. She had kept an anxious eye on him as he circled the room with Maithili. He wasn't jiggling the baby as she had expected. Most men did that. She thought she heard him singing softly to her. Before she could finish her coffee, he was back. Maithili had slept off, curled comfortably against his chest.

'You have children of your own?' she asked.

'No, I'm not married,' he replied. 'I look after my cousins' babies when they visit and also babies of the workers...'

'You don't mind...?' she gasped in surprise. She had discovered by then that he was not a community worker but part of the management of a community NGO. Provincial set-ups usually had a rigid hierarchy, and it was unthinkable that a management person, especially a man, would offer to babysit the children of grassroots workers.

'I like babies,' he said. 'I think of their minds that are without prejudice and preconceived notions. They're so pure!' he had added, managing to sound sincere in spite of spouting such a twee sentiment.

She couldn't help but contrast him with her Empower colleagues who, in their natty attire and branded sunglasses, would have been better occupied selling tobacco to yuppies. At the recent conference, too, he hadn't seemed bothered at all about not having found a room at the fancy hotel, where most of the other delegates were put up. She noted the frayed cuffs of his blue shirt as he waved away such bourgeois considerations: 'The guesthouse is more central. I only have to sleep there, anyway.' She knew for a fact that the guesthouse was quite rundown. But she also overheard him saying to another delegate that he was quite comfortable staying there except for the temple bells that woke him up at an unseasonable hour. 'Shouldn't there be a law against religion hurting secular sensibilities?' he had joked. Was he really an atheist! People of his kind are usually believers at heart.

Dini pulled herself up. Activists like RS were becoming increasingly rare in the NGO sector—or anywhere for that matter—and that was a fact. She had no right to think of him so condescendingly.

How would he be as a lover? Had she lost her mind! Kenny appeared before her eyes. Kenny still mattered, didn't he? For eight years, he has been a regular visitor to her home, but they were not together anymore. He would bring gifts for Maithili, spend time with her, teach her songs. Last time, he had brought Dini a couple of tops too. After gifting them to her in a pretty bag, he looked at her expectantly: 'From Dubai; I went for a gig last month.' 'Oh thanks, Kenny, how is your girlfriend?' she had shot back.

Did Kenny think she would be available whenever he wanted? The only reason she didn't have a boyfriend was because since Maithili, she hadn't felt the need for one.

She had often enough discussed her lack of desire with her two closest women friends. Raji was a banker, single and much older; Namrata was her age and lived with a woman. Both of them were in Mumbai.

Raji would agree that there was nothing amiss in her life: 'There's no point in forcing yourself to go out with a man just because it is something everyone does, Dini.'

But Namrata would sound doubtful: 'But how will you know whether or not you desire a man unless you go out with him at least once?'

Raji would go on to insist that people tend to project loneliness on to those who live differently—especially women without men. 'It is a kind of trap to get into a relationship because everyone else is in one,' she had said last time.

Was she falling into the trap of wanting a 'normative' life? Dini asked herself.

Her headache had more or less evaporated. She knew she should get out of bed and finish working on her report. But there were still a few things that needed settling.

Dini brought out Kenny's presents from the drawer in which she had stuffed them. She shook them out. The green top had a rich colour, but it was kind of slinky. Dini liked wearing cotton, which she could starch and steam iron, but on an impulse, she tried the top on. It had a halterneck and deep armholes; her bra peeked out. She pirouetted in front of the mirror. She would never wear it—it made her look like an executive in a multinational. Or was halterneck not quite corporate wear? An executive on a holiday, in that case! She tried the pink one—it was transparent and had a lot of lace.

Yuck! She took it off immediately.

Cupboard settled, Dini made for her desk but found it difficult to get started on the report.

RS was attracted to her, she was thinking about him—where was the problem? She stopped short. A relationship with someone like RS? He belonged to a different world. He had grown up in a village, he came from a Scheduled Caste family.

But she had abdicated caste and her Brahmin identity conclusively, hadn't she? And that too on the day she met RS for the very first time at the selfsame meeting. It had been serendipity all right!

The incident was engraved in her memory. That day, her father and his formidable older sister—'Akka' to the entire family—had visited her Delhi home for the first time to meet 'Dini-ma's adopted daughter'.

Childhood conditioning had compelled Dini to drape a heavy Kanchipuram sari, wear the orange flowers in her hair—after all, Akka had brought them all the way from Mumbai—light the lamp at a hastily put-together puja altar, and put a sandalwood mark on her forehead.

Akka was acting more cussed than usual. 'No, I will not eat before the puja; no, not even a glass of water!' she declared as soon as she arrived. She proceeded to bring out countless objects like idols, diyas, bells, incense sticks, bowls, sandalwood, some grass, sweets, consecrated water, etc., from her suitcase and then started a kind of puja Dini had never witnessed before.

All this was done without any explanation, though her father seemed to be privy to whatever was happening. Akka recited from a tattered book with a garish cover and performed bizarre rituals. She would stand up, circle Dini and Maithili, and ring the bell at intervals. Maithili seemed to be her focus. Akka dotted her forehead with sandalwood paste and took the lit diya precariously close to her again and again, first to her little feet, then her stomach, her arms. A suspicion that her fanatical aunt was indulging in some newfangled voodoo to purify the presumably non-Brahmin child began to trouble Dini.

Hadn't Akka been at her relentlessly with her spectacularly ill-timed calls from San Jose ever since she found out about the adoption? 'Dini-ma, but we need to find out about the background of the baby. Caste is not superstition; it is a scientific matter. Now all American doctors say heredity and genes are of utmost importance!'

As the diya approached yet again, Dini got up abruptly with the baby. Akka paused the puja at once: 'We'll begin again after the baby has had a nap. We need half an hour more.' Her worst suspicion confirmed, Dini surprised even herself by announcing that her baby would not be brought up as a Brahmin: 'Akka, let me make this clear. Maithili is going to choose her religion when she is an adult.'

After that, she had left home with Maithili without even taking the time to change into normal clothes. She wanted no part of the enervating scene of her father pleading with his sister to forgive her high-strung niece.

She had marched into the office in all her Iyer finery, with a baby at her hip, and ran into RS. Starting out as her mentor for grassroots work, he was now intent on changing his role after eight years.

No, caste was definitely not a consideration for her anymore. Kenny, too, was Catholic, though an upper-middle-class Naga man was very different from a rural Scheduled Caste man who wore his origins on his frayed sleeve. RS spoke English carefully. It would be obvious to anyone that it wasn't his first language. A relationship with him would be very awkward socially, she conceded in her mind.

Dini realized she had been staring at her computer screen for ten minutes and not written a single word. All that she could think about was RS: his sheen, his smell, his texture. She felt an unfamiliar excitement. It wasn't about a relationship; it was about bodies—it was indeed about desire. She wasn't committed to Kenny. It had been over between them for ages. She was a free bird.

She felt daring and somewhat light-headed.

She wasn't a coward.

It was perfectly normal for a woman of thirty-seven to desire sex occasionally.

She dialled RS's number.

■

It did not take long for Dini to set up a dinner meeting at the dilapidated guest house with a startled RS. 'You want to come here?' he asked, incredulous. After assuring him that he had understood her correctly, she feverishly engineered a sleepover for Maithili at her friend's place. The friend's mother was also surprised: Dini was known for being possessive of her daughter and insisting on having sleepovers only at her own place. However, it was finalized quickly.

■

Dini knocked on RS's door with some irritation. The guest-house attendant had followed her and was watching with undisguised curiosity.

RS opened the door immediately.

'Hi, RS,' she said breezily. 'I hope you have two chairs and a table...' she added for the benefit of the curious attendant.

'Eh!' replied RS, hopelessly confused.

'It will take us a couple of hours to finish the report. I

haven't been able to get very far,' Dini said taking out from her bag the scratch pad that accompanied her everywhere. 'I don't want to sit on the floor.'

'I didn't...' tried RS, still at a loss.

'We can use this stool,' said Dini striding into the room. 'Go and get another chair,' she said to the attendant who was looking bored now.

'No chairs,' he replied.

'There must be another stool, like this one,' Dini persisted, beginning to enjoy herself.

'No more stools,' he replied trying to back off.

'Naresh Bhai, have you made the dinner I had requested?' RS asked. 'We have to do a lot of work,' he continued as Dini felt laughter bubbling within her.

'Dal and bhindi,' the attendant replied sullenly. 'No paneer.'

'Okay, get us the dinner then,' said RS.

'After that, you can look for the stool,' added Dini but she was speaking to his fast retreating back.

'Oh RS, should we go out for dinner? There is no paneer and I had okra—bhindi—for lunch,' she asked perversely. She couldn't help it.

RS looked at her carefully, 'The food is quite fine here actually. Naresh is not a bad cook,' he replied.

'And there's no place to sit,' said Dini. 'How will we write the report?'

There was a long silence. Then, RS said gently, very gently, 'I can take this chair. You can sit on the bed. We can use the stool as a table. This report... of the conference?... I wasn't quite sure why we...'

'But of course, we must write it,' replied Dini, trapped in her own act.

'Okay, yes of course,' replied RS. 'I can send you a draft once I get back. But where...'

'Then why did you call me here?' she asked, a little breathlessly.

'I didn't...' He began and then stopped abruptly. 'I thought we could discuss it... generally.'

'Oh... Okay, let's discuss generally. There isn't a chair for me, anyway.'

Dini knew she was making no sense. The laughter bubbling within her was threatening to spill out.

The attendant was back with a big tray covered with a tablecloth. Dini noticed it was washed and ironed. He kept the tray on the stool.

'Naresh Bhai, can't you get us another stool from the next room?' RS asked him. 'We have to finish some important work.'

'All rooms locked. No stool outside,' replied Naresh. 'My duty is over too.'

'Who will come for duty after you?' Dini asked.

'Peon. He doesn't know anything about furniture,' Naresh replied sullenly.

'Okay, Naresh Bhai, it is fine. Don't worry,' said RS as Dini coughed to stifle her laughter. What was wrong with her!

After Naresh left, closing the door after him, Dini wanted to run and hide. She wanted to throw herself onto RS. The room was so silent.

'RS, are we going to submit this report to the President of India?' she blabbered.

'But why such an elaborate charade?' RS was asking her, not smiling even a little.

'Naresh was very curious?'

'So what?' RS was looking at her full in the face.

'I don't want Naresh talking about us,' Dini replied unable to meet his eyes.

'But what would he talk about?' RS asked again. He had drawn his chair close to the bed. He was so near.

'Should we eat?' she asked, breathless again.

'I am not hungry,' RS said softly, taking her hand into his.

Dini thought of the clove-and-eucalyptus mouthwash she was carrying in her bag. Should she try and slide out to the washroom? But RS's hand was caressing, doing exciting things. She tried to stand up.

'Dini, I have been waiting for this for years,' he said. She was so close to him, so close.

'To have dinner with...' she started to say but he took her into his arms.

'Nine long years,' he said.

'No, eight... More like eight weeks, I mean,' she could barely speak. 'A woman always knows. You never—'

'You were wearing a blue-and-orange silk sari and you had flowers in your hair.'

Dini baulked at the vision of the stereotypical Indian womanhood his words conjured. Besides, his memory was irritatingly accurate.

'Orange flowers. I wondered from where you had got them. They are available only in the south of the country.'

Except when an aunt, who should have stayed put in California, puts them into three plastic bags and boards the flight from Mumbai to Delhi, as though arming herself with grenades to carpet-bomb the carefully cultivated identity of her niece. What had he thought of the sandalwood mark on her forehead, the giveaway caste marker?

'Why didn't you tell me before?' she stuttered. It was difficult to be playful with the breath knocked out of her.

'What—that I fell for you that day?' he asked, releasing her momentarily to look at her.

'Yes,' she answered. His pupils were the inkiest ink ringed with brown-black.

'You were dressed so traditionally and you had Maithili with you; I assumed you were married. Taken!' he replied, still not smiling.

'So how did you find out I was... not taken?'

'You told me. You sent me your details, remember? For the reimbursement form we needed to fill? And I have never heard of a boyfriend.'

'Inadequate data,' she tried to tease. His arms felt hard and sinewy, as though hewn from rock.

'But conclusive. The data I have on you better be conclusive!' he replied fiercely. 'Intelligent, independent, brave... Beautiful. You are so beautiful, Dinitia,' he whispered, tracing a line softly from her neck to her shoulder, making her break out in goosebumps.

'It can't be conclusive... We women are changeable,' she managed before his lips locked on hers.

Where had he learned to kiss like this? Dini had never experienced such power combined with so much reverence. He smelt of the earth. He felt sculpted and smooth but handled her like porcelain.

'You will have to make up for all the lost time.' She demanded to be explored, to be taken. Soon, she was the votary, worshipping his perfection. He was like the ever-rising brightness of midday. He smelt of sun-kissed rocks; he tasted of warmth.

Afterwards, he insisted they sleep in each other's arms. It was as though he couldn't bear to let go. Dini had heard that men hated cuddling. Kenny too would resolutely turn over to the other side. But this was the limit of her experience in the field. She had never known such intimacy. Of course he didn't snore, Greek gods don't! But when he turned his face trustingly towards her in deep sleep, snorting in a comic fashion, the spell was broken at last. She eased herself gently out of his embrace and giggled softly to herself before falling asleep.

■

It was only in the clearer light of the next morning that Dini became aware of the social dimension of their situation, the meanness of the room and the pettiness of the world he lived in.

'Hey RS, I must go. I have to pick up Maithili from her friend's house,' she said, jumping out of bed at five-thirty. She wanted to leave before Naresh arrived at his desk.

'Of course, let's go. I'll take five minutes to get ready,' he replied, having got up with her.

Dini froze in her tracks. 'You don't have to come, RS. It is still very early in the morning. Get another couple of hours of sleep,' she added, managing to make it sound light and airy.

'Dini, this is something that I want to do,' he insisted.

She had to think on her feet, 'You know Maithili, RS. She is a little precocious. She will ask all sorts of questions.'

'She has met me before, hasn't she? I'll just be visiting your home for the first time,' was the reply. He already had his clothes on and was looking at her expectantly. 'You can tell her we are very good friends.'

'Yes, but what's the point?'

'What do you mean?'

'She'll want to tell me everything that she's done since last evening right away. She'll demand my full attention. You'll just get bored,' Dini demurred.

'I won't. I want to get to know her too. Really, Dini, I do.'

'Oh RS... You know children can get resentful...'

'I know that. But it's possible to reason with them. You can tell her that I insisted on coming along to meet her.'

'I see no reason for telling her anything at all,' Dini parried, a little impatient by now.

RS turned on her. 'Did you actually say this, Dinitia?'

'What have I said, RS?'

'That our relationship is nothing at all.'

'It's not a relationship.' The words were out before she could bite them back.

'Then what is this, a casual fling?' he was livid.

Dini felt a gulf open up between them. In his code of conduct, flings were obviously anathema. What was she to say!

'RS, listen. Please don't be angry. I didn't say it's nothing. We've just...'

'Just what?'

'Look, we've just spent a night and...' She really didn't know how to begin explaining.

'Just had a one-night stand, tenth–twelfth–thirteenth in the series that you are having?'

'You are insulting me,' she said softly, preparing to leave.

'And you, what about you? I say I want to get to know the daughter of the woman I just made love to and she replies "what's the point".'

'We are not getting married,' she spat out in spite of herself. 'We just fucked.'

He surprised her by catching hold of her shoulders and shaking her violently. 'Fucked, just fucked... Is this what this means to you? The elite Brahmin woman! The body of the untouchable to be used and abused—never accepted, never adopted...'

Oh God, of course he had noted the sandalwood mark on her forehead; he had known all along! He had never brought up the issue of caste all these years. But how could she have imagined that it could ever be overlooked? How could she have been so naive? From his perspective, she came from the oppressor class. Come to think of it, she did actually. The long history of oppression cannot be negated just by the enlightened views of a single generation. It was the same all over the world. But what the hell did he mean by 'adopted'!

'RS, this is so unfair... How did caste come in? You know how much I respect you ... the work you do,' she mumbled, her ever-ready temper doused with uncharacteristic remorse. She was troubled enough to desist from pointing out that he was gripping her so hard that she would have bruises. And did he realize that this kind of behaviour was punishable under domestic violence!

'Is this the way you show your respect? By not letting me even meet your daughter?' he was saying.

She was desperate by now; she couldn't bear to hurt him like this!

'RS, please. Please listen to me. You have to understand that I am a single woman bringing up a daughter in a very middle-class colony... People can't be allowed to say things about my "character". Maithili is very young; she will talk. She can get very hurt, you know, if it gets around that her mother has a close male friend. Look, we've just started. Who knows where this relationship will go... You may find somebody else tomorrow. Then what will I say to Maithili?'

She allowed herself to be gathered in his arms and kissed once again—gently, lovingly, apologetically. Protestations of eternal love followed. How could he even think of looking at another woman after this heavenly night? Yes, he had been an unthinking bastard. She was the bravest, loveliest creature he had ever met and he would personally, with his bare hands, throttle anybody who dared to hurt or insult her or her daughter. Oh, could she forgive him for his boorishness. What did he know! He was just a villager, un-evolved, mostly self-educated! He knew nothing about the constraints of a single mother. But now it was going to be his mission in life to ensure their well-being.

It had taken an hour for her to get him to the point where he 'understood' that their relationship could not be revealed to her daughter so precipitately—no, not even hinted at! But of course he kissed her long and hard again before she could leave.

July

The Odd Semester Begins and
Odd Things Happen

During her first summer vacation as the 'woman alone', Shailaja found that she had fallen into a routine—early to bed, early to rise—for the first time in her life. The only person she was meeting regularly was Mrs Gandhi, who proved invaluable with practical advice about setting up a home. Nevertheless, the hot days felt full with many unfamiliar chores to accomplish, and by evening, she was too tired to obsess about issues of identity and existence.

This last evening of the vacation was no different, and after a good day's work, she, as usual, escaped—this time to a murky underworld where incredibly muscled and tattooed goons kidnap young girls to sell to oil sheikhs. Alongside watching TV, she was eating her very early dinner and a delicious languor was stealing over her. The spicy paneer matar and the thin, light *phulka*s were great accompaniments to the wronging of white innocence. Before she knew it, she had downed three phulkas, and Rajni ki Ma was at her side with the fourth.

'No, I don't want more.' As she was remonstrating, the doorbell pealed. 'Please see who's come, Rajni ki Ma.'

'*Memsahib hain?*' she heard a man's voice ask, and with her heart racing, she rushed to the door.

'Hi Shailaja, I was passing by and thought I would ask how you're settling down.' It was indeed Ranjan at her doorstep.

'I'm quite all right, Ranjan,' she replied airily, basically for the benefit of her inquisitive domestic help. 'Do come in.'

He stepped in and continued blithely, 'All settled? It can be difficult in the beginning. I can see you have got yourself a slave already. I came to check if there's anything you need.'

He was concerned about her like he would be about a distant relative. Rajni ki Ma was listening avidly. Shailaja thanked her stars he was speaking mainly in English.

'Nice place you've got,' he said looking around. 'Quite spacious! I can see Delhi University looks after you guys quite well,' he joked.

He was trying to behave as though they were casual acquaintances. They had spent thirteen years together.

'Yes, thanks Ranjan,' she managed at last, willing herself to turn into stone.

'Get some water,' she said to Rajni ki Ma.

'Here are the keys of your car. I've got it along. Why did you leave it behind?' he was remonstrating. 'It must be inconvenient to travel all that distance by public transport.'

'It's not a problem,' she replied icily. 'Uber goes everywhere these days. It's also quite easy to get buses and autorickshaws from here.'

He placed the car key and the papers on the table just as Rajni ki Ma, uncharacteristically subservient, reappeared, bearing a glass of water on a tray.

'When does your college begin?' he asked.

Didn't he know? Didn't he remember how she used to bewail the end of vacation!

'Tomorrow. But it's fine, I don't want the car,' she heard herself say.

'Come on, Shailaja! Don't be childish,' he replied. 'We are still friends.'

He wasn't affected, his heart wasn't aching. 'I have to prepare for an early morning class, Ranjan. It's quite late,' she said, cold and hard.

'Shailaja, really!' Visibly embarrassed, he looked at Rajni ki Ma and got up, frowning. 'Look, I always thought of it as your car. Besides, it is registered in your name. You can sell it off if you don't want it.'

'No, thank you. I don't want water,' he said to Rajni ki Ma.

'You've finished, so you can leave too,' Shailaja said to Rajni ki Ma as soon as he went out of the door.

■

It was difficult to stem her tears that night.

'Shailaja, why are you leaving? If anyone has to go, it should be me,' Ranjan had said to her when she told him about her decision to leave the Defence Colony barsati. He had come home after almost a month.

'I want to start again on a clean slate...'

'Oh, such a child! There aren't any clean slates in life unless of course we die and are reborn. We have been together for twelve years...'

Tears started to flow.

'Thirteen, Ranjan. I was twenty-two...'

'Yes, a baby. Stop crying... It's not easy for me, you know.'

'Then don't do it.'

'Shail... Look, I didn't mean to start anything with Diksha...'

'You couldn't help yourself, could you? A beautiful woman twenty years younger,' she had sobbed.

'You were—are—beautiful too… I still think of our first meeting. You looked like a startled fawn.'

How soft but lethal that inadvertent blow!

'Go away, Ranjan…'

But their relationship was destined to end that way, wasn't it? Could she have done anything differently?

Ranjan and she had met soon after she finished college. Fresh after an MA in English Literature, she had just started her MPhil. Her parents were vociferous in their criticism. This MA anyway qualified her for nothing—she was, in their opinion, simply wasting her time. What was the point of studying more English if all that one would do is become a teacher? They started suggesting suitable boys as soon as she refused to take admission in MA Economics, for which they had sent her to Delhi in the first place. Shailaja would flinch every time her father produced his winning cards: 'Six-figure salary, Shailaja' and 'Only son and no responsibilities!' and 'Banker, engineer, doctor'.

If she had listened to them, could she have had a different life? She could have owned a flat in Vasant Kunj. It would have been easier than being single and alone. But did she really want to be like Mrs Gandhi or Mrs Jain? Or like her younger sister who juggled a full-day job with cooking and caring for her children and husband, and had no time to get her arms waxed, or even find fault with her older sister anymore?

When her parents heard that she had moved in with a film-maker without a wedding ceremony, the remnants of their hopes were dashed. Their older daughter was bringing such shame to the family. So free, so loose! Her father made a desperate attempt to salvage the situation; he came to Delhi to remonstrate with her. 'Is he married or what?' 'He is so old. Surely, he must have been married before.' 'Then why can't he just marry you?'

But she had newly learnt to laugh disparagingly at the great Indian wedding: the vulgarity of video cameras capturing the bling-and-rhinestone, the Christmas-tree costumes; the meaningless march around the sacred fire; and the hard reality of legions of strangers wolfing down meals procured at many thousands per plate. 'Oh Shailaja, weddings are the celebration of middle-class tastelessness! You can't submit to it only to please your parents,' Ranjan said to her. 'We can arrange a civil marriage in court; it will take ten minutes,' her father pleaded. 'But why is a wedding necessary? Isn't it enough that we are committed to each other,' she countered. 'Arre, this is India, *beta*. Women need security here!' And the most hurtful one: 'Since when have you become such an iconoclast? You were never like this.'

Parents always know.

But she had told her father she didn't care a hoot for what people thought. No, she wasn't doing it to hurt her family, they must understand. It would be immoral to force Ranjan to do something he didn't believe in. What kind of partner would she be if she didn't understand his principles! Did her father want their relationship to be defeated by society before it even started? If they loved her, they would understand. Her father had shaken his head in despair and demanded to meet Ranjan. There was more of the same at dinner at the India Habitat Centre. With a few silken phrases and a discourse on the essential unreliability of human life, Ranjan managed to staunch the stream of arguments and objections that were, by then, threatening to overwhelm Shailaja. She looked on as her sensitive, unworldly boyfriend won the day, rendering her father, the crusty retired bureaucrat from Uttar Pradesh, speechless. 'Ultimately it is Shailaja's decision—not yours or mine. I will do what she wants me to do, Mr Sharma.' Shailaja felt a little sorry for her father. 'Believe me, I am not making a mistake, Papa! You must tell Mummy you have seen for yourself that I am happy,' she said to him.

Yes, she had been happy with Ranjan for thirteen years, everyone could see that—until happiness ended one fine day. Just like that!

The day she realized that Ranjan had stopped looking at her! He failed to notice her newly shaped eyebrows, plucked into deep arches that gave her a quizzical expression. The trendy beautician had remarked, 'This gives you attitude, Madam!' She strutted around Ranjan; her own eyes questioning desperately—but there was no reply. During the last few months of being together, Shailaja took to speaking too loudly: look at me! Their friends were startled when she split their eardrums with her cheery phone calls too early in the morning. In those neurotic days, Shailaja came up with millions of plans—films, weekend trips, picnics. So uncharacteristically persuasive was she that friends capitulated in sheer surprise. 'Full of energy these days, aren't we, Shailaja!' The friends left her, but she still had the photographs, forged proofs of their togetherness. It was Ranjan's smart set: well-dressed, well-heeled! In spite of so many holidays together, they never really became hers. She was left only with the pictures. Precariously on a rock, stream bubbling, beer cans with golden liquid spouting, or snow-capped mountains and hysterical laughter in a raft. Ranjan's arm around her, as though to protect her. All lies. She knew it was over much before she found the birthday card with the lipstick kiss and the giveaway message.

It was almost morning when she finally drifted off to restless sleep.

■

Shailaja woke up reluctantly with the phone alarm at six in the morning and switched on the pump. The first day of the odd semester! She hadn't got much sleep, but she was still looking forward to meeting the students. She had worked quite hard in the vacation: reading *Gone with the Wind*, word by word, and photocopying and collating secondary material. Preparing for the new course on popular fiction had given her an insight into romance; teaching it would be therapeutic, she told herself firmly.

The morning passed too quickly with the ever-voluble Rajni ki Ma. She laid out Shailaja's green chiffon sari on the bed. A gift from Ranjan in a previous life! Or had it been just last year?

'Didi, wear this today,' she commanded.

'I have to go to college. This sari is thin and transparent. It is for the evening.'

Rajni ki Ma started off another tirade about single women dressing like widows and driving away men from their doorsteps.

'One should not fight all the time. It can't be his fault totally. Can one clap with one hand? After all, he came and gave the car, didn't he? Who gives away something so expensive! You could have talked to him, offered him something to eat. There was enough food and I could have made more. As it is, you people eat so little…' She went on. Shailaja thought she had a point but she still hung the sari back in the wardrobe and took out a yellow salwar and a grey kurta instead.

Rajni ki Ma made a face. 'Uh, not even matching. Other madams have everything matching, even sandals. Buy some new clothes, no!'

Shailaja emerged from her new home. She felt young—about five years old. The *poha* Rajni ki Ma had prepared for her—the Maharashtrian way, with peanuts, curry leaves and a dash of sugar—had been piquant with green chilies. She really enjoyed breakfast in spite of the heartache. Her class began at ten-thirty. It was a good forty-minute drive from Vasant Kunj to college. Shailaja shot out of the parking; it was ten already.

But then she had to brake rather precipitately. A huge water tanker was squatting right outside the parking in the middle of the narrow road to the colony gate. What was she to do? As usual, there were cars parked on both sides of the lane all the way till the gate. The parking areas inside the colony were woefully inadequate to contain the Indian automobile revolution that had resulted in two-three cars per flat. With the tanker standing where it was, it was a complete roadblock. In fact, the sides of the tanker were brushing the parked cars on both sides. Shailaja honked. A woman resplendent in a parrot-green dressing gown appeared from the thicket at the side of the road. 'Two minutes, Madam,' she said.

Shailaja noted that the huge pipe that emerged from the underbelly of the tanker and vanished into the hedgerow was vibrating. It was dispensing water into one of the monstrous black storage water tanks behind the hedgerow. The tanker was, no doubt, from the state water department and had been sent to pacify the irate residents. Water was supplied for only half an hour that morning.

Another woman in a frilly pink nightgown arrived on the scene and said to parrot-green, 'I called the tanker. How is it that you are taking water before me?'

It was Mrs Gandhi underneath the pink frills. But she did not even look at Shailaja. She was busy holding her own with parrot-green.

'If you keep sitting inside having tea, the whole world is not going to wait for you,' parrot-green attacked.

'I had called the tanker,' repeated Mrs Gandhi.

'So what, I had called him yesterday and the day before, and you took water before me both days.'

Shailaja stuck her head out of the window. 'Nilima-ji, it's me.'

'There is not a drop in my home, and Mr Gandhi has to leave for work,' she said turning to Shailaja at last.

Mr Gandhi? Husband… Wow! 'So do I, Nilima-ji. I have work too. My class begins in twenty minutes,' said Shailaja poking her head out further. 'Please move the tanker and let me pass.'

Both the women looked askance. 'Not a drop of water,' repeated parrot-green.

'This is emergency, Shailaja. One day the children can wait for five minutes,' said the betraying Mrs Gandhi.

'You know I teach in a college. And can't the water wait five minutes?' Shailaja persisted.

'No, it can't. Why should we ask the tanker to move? He got here first,' replied parrot-green querulously.

'I will lose my job,' Shailaja pleaded.

'Teachers in Delhi University are always late,' said the treacherous Mrs Gandhi as her partner-in-crime nodded her agreement. 'Nobody ever loses job. You only said!'

'That's not true. Like in every other job, there are some who are conscientious and others who aren't,' replied Shailaja, cursing herself for bitching about her colleagues to all and sundry.

'It is a good job for women,' conceded parrot-green. 'You're a woman. You must understand the kind of problems one can have without water,' she continued in a sisterly way.

'I'm not telling you to not take water; I'm only requesting you to let me pass. Where is the driver?' said Shailaja, feeling a little desperate now.

'How do I know? He must be around,' replied parrot-green.

'Don't get so impatient, Shailaja. Try and see it from Mrs Malhotra's point of view,' said Mrs Gandhi brokering Buddhist peace. She had been nattering about her 'new way of worship' all through summer.

By then, there were three cars honking behind Shailaja. Somebody yelled, 'Which motherfucker is blocking the road today?'

Mrs Gandhi and parrot-green looked at each other and, in unspoken agreement, disappeared behind the hedgerow like exotic birds startled by rude tourists in a bird sanctuary.

'Nilima-ji, I will get very late,' whined Shailaja but she was talking to thin air.

A man strode out of the car, 'Inconveniencing everybody!' he hollered. 'Blocking traffic at ten in the morning! Driver!' he called.

Nothing happened.

'Whose tanker is this?' The man demanded.

'There were a couple of ladies here a minute ago,' said Shailaja, trying to help.

The man gave her a scornful look. 'Mrs Gandhi!' he growled. 'She seems to have a swimming pool in her flat. Water came for an hour in the morning; still this truck from Jal Board has to be called!'

'I think the water came for just half an hour this side. There was also this other woman, Mrs Malhotra… In fact, she was taking water,' the ever fair and loyal Shailaja tried to explain.

The man paid no attention to her. He walked to the tanker and turned off the water supply; the fat tube stopped vibrating. Shailaja wondered about him, obviously a man of consequence. His tummy protruded so confidently, like that of her college principal. A thin boy emerged from the thicket. He looked about fifteen.

'Move the tanker, you son of a bitch. Next time I'll get you arrested,' the man commanded.

The boy jumped into the driver's seat and the tanker began to roll back.

Law of inertia: roadblocks in Vasant Kunj don't move without the use of rude force.

I should have got out of the home earlier, rued Shailaja. She would be very late.

Law of inertia: Rajni ki Ma won't stop unless there is an equal force against her.

She was trapped between the home and the world, powerless, helpless! Panic had her stomach in knots, the road seemed to rise to block her way, the trees on either side gesticulated menacingly. The big tanker was challenging her to pass from the narrow alley that it had created by rolling back just a couple of feet. The car behind her was honking. She breathed deeply, released the clutch and wove her way around the monster. The car nipping at her heels seemed to snort derisively at her lack of expertise.

She had learnt driving just a couple of years ago; Ranjan's driver had taught her. They had bought a second-hand car for her commute to college. She hadn't used her skill much because the driver was usually free to drop her to college in Ranjan's brand new sedan. But at least she could drive and had a car, Shailaja told herself, in an unconscious echo of Mrs Gandhi's Buddhism.

While Shailaja drove shakily to college, Mrs Gandhi shut herself in the bedroom. The water tanker had gone away in a huff without piping the precious liquid into her storage tank; it was less than half full as of now. There would be virtual crises in the home by the evening. She had wasted half an hour pleading with the sulky driver but he was adamant.

'Madam, we also get insulted; we can't take so much scolding in the morning… We are human beings too.'

Even the hundred-rupee note she waved in his face did not work. She returned home and yelled at Rajni, who was running her usual 'Niagara' to attack the dirty dinner utensils stacked in the sink. 'From where should I get water for this kind of luxury? You people make me buy water every day. Should I deduct the amount from your salary or what?'

Sunil irritably asked her to lower her volume. 'This house is noisier than Sadar Bazaar.' Then he rushed out, leaving the bathroom tap running. They must have lost six to seven buckets before she spotted the water draining while on her daily round to check for drips and leaks.

Feeling wronged and indignant, she refused to respond to her mother-in-law, who was asking her why her son left without having breakfast; who was going to look after his health if his own wife became so bad-tempered in the morning?

She hadn't even had the time to bathe up till now, and all that Sunil did was insult her in front of his mother and the servants. Everybody was out and pretending to do important stuff—Sunil was in his office where there was that secretary, Reeta.

Neeru was in school. She had left early, also without breakfast, which was usual, but without bathing as well. She would demand several buckets of water for her beauty bath in the evening. The two younger children were at school and playschool, respectively. The crotchety old woman, after getting no reply from her, started ringing the puja bell furiously. It was left to her to check on taps and clean up after everybody.

She, too, should take up a job and leave the household to its devices. She could take to teaching children too, couldn't she? How youthful and confident Shailaja had looked driving the car. Well-ironed cotton salwar-kameez and light lipstick!

She had always wanted to look like that. But where did Shailaja get the car from? There had been no car all this time. Teachers earned money even when they stayed at home on vacation! Mrs Gandhi caught sight of herself in the dressing-table mirror. The face that sat atop the mountain of pink frills looked drawn and pale. The roots of her hair shone silver. If she stopped dyeing her hair, it would be a shock of white, not the kind of silver-streaked cloud that adorned Shailaja's head. 'This girl—Sheela... Shailaja—you keep talking to, what does she do?' Sunil had asked, sounding deliberately casual last evening. Girl indeed!

Shailaja must be as old as her, if not older. Mrs Gandhi had got married early. She was a slip of a girl then; she used to look even younger than twenty-two. This household had made her an aunty!

After marriage, she had come into the family home, which was a small flat above a shop in Sadar Bazaar. There wasn't even a cupboard to call her own. Their bedroom was also the ironing station and storage place for household linen, so people were in and out of it all day. It was only late at night that they were allowed some privacy. To add to that, every now and then, Sunil's mother would wonder loudly for all to hear how parents could be irresponsible enough to bring up their daughters without teaching them even the rudiments of housekeeping. 'Now, our Nilima would have ruined two kilos of milk trying to set curd without warming the milk properly.' 'Our Sunil is so unworldly; we were hoping his wife would knock some sense into his head, but our daughter-in-law has turned out to be hundred to his ten. She pays fifty paise per blouse to the dhobi when there are two imported steam irons in her own room.'

Her mother-in-law put all the responsibility of running the house on her, made her neglect her looks right from the beginning. It was no wonder that she put on weight.

In tears almost every day due to the taunts directed at her by the in-laws, she left for Assam six months after the marriage. Mrs Gandhi relived her one and only triumph over Sunil and his family. Her father was so supportive when she sobbed out her trauma. In spite of her mother's injunction—'it is girls who have to adjust'—he wrote to Sunil's father in flawless English stating frankly that they had not given their daughter to the Gandhis so that she should be put to work like a servant. Had they known that there was such an acute problem procuring household help in Delhi, they would have given a couple of 'domestic helps' as well in dowry. She loved the expression 'domestic help'. Sunil's family came—his mother, father, brother, sister and he—all the way to Assam to fetch her back. She recalled their sheepish faces as they sat in the gracious sofas of their company bungalow, nibbling at the snacks served by the housemaid and the butler. Sunil even whispered 'I am missing you' when nobody was looking. 'We'll move to our own flat, I promise,' he said.

She would never get her Assam days back. The patriarch who could write such wonderfully biting letters was dead, and so was her mother. Her brother and his wife lived in a flat in Guwahati, and they had made it clear that there was no space in it for a sister seeking even temporary refuge from her marriage. She felt a pang of nostalgia. She would do anything to go back to Assam and hear her father speak in his reassuringly anglicized accent and feel the breeze from their garden on her face. Couldn't the Buddha turn the clock back for her? But why would he do that? She hadn't even had the time to chant this morning.

At the last Buddhist meeting, a member had given her a phone number. 'This is our leader's number. If you have any problems and need advice you can call Navneeta Singh.' Mrs

Gandhi dug out the scrap of paper on which she had written it down. But such women would not understand, would they? They had careers and fancy jobs! Dinshee, for instance, was so busy always! But Shailaja worked too and it was possible to talk to her. Would Navneeta be like Shailaja and have the patience to listen to her?

Navneeta's voice was soft and gentle on the phone. A bit like Dinshee's, but kinder.

'Nilima-ji, how are you? I have heard so much about you from the other members—Mrs Malhotra, and—'

'Navneeta, I am chanting regularly but I'm having problems,' Mrs Gandhi said, taking the bull by the horns.

'Yes Nilima-ji, tell me.'

Mrs Gandhi was suddenly tongue-tied.

'Our problems lead us to Buddhahood. We must thank those who are creating these problems for us,' encouraged Navneeta softly.

'It is my mother-in-law. Now she is ringing the bell so loudly and making such a racket. It is not possible for me to chant. All morning she has prevented me.'

'This is indeed a problem, Nilima-ji. But tell me, what time does she do her puja?' Navneeta was sounding very sympathetic. She might also be living in an extended family.

'Very late, at eleven. I tell her again and again that puja should be done in the morning. But all morning she is busy interfering in the kitchen.'

'Oh-oh-oh! This is so bad, Nilima-ji.'

At last there was somebody who appreciated the kind of problems she had to face. But Navneeta was continuing, 'I suppose she is old... Nilima-ji, we can't expect the old to change, can we? It is up to us to make adjustments and inspire older people to follow the true path. I would advise you to do your chanting before she gets up—early in the morning. Set her an example. Morning is a beautiful time to chant. I chant at 6.00 a.m., as soon as I get up, and I can't tell you how effective it is. I feel one with nature, with the entire environment.'

'But children's tiffin, husband's breakfast… This is the time when—'

'Yes, of course, this is a mother's duty. How old are your children?'

'My oldest daughter is fourteen; then there is another one, she is eight. My son is very small, just three…'

'So, won't your eldest daughter chant with you?'

'No, Neeru is not interested in all this—young people, you know. They are only interested in clothes and parties…' Mrs Gandhi could not bring herself to describe Neeru's habitual contempt towards everything her mother did.

'Oh, she will come around, Nilima-ji. I would say keep telling her about the practice. We have a lot of young members. Some of their meetings are held separately. And your two small ones are at such lovely innocent stages in their lives. Nilima-ji, it will shape their character if they hear their mother chant before they leave for school.'

'But their tiffin… And then Sunil is so fussy…'

'There must be a cook who makes the tiffin and breakfast?'

'No, the cook comes later to make lunch—I do the breakfast myself…'

'Oh Nilima-ji, it is wonderful that you make breakfast for the whole family. But you said your mother-in-law likes to supervise?'

'She only likes to order the servants around. It is a constant interference.'

'But why not let her do it?'

'You mean I let her run the kitchen?' This was no good, Mrs Gandhi thought; Navneeta was being impractical, like Dinshee.

'Only when you are chanting, of course—just for half an hour or one hour in the morning and then in the evening for a shorter period. Get away from domesticity. Call the cook earlier and ask your mother-in-law to supervise. After all, isn't she the children's grandmother and your husband's mother? She will be gainfully employed and you will get time for yourself.'

Mrs Gandhi was dumbstruck at the idea of using her mother-in-law's interference profitably. Navneeta went on, 'You know, there is Mrs Verma in your group. She had the same problem. Her mother-in-law wanted to cook for Mr Verma. I advised Mrs Verma to let her do it and also chant for her happiness. They used to have fights every single day, but now they are the best of friends. Can you believe it? Her mother-in-law actually makes breakfast for her as well. Nilima-ji, you too chant for the happiness of your husband's mother.'

'But her happiness is making life hell for me,' muttered Mrs Gandhi.

Navneeta sighed at the other end. 'Poor woman! She needs your help in transcending the low life condition she is creating for herself. We can never be happy by making other people unhappy.'

This was not going the way she had hoped, but Mrs Gandhi persevered. 'If I chant in morning, my husband and everybody will come to know.'

'Don't they know already?'

'Oh no, mother-in-law is quite deaf and Sunil goes to office every day—even on Sundays these days. And anyway I close the door when I chant, or I go to a member's home. Nobody in the family knows.'

'But Nilima-ji, they should know. Your family deserves to

know that you are on the path to Buddhahood. It would be good karma for them to hear you chant. In fact, your aim should be to make everyone in the family chant with you. But tell me, how is it that they don't know yet? Don't you have the Gohonzon?'

Mrs Gandhi had not even thought about installing a Butsudan that contained the Gohonzon with the magic words: 'I devote myself to the Lotus Sutra of the Wonderful Law.' You were supposed to chant the mantra repeatedly in front of the Gohonzon—the mandala of ancient Chinese characters—for at least ten minutes, twice a day.

'No,' she whispered.

'You have been chanting so regularly and attending all meetings. Since when have you been chanting?'

'Two and a half months.'

'Oh, just two and a half months! Usually we take applications for the Gohonzon after six months of regular practise. But sometimes we make an exception. Nilima-ji, I am so glad you called me. The enshrinement of the Gohonzon brings great luck to the household. You must begin preparing for it.'

Mrs Gandhi had attended an enshrinement ceremony. It was very impressive; lots of loud chanting and followed by a big tea party—two sweets and three savouries. Why couldn't she hold a ceremony like this in her own flat! Mrs Gandhi tried to imagine what her mother-in-law, her husband and her eldest daughter would say if she declared openly that she was becoming a Buddhist.

'You must tell your family about the practice and prepare them for the Gohonzon too,' Navneeta said.

In fact, neither her mother-in-law nor Sunil would be able to object as this was religious activity in keeping with theirs, and not conversion to another faith. All this had been explained at the meeting. Mrs Gandhi began to get excited. She would organize the enshrinement ceremony and call her kitty-party friends. She would also call Dinshee and Shailaja. She would have it on a Sunday so Neeru and Sunil are around too. They would be impressed by Navneeta and all the other Buddhist ladies. Although these days Sunil had taken to going out even on holidays...

In flawless English, Navneeta was outlining the process of having the enshrinement ceremony. Mrs Gandhi couldn't wait for Neeru and Sunil to meet her new friends. So many of them were working women and spoke so well.

'Navneeta, you will come to install it in my home, won't you?' she asked.

'Oh sure, Nilima-ji. Very gladly. But I must warn you, sometimes it takes a while before we can have the enshrinement,' replied the well-spoken Navneeta.

Mrs Gandhi was strangely elated and peaceful the whole day. When the water ran out in the overhead tank at five in the evening, as she had known it would, she quietly pumped up the remaining water from the storage tank and called Bahadur to the kitchen to tell him to let everyone know. He had been getting ready to protest his innocence in the matter but she didn't raise her voice even once; he gaped at her in surprise and fled before she could change her mind. She heard him yell at Rajni to stop throwing water in the verandah outside and then remonstrated with Ganesh, who was asking his doting grandmother to fill the plastic tub in the bathroom so that he could splash in it.

While Mrs Gandhi plotted her enshrinement, Shailaja, whom she had been instrumental in getting delayed for work, was driving to college with the sinking feeling that she was going to be unpardonably late for class.

She felt indignant. She had been foolish enough to commend Mrs Gandhi for attempting to rise above petty, everyday affairs. Obviously, all her talk of Buddhism hadn't made a dent in her essential self-centredness. And that husband of hers for whom she was aggressively procuring water—did she know what all he was up to? She had had a taste of his Casanova behaviour and knew exactly how much *he* was invested in the marriage.

This was a couple of days before the vacation ended. Shailaja began recalling the incident in her mind to take the edge off her anxiety. Mrs Jain had been bringing up the issue of the rubber plant again and again. 'My rubber plant was two feet high, Shailaja. Just letting you know. You must have settled down by now and will have the time to go to the nursery.' Shailaja had taken herself to the nursery to buy the dashed thing before she got busy with her teaching, though Rajni ki Ma had been giving a contrary opinion. 'Did you even see this rub-badd plant? How do you know it was there?'

She found an impressive specimen in the neighbouring nursery, but bringing it back home proved to be quite a challenge. The Uber driver flatly refused to carry it in the dicky. It was only the fourth autorickshaw driver who agreed to take her with the two-feet-tall plant in a cement pot to Vasant Kunj, but only at three times the usual fare.

There she had been in the colony car park, where the autorickshaw had disgorged her and the plant, and the afternoon sun was beating down. Why hadn't she thought of how she was going to get the plant up to Mrs Jain's flat? It weighed at least thirty kilos; the autorickshaw driver had complained loudly while depositing it there. It was the middle of the day; there was no guard or any other potential help to be seen.

The parking was deserted except for a black, stately sedan and its driver who seemed ready for take-off in the driveway. With the car AC running, the driver was probably waiting for the memsahib-sahib to emerge from one of the flats.

'*Bhaiya*, would you know where the guard is?' she asked politely.

He paid no attention whatsoever. He couldn't have heard what she was saying, but he didn't bother to lower the window to find out either.

Shailaja had tried to move the pot; it wouldn't budge an inch. The driver had kept watching her superciliously.

At last reaching the college, Shailaja parked quickly in the college parking and began walking to her class, which was wickedly in the block farthest from there, still thinking of her first meeting with Mr Gandhi.

As she had stood nonplussed in the colony parking with the outsize potted plant, a man with a slim briefcase arrived on the scene. Seeing her, he stopped short. 'Any problem, Ma'am?' he asked.

It was Mr Gandhi. There was a picture of him getting some sort of office award prominently displayed in the Gandhis' drawing room and she had seen him pass by a couple of times in the colony. She noted his fresh, creaseless clothes and mentally credited Mrs Gandhi for the excellent *press-wallah*. But if she could kit her man out so well, whatever happened to her while selecting her own wardrobe—all those gaudy, bling-saris and peacock-plume salwar-kameez! Alternately, if the man actually took time out to choose his own clothes, couldn't he also advise his wife to tone down her colours?

'Mr Gandhi, how are you? I was looking for the guard to help me carry this upstairs. But I can't seem to find him.'

'Oh, you know my name! This is not fair, as I don't know yours,' he had said, looking at her in a particular way.

'Yes, I know Nilima-ji and the children very well. I am Shailaja; I live in the building across—on the top floor.'

'Oh, so you are the new girl who has moved in recently. My wife mentions you very often. But you have never visited us.'

'I have visited Mrs Gandhi a couple of times. But you've not been home...'

'Next time, you must come while I'm there,' he replied, openly paying court. 'Ramprasad, go and get the guard,' he said in a rather imperious manner to his driver.

The driver leapt out of the car and went into a little thatched structure that stood right behind the carpark. He reappeared with the guard in tow in two minutes flat.

The guard assessed the weight of the pot by going around it and then shook his head. 'Madam, I have a backache; I can't carry it up. Even now I was resting...'

'I'll hold it from one side. It has to be taken only till the first floor. To Mrs Jain's,' she offered, desperate to get out of the awkward situation.

'Please allow me to handle this, Shailaja,' Mr Gandhi had replied. 'Ramprasad, you lift the pot from one side,' he ordered the driver. Then turning to the guard, he said curtly, 'Surely you can help now; pick it up from the other side.'

Shailaja had looked on as the uppity driver and the recalcitrant guard picked the pot up jointly and began to lug it up the stairs

'Thank you so much, Mr Gandhi,' she said to him, a little embarrassed.

'It would be nice to have a potential weight-lifter for a

neighbour,' he had replied, grinning even more flirtatiously. 'But I couldn't stand by and watch you break your limbs...'

Even more than his exaggerated courtly manner, it was his eyes, Shailaja thought. All the time, they had buzzed around her. She knew he was taking note of her understated kurta and cigarette pants. He also noted that the beige-and-blue print of the kurta was trendy, the pants expensive and a perfect fit, her sandals branded leather, the brown lipstick luxury, and her eye make-up subtle. Which secretary in a too-short skirt was the recipient of his gaze usually, she had wondered even then. Of course, he had grabbed that opportunity to procure her mobile number and was since persecuting her regularly with senseless forwards.

And his clueless wife, whom she felt so sorry for, thought the world of him—Mrs Gandhi had betrayed their fledgling friendship to get water for His Highness without a thought.

Lost in indignation, Shailaja suddenly caught sight of the principal in the corridor.

'Good morning, Dr Dhar,' she said, switching off her frown and trying to smile.

'Good morning, Miss Shailaja Sharma,' replied Dr V.K. Dhar. Mercifully, he walked on without asking what she was doing running in the corridor well after the third period had started.

Would he go into her office, check the timetables and draft a termination notice? Shailaja tried to calm herself by whispering 'irrational'. This was an irrational fear. To throw out a college teacher of more than ten years, he would need to serve a memo or a chargesheet at the least. Nothing so gargantuan had happened to any teacher in her college—or for that matter, in the entire university. Besides, it was the first day of college after the vacation. Some teachers wouldn't have even started teaching.

However, she couldn't run away from the fact that her

position was still unstable. The college had renewed her appointment every semester but still not given her permanent tenure. Now that her circumstances had changed so much, she needed to establish her sincerity and not be caught coming late for a class.

It was ironic that this job had become so important for her. She had not been too happy to accept a position in what was widely considered to be a down-market college but had done it only at Ranjan's insistence. Even temporary jobs are difficult to come by, he had said.

■

There they sat in a row, waiting patiently for Shailaja. Eight students—all girls!

Solid middle-class families sent their wards to Deendayal Sanatan Dharma College with the expectation that they would be taught by no-nonsense matrons and venerable male 'professors'.

'I don't think you should talk about us in the staffroom,' Ranjan had cautioned her, surprising her with his practical sense.

'I wouldn't want to lie,' she protested.

'Discretion is the better part, sweetheart. Just be discreet till you get a permanent job,' he argued.

However, there had been no occasion to talk about her personal life as she didn't make any friends in the staffroom. After she refused to be drawn into their boring union politics, the few younger, politically aware teachers also kept their distance. The older male teachers kept to themselves anyway. The aunty-types stared at her—a few of them askance—at her attire.

'You don't seem to possess any Indian dresses,' one of the senior 'lady' teachers observed stonily a fortnight after she joined, disapproving of the smart but casual trousers she had worn to work. 'The sari and salwar-kameez suits are graceful dresses and most becoming in the teaching environment.'

Shailaja had quietly bought some 'suits' the very next day. 'The workplace is going to occupy a very small space in my life,' she had said to Ranjan. 'It's not my type. I'll do other things alongside.'

Ten book reviews in newspapers in those many years. Her accomplishments did not make for an impressive CV.

And here she was, almost half an hour late for a class on popular fiction.

Six out of the eight students also wore salwar-kameez. The kind of clothes mummy would buy. In this day and age and in Delhi, fumed Shailaja. How would she teach these girls about desire and its fulfilment, about flights of fantasy, about daydreams realized in fiction, about the purgation of reality? She looked at them closely. Two were wearing jeans and one a lace top. There was hope. Besides, it wasn't only about appearances; her reading of feminist criticism had taught her that, hadn't it?

'Ma'am, there are ten of us in this class. There are also two boys, but they are absent today. All others have gone for the other option.'

'It seems Popular Fiction is not too popular here.'

'No Ma'am, actually there were twenty students who wanted to opt for this paper. But then Dr Reena Singh said this morning that this is a light paper and not really about Literature. She also said that the other option that she is teaching is more scoring, with marks going up to 85 per cent. So the students withdrew their names.'

Shailaja was not overly surprised by this information. It was in keeping with the teacher-in-charge's inconsistent ways.

'On the one hand, it is good that we will be a small,

intimate group. On the other hand, it is ironic that we will be a select group trying to study literature that is neither "small" nor "select". Okay, so let's begin with the concept of popular fiction. How do we understand the word "popular"...' began Shailaja.

As she started her lecture, doubts began to assail her mind. She had over-prepared for this course. But how would she explain the purpose of commercially produced fiction—with narratives designed to 'mesmerize the mind and send it on vacation', according to some critics—to students who read hardly anything beyond what was prescribed, and sometimes not even that? A book was but a necessary evil of existence to these young people who belonged to set-ups perhaps not very different from the milieu that was her own now. There was one small bookshop in Vasant Kunj, usually deserted. Did Mrs Gandhi and Mrs Jain, for instance, possess or read any books? What if she had presented Mrs Jain with a red-and-gold edition of *Gone with the Wind* instead of a rubber plant?

Shailaja decided to start with the amazing popularity of the romance.

'But *GWTW* is boring,' exclaimed lace-top Amulya.

'It just goes on and on,' agreed salwar-kameez Najma.

GWTW indeed! Shailaja had hoped that the girls would respond enthusiastically to a love story. Ten years of teaching had prepared her for the unforeseen in class, but the summary dismissal startled her. Most of them had not read beyond the first hundred pages.

'Don't you girls like love stories? Don't you have boyfriends?'

Equal numbers of yes-and-no and giggles. No, they had not heard of Barbara Cartland. Yes, they were aware of Mills & Boon. Boyfriends? Hee hee!

'In a way, *GWTW*'—what the hell, she would also use the acronym—'is the mother of romances.'

The girls shuffled their feet.

'Chick lit! What about chick lit? Are you familiar with stories about single women?' she asked, a little desperate.

There was silence, some giggling, and then the answers started to come in.

'Ma'am, *Sex and the City*!'

'Ma'am, *Bridget Jones*!'

Thank God for globalization, for technology that kept so many genres alive simultaneously.

'Chick lit is the latest avatar of the romance genre,' Shailaja informed the class.

'Ma'am, it's different... *Bridget Jones* was not like this.'

'What do you mean?'

'Ma'am, it was funny. *Sex and the City* was funny too.'

'Yes, and *GWTW* is not, I agree. But don't you think that Bridget Jones and Scarlett O'Hara are both focussed on love and marriage in the same way?'

'Ma'am, Scarlett keeps getting married.'

'She has children but she goes on chasing men.'

'So you think marriage kills romance?' Shaila countered daringly.

The girls were silent. After some time, salwar-kameez Najma said, 'It's no fun after marriage.'

Shailaja wondered what she meant.

'Ma'am, can't we begin with Agatha Christie?'

'Is it because you prefer murders to marriages?'

Giggles. 'No Ma'am, it's slimmer.'

But it was romance she wanted at the moment—the tall, dark and handsome Clark Gable and the promise of a sequel. And of course feminist criticism about why she wanted to read all this so much!

Unfortunately, this therapy of hers would involve these

eight students. These young women had a full life beyond the classroom. Even if they didn't have boyfriends, they had hope and, of course, screens that promised sex and the city. She needed to change tack.

'Have you seen the film *Gone with the Wind*?' she asked.

There was excitement in the ranks as they consulted each other. Is there a film? Which film? 'No, Ma'am.'

'Now Vivien Leigh, who played Scarlett O'Hara in the film, had a nineteen-inch waist.'

Oohs and aahs! She heard the term 'size zero' being bandied. She had at last caught their imagination.

'We can watch the film together,' she offered.

There was unanimous assent and approbation.

'Ma'am, we're sorry for not having read *GWTW*,' said Krishna.

'We took the paper because you are teaching it,' said Najma.

'Oh!' exclaimed Shailaja, taken aback.

'Ma'am, we loved your classes in the first year,' added Amulya.

Shailaja tried not to look ridiculously happy. 'We can't begin class till you've read something. Can you finish reading the book by next week? Until then, we'll watch the film and have general discussions!'

'Yes, Ma'am, thank you, Ma'am,' said her newly constituted chorus.

'Also, use this time to think about love. What is it that women associate with this word? Is it different from the way men understand it? You could ask your boyfriends what they understand by the word love,' she added recklessly.

Giggles. 'You're cool,' an undertone, a whisper, an aria—a benediction.

It was something to hold on to, Shailaja told herself, as she sat in the staffroom demolishing a samosa. She crumbled the crust and beat it into the spicy potato filling. It was good, especially when accompanied by the tamarind chutney. The college canteen did few things well—the samosa being one of them.

In a very different space from Vasant Kunj and DDSD College, at the crises centre for women in Nizamuddin, Dini was mulling over the new, unexpected development in her life.

She had reached the Nizamuddin centre fifteen minutes ahead of time, as was usual with her. Of course, to call the space where she was seated—on a rickety chair in front of a wobbly table—at the centre of anything was to stretch formal definitions. She had worked the crises centre into the project even though there had been no money for it. It was a bare room with minimal furniture, provided by the community for two hours every week. She represented her NGO on a weekly basis here, lending a listening ear to the women. It was something she cherished doing. The real need assessment, the real work, she believed, took place in such interactions. Statistics and reports can be made to lie but a woman with a bursting heart is another matter. Dini treated the stories that made their way to her with the utmost care. She would note them down in her register scrupulously, word for word, filing them under general headings like child abuse, incest, marital rape and sadism/perversions.

But today, the register that she would normally read and annotate again and again was still lying unopened on the table.

'We can meet only after two months now, Dini. I am going to New York for that six-week training programme I told you about,' RS had said yesterday, looking quite forlorn.

He had come to Delhi three times after the guest-house rendezvous. He had stayed at a friend's vacant flat in the nearby Munirka, and they had met in complete privacy. He called every day, sometimes twice a day. Almost nine years after the brief affair with Kenny, she had landed herself an ardent lover.

She was day-dreaming. It had been equally exhilarating with RS the second, third and fourth times. He adored her so obviously. He made it all about her. Neither did he look into the mirror obsessively, nor did he speak at length about himself, which was such a contrast to the men she had been accustomed to.

All the men she knew, especially those in her office, were so full of themselves. But RS was reticent about personal matters. His conversations were about social hierarchies and liberational ideas, about his current project that sounded path-breaking. He was working with a community that was classified under 'criminal tribes' during the British period. They were still tainted by the stigma and led an uneasy, subterranean existence in tightly knit groups. He had put together a plan of village tourism, and his NGO was training some of the young tribal men to act as guides not only to the monuments in the vicinity but also to the rural ways of life. His New York trip was geared towards fine-honing the training programme he had designed.

It had been a Herculean task for her to get him to talk about his family, but her persistent questioning led her to discover even more things to admire about him.

'My mother got married at fourteen, like all other girls in our community,' RS had told her. 'She gave birth to six children one after another, but none except my oldest sister and I survived. That's usual too. My sister was the apple of her eye—her first child!'

'Did she love her more than you? But you were the boy of the family?' she had asked.

'Yes, but Samta, my sister, was exceptional. She was very pretty, very bright. My completely illiterate mother recognized this and exulted in it. Against all family pressure to send her to graze cattle, she got her admitted to school. Samta loved school—like me—even though they would make us sit away from other students. But the school master was very encouraging to her; he too realized that she was head and shoulders above everyone else in the class.'

'What happened to her?' Dini asked, dreading what would come. Didn't she know about the lives of girls in bastis?

'She was barely thirteen when my father decided to marry her off. He had taken money from the groom's family. My mother pleaded with him—let her study, let her have a life. But he wouldn't listen. My mother even brought the schoolmaster to our home. I remember him pleading with the entire family that Samta should be allowed to complete her school education, that she could get a scholarship. He was from the city, so nobody listened to him either. My sister got pregnant immediately after her marriage. She was not even fourteen when she died in childbirth.'

RS's face had darkened. Dini put her arms around him, but he went on with his story: 'My mother almost lost her mind. I remember her crying non-stop for days. She kept blaming my father for her daughter's death till the day he died. She tells me that I should not let such a thing happen to any young girl, that it's my responsibility to prevent this from happening in the community...'

'Your mother sounds exceptional, RS,' she had exclaimed.

'She's no ordinary woman. I told her about your work. You can't imagine how excited she is. She's an instinctive feminist, Dini.'

Had she found the only man in the world who gravitated towards feminists naturally, Dini wondered. How she would love to meet his mother! On a mental flight to faraway Rajasthan, Dini suddenly realized that Jamila had parked herself on the chair opposite hers and was demanding her attention. She smiled brightly; she loved this woman. Jamila was a potential change-maker too.

Jamila had come to the basti ten months ago after marrying Parvaiz, a construction worker who lived there. She worked in a readymade garments factory and earned a little less than eight thousand rupees a month, working nine hours a day on an average. The factory was far—in Gurgaon—and it took her at least two hours to get there by bus; the return journey could be anywhere between two and a half to three hours, depending on the traffic. Jamila had told her that she got married in the hope that she would be able to exchange her gruelling schedule with softer domestic work that she thought would come as a corollary to marriage. However, when she had brought up the subject, her husband told her categorically that an average looker like her should not expect to lead a life of leisure. 'I haven't married you to increase my responsibilities; a man marries for betterment of his situation.' So, for Jamila, marriage had meant getting up an hour earlier than she used to, working longer in the kitchen under the tutelage of an exacting mother-in-law, and providing sex to her husband whenever he wanted it—every night, twice, thrice. It amazed Dini that Jamila could play the fool—mimicking the nasal sanctimonious tones of her husband—to the giggles and chuckles of other women.

However, today Jamila was not smiling.

'Dini Didi, close the door,' she said.

Dini got up and did as asked. It was not an unusual request in the basti.

'You have to take me to a doctor,' Jamila said.

'Why, what's happened to Romola Aunty?' Romola Batra was the gynaecologist to whom all women in the basti went in time of need.

'No, no, she knows my mother-in-law. I have conceived again.'

'Again?'

'Third time. First two times it came off easily—I had the medicine this friend of mine had told me about and next morning, all out and clean.'

'Jamila Behen, you know it is bad for you…'

'Bad—but who will look after a bawling baby?'

'You can't keep having medicines to abort. It is risky.'

'Baby would be more of a disaster.'

'You don't want a baby?'

Jamila struck her forehead with her hand and replied in a mocking tone, 'Didi, am I working in an NGO and earning fifty thousand like you to want or not want?'

Dini sighed; she earned much more. 'Won't Parvaiz Bhai understand? Should we get the women to speak to him?' she asked.

'Oho Didi! Does it even matter what he understands? If I don't go out and earn, who will pay for the food? Who will pay for his clothes, his card games?

Dini bowed her head with the unexpected pain that did not let her breathe. Jamila was right. The factory would probably give her some maternity leave, but it had no crèche—none of the factories had a crèche. A baby in Jamila's life would only mean more responsibility, one more mouth to feed…

'I'll take you, Jamila Behen, but you have to promise one thing.'

'Dini Didi, my life is here for your taking.'

'No, Jamila Behen. Both of you have to start on birth control.'

Jamila burst out laughing. 'You mean Parvaiz?' She mimicked him: '"It is close to a year, Jamila. Ammi is waiting for a grandson. People will think there is something wrong with me unless you have a baby soon." He's waiting to prove his manliness to the world, Didi. He'll never agree.'

'Then you…'

Jamila struck her forehead again. 'Yes, yes, yes, I don't have to prove anything to anyone, Dini Didi. I am too busy trying to make ends meet. If neighbours accuse me of being a transvestite because I can't have children, I'll just laugh at them. Till last month I was on the pill, but my mother-in-law opened my purse and saw them. They beat me black and blue… I promise I will be more careful in future.'

Dini felt tears pricking her eyes.

'Promise, Didi,' Jamila repeated. 'I made a mistake this time. I promise it will not happen again. I'll keep the pills in the factory.'

Dini nodded, pushing the tears back.

In spite of strict instructions from her organization against encouraging the 'partners' in 'culturally unacceptable activities', she knew that nothing would stop her from helping Jamila get an abortion and, subsequently, a regular supply of birth control pills.

Dini returned to office and worked passionately on her report the rest of the day. A couple of colleagues were going to a bar in the evening. For the sake of form, they asked her if she would like to come along. 'Oh, I wish I could, but I have to get home early,' she replied, also for form's sake.

September

Buddhism and Demons

Since she resolved to hold the enshrinement ceremony at her house, Mrs Gandhi had acquired a purpose and, in its pursuit, scored a series of 'victories'. This Sunday, she woke up early, feeling particularly energetic because her enshrinement was to be held a week from now. The Gohonzon had arrived from Japan. She was incredibly lucky to get the holy scroll so soon, Navneeta told her. It must have been her good karma that the district chief just received a scroll intended for someone who had to leave the country suddenly.

However, it hadn't been easy to reach the point of its installation in her home. There had, of course, been the string of predictable objections from Mummy-ji. But we are Hindus; nobody in our family has ever done this kind of thing; people will say you have converted. And also, why are you getting this Buddhist mandir? We have our own puja-ghar, don't we? You can put the Buddha into it too. If you want to chant, you can do so quietly. Why does everyone have to know?

There had been many visits to her home by the Buddhist brethren, especially Navneeta, who engaged in long discussions with her. One by one, her mother-in-law's arguments were tactfully countered and the vision of an all-encompassing faith presented in all its glory. 'All of you, very welcome,' she would mutter every time the impressive Buddhist 'madams' visited. Seeing the old woman at a loss for words warmed Mrs Gandhi's heart even more towards her new fraternity.

Of course, in deference to the Buddhist insistence on a harmonious family, she was also making the Herculean effort to be nice to Mummy-ji.

'Mummy-ji, get chickpeas made today. I had soaked them last night. Tell Bahadur to not put too much chilli but do get him to darken the curry with tea leaves, like you used to do,' she said to the old lady after many rehearsals with Navneeta. Taken aback, the old woman looked at her suspiciously. 'Where are you going so early in the morning?' she asked, her voice choked with misapprehension. 'I am not going anywhere, Mummy-ji,' Mrs Gandhi replied with a snort of unaccustomed merriment. 'I thought I should do my prayers at this time. You used to make chickpeas so well. You can train Bahadur.' Remembering what Navneeta had said, she even added, 'Because of you, I can think of praying in the morning. I realize how lucky I am to have you with me.'

The success of the old woman's cooking went far beyond her expectations. 'This was *chhole* as it used to be made years ago in our home!' Sunil exclaimed. His favourite child, Neeru, was at once motivated enough to try it out without insisting on her salad and burger. Mrs Gandhi couldn't stomach this street-food kind of cooking that the older woman did, and had pulled away the chhole from Ganesh—'Mummy-ji, his stomach is delicate.' But overjoyed by the rave reviews from other family members, the old woman did not pay attention. Teenu, the easiest to feed, was excited enough to take them in her tiffin the next day. 'Mama, I dared my friends to eat my tiffin. You know, Anita started to cry because of the chilli; it was so funny.'

There was no stopping Mummy-ji since that day.

It was all for the better, Mrs Gandhi conceded in her mind. With Mummy-ji fruitfully occupied, her own mornings had become more peaceful. Of course, she still had to wait for the family to leave before doing her chanting, but there was time enough to bathe, dress and even go for a walk in the park.

She padded out of her room carefully. Ganesh was fast asleep in her bed. And so was Sunil—on the other bed in the room. Navneeta had asked her to continue chanting for him—now increased to half an hour every day from the initial ten minutes. 'He seems to be undergoing something transformative, something big. If you chant for his happiness, you will understand him much better.'

Sunil, in fact, had been behaving even more strangely. Just last week, he ordered new twin beds from one of the furniture shops in Munirka. He insisted on replacing their double bed with these. In fact, the *thela* that brought the twin beds carried away her beloved double bed in spite of her protests. It was given by her parents at the time of their wedding. 'But these Munirka beds are new and of better wood,' Sunil had asserted. 'You are very restless; I can't sleep because you toss and turn so much. And then Ganesh also kicks around,' he added.

The two beds, with a bedside table in the middle—arranged in this way on Sunil's insistence—occupied most of the bedroom now. The sole table had Sunil's watch, wallet, card case, etc., on it. She had to keep even her bottle of water on the floor. There was no space for her multi-vitamin and calcium tablets either, as the drawer was overflowing with Sunil's knickknacks. Besides, she had to sleep on her side all night as her twin bed was not wide enough to accommodate Ganesh. It was so inconvenient. She told Navneeta that it was not in her nature to question her husband or be suspicious. She was ready to put up with this arrangement—even though it meant buying new bed linen and putting away all her lovely double-bed covers—but Sunil should have at least thought of what the servants would say. Bahadur grinned when Rajni asked outright why Sahib and Memsahib had taken to sleeping like brother and sister; she had not seen anything like this in any of the other six households that she had worked in earlier. Taking care that Bahadur was within earshot, Mrs Gandhi witheringly informed her that all foreign countries—England, America and France—had sleeping arrangements like this, and this new fashion was only now coming to India. Besides, once Ganesh grew up, they would go back to the double bed. But the help had got a chance to sneer, hadn't they?

Having her tea at the dining table and ignoring the din in the kitchen being created by Mummy-ji and Bahadur, who now came early in the morning and made breakfast as well, Mrs Gandhi was lost in thought. 'Your relationship karma will improve with chanting,' Navneeta had predicted. She must be right; she had so much experience. A couple of times, both Sunil and Neeru had appeared to listen when she repeated what the 'madams' had said to her mother-in-law: 'This is not worship of any deity. It is directed at the power that lies within each of us. Think of the Gohonzon as the Buddha in the mirror.' Neeru rolled her eyes and looked heavenward, but Sunil almost nodded. Mrs Gandhi took care to inform them about the ceremony and casually added that with so many important English-speaking people coming, it would be a big help if they were around. Sunil muttered something about his lack of belief in 'all this' but didn't refuse outright. Happily, the news of the enshrinement got Neeru excited: 'My classmate, Saurabh, was telling me about it. His mother is a chanter. I'll invite him also.' Mrs Gandhi had felt so grateful for her daughter's interest that she almost overlooked the evident fact that her adolescent daughter was close friends with a boy. She resolved to take the matter up sometime soon.

Mrs Gandhi bathed and dressed quickly and quietly. Sunil and Ganesh were still fast asleep. When they woke up, Mummy-ji would see to their breakfast and that of the girls. She could focus on completing her invitations for the event. She had already invited all the women from her kitty party and those in the neighbourhood to whom she had carried the message of the Lotus Sutra. They were so friendly and forthcoming. Mrs Awasthi's sister was undergoing a divorce and Mrs Arora's son had got himself a Christian girlfriend. Poor Mrs Gupta had joined the practice three years ago but left depressed and disheartened when her mother was diagnosed with cancer. Yet, when Mrs Gandhi visited her a couple of times, she chanted with her and promised that she would start again. This was a tremendous victory, Navneeta said.

She had also visited Mrs Jain, who seemed to be spending all her time fighting with the neighbours about her plants. As expected, she had a host of objections to chanting. 'Oh no, not even for ten minutes!' She was a Jain and the follower of Mahavir Bhagwan; it would be sacrilegious for her to chant the mantra of a rival practice, she argued. This was Mrs Jain through and through. But Mrs Gandhi was not going to give up on her. She cross-checked with Navneeta, who clarified that followers of any religion, including Jainism, might chant. 'Aren't all religions ultimately different paths to the same Truth?' Mrs Gandhi had promptly replayed the wisdom to Mrs Jain, who continued to look sceptical. 'I'll ask the priests at my temple,' she retorted. Mrs Gandhi scoffed—as though those illiterate priests would know more than Navneeta.

She told herself that she would not allow herself to feel discouraged and would invite Mrs Jain warmly for the event once again. Navneeta had told her that one had to be persistent. It was not easy to make people realize what was good for them. She had also assured Mrs Gandhi that she would chant for her victory and that Mrs Gandhi should challenge herself by taking the practice to those who really needed it. She meant to introduce the practice to at least two to three suffering women this week. This was her promise to the Gohonzon. In return, the Buddhist powers would make Sunil attend the enshrinement, that was the deal. She was chanting night and day for his presence at her special occasion.

Her thoughts ran to Shailaja. She needed the practice so much more than the others, who at least had stable marriages or families. It was such a pity that she was avoiding her these days. Mrs Gandhi decided to not be deterred. Women who lived alone just did not realize the pressures of running a household! Of course, there was Dini too, who didn't seem to know how unhappy she really was. But Mrs Gandhi felt she needed to strengthen her practice further before tackling the risky task of trying to make Dini chant.

Should she chant in the bedroom before embarking on her mission to Shailaja's third-floor flat, she wondered daringly. She settled down tentatively on the little carpet. Sunil snorted in his sleep. It might not be a good idea to wake up Ganesh so early. Also, it wasn't time yet to try and shower the benefits of chanting on her husband. Mrs Gandhi decided to take a round in the park and recite her morning Gongyo with Mrs Malhotra before going to Shailaja's. She was likely to be home because it was a Sunday.

■

It seemed to Mrs Gandhi that Shailaja was looking pale and drawn. 'Something happened. You not looking well,' she said as soon as Shailaja opened the door to her.

Shailaja sighed. 'Yes, I'm not feeling too well; I was lying down…'

'What? Period pains?'

'No—yes…' She replied, looking embarrassed—as though Mrs Gandhi was a man!

'I too get these cramps. I have homeopathic medicine for them. Should I send it?' Mrs. Gandhi asked her.

'No thanks, Nilima-ji. I'll be fine if I rest…'

'You can come to my home; rest there. No problem at all. I will make some green tea,' she tried to persuade the other woman.

'No, don't worry, Nilima-ji, I have green tea.'

Mrs Gandhi settled down on the sofa. She was visiting Shailaja after a two-month gap; that's when the unfortunate water tanker incident had occurred. The drawing room was still quite bare, but the mismatched furniture was arranged in a way that looked quite stylish. There were pretty, bright curtains on the windows. Rajni's old and decrepit mother was doing a much better job of dusting and cleaning than her youthful daughter. Mrs Gandhi took a mental note to speak to Rajni sternly. Shailaja was still standing and looking at her expectantly, but she didn't want to reveal the purpose of her visit so precipitately,

'Oh, sit no, Shailaja. I came to talk,' Mrs Gandhi began.

'About what, Nilima-ji?'

'Is all well? Are you settling down well in the colony? I have been so busy, we haven't met.'

'Oh yes, Nilima-ji, I have settled down quite well. The only problem is with logistics. The colony is so chaotic in the mornings, what with tankers jamming the road; it is quite a challenge to reach work on time,' replied Shailaja.

'Yes, that day I thought you looked so worried... You must relax, offer everything to the Buddha,' said Mrs Gandhi. If only Shailaja would do this. 'I heard you had some problem with Mrs Jain too.'

Shailaja looked as though she couldn't understand her.

'Mrs Jain was saying that you lock up the terrace and she has no place to dry her laundry. Shruti used to allow her to use the terrace. I tried to explain to her that everyone is different and she should understand and not criticize,' tattled Mrs Gandhi.

'She spoke to you!' exclaimed Shailaja. She looked very surprised, Mrs Gandhi thought. But of course Mrs Jain would speak to her. They had known each other for ten years.

'You know, Shailaja, we think our own problems are the worst... But that is not true. I was fighting with Mrs Malhotra... I felt that I didn't get water because of her. I called her selfish, but it only hurt me. I then chanted for her. I realized that she too had many, many problems. Even more than mine. Her sister is undergoing a divorce; her father-in-law has been in bed for a month. So much money they have to spend on care... Only now her son has got a job because of chanting. Earlier, she too was angry with me and wouldn't talk. But the other day, you won't believe, she called me when the tanker came. She said you take water first!'

'This is quite a big change,' said Shailaja. There seemed to be tears in her eyes.

Mrs Gandhi got up, sat next to her and took her hand into her own. 'Chanting can change everything. Who doesn't have problems? I am thinking you must have had problems, very big problems—the divorce and all—and nobody to share...'

'Oh,' said the poor woman, taking away her hand. 'Aren't there problems in all relationships—in your marriage, for instance?'

'You so right. The Buddha said life is full of problems, and our biggest leader in Japan, he says that problems are opportunities. Just this morning, a member sent me this quote.' Mrs Gandhi pulled out her phone, and before Shailaja could say anything, began reading out the message, '"Life isn't always smooth. If it were, we would never grow and develop as human beings. If we succeed, we are envied; if we fail, we are ridiculed and attacked. Sadly, this is how people are. Unexpected grief and suffering may lie ahead of you. But it is precisely when you encounter such trying times that you must not be defeated. Never give up. Never retreat."'

Shailaja was silent, as though trying to understand the profundity. It wasn't easy, but Mrs Gandhi wasn't about to give up.

'Isn't this helpful? Chanting makes us accept our problems. These daily quotes are very good. So I was telling you about my problem. Now Sunil, he is so nice in every way, but…' Mrs Gandhi faltered a little.

'But what?' Shailaja asked.

Mrs Gandhi felt touched. Shailaja was interested in learning about her situation even though it seemed she had been weeping; even though she was so much worse off being divorced and alone.

'Sunil has changed. It was different when we got married. We used to spend so much time together. Now he is busy and sometimes I feel he does not care,' Mrs Gandhi explained as she did to everyone these days.

'Oh Mrs Gandhi!'

'I feel he is not taking me out anywhere because he is ashamed. I used to only cry and blame him. So much time I wasted in blaming him for calling me fat, forgetting my birthday…'

'You must have felt hurt; it is natural to blame then,' Shailaja replied.

'But we must make an effort and rise above blaming–shaming. The Buddhist leader told me to chant for him. I chant and chant... Now I am beginning to see things his way. I realize he too needs me even if he forgets. He doesn't even know in which class Teenu is. He asked me yesterday. He knows nothing about the household, and his mother, she is old,' Mrs Gandhi found it increasingly easier to talk about family matters these days.

'But Nilima-ji, he should remember your birthday and—'

'He will, he will. I am confident. I am the only wife he has. I chant for this. But I also chanted for you this morning. I said to Gohonzon, give her all happiness. Then I felt I must come here and chant...'

'Oh Nilima-ji, really, you don't have to do this. I know you are busy.'

She was being so formal, but Mrs Gandhi could see how grateful she was feeling.

'Shailaja, no problem it is. I have finished all my work. And my mother-in-law... You know, I chant for her also. You won't believe, she has started to help me. Now I can go out of the house any time. I came to spend half-hour with you.'

'Oh Nilima-ji, this is so kind of you. It would be wonderful if we could spend that much time together but I am having some guests over...'

Mrs Gandhi knew this was not true. Shailaja had not bathed or dressed; how could she be waiting for guests? The Buddha alone would know why she was lying. However, it was important to release Buddhist vibes in that space, otherwise she would have to climb all those stairs again this week.

'Shailaja, let's chant till guests come. That will be enough, even if it is ten minutes. You know I am going to get my own Gohonzon on Sunday. I've come to invite you for the enshrinement...'

'But Nilima-ji, I don't believe... I am sure one must not chant without belief. I'll come for the enshrinement, of course...'

'Good, you will come to know more about the practice as leaders will be there. But let me tell you, leaders say you begin to believe automatically after you start chanting.'

'But also, I don't know what the chant means. Surely we should know that before we start the practice?'

Mrs Gandhi was prepared for this. She whipped out her phone again. 'See, I have the Great Sage's own words about this: "Those who chant Nam-myoho-renge-kyo, even without understanding its meaning, realize not only the heart of the Lotus Sutra but also the main cord, or essential principle of the Buddha's lifetime teachings."'

As Shailaja was fidgeting, she broke off. 'Okay, I won't read the whole thing. I will forward it to you.'

'Okay Nilima-ji, let's chant for five minutes. I have to get ready for my guests after that,' said Shailaja with a sigh.

Poor woman, always sighing, thought Mrs Gandhi. But she felt a gush of happiness. This was definitely another victory. She would chant in gratitude for this. She would also narrate this experience at the next discussion meeting. Shailaja had been so reluctant in the beginning, and she had feared that she would only sulk about the tanker. But thanks to the Buddha, everything had gone well. She was able to give Shailaja the wonderful gift of chanting. Even if it was only for five minutes.

After Mrs Gandhi left, Shailaja grinned to herself. Mrs Gandhi truly belonged in a Charles Dickens novel! But it wasn't unkind laughter. After all, she had not taken any payment for getting the tripping power line repaired by her electrician; Shailaja had been very grateful for that. Her Buddhist spiel wasn't altogether fraudulent either.

Shailaja's mind was anyway happily occupied with her work. She was planning to check out the new book of essays on *Gone with the Wind* that she had borrowed from the university library over the weekend. In her ten years of teaching, she had never had such an enthusiastic response from her students, nor had she prepared so avidly for her classes. Her teaching was going spectacularly well.

Her mode of talking about everyday life—including her own—had earned her many fans. She began by encouraging the students to explore why they identified with Scarlett O'Hara. 'Have you asked yourself why you are able to "understand" and empathize with a woman whose life is so different from yours? What is the point of connection?' she asked in the last class. After fifty minutes of discussion, some students proposed that it was the importance of men in their lives that connected women from such different backgrounds. 'It's the same for women everywhere,' Najma said. Krishna contradicted her with a good point about 'the hegemonic Anglo-American discourse that took no cognizance of cultural differences'. So, she held a group discussion on Anglo-American romances as contrasted with those in Bollywood films. But Shailaja also indicated that love could be transcendence, a mode of protest, and, most importantly, a kind of fantasy that critiqued relationships as they existed in society. By celebrating an imaginary partnership with a tender, caring man, women were also giving expression to their innate desires. She was aware that she had built romance as a post-feminist force in her classes, not knocked it down as escape and mindless reading like the senior members of her department did.

Ironically, the eight girls adopted her as their love guru, seeking her outside class hours to narrate their experiences with boys. Moreover, students from other colleges started to come to attend her class discussions. Dr Reena Singh, the teacher-in-charge, was livid about the 'extra' classes the second-years had been arranging with Shailaja: 'These girls are bright and impressionable. They should be spending their time in worthwhile pursuits instead of discussing love and romance all day.' At a department meeting, she declared that she would draft a letter to the university, requesting them to drop such lightweight readings from the syllabus. Shailaja saw a couple of suppressed smiles among the younger lot of teachers and felt triumphant.

■

Shailaja left really early for college on Monday as traffic, for some reason, was particularly bad at the beginning of the week. She had had to forego Rajni ki Ma's breakfast but reached in time to order an oily bread pakora from the canteen. She was wanted in the principal's office, said the peon just as she was counting the change to pay the canteen boy. With some trepidation, Shailaja lugged herself from the staffroom to his office on the first floor. It wasn't very often that the principal summoned teachers to his office, especially lowly temporary teachers like her.

Shailaja hated the way so many of her colleagues were smarmy around the principal. The worst was how some women teachers even sprang up to attention when he entered the staffroom. Over the last ten years, he had embellished his position shamelessly—he had renovated his office with glass and steel and appointed a smart female receptionist who sat in a little cubicle outside and ushered in colleagues and students one by one. Principals of Delhi University colleges did not, as a rule, surround themselves with such paraphernalia. Dhar, with the tacit support of the college governing body, chaired by his political mentor, had set himself up like the CEO of a minor corporate.

'Good afternoon, sir,' she said, a little hesitantly. For one, she hated calling him 'sir' like other teachers did. It seemed feudal. Two, Dr Dhar was, in her opinion, a bit of a 'megalo'. 'I am sure he practises his smile in front of the mirror,' she used to quip to Ranjan, and sometimes even mimic the way Dhar performed being gracious.

She sat down primly on the chair opposite him, across his vast desk, hating herself for feeling so nervous.

'Yes, Ms Sharma, so how are you keeping these days?'

'I am fine, Dr Dhar.'

He guffawed, 'Dr Dhar!'

'I mean... Sir...'

'No, you can call me Dr Dhar if you like. My name, you know, is Dinesh. You can even call me Dinesh. You English-wallahs are very informal, aren't you?'

'No, Dr Dhar Sir...'

'What's in a name? That which we call a rose, by any other name would smell as sweet.'

Shailaja nodded, baffled by the inappropriate quote and also by the fact that he had got Shakespeare right.

'So Ms Sharma, there is a complaint against you'—he suddenly looked severe—'from Dr Reena Singh, respected senior faculty.'

Shailaja's heart missed a beat. The woman was incorrigible. When had she decided to go and tell tales about her? Hadn't they spoken to each other just yesterday? Besides, she hadn't been late all of last week.

'It is to do with your teaching. It seems you are teaching this ... love story...' He held out a paperback edition of *Gone with the Wind*. It had a lurid red cover. On the front was Clark Gable about to kiss Vivien Leigh, who wore a red off-shoulder dress that revealed a lot of bosom. In Dhar's hands, especially with his thumb on Vivien Leigh's bosom, the book looked vulgar. 'Do they teach cheap love stories in English Honours these days, not Shakespeare and Milton?'

'Yes—no, sir. *Gone with the Wind* is in the course. It is prescribed by the university. It is not a cheap romance; it is a classic. The paper is called Popular Fiction.'

'But in English Honours, you must teach Great Literature. I read Shakespeare in a subsidiary course in BSc. But I still remember his immortal lines. You saw for yourself. But I have heard you have other views. Dr Singh says you insisted on teaching this course even though it is optional. She also feels that the way you are teaching the book is too open.'

'Sir, I don't understand...'

'You talked about your boyfriend in class. This is bad influence on our young students,' he declared.

'I—'

'Two boys from your class complained to her.'

'But they have not attended any classes. They came once in the beginning of the semester.'

'They told her you are always late for classes and they found your lectures embarrassing. I have myself seen you going in twenty-five minutes late,' he said.

'Sir, I teach the syllabus—what English teachers teach all over the world. The students are responding very well. I am taking extra classes, in fact.'

'There are only eight students in the class, I am told. There were ten and two dropped out. We must not offer this course next time. Extra classes are fine, but you can't be late for your regular class. It is the regular class that is on the timetable, isn't it? How do we know about extra classes with eight students—whether they even take place or not?'

'You can call the eight girls and ask them,' she replied, hating herself for sounding so defensive.

He shook his head. 'But two students have complained. It is my responsibility to enquire. But you can't talk about boyfriend in class; this is India. And, of course, you can't be late for class.'

'Sir, I have recently moved to a new place—'

'With boyfriend?'

Shailaja was stunned. Had he just asked her whether she was living with her boyfriend?

'He should drop you to college—at least first few months—' observed Principal Dhar.

Shailaja sat quietly, feeling her heart sink to her shoes. There was silence for quite some time. When she looked up at last, he seemed to be ogling her breasts.

'The governing body of the college is old-fashioned. You know, they wouldn't approve of a live-in,' he went on.

Shailaja found her tongue at last, 'I live alone in Vasant Kunj.'

'Oh, this is bad. It must be lonely.' It seemed to her that he was looking at her breasts again. She wished she had not worn the kurta with a slightly deep neck line.

'I am broad-minded. Of course I am married, but my wife, you know, she is very understanding. She spends her time in puja-paath, you know... She is not interested...'

Shailaja felt as though molten lead was being poured down her ears.

'I will try and explain to the governing body,' he continued, suddenly business-like. 'I will try and argue for your continuation in college. Have you given your new address to the office?'

'No...'

'Please give it to my PA as you go out. The college should be able to contact you whenever you are needed.'

'Yes.'

She got up slowly. He seemed to be stripping her with his eyes.

'Does your boyfriend not even come at night anymore?' he leered.

Shailaja felt herself going red in the face. 'What kind of question is this?' she spat out.

'Vasant Kunj is not very safe, Ms Sharma; you should be careful, especially at night. If there is a man around, anti-social elements keep away.'

'I can look after myself, sir. Thank you,' she hissed.

As she was leaving, she heard him laugh softly.

■

This couldn't be happening, Shailaja's mind whimpered. The principal of her college couldn't be treating her like some cheap woman he could take advantage of. When did she get reduced to this? She would complain about him; she would get him beaten up... She was not without resources; she was not without people who would take care of her.

She drove back home on auto-pilot, cutting through traffic like knife through butter.

Alone in her flat, her mind shot to Ranjan. But he was no longer her boyfriend!

Ranjan had come to her with the car. They were still friends, he said that. He still cared. She was older, so a little less attractive—but still attractive. Shailaja felt an uncontrollable desire to hear his voice. He would do something; he would protect her honour.

She put a call through to him with some trepidation. Her heart was beating so loudly that she was almost afraid he would hear it throb in her voice.

'Oh hello, Shailaja.' He sounded stiff. 'Are we talking to each other?'

'Ranjan, I'm sorry. I have been meaning to call. That day when you came I didn't mean to be rude, but it was late and there was the maid…'

When he didn't reply she repeated, 'I'm really sorry, Ranjan. But how have you been? How are things with you?'

He drew a deep breath. 'I can't complain.'

When there was silence at her end, he continued, 'We are planning to travel soon. It's been hectic—for Diksha more than for me. She did a crossover film with an American director and it was very tough. Six months of very hard work.'

'And your own work?' Shailaja asked at last.

'I've been busy. I just finished three assignments in Mumbai. I've applied for funding to make a documentary on Kashmir, and I expect it to come through very soon. And after that we'll travel.'

But that was their plan made in the early days of their romance. They were going to see the world together.

'When do you expect to leave?'

'In two–three months—for Europe. But I'll be going to Kashmir day after tomorrow. Tell me about you. How's college?'

'Bad! I want to resign,' Shailaja said.

'I suppose you were never serious about teaching.'

The only thing she had been serious about was her life with him—didn't he know? Shailaja felt her heart dissolve in pain.

'The Principal… He … made a pass at me.'

'Oh Shailaja!'

'Ranjan,' she sobbed. 'He kept looking at me and it was so humiliating.'

'Did he try to touch you or something?'

'No, but... He asked whether my boyfriend lives with me... And... He asked for my address...'

'Oh Shailaja, this sounds bad. But the college would have your new address anyway. Isn't that so?'

Sobs racked her body.

'Call a friend over. You shouldn't be alone if you're feeling like this.'

'Can you come, Ranjan? I need to talk ... so desperately...'

There was silence at his end. But then he said, 'Of course I can drop by. We can meet. Let me see... I should have some time tomorrow before I leave, or...'

Shailaja felt her heart ache—it was physical. He wasn't going to get into his car right away.

She forced herself to sound normal, 'Yes, actually it's not so bad. Some practical considerations need to be worked out and I was hoping... I'm going to resign...'

There was silence at his end.

'Shail, I hope you are not overreacting,' he said at last.

'What do you mean?'

'I mean your princi, if I remember right, is not very ... sophisticated, you know. In fact, he is quite provincial. He is not very confident speaking in English. You know, he might not have meant any of this.'

'Ranjan... How many ways are there to interpret what he said?'

'Look Shail, don't do anything in a hurry. That's all I would advise.' There was silence for some time.

'Shail, Diksha has just come back from Singapore. Can I call you later?'

'Okay,' she said, the word 'crushed' dancing in front of her eyes. 'We can talk later...'

But he had called her Shail! Was it true that Diksha had walked in at this very moment with her strawberry curls and her pout, wheeling in her Gucci luggage, and looked at him accusingly? Or did he just not want to talk to her anymore? Why did it matter so much to her one way or the other?

'Shail, it'll do you a lot of good to think about all this calmly. And remember, you don't need to do anything in a hurry. We'll talk of course.'

The night was long. She slept fitfully and wept at intervals, wondering whether the ache she felt would leave real, live scars on her heart.

September

The Activist in Love

Dini woke up earlier than usual. She loved the thirty minutes of solitude when she sipped her morning coffee. She sat in her favourite chair—an old swivel chair with a high back-rest that she had picked up from the clearance sale at her office—and gazed out of the window. Once, she had seen a parakeet with a big marigold flower in its beak, sitting atop a tree. The deep green of the ashoka leaves, the glowing yellow-green of the ring-neck parakeet, and the glorious orange-gold of the marigold—a cosmic photo op! She had held her breath in sheer awe. It felt like the affirmation of her activism against the cutting down of trees.

Surprisingly, RS had taken a contrary position. 'Look, broadening of roads is a necessary evil. We have chosen a mode of progress that is factored on urbanization. We can't suddenly invoke a rural idyll in the middle of the metropolis,' he observed.

'But trees are beautiful; they have so much life in them. It is criminal to chop them off so brutally,' she countered immediately. 'Besides, we have to worry about the environment in this time of global warming.'

'You are a pantheist, like your Aryan ancestors,' RS

teased. 'You just use the language of modern environmentalism.' Perversely, she ordered a dish of mutton seekh kebabs at the JNU dhaba where they were having dinner. But when she retched at the first bite, RS took the dish away from her. 'Let's find a better way for you to lose caste,' he had said, eyes sparkling.

Dini realized she was smiling widely to herself. She turned on her ancient two-in-one, waiting for the mellifluous Raga Hindolam to work its magic. RS was reaching Delhi in the afternoon and they would meet at the Munirka flat again. She had missed him a lot, though he had called regularly from New York. Should she take a present for him, she wondered. He had got her a red-and-black *bandhani* dupatta last time; before that, a puppet he had selected from those made by the puppeteer community in the village; and before that, besan laddus made by his mother in a steel container that now sat on her kitchen shelf, as well as several other things for Maithili. He was unapologetically romantic. Embracing the unaccustomed joy she was feeling, Dini attempted an *alaap* along with the recorded violin music—*sa ga ma dha ni sa*...

■

She bought him a silk scarf on way to Munirka from her office. It was deep green with blue lights.

'It's not my birthday,' RS said, peeling off the packing the moment she gave it to him. 'What is it? How should I wear it?'

She put it around his neck and made a rakish knot. It looked striking against his grey cotton tee-shirt. Very smart! RS studied himself in the mirror, took the scarf off and tied it around his head like a Rajasthani turban. In spite of himself, he was grinning like a young boy.

'What do you think of my turban?' he asked her.

'You look like a bridegroom,' she replied, giggling too. How youthful he looked when he laughed! She knew he was above forty.

'How was the training programme in New York?' she asked him.

'It's so difficult to fit one's work in the format of goals, objectives and results that these modern-day trainers keep coming back to. But you work in an international set-up, so you would know how to negotiate that,' he replied. 'It's not the way I think about my work.'

'Why did you go then?' she asked him.

'Oh, it was useful, alright. There were some great lectures on life skills and life audits. It was very good to meet participants from other countries—Kosovo and Ireland particularly! Besides, the trustees were very keen that I publicize our new Tourism from Below Project!' he replied. 'I got a great response from everyone, by the way. This girl Niamh—from Ireland—wants to visit the project and work out a partnership with us.' He broke into a sheepish smile. 'I had a tough time with her name,' he admitted endearingly. 'No connection between the spelling and the way it is pronounced!'

Dini smiled. 'When does she want to come to India?'

'In January next year. She is fascinated with India—asked so many questions, especially about Indian families. She watches a lot of Bollywood films. She was quite surprised when I told her I wasn't married. I told her about you and she asked at once when we intended to marry. She's very keen on attending an Indian wedding,' he replied.

'RS, tell me why you aren't married.' It was a question she had been meaning to ask for a long time. It couldn't have been easy for him to fend off the millions of proposals that must have definitely come his way.

'Hmm! What do you think of marriage?' RS asked drawing her into his arms.

'I don't think much of it,' she replied.

'Yes, it is a bourgeois institution, isn't it? This is one reason I didn't marry,' he said nuzzling her shoulder.

'Is there another reason too?' she asked breathlessly.

'Yes...' he replied.

'Are you going to say the predictable thing now?' Dini asked even as her heart raced.

'And what's that?'

'That it's because you didn't meet someone like me...' she teased.

'No, I wasn't going to say that,' he said.

'Then what—' she asked, disappointed in spite of herself.

'I was going to say that at last I've found a good reason to marry. I'm going to propose,' he said. 'Let's get married, Dini.'

'Just because Niamh asked? Don't be silly.'

'Silly? Why is it silly?' he asked, a little edgily.

'I don't believe in marriage. You don't either. We are together because we want to be together,' she replied meaning every word. 'Isn't this enough?'

'Yes, this should have been enough for me,' he said caressing her, as though newly amazed by her perfection. 'But it just isn't anymore.'

'RS...' she said, wondering how it was possible to feel elated and distraught at the same time. 'We've been together for only a couple of months.'

'It's also my mother,' he disclosed at last.

'You mean you have told her about me, about us?' Dini was shocked. His mother must have been beside herself with rage and disappointment.

'Yes, of course!' he replied, matter of fact.

'How could you?' she asked, stepping away from him.

'What do you mean?' he asked.

Did he not see that their relationship could never be divulged to families? That it was impossibly fanciful? 'You don't expect her to ... understand, do you? I know my father won't,' Dini tried.

'I don't know what you mean, Dini. She made those laddus for Maithili after I told her. She's waiting to adopt both Maithili and you. She has been telling all the women of our community that her son has been very clever and is polishing off ghee without having bothered to buy a cow,' RS replied.

'What does it mean?' she asked, intrigued by the saying in spite of the conflicting emotions assailing her.

'It is a local expression that means that I haven't had to strain myself to get a family. I will get the entire package ready-made.'

An older woman clad in a black ghaghra declaiming to a gathering of whispering women! In Dini's mental picture, all of them were wearing silver jewellery; some were giggling and covering their faces with their *odhni*s. RS was very dark with glowing mahogany skin and gleaming jet-black hair. His mother probably looked like him. Her own father was fair, very thin and austere. She felt his shock and disbelief in her own body. Oh no!

'But you should have talked to me before telling her,' she whispered.

RS paid no attention to it. 'Dini, my mother still lives in the untouchable section of the village in a small two-room house. But for her, it is a palace. She tells everybody that her son has been to the US and become a big man and now she can afford to live in a pukka, white-washed house. Ever since she heard about you, she has started planning my wedding. She wants to invite everyone in the village, the high-caste people as well... She tells me they will come to the untouchable section because now I am a big man who gets invited to "Amrika".'

'But marriage can't be...' she tried to say.

'It can be whatever we want it to be,' RS replied firmly.

'What do you mean?'

'I have been thinking about us... Our marriage won't be the usual bourgeois thing. You and I together—we can give it a new meaning. Don't you think that this divided world needs more unions like ours? It's not okay to hide our relationship like a dirty secret. We need to make it public. Come with me to my village and you will understand what I mean.'

Dini couldn't think of how to contradict this, especially as her body had cleaved to his again, as though of its own volition. But how would he respond to her father? In fact, what would he think of her if she were to tell him about her vexed negotiations with her origins, her childish rebellions? However, there was little time to work all this out in the space of the three hours they had together that day.

■

When Dini got back home, Rani was playing carrom with Maithili.

'Hi sweetie,' Dini said, her spirits lifting at once at the sight of her daughter's head bowed over the board game. Maithili's abundant hair fell into natural ringlets, and Dini loved to get it cut in a way that enhanced the curly effect. Maithili looked up and smiled, saying, 'Mama, Raji Aunty called half an hour ago on Rani Didi's phone.' Dini noticed a spot of red on her chin. Tomato ketchup—they had been eating French fries. She wiped it away, her heart melting with tenderness.

'Raji Aunty was saying she couldn't contact you,' Maithili was saying.

'I went to meet RS Uncle,' Dini blurted out. 'My phone was on silent.'

Maithili did not say anything.

'I told him he must come and spend some time with you when he visits next,' Dini pressed on.

'No, don't call him,' Maithili replied.

Dini wondered what to say to her daughter.

Maithili had behaved so badly when RS visited them. She had turned to ask why he was in the living room, why he was not sitting in the kitchen with Rani Didi. RS was simply confused by the question, but Dini caught on that due to his dark skin and frayed clothes, she slotted him as someone like Rani. She was taken aback. Hadn't she brought up Maithili to be conscious of Rani Didi's rights, and by extension, the rights of the working classes? The child knew about her mother's work in the bastis. Why was she behaving like Teenu or any other Delhi brat! She had tried to talk to Maithili later but wasn't very successful.

'RS was asking about you. He was asking me when we will visit Rajasthan,' she tried again with her daughter.

'I don't want to go,' replied Maithili.

Dini sighed. This wasn't going to be easy; RS was unaware of the kind of upset he could cause.

Just before he had left for New York, he got her papier-mâché heads—intended for hand-made dolls—created out of waste paper by out-of-school adolescents in his project area. 'Dini, these heads are so stunning. Look at these eyes. So lifelike! Maithili will love them!' Dini knew better but distractedly arranged the heads in a wooden bowl on the dining table. When the child caught sight of them later in the evening, she shrieked in sheer fright. 'Mama, people's heads, look! Murdered people!' She refused to touch them.

Dini had to persuade her over several days to give up the horrifying image of severed heads. She arranged them on little platforms behind a Lego wall. She explained in detail how children who were made to graze cattle in Rajasthan villages and did not have any opportunity to play with toys made them. After weeks of such stories, Maithili at last unbent to play with them. Now they were village folk looking over the Lego wall, waiting for their teachers to arrive.

'Maithili, what did the children who graze cattle do today?' she asked her daughter, pointing to her Lego installation.

'They were playing in the fields. Rani Didi has gone to make food for them now,' Maithili replied.

'So the teachers we sent from Delhi didn't reach them. Poor children! It seems to me they will remain illiterate,' Dini persisted.

'We'll go and teach them, Mama. I'll also take my toys for them.'

'RS is the one who knows all those children. He'll have to take us to them,' she reminded Maithili, seizing the moment.

'Okay, you ask him and we'll go,' Maithili said. 'We'll take Rani-di too.'

It would work out ultimately, Dini told herself firmly as Maithili ran to the kitchen and began to natter to Rani about Rajasthan villages and children who stayed with cows and goats all day. The lapse had been on her part. Their social circle up till now had comprised only the English-speaking alternate elite. Besides, Maithili had asthma, and Dini was mortally scared of taking the child to a place where the symptoms could exacerbate. She really should have been more vigilant and arranged at least a few visits to the basti for her in good weather.

'If we don't attempt to transcend caste and class divides, who will?' she had argued with Raji the last time they had talked about RS.

Dini sat down with Maithili to knock around the carrom men. 'Mama, be careful,' warned Maithili. She would always want to capture the queen disc right from the beginning of the game and protest loudly if Dini's striker even touched it.

'You know I won't aim for the queen,' Dini reassured her automatically. Usually, she would try and inculcate a sporting spirit in her daughter. But somehow it didn't seem so pressing right then.

■

The doorbell rang and Rani ran to get it. She returned with Mrs Gandhi. Dini suppressed an involuntary groan.

'I was sitting on the bench with Mrs Malhotra and saw you returning,' she said. 'Working late so much? Oh hello, Maithi. You playing carrom. Teenu also likes to play; she is so good.' Mrs Gandhi was unusually effusive, Dini thought.

'Hello Aunty,' replied Maithili. 'Mummy is playing with me,' she declared.

'But Mummy is not a little girl,' said Mrs Gandhi disingenuously. 'You come and play with Teenu.'

'Mummy plays carrom very well,' insisted Maithili.

'Now your mother does everything well. Nobody like her—' began Mrs Gandhi.

'I meant to tell you that Maithili liked the kheer she had at your place yesterday very much, Mrs Gandhi. You make it often?' Dini interrupted, steering Mrs Gandhi away from the dining space. 'Let's sit in the living room. Maithili, you continue with Rani Didi and try and get the queen. I'll join you in fifteen minutes,' she added pointedly.

Maithili pouted but did not protest.

Mrs Gandhi was going on, 'You too have had my kheer,

haven't you? I was telling Neeru it's my speciality. But she keeps saying it is an old-fashioned dish. Nobody has kheer these days and you keep making it… These teenagers!'

The way Mrs Gandhi's eldest daughter spoke to her never failed to make Dini flinch.

Mrs Gandhi settled on the sofa, and Dini braced herself.

'Since that day only, when I brought kheer for you, I have been thinking of coming to you. It was a misunderstanding,' said Mrs Gandhi tentatively.

'What?' Dini asked, knowing full well that she was talking about her husband's affair.

From the corner of her eye, she saw that Rani had brought another plate of fries from the kitchen. Maithili wouldn't have any dinner if she stuffed herself with unhealthy snacks so late in the evening. She would need to have a talk with Rani.

'I asked Sunil about the diamond ring. He got really angry,' Mrs Gandhi began narrating her story in an indulgent tone.

'Why was he angry?' Dini asked perversely.

'He said how we can have a marriage if there is no trust. It is true!'

'Did you tell him the reason for your suspicion?'

'Yes, but he said that Reeta, his secretary, had gone with him to the jewellery shop when he went to pick up my set and she bought the ring.'

Dini sat quiet. No, she wasn't going to take the bait. She knew what Mrs Gandhi was after. It was the same story with so many women. If this explanation satisfied Mrs Gandhi, she would be the last one to assume the responsibility of naming it for the bollycock it obviously was.

'He said he wanted to get the gold set himself and that was why he went to the store. Reeta went with him as they also had some official work nearby,' Mrs Gandhi repeated, looking at her expectantly.

Dini stared back unflinching. 'So, Mrs Gandhi, then everything is sorted out, isn't it?'

'Yes, Dinishee-ji, thanks be to the environment'

'Dinitia,' Dini corrected, wondering why this philistine, who advocated that all trees that were plebeian be removed from this elite neighbourhood, was talking about the environment.

'Buddhism teaches that there is the Buddha in everyone and one must believe the best of everyone,' preached Mrs Gandhi to Dini's further bemusement.

There was a very long silence which Dini used to get some nimbu-paani and *murukku* for her guest. 'You want murukku?' she asked her daughter. 'This is homemade and very healthy,' she said sternly to Rani. Maithili shook her ringlets vigorously to refuse and said, 'Mama, I've taken the queen twice.'

'Five minutes, Maithili. I'll come before you take the queen for the third time,' replied Dini.

'But I am thinking that secretaries must be getting a lot of money. Do they?' asked Mrs Gandhi munching on a murukku.

'I don't know, Mrs Gandhi. Every office is different.'

'This Reeta has so much money to buy jewellery and she is also supporting her mother and brother,' said Mrs Gandhi. 'I am thinking I should have also taken a job...'

'You could explore, Mrs Gandhi. You must. You have an MA in History, right?'

'I have forgotten all history,' she sighed, amazingly accurate for once.

Dini had learnt to be comfortable with silences. It was not a good idea to hurry women. The confidences followed their own pace, interspersed with retractions, denials, lies. Mrs Gandhi had been close, very close...

But her next observation had nothing to do with her own

life.

'Do you know the woman who has moved into 1288?'

'The top floor, across your flat? No.'

'She must be your age. Also working like you. A divorcee. All alone. No children, nothing.'

'Yes, Mrs Gandhi. There are a lot of single women.'

'But so sad to be alone, no? She could have had children as big as ours—as mine, I mean. You also had Maithi late, no?'

'Late?'

'One must have children while body is still young—in early twenties; you must have been almost thirty, no?'

'It doesn't matter these days.'

'Her hair is grey already. Childbearing age is past...'

'Oh, we don't know that. Women are having children well into their forties and even fifties now. And it's possible she didn't—doesn't want children.'

'I can see she wants. Women need children. Your husband is always out but then you are happy because of Maithi, no? Good you had her when you did. I am thinking that I am so fortunate to have Neeru, Teenu and Ganesh.'

'Mama, Rani Didi is cheating,' yelled Maithili. Dini got up and brokered peace between them by winking at Rani and returning to the board the queen that she had captured. She wanted to know more about the single woman.

Mrs Gandhi seemed lost in thought when she returned to the sofa.

'Does she seem unhappy?' Dini asked.

'Who, Teenu?' asked Mrs Gandhi, having already forgotten the lonesome woman of 1288.

'Teenu is such a cheerful kid, Mrs Gandhi. I am asking about this single woman.'

'No, she too laughs and all. But she talks to herself.'

'I think a lot of people do,' replied Dini in an abstracted manner. She was thinking darkly about women's lives.

'You know, Dinshee, I was teaching Ganesh Moral Science and there was this story. That one can be jealous of people with new shoes till we meet somebody with no legs.'

'Eh?' exclaimed Dini, perplexed.

'You know grass is always greener in other fields. Doesn't Maithi have Moral Science?'

'No, her school doesn't have it. Is all this from Ganesh's textbook?'

'No, from Teenu's. Ganesh is in playschool. I just read some nice lessons to him. I think Moral Science should be taught in all schools. It is more important than Math and Science. I am learning from it too. I have joined this Nam-myoho-renge-kyo group also. Spiritualism is so important. Now I'm getting my own Gohonzon.'

'And what do you do in this group?' Dini asked.

'People talk about their lives and then we thank the Buddha for our blessings, and then we chant Nam-myoho-renge-kyo to the Gohonzon.'

'What did you say?'

'Nam-myoho-renge-kyo. Should I write it down for you?'

'What does it mean, Mrs Gandhi?'

'Oh, it is the title of the Lotus Sutra in Japanese. You must join the group, Dinshee. You chant for Maithi's father to come home.'

'Chant for what?' Dini asked dangerously.

'I mean you want Maithi to have father, no? Or you divorce and marry again,' replied Mrs Gandhi daringly. 'Women like you have choice even at your age. I only have Sunil.'

'Oh, okay, I will think about it,' Dini replied, for once defeated by Mrs Gandhi.

'You come next Sunday for my enshrinement and there will be leaders there who will tell you more. Shailaja—from 1288—she's also coming.'

'Which leaders are these, Mrs Gandhi?'

'Buddhist leaders,' she replied.

'Who are they?' Dini gasped, imagining an array of Buddhist monks with shaven heads in Mrs Gandhi's drawing room.

'Just ordinary people like you and me,' replied Mrs Gandhi.

But asking that question proved suicidal for poor Dini. Cannily, Mrs Gandhi sensed her advantage and began talking non-stop about the practice. It took a good half an hour, a promise that she would attend the enshrinement, and a tantrum from Maithili for Dini, to reverse the stream of domestic spirituality and wisdom that she had unwittingly unleashed and send Mrs Gandhi back to her cheating husband.

September

The Enshrinement

On Sunday, the day of her enshrinement, Mrs Gandhi woke up with a sense of anticipation coursing through her. The Butsudan in which the Gohonzon was going to be enshrined had arrived from a shop recommended by the Buddhists. It was not ornate; in fact, it was too plain. Navneeta had explained why it needn't match the furniture: 'This will make the holy spot in the home, Nilima-ji. It is only right that it should be different from other things in the house.'

The carpenter would come and install the Butsudan by noon. The enshrinement ceremony was to be held later in the afternoon. She was reminded of her birthdays in Assam when her father would solemnly hand her a present first thing in the morning. It wasn't as though there had been no other celebrations in her life. She had duly celebrated wedding anniversaries, Sunil's and the children's birthdays, her mother-in-law's fasts and religious festivals. A wife and mother should never try to be the centre of attraction, her mother had taught her. But today, quite legitimately, she was once again going to have a function just for herself, and even her mother, had she been alive, wouldn't have been able to object to it.

The first important step was to find an appropriate place for the Gohonzon. The wall on which it would be installed had to be empty of all pictures, calendars, ornaments. Also, there had to be place in front of it where the faithful could sit and chant. They were woefully short of room: the three bedrooms were chock-a-block with furniture; Neeru had been asking for a separate bedroom as she hated sharing one with Teenu. Soon, Ganesh would demand a room of his own, even though he was still sleeping with her. Even the corner of the lane behind their house, which they had encroached upon by building a 'temporary structure' with single-brick walls and a green fibre-glass roof, was full of boxes, trunks and toys.

In the beginning, it had seemed to her that there was no room—no room at all for the Butsudan. Then it occurred to her that there was the living room. She was startled by her own daring. The living room was the centre of the household. But, of course, nobody would be able to say anything against a religious object. Navneeta had told her that the Gohonzon should be installed in a special place: 'There is no concept of monasteries or monasticism in this form of Buddhism; you chant from your home. The Butsudan is like a little temple.' When Mrs Gandhi told her that she was thinking of installing it in the living room, she agreed enthusiastically and said that in such a prominent place, it would benefit the entire family and the guests as well.

Sunil was livid.

'Nilima, you can't have your Buddhist temple here. It will look awkward,' he said when she was taking down his photograph in order to clear the wall.

'There's no place anywhere else, Sunil,' she replied. 'I'll put your picture in the bedroom.'

'What about Mummy-ji's room—next to her temple?'

'There's a cupboard and an almirah there. There's no space for a calendar even!' she replied hurriedly. 'That room is so small. Where will people sit when they come for the enshrinement?'

'Then don't have the enshrinement,' he snapped. 'Whoever puts the temple in the living room for all the guests to stare at! And you're saying it is not even a proper temple.'

'But Sunil, what will everyone think? I have invited so many. It will be bad luck to cancel,' she countered, her heart sinking.

'You should have thought about it and talked to me earlier. There are still two days. Cancel the thing,' he insisted.

Unexpectedly, Neeru piped up, 'Papa, it will be bad luck. My Math test is on Tuesday and Mummy is going to chant for me.'

Mrs Gandhi had at once thanked the Gohonzon in her mind for her foresight in inviting Neeru's classmate and his mother for the ceremony.

'Mummy-ji too has been preparing for it all week. If you want to cancel it, you must ask her first,' she added for good measure.

'Papa, please! Everyone has it in their living rooms only,' Neeru had pleaded. 'Mummy's Butsudan is quite small and will just hang on the wall. Saurabh says theirs is really big—like a full-size cabinet—and the whole family sits in front of it when his mother chants. He was telling me his father got a promotion one month after the Gohonzon came.'

Sunil walked off in a huff but didn't mention cancelling the ceremony again. Also, Mrs Gandhi overheard Neeru asking him to be there to meet Saurabh and his mother: 'They're coming all the way from Dwarka to meet you!' So the chances of his being there for the ceremony were good. But why did the boy's parents want to meet Sunil?

Frowning, she got out of bed and went into the kitchen,

intending to get her morning tea. To her surprise, she found that her mother-in-law was pottering around in the drawing room.

'Have you had your tea, Mummy-ji?'

'Oh yes, I have been up for more than an hour'.

'Couldn't you sleep?' she asked.

'Oh, you know I don't get much sleep. I did my puja early, because it is Sunday. Now, on other days there is so much work—tiffin, breakfast...'

Mrs Gandhi did not bother to contradict her. A major part of her mother-in-law's overseeing amounted to sitting on a plastic chair right outside the kitchen and shouting each and every instruction five times to the hapless cook. But there was no harm in letting her believe that she was running the show.

'Mummy-ji, hasn't Bahadur come yet?' She could see no sign of her cook, who should have reported for duty half-an-hour ago.

'I sent him to get cauliflower.'

'Why do we want cauliflower?' Mrs Gandhi asked, irritated that the old woman had sent off the cook just when there was work to be done for the meeting. 'There are so many other vegetables in the fridge. He must prepare for the afternoon.'

'Oho, for that only. We will fry some pakoras—cauliflower, onion and potato pakoras. You know Rajni got me *kankaua* yesterday. They call it something else here—*kanchara* or something. I have told Bahadur to soak the tamarind for the chutney.'

Her mother-in-law's latest obsession was kankaua. Ever since she found out about the enshrinement ceremony, she had been after the whole family repeating the name like a rosary, as though if she didn't get it now, she would not attain deliverance! Apparently, kankaua grows wild only in this season and so everybody should leave whatever they are doing and scour the greenery in Vasant Kunj to procure it for her. Neeru had at last looked it up on the Internet. This was a plant called 'wandering jew'. To Mrs Gandhi, it sounded dangerous. However, the old woman was intent on making pakoras of its leaves.

'Mummy-ji, nobody will have pakoras. And this kankaua— we don't know if it is safe. It might poison everyone. I am making healthy snacks: steamed *dhokla* and baked samosas.'

'Heh, how can kankaua poison? We have eaten it for years. Pakoras are very nice in the beginning of winter,' insisted the old woman.

'It is still so hot. Besides, what is the point of making something nobody will eat?'

'I will serve; they will eat. I know Mrs Khanna will have. She was telling me that it has been ages since she tasted kankaua.'

'But Mrs Khanna is not coming...' As Mrs Gandhi spoke, it came to her in a flash that the old woman had invited the neighbours and God knows who all for the ceremony.

'Mummy-ji, this is a holy meeting, not your *jagraata*.'

'Your madams said it is like our kirtan and jagraata only! They are holy too, no? The neighbours should also find out about new worship. So I asked everybody. Your baked samosas are so bland! There should be something spicy with tea.'

Mrs Gandhi was on the brink of tears. The old woman could still be trusted to spoil everything for her. These neighbours would not blend with the Buddhist group at all. Mrs Khanna and Mrs Rajoria were old and loud. They would cough and sneeze. Worst of all, they might even belch and fart, especially after consuming hot pakoras. What would Navneeta think? And she was bringing 'Khosi'—Mrs Khosala—who worked in a bank and spoke only in English.

Her mother-in-law had a duster in her hand and was going around the drawing room tapping furniture. She was actually moving around without her walker. Mrs Gandhi felt an uncontrollable urge to push her out of the room, out of her life.

Just then, Bahadur walked in, bearing a huge cauliflower like a trophy.

'Where did you disappear? Make my tea,' Mrs Gandhi said sharply.

'Madam, it is so difficult to find cauliflower in this weather. All the heads are eaten by insects. I had to go right up to the Mother Dairy. With great difficulty, I got this for one twenty rupees.'

'Are you mad?' screamed the old woman before she could say a word. 'Is this a vegetable or gold and silver? How long it takes to earn this much money! You see sahib is busy from morning to night, and you go out and throw one twenty rupees!'

'Mummy-ji, you only said that kankaua tastes best with cauli—' began Bahadur.

'In which world are you living, Mummy-ji? Is it possible to buy gold and silver with one twenty rupees? Now you let Bahadur do other work,' snapped Mrs Gandhi. 'If the whole neighbourhood is coming, we will need to make more than your kankaua pakoras.'

She swept back into the bedroom where Sunil was still snoring and felt her spirit sag. With the old woman dusting the drawing room so aggressively, there was again no place for her to chant. This was supposed to be her special day.

She locked herself up in the bathroom and dialled Navneeta's number with some trepidation; it was still very early.

'Good morning, Nilima-ji. How are you on your special day!' Navneeta's voice was soft and soothing, though a little sleepy.

Mrs Gandhi found herself sobbing out the story of the stressful morning to her leader.

'It is my special day but look at my condition; no space for me anywhere in this house,' she concluded. 'Even now I have to call from the bathroom.'

Navneeta listened attentively and made soothing sounds as she always did. 'Oh Nilima-ji, don't be nervous, everything will go well. You'll have more people than less, and it's good that so many will get the benefit of the chanting. Now that the space for the Butsudan has been decided, you must chant only there. If it disturbs others, tell them that you are praying, and it will get them good karma if they listen to you.'

Mrs Gandhi tried to explain why this wouldn't work, but Navneeta was not to be dissuaded. 'We have to claim our place in the house in order to worship,' she asserted. 'Mark my words, you will feel much better after you chant loudly and clearly.'

Mrs Gandhi heaved herself up and went back into the drawing room. The old woman, standing in the dining space, was instructing Bahadur at the top of her voice, 'Very thin layer of besan, otherwise, the taste of kankaua will be drowned.'

'Mummy-ji, you will have to close the door of the kitchen and speak softly because from now onwards I will be doing my chanting here,' she said firmly.

'Chanting?'

'The Buddhist prayer—like I do every day in my room.'

'But the madams are coming. Dusting needs to be done. You can chant after they come.'

'I am supposed to chant for a much longer time today.'

'But today they will put the mandir. Right now there is no priest. What if you do things incorrectly before the big puja?'

Mrs Gandhi drew herself up. 'There is nothing incorrect. It is the intention that matters. There are no middlemen in this faith.'

'Oh,' said the old woman, falling silent. But then she added, 'It is like this in our religion also.'

'Bahadur, take care that nobody disturbs me for half an hour,' said Mrs Gandhi firmly.

'Yes, Madam,' replied Bahadur deferentially. He had been listening avidly to this exchange.

The old woman picked up the duster and retreated into the kitchen. 'Now, speak very softly and tell that girl Rajni also, when she finally appears,' she said in the loudest whisper possible. 'Madam has already started the big puja.'

Shailaja felt battle-weary as she descended the stairs for Mrs Gandhi's enshrinement. She was still in shock from her humiliation at the hands of the principal. Of course, she had heard these things happen to working women, but that didn't make her feel any better. Besides, Ranjan had gone off to Kashmir without coming to meet her.

She had tried to discuss the issue with the more politicized faculty, though she had always been wary of them. Sachin and Anita were scruffy, impassioned, and likely to demand 'ideological' support for issues ranging from the rights of contractual labour to the resolution of the conflict in Palestine. They were the kind of people Ranjan would call 'earnest bores'. They hated the principal. When she told Anita about his 'inappropriate' reference to her personal life, the latter started out by being excited about the opportunity to fix the slimy Dhar. But too quickly she began to bewail the collapse of committees against sexual harassment under the present regime. 'I am not advising you to not complain. If you complain,

I will support you and so will Sachin. I don't know about the rest. But I want you to be fully cognizant of the situation before taking a step,' she advised.

Indeed, Shailaja had noticed that after the new VC took over three years ago, Anita and Sachin started to lose ground. 'The VC is unleashing a reign of terror and our principal is his special man. They are trying to institute cases and inquiries against all teachers' union activists. Sachin and I are marked people in this college. People like Reena Singh are bound to take advantage of the situation,' Anita had told her some time ago.

At the last faculty meeting, the teacher-in-charge Reena Singh had ticked off both Sachin and Anita for not teaching the new courses—that the VC had imposed—with the seriousness they deserved. Shailaja waited for the duo to spring at her and suck out her life, but Anita only resorted to sarcasm: 'Dr Singh, why don't you give a demonstration on how to teach students about the Delhi metro? We can all benefit from your experience of formulating the course.' Reena Singh had not bothered to reply.

To add to her anxieties, at home early this morning, she had had a spat with her old tormentor, Mrs Jain. Mrs Jain was insistent on drying her clothes on the railing right outside her door: 'You have started to lock your the roof terrace. But anyway this is better. I can keep an eye on my clothes here.' Shailaja tried to reason with her and even offered her roof terrace again, but it was the railing she wanted. 'I won't be able to see them on the roof. I lost a couple of socks last time. They were imported—from Marks & Spencer! Don't know who took them!' Shailaja decided to concede defeat, though she hated the sight of the neighbour's clothes right outside her door.

But this morning, when Mrs Jain's help came upstairs with the washing in a bucket, the battle was unwittingly resumed by Rajni ki Ma, who happened to be industriously dusting the iron grille gate at the entrance. She didn't like Mrs Jain's help, who was related to her daughter's husband and was always uppity with her. This was her chance to get even. 'No, no, Madam is expecting guests. And it is not even raining any more. Remove those pot holders and pots from your own railing and dry your clothes there,' she belted out.

The help went back sullenly, but Mrs Jain called up Shailaja at once: 'My in-laws are coming next week. Bed linen has to be washed and dried before that and then when they come, there will be even more clothes. You have no pot holders or any greenery on your railing. And anyway it is DDA property and outside your flat technically. The railing belongs to everyone!'

This came from a woman who had colonized the entire railing and the landing with her pots! Of course she sent her help back yet again with the selfsame washing. All the Jain socks, big white cotton bras and colourful panties were now fluttering right outside Shailaja's door. Rajni ki Ma was grumbling non-stop about her pusillanimity in dealing with the neighbours 'who don't even go to work and are not even educated! What use are all your degrees?'

Little did Rajni ki Ma know how completely useless her education was proving to be, Shailaja thought to herself as she dragged herself to the enshrinement. As luck would have it, she almost walked into Mrs Jain there. She looked triumphant but gave Shailaja a withering look. In a pointed manner, she beckoned Ganesh, bringing out a chocolate from her capacious bag.

'Oh Shailaja, welcome,' said Mrs Gandhi appearing at the entrance at the same time.

Shailaja had never seen Mrs Gandhi beam so much before. She was draped in a shiny mauve sari and wearing a gold-and-pearl necklace and earrings.

'Wow Mrs Gandhi, you look so festive,' she exclaimed.

'Light colour. Good for the afternoon,' Mrs Gandhi replied cheerily and turned to respond to Mrs Jain, who was aggressively demanding her attention, no doubt to exclude Shailaja.

Shailaja had an unexpected longing to be like all the other women in the room, with their jewellery and shiny saris. Even Mrs Jain was dressed in blue silk. Acutely conscious of her cotton salwar-kameez, she walked to the back of the room trying to find a corner to hide.

Mrs Gandhi's drawing room seemed transformed. A small cupboard-like altar was affixed to the wall facing the entrance and furniture was shifted to the sides. There was a floor-seating arrangement with mattresses covered in white sheets. Shailaja noted that the peeling wallpaper was stuck back, even though the golden paisleys had gone a bit askew in the process. The erstwhile abandoned film-set of a room now looked ceremonial, as though ready for a wedding. It was already full of women. Perfume mingled with incense, making the air headier. Shailaja started to feel restless. Mr Gandhi and Neeru passed by. He smiled at her and lifted his hand in salutation as Neeru, wearing a short red skirt, glared in her usual belligerent fashion.

There were still ten minutes to go and Mrs Gandhi's guests were trickling in one by one; she seemed to have invited the entire neighbourhood. It was easy to distinguish the Buddhist fraternity as Mrs Gandhi was ushering them to the front, right next to the cupboard altar. Shailaja noted how different they looked from the others. The Buddhist women were dressed casually, in jeans and salwar-kameez. In fact, she would have blended rather well with them. They were casting slightly bewildered looks at the festive crowd.

One of the seemingly Buddhist women came and sat right next to her. Shailaja noticed her school-girl hair immediately.

What could have been voluptuous ringlets were pinned away from her well-scrubbed face. She was dressed down with vengeance. She wore a faded red tee-shirt and a printed salwar with it.

She smiled at Shailaja. 'It hasn't started? I thought I was late.'

Shailaja consulted her gold watch. 'No, it's not time yet. The chanters are in the first row.'

She grinned. 'I am not a Buddhist. I have come to support Mrs Gandhi. Are you a chanter?'

Shailaja was surprised. Was she really Mrs Gandhi's friend?

As though reading Shailaja's mind, she continued, 'Our daughters play together.'

She looked way too young to have children as old as Mrs Gandhi's, thought Shailaja.

Shailaja and Dini introduced themselves to each other just as the sound of chanting rose like a wave from the other end of the room.

October

Friendship and Longing

Shailaja heaved a sigh of relief when the week-long mid-semester break began; she was looking forward to a whole fortnight of not going to college. The joy she had been deriving from teaching was destroyed after the incident with the principal. She couldn't help but censor every word she uttered in class. Her students seemed to have sensed a distance and were being rather subdued as a result. She had gone back to feeling isolated in the staffroom as well. So when, on the first day of the break, the principal's PA called Shailaja asking her to come to college on Wednesday for admin work, she found herself lying. 'I am in Kanpur. My mother fell ill suddenly. She's admitted,' she improvised. 'Madam, you should have informed the college before going out of town. I will tell Principal Sahib,' replied the PA.

Would Dhar make an issue of it? Shailaja asked herself nervously. How she wished Ranjan would return quickly from Kashmir. She had talked to him twice over bad network, and he had promised to visit as soon as he returned. In the meantime, she could crosscheck the process for making a complaint against sexual harassment at the workplace, just in case. An activist—like Dini—was bound to have a lot of information on it. Shailaja had been pleasantly surprised to get a call from Dini a couple of days after the enshrinement, asking her to drop by for coffee: 'If you like real coffee, otherwise tea!' It would be nice for her to go out, thought Shailaja. The only other person in Vasant Kunj who was inviting her home rather resolutely was Mrs Gandhi. But, of course, she had an ulterior Buddhist motive.

Dinitia—'Call me Dini, please'—had been unequivocal in denouncing 'this spiritual clap-trap' at the enshrinement itself.

'But why is it in Japanese that no one understands? What is the merit in repeating something a million times in it?' she had declaimed loudly, making Shailaja acutely conscious. The woman on their left was eavesdropping openly.

'It comes from faith and I don't think faith depends on understanding,' Shailaja hissed. 'Besides, one can check out the meaning if one wants.'

'So why not chant in a language one understands?' Dini countered at once, not lowering her voice even a little. 'It is so obviously intended to be an abracadabra kind of thing! All this is to push people into superstition. Human beings are essentially rational beings—I mean, if they aren't, they should at least try to be.'

At that time, Shailaja held her peace but after the enshrinement, on their way out, she couldn't resist saying, 'Mrs Gandhi is looking so much happier. This practice seems to be working for her.'

Dini tossed her head as though to flick back imaginary hair falling into her eyes. 'I think she is happy because it is giving her an opportunity to make friends.'

'Does it matter what the real reason is? Isn't it more important that she is happier than she was before?' Shailaja replied.

'I think reasons matter. They always matter. I hate it when

gullible people are tricked into such things. Religion feeds on human suffering—I hate that!'

Anyway, whatever her convictions might be, she seemed extremely nice. When Shailaja accidentally mentioned her 'former boyfriend' as an instance of the only other atheist she knew, Dini had not stared or looked at her in a questioning manner. In fact, she went on to ask matter-of-fact questions about him. It turned out that she had seen Ranjan's film and had heard about him through 'a cousin, thrice removed of a friend'. 'No, I don't know him personally. We have never met,' she added before Shailaja could ask. But Shailaja felt a connection forge between them.

She realized how much she wanted to say Ranjan's name out aloud. She would pay Dini a visit in the evening.

■

The door swung open as soon as Shailaja rang the bell.

'Hi Shailaja,' said Dini. 'I just walked in myself; haven't even changed! Would you like some coffee right away?'

Shailaja couldn't help but stare. Dini was wearing a top that must have once been green with the same printed salwar she had worn to the enshrinement. Did she dress like this for office?

Seated in the living room, Shailaja looked around her. The sofa was spartan with thin cushions, and the coffee table in the centre of the room was completely uncluttered. The flat was exactly like hers—just as DDA had constructed it, with iron windows and cheap wooden doors—scrupulously clean, but done up rather unimaginatively. There were various kinds of toys and word games stacked in a corner and a carrom board, set up and waiting to be resumed, lying on the dining table.

'Here is my special filter "kapi"!' said Dini, reappearing in record time with two sets of stainless steel tumblers and a plate of murukku on a tray.

Dini was definitely 'Madrasi', with her curly hair oiled and tied back, and just a hint of the land beyond the Vindhyas in her accent. She confirmed it over the wonderfully aromatic coffee by identifying herself as a 'South Indian' from Palakkad who had grown up in Matunga, Mumbai. 'It is a Tamilian ghetto. I had a completely non-North Indian upbringing,' she confided.

She was surprisingly easy to talk to, and very soon, they were deep in conversation.

'How do you find living in Vasant Kunj, Shailaja? Mrs Gandhi told me you're staying by yourself for the first time,' Dini asked.

'It's nice, but at times it gets lonely... There are only these avoidable men.'

Dini laughed, 'Oh, these over-friendly men of Vasant Kunj! Just swat them away. Most of them are cowards anyway. But of course, if they trouble you, you must report them.'

'How does one know if the issue is serious? I mean... not in Vasant Kunj, but if there's a remark from one's boss... How does one know whether or not he meant it as a pass?' Shailaja asked.

'I think the woman is the best judge. If it feels offensive, it is offensive. There are internal complaints committees at all workplaces now. But if you give me a specific example, I'll be in a better position to answer your question,' Dini replied looking business-like all of a sudden.

Shailaja retreated at once. 'No, there's nothing specific, just a feeling...'

'Women need to trust their feelings in such matters,' Dini insisted. 'Sexual harassment is basically any unwelcome sexually determined physical, verbal or non-verbal conduct. If you think there was a sexual intent in what he was saying or doing, you must act.'

'The principal—he mentioned my boyfriend and then he kept looking at me... He mentioned his wife and how she is very religious. He added in a meaningful way that she isn't "interested". He didn't specify in what, but there was no doubt about what he was implying. He also asked for my address, and then there was a call from his office for me to come and do admin work in his office during the holidays,' Shailaja explained with some difficulty.

'He had no business to mention your boyfriend or his wife's lack of "interest". Very inappropriate and suggestive! Shailaja, you should make a complaint to the ICC.'

'The members of the ICC are nominated by him. They are not likely to—' Shailaja began.

'There is an external member too, Shailaja. I can find out who that is in your college,' offered Dini.

'You know I've just started to live on my own. It's overwhelming—at times I feel insecure. I feel I might be over-reacting,' replied Shailaja. The process seemed too demanding.

'His behaviour seems quite objectionable,' Dini said. 'The man is a lecher, alright.'

'You don't think it's my insecurity?' Shailaja asked.

'No, I don't. That's what men, and even other women, make single women feel about themselves. Single women are always accused of abnormal, irrational behaviour,' Dini declaimed, offering her more murukku. 'Our society overrates marriage and biological families.'

'Ah, you know, you sound like my boyf—my ex-boyfriend Ranjan. Remember I told you about him?'

'Yes, the film-maker Ranjan Dey. His film on widows was

quite good. It was definitely a challenge to patriarchal notions of family.'

Ranjan's award-winning film titled *Widows of Banaras* had become quite popular in the NGO circuit. For all the wrong reasons, Ranjan would complain. These activist-types presume to have a solution to everything—as if everything can be understood! Art should attempt to penetrate virgin areas of experience. When an artist begins to operate habitually within politically correct limits, he indulges in boring daily-ness. The bloody voice in her head! Ranjan's sexual metaphors were so seductive. Dini was just the kind of viewer of his award-winning film he would have denounced.

'So, does Ranjan agree we overrate the importance of men? That's honest,' Dini said.

'He thinks we carry on mindlessly with social conventions,' Shailaja answered.

'You mean with things like marriage?' Dini asked.

'Yes. There was a lot of pressure from my family even in our case,' Shailaja replied, not knowing how to carry on. 'Now I wonder whether they had a point.'

'Marriage is basically a social commitment, isn't it?' Dini said gently. 'A relationship can end even if one is married.'

'Yes, but I suppose if there was a family—children—my life wouldn't have changed so drastically,' Shailaja found herself admitting. It was easy to be honest with Dini.

'Do you really think so?' Dini asked. 'Children can also complicate a breakup because they are so vulnerable. Besides, time and again, it is women who have to take on their responsibility. Shailaja, tell me something—did you really want a conventional marriage, children, family, etc.?'

'I didn't. Not when we got together. But now... When I see a family—even like that of Mrs. Gandhi's—I feel...'

'Oh, no, no, Shailaja. Mrs and Mr Gandhi are hardly a couple to emulate. And Ganesh... Would you like a son whirling like a dervish on his tricycle?' Dini asked, her eyes twinkling with mischief.

'No,' replied Shailaja at once. Both of them looked at each other and started giggling.

'We idealize the normative family too much. We have to remember it's an institution like any other—and a lot of power play goes on there as well,' Dini said after a while. 'The family is a patriarchal set-up, Shailaja, whatever one might say. At least in our country.'

'I suppose it is. This point came up during the discussion of Ranjan's film in Bellagio. You know, Bellagio on Lake Como in North Italy? We had gone there.'

'Oh, did he get that fancy American residency?'

'Yes, for a month.'

They had gone to the Bellagio residency two years before they split. It had been like a honeymoon! It was the most exquisite place Shailaja had been to in her entire life.

'A friend was telling me to apply for it. The residency is for social practitioners, isn't it?' Dini asked.

'It's not exclusively for social practitioners. There are other categories like "culture" that includes art and literature; then there's academics. Ranjan doesn't like to be called a social practitioner or an activist film-maker. He applied under the social practitioner category only because it is relatively easier to get through in that than in the other sections. There's too much competition in culture and academics,' Shailaja explained.

'Yes, I suppose. But what's the problem about being called a social practitioner, especially if one is making a film on widows and availing of the category for a residency? I would think it is a compliment.'

'Ranjan used to say—says—that Art is, or should be, primarily Art.'

'You agree with him?'

'I think that it is not a very useful distinction—between activist film-makers and art film-makers.'

Dini sighed. 'Yes, I would say all good art should be activist.'

'Ranjan says that the socially useful aspect is incidental. His aim in making the film was to capture the rhythm of the lives of widows, most of whom are outsiders to Banaras.'

'I didn't hear any rhythm, I only heard the rising notes of pathos—the series of betrayals and abandonment by brutal families. Most of them admitted on screen that they didn't want to be left there to wait for death! Families can be so cruel,' Dini said.

'But he didn't set out to critique the Indian family,' Shailaja insisted. 'Social change was not his aim. He was focussing on their daily existence—he said there was a kind of spartan beauty in that kind of minimalist life.'

Dini made a strange noise that sounded like 'pah!'

Shailaja decided to let it go; she didn't know the other woman well enough to argue more. 'But you must apply for that residency,' she said instead. 'It was incredible. We stayed in a lovely villa on Lake Como for a whole month. We had a big room and a study all to ourselves. They would pack us picnic lunches and we would take the boat and spend the whole day in some beautiful park. I was so lucky to be able to go along. Ranjan says there aren't that many residencies where one can take one's partner.'

'Were you involved in making the film, Shailaja?' Dini asked.

'Very little,' Shailaja gulped. Dini had a way of asking sudden penetrating questions. She had been with Ranjan for the entire shoot. 'I helped with the research and the commentary. My name was there.' She had been a little disappointed as none of their friends noticed her name in the rolling credits.

'I don't suppose they will allow children in the Bellagio residency?' was the next unexpected query from Dini.

'No, I don't think. But you might want to take a boyfriend or a husband along.'

'I have been on my own basically,' Dini said, looking at her strangely. 'It's been quite good.'

Just as Shailaja was about to ask a question, a little girl walked in. A young woman, obviously her caretaker, followed.

Dini introduced Rani and Maithili to Shailaja. 'This is Rani, Didi to Maithili and my helper. Maithili is learning Bharatnatyam,' she added proudly. Shailaja, after a glance at the little girl, concluded that she was adopted: Maithili's features—almond eyes and a little snub nose—spoke of the northeastern region of the country. It was difficult to imagine Dini with a husband anyway. It would be quintessentially feminist-activist to have circumvented any male interruptions to the mother-daughter idyll. 'What is worrying is that they open their mouths and platitudes roll out. One always knows what such people are going to say and do!' But in spite of Ranjan's echoes in her mind, Shailaja found the female space of Dini's home very restful.

As they said goodbye, she invited Dini to her flat over the weekend for a 'North Indian' meal prepared by Rajni ki Ma.

Dini had gone to the enshrinement with the express purpose of looking out for the 'single, lonely woman who talked to herself'—so described by Mrs Gandhi. Just as well I am there for her, she exclaimed to herself after Shailaja left. She seemed to be in a bad situation, all right. The incident with the principal sounded traumatizing. And that too after being let down badly by the arrogant prick she was involved with! Should she have denounced Ranjan more, Dini wondered.

Right from college days, Dini had been counselling successfully for breakups. 'He's different from other men,' all the smart, bright girls would claim in the beginning while describing the most stereotypical acts of male selfishness. Shailaja's obsessiveness over Ranjan also bordered on pathological. She took every opportunity to talk about him and seemed to derive her entire value system from his vacuous observations. Could she get Shailaja to think like an autonomous human being? Awaken in her some agency? Could she get her to act against that principal?

Shailaja had visibly relaxed by the end of their meeting. However, rather than feeling successful, Dini felt troubled and upset! To Rani's delight, she ignored Maithili's demand for lasagne that she would have made herself and instead asked her to make a cabbage kootu and steam some rice. Rani loved to practise the 'Madrasi' dishes Dini had taught her. Besides, whenever she cooked, Dini invariably asked her to stay over for dinner, and she enjoyed sitting at the table with Maithili and Dini.

'There are yesterday's noodles in the fridge. You can have them,' Dini cajoled Maithili. 'Also, I have made marble cake. It's orange and chocolate.'

The cake distracted Maithili, and she demanded to have it before dinner. Dini allowed it reluctantly. She had made the eggless cake from scratch with yogurt, whole flour and jaggery. It should be healthy enough, she comforted herself.

She stationed Maithili in the dining space with the promised cake and a podcast of the Mahabharata, and made for her room. Her counsellor self that had just done a good session with Shailaja was now demanding to confront her. Ever since RS brought up the question of marriage, hadn't she lost focus, she asked herself. When Shailaja was describing Bellagio with so much nostalgia, she had found herself fantasizing about a 'barca' cruise on Lake Como with RS. What did it say about a person like her to let foolish desires cloud her judgement? How could she have let the situation slide to this extent? It was with the greatest effort that she had made her signature assertion to Shailaja, 'I have been single and it's been good.' In fact, the ever-perceptive Raji had asked her last Sunday during their weekly conversation on phone, 'Are you quite sure this is a fling, Dini?'

Her phone rang, showing RS's name. He must have just finished work. She put the phone on silent. She would need to tell him it's not possible—their relationship had no future.

Instead of lying down on her bed, Dini sat stiffly at her table, doodling on a notepad.

'It's not to be, RS. If my father finds out, he would die by suicide,' she muttered. But how could she say such a thing to him? He would only hear centuries of mockery in her rejection: *your ancestors—men and women—gathered other people's shit and walked the streets with baskets of it. My ancestors quailed at the thought of even the shadow of the shit-gatherers falling on them. They were refined, top-notch Brahmins with sacred threads and caste marks. All day, their women encircled them to prevent potential pollutants from getting anywhere near their sacred intellection. I come from that lineage.*

There was already the issue of her adopted daughter between her and her father. Besides, Maithili was difficult, very difficult. She might not be Brahmin, but she was definitely a spoilt upper-class brat.

Dini reminded herself that she had duties towards her father and daughter. She would have to define the boundaries with RS—and do it fast. Even if it meant that she would be acting like a screwed-up, casteist, classist bitch!

Why was she doing it to herself? Hadn't it started out as only sex for her? And sex is not a social responsibility, is it? She was not bound to carry on with a Dalit man just because—just because he is a bloody unselfish bastard who needed to be protected from his own naivety. How had she got herself into this royal mess?

Before she could dial RS's number, Rani came into her room to announce that dinner was ready.

The next hour was taken up in having dinner with Maithili and Rani, and listening to two tales from the Mahabharata with Maithili after Rani left.

'Mama, what does ab-duct mean?' Maithili asked her sleepily when Dini tucked her up in bed at last.

'Abduct means kidnap; take somebody away by force.'

'Mama, why does Arjuna abduct Subhadra?'

'He falls in love with her and she's already spoken for. It had been decided that she would be given in marriage to Duryodhana. That's why, Maithili. This is a story from long ago.'

'Will someone abduct me?' Maithili asked.

'No, of course not, baby. You're going to grow up into a strong woman and nobody will dare to abduct you,' Dini replied.

'Did Kenny uncle abduct you, Mama?'

'No, Maithili, of course he didn't. Men don't abduct women anymore. If two adults want to be together, they don't have to seek anyone's permission. People have the right to choose their partners. Now go to sleep,' Dini said.

Ruminating, she went back into her room. Maithili was growing up; she would soon start asking questions about relationships. Kenny Uncle doubling as an occasional visiting father wouldn't satisfy her forever. This was the worst time she could have chosen to complicate her life with RS. But he had been so attracted; so persistent!

RS wouldn't have started anything with her if he knew her life story, said the contrarian voice in her head. It was she who had seduced him. Once he got to know about her life and her highly controversial choices, it would be over with a bang. The fantasy would explode—both his and hers. She needed to do this. It was time for bitter truths, for black coffee!

Steeling herself, she dialled his number.

'RS, I have to tell you something,' Dini said, aware that she sounded like a tragedienne in the penultimate act.

She was suddenly not able to carry on.

'Dini, what is it?'

'I was... am... I can't...'

'You had a relationship with a woman?' he asked gravely.

Dini shook her head impatiently—*How did another woman enter the picture?*—and then broke out into a bitter laugh. What was it with *everyone*? Just because she had theorized the erotic aspect of women's friendships in a couple of seminars, they took her for a closet lesbian. Even her own boyfriend!

'Good heavens, RS, you of all people... Really! If I had fallen in love with anyone else, would I be apologetic about it or hide it from you? I have never even had a relationship with a woman!'

'Oh Dini,' he said with audible relief, 'but didn't you say that sexual identity is fluid?'

'It is, but that's not what I want to discuss. *I want you to know that Maithili is not adopted. She is my biological daughter*,' Dini said in a rush.

'Eh?' he asked, perplexed. She could hear him sip tea. He liked to have it last thing at night. Prakash-ji ('Birbal to my

Akbar', he had once proclaimed grandly) must have made it for him after dinner.

'I was lying when I said—when I actively suggested... that Maithili was adopted,' she repeated.

'Is she Kenny's child?' he asked, having worked it out at last.

Like everyone else in office, he thought she had adopted Maithili from Shillong. Everybody also believed that Maithili's 'Uncle Kenny' was her godfather and connected to the orphanage from where Dini had got her. It always surprised her that nobody suspected that they had been in a relationship. Even those colleagues who prided themselves on being able to smell a liaison even before it started had allowed the delicious scandal to pass by unnoticed. Was it Kenny's appearance—the almond eyes, the schoolboyish air—or was there a visible lack of frisson between them?

'Yes,' she replied. 'Maithili is our biological daughter.'

It seemed the phone would be silent forever.

'You and Kenny were...?'

'Yes, we had an affair, RS.'

Nine years ago, as her mother lay dying, she had started an affair with Kenny at a week-long holiday in Goa. Dini, the graduate from TISS, Mumbai—with a degree in social development—transformed into a silvery aquatic creature seeking a mate. She spent the entire week sporting luxuriantly in the sea, in the hotel pool, in the big tub in their bathroom with her curly hair spread behind her. She was a body with a bottomless appetite. Kenny, the guitarist, was taken aback by her desire but upped his act to match hers. He told her that sex with her was like playing the double octave skilfully, consummately. She had had no idea what he meant but told him categorically that she wasn't a guitar! For some reason, that had made him laugh.

She had laughed with him but the reality check came later, much after those seven days of hedonism, much after she thought they had bid a final goodbye. She could still hear Kenny: 'Was it the butterfly that died in the act of love? But human beings were condemned to consequences.' The masculine vocabulary of evasion! Kenny quoted the lines to her without acknowledging the source when she called to tell him about her unexpected pregnancy. Dini knew at once that the words weren't his and as he was reading Graham Greene, the Catholic writer for whom abortion was a sin and whose novels, set in far-off Oriental lands, invariably included men tormented by the impossibility of committing to unsuitable relationships that they formed there, it hadn't been difficult to guess from where they were plagiarized.

RS was taking an age to reply. She waited for the storm to break. She waited for him to charge her with immorality, call her a high-class whore. Wasn't he provincial and judgemental? Wasn't he scandalized that she could contemplate casual flings with no long-term commitment? His outrage would uproot every tender sapling he had planted in her heart.

'So, you mean Kenny and you didn't marry but went ahead with the baby?' he asked at last.

'Yes, I made that decision. He wasn't ready for a baby. He wanted to work on his music career.'

'Bastard!'

'No, no, it wasn't like that. It wasn't that kind of relationship. I knew I didn't want to spend my life with him. He asked me to marry him when I told him about the baby... I was the one who refused.'

She had toyed with the idea of agreeing to marry Kenny. However half-hearted, he had proposed, all right. But how could she marry a man whose name was going to be mispronounced for sure by her father? She had imagined her father's stricken tone as he spoke on the bad WhatsApp connection to her aunt in California: 'Akka, she says she is going to marry this boy Ken-ny. Yes, he is Scheduled Tribe, ST, from Nagaland. Yes, of course Nagaland is a part of India, Akka.'

Besides, Kenny had persecuted her with contradictory statements: 'Let's be practical,' and then five minutes later, 'It would be a mortal sin to get rid of the foetus.' He would get into quite a state. It was his fault entirely, he moaned. Oh, what was he to do! He was an irresponsible bastard.

She didn't care a jot about his religious scruples but she knew she was going to go ahead with the pregnancy. She wasn't going to do the 'sensible' thing girls in her situation were supposed to do: go to a cold place and get rid of what she found growing in her womb. There had been too much dying around her. No more! Her family had been engulfed in a miasma of death for the last three years. As cancer waged its guerrilla warfare in her mother's body, she had known ultimate despair. The baby was her chance to unlearn the lessons of dying, to hope again.

'But then why does Maithili call him "Kenny Uncle"? She told me Kenny was her favourite uncle,' RS was asking. His voice sounded muffled, as though he was speaking from far, far away.

'We wanted to keep things simple for her. Didn't want her to be subjected to uncomfortable questions,' she replied unconvincingly.

It had actually been solely Dini's idea that they smudge the fact of Kenny's paternity and say that the baby was adopted. 'Only for the time being!' she had consoled him when Kenny looked askance.

It was not easy to explain all this to RS. As she told her story in broken sentences, Dini was keenly aware of the deep misery she was experiencing. Her heart cried out for him to try and understand; her mind told her he never would. Besides, she didn't really want him to understand, did she? Their relationship was ridiculous, impossible even.

'How old were you then?' he asked.

Why did he want to know how old? Really! 'Twenty-nine,' she replied.

'Dini, this is a lot for me to take in. Why didn't you tell me all this earlier?' he asked.

'I don't know... It didn't seem relevant...' she replied.

'I can't understand how it is not relevant. Did you manage to hide it from everyone? What about your family? Surely your father knows?' his voice rose.

'My father doesn't know; he was in the US at that time. Nor does anyone else in Delhi. Only my two friends in Bombay know. You're the first... I'm sorry I didn't tell you before,' she managed.

There had been a series of deceptions. Her closest friends, Raji and Namrata, helped send off her unsuspecting father to California. 'Mr Srinivasan, you need a change of scene. You don't have to worry about Dini. She has got a job offer from an excellent NGO in Delhi, and she will stay with friends initially. Both of us have families there.' She then moved to Delhi, far away from her own family and the Iyer community.

Kenny, too, played his assigned role in the charade. In fact, counselled by Raji on an ongoing basis, he made himself quite helpful in the final stages of her pregnancy without revealing his connection to it to anyone. However, once the baby was born, she became only surer that she didn't want him around. 'I must make something of myself,' he said while holding in his arms the most magical being he was instrumental in making. 'I understand. I have no problems managing the baby on my own,' she had replied.

To her father and Akka, she introduced her daughter over the phone as an abandoned newborn from Shillong, whom she had decided to foster. A couple of months later, she joined her new job at a 'politically correct' international NGO. She ticked 'single' against marital status, declared her father and daughter as family, and no questions were asked there.

'Dini,' RS said. 'Please stop crying.'

Dini wasn't able to stop.

'Please Dini, it's okay.'

'No, it's not okay,' she sobbed. 'I've lied to everyone.'

'This is just not the way to have this conversation,' RS replied with a catch in his voice. 'Please don't cry. I was taken by surprise. I shouldn't have... Look, I'll take the early morning bus tomorrow.'

She couldn't believe her ears, 'Bus to where?'

'To Delhi, of course. I need to apologize to you in person. You stop crying and go to bed, please,' he said.

Dini put the phone down as if in a trance.

She was feeling light and hollow-boned. There was nothing to keep her chained to the mundane, the everyday. Like a bird, her heart was poised ready for flight into the blue unknown as she waited for dawn.

That evening, Mrs Gandhi finished her Gongyo and settled down on the sofa to enjoy the brief period of calm before the children returned. Bahadur was making 'rara mutton' under her mother-in-law's guidance, and the entire flat was suffused with the aroma. Ironically, her home had become more her own after she handed over the kitchen to her mother-in-law. She had hardly used the living room earlier. In fact, she never used to have the time to relax. All that had changed—thanks to the Buddha, she said inadvertently in her mind, and then bit her tongue in a bid to take it back. She had been told categorically that one wasn't supposed to address the Buddha like this in the practice.

Her enshrinement had been a tremendous success—even the kankaua pakoras were much appreciated. Everyone she had invited turned up, and the icing on the cake was Sunil's presence throughout. He had a long conversation with Navneeta and Mrs Khosla, and she saw him giving his business card to both of them. They must be important professionals. She felt very proud to have them as her friends. Later that evening, Sunil and she—like the couple they were—also talked to Saurabh and his mother, who came in their chauffeur-driven car all the way from Dwarka. Such a nice woman! She brought her flowers and a set of Buddhist holy books. Saurabh, too, looked very well behaved, like a boy from a decent family. But, of course, she would have to make sure that Neeru stayed within her 'limits' in that friendship.

Mrs Gandhi's nostrils were beginning to tingle with the strong smell of garlic and onions frying in mustard oil.

'Mummy-ji, please close the kitchen door. Even the neighbours can smell the mutton cooking,' she said to her mother-in-law.

'Oho, it is only mutton, no? And there are no guests in the house! Sunil loves this dish,' Mummy-ji yelled back. 'If I close the door, I will die of suffocation,' she added.

'No chance, ji,' she whispered with a sigh, wondering when Sunil would come home. Things were changing but too slowly. With the Gohonzon at the heart of the home, wasn't it time for their relationship to pick up?

Just then the doorbell pealed, and Sunil entered with the

driver, carrying his briefcase, in tow. It was only seven-thirty. She remembered to thank the environment this time, and not the Buddha! 'The Buddha is not a deity; he is within us,' Navneeta had explained.

Sunil was looking a little pale, she thought. 'Would you like green tea?' she asked him.

'There's green tea in the house?' he asked, surprised.

'Yes, of course. I have a cup every day. Good for dieting,' she replied.

He nodded and she went into the kitchen to make it for him. When she emerged, he was talking on the mobile. He sounded agitated, so she kept the cup on the peg table nearest to him.

'We can get a loan from the bank, can't we?' he was saying.

The answer didn't seem to please him too much. 'I don't think it is a good idea to hold up the bonus. The secretarial staff works just as hard as anyone else.'

Mrs Gandhi felt worried. Diwali was coming. It would be very bad if there was a problem with Sunil's salary.

'Some problem?' she probed.

'Which tea is this?' he was asking.

'From Guwahati. Rahul had sent some boxes,' she told him. Her brother didn't believe in giving expensive gifts but he did keep her in regular supply of tea. After a while, she asked him again, 'You are having problems with money?'

'No, nothing! Finance department is delaying some bonuses.'

'Yours too?'

'No, no, the secretarial staff's. I was telling them it's—why are you asking?'

'I will chant for the bonus,' Mrs Gandhi said. That Reeta was secretarial staff, wasn't she? 'Reeta must be worried?'

'Reeta? Why are you asking about Reeta?' Sunil asked, slightly irritated.

'You told me, no—she's paying for brother's education and mother's ill too. Must be needing money.'

'Everyone needs money this time of the year. But why this interest in Reeta?'

'When we chant, it is better to have specific goal. Am thinking I will chant that Reeta gets money for her family,' Mrs Gandhi offered. Navneeta had asked her to chant for her enemies.

'Nilima... You really think chanting would help?' he asked.

'Cent percent!' she replied. 'I chanted for you to come for the enshrinement and you came, no? And today also.'

'You chanted for that?' he sounded incredulous.

'I did fifteen hours. Navneeta told me to do.'

'You told Navneeta that I—that you wanted me to come for the enshrinement?'

'Yes, everybody talks about their lives at meetings. I said he works also on Sunday and asked Gohonzon to make you free that day,' Mrs Gandhi replied. It was feeling so nice. They hadn't talked to each other like this in several years. 'People talk about work too. Khosi—Mrs Khosla—is so high up in the Bank and she—'

'In which bank is she?' Sunil cut in.

'Standard Chart—'

'Do you have her number?'

'Mrs Khosla's number? Yes, we all have each other's numbers. There's a WhatsApp group—'

'Forward me her number, will you? Why didn't I think of...' he was muttering.

A little mystified, Mrs Gandhi dutifully brought out her phone. As she pinged him, he turned to her smiling, 'Your chanting might really help.'

'It always does,' she replied automatically. She was trying to work out why her husband was so tense about the nonpayment of bonus to the secretarial staff.

But Sunil was speaking to Mrs Khosla on the phone: 'Doesn't Stanchart have a special scheme for entrepreneurs?'

'She's been with the company for five years. I can stand surety if you like,' he said.

So Sunil's worry had been for that Reeta! He was a considerate boss; she shouldn't think otherwise.

'By the way,' Sunil turned to her and said, 'Reeta is starting a new venture. I've spoken to Mrs Khosla to expedite her loan. You must chant that this works out. And mention it to her next time you meet.'

He went into the bedroom humming a Bollywood number and she heard the bathroom door close.

Mrs Gandhi sat down in front of the Gohonzon with mixed feelings. She was feeling negative about Reeta. She must seek guidance from Navneeta again. However, until then, she knew that she must compel herself to chant for Reeta's family. Her brother must get educated and her mother must receive good care—even if the 'environment' makes it happen through her husband. They are not responsible if she behaves like a slut! Ultimately, Sunil will realize...

Bahadur came to inform her that the mutton was ready and the table laid. She nodded and continued chanting, willing the Buddha in her to take away that unreasonable heaviness from her heart.

It was evening of the last day of the mid-semester break, and Shailaja knew that a madly busy time awaited her: finishing the courses, evaluating assignments, discussing these with the students, and submitting the marks in triplicate to the office. She was not looking forward to going back to college at all. What if she were to resign and try and get an appointment in some other college, she asked herself. Vacancies did come up at this time precisely because of the overload of work. She would prefer to spend time sweating it out in another college rather than in DDSD—or would she? Having spent ten years in the same establishment, she had no idea what a different environment would be like. Other colleges might have their own Dr Dhars, for all she knew. How she wished Ranjan would visit so that she could discuss this entire sorry state of affairs with him. He had not come to her flat after the unfortunate incident when he brought her the car, though he had promised her that he would. He must be back from Kashmir.

Dini had broached the topic of sexual harassment again when they had dinner together last evening.

'The principal should know better than to comment on your personal life,' Dini said. 'I found out about the external member in your ICC. I know her. She's quite sensible and can be relied on.' 'Look, even if you don't make a formal complaint against the principal, you must make a noise about it. You know these bullies... If you don't take them on, they just get emboldened. I would say look for a way to confront him.'

Shailaja wondered how to go about this. Not only the ICC but all committees in college were nominated by the principal. How should she make a noise? Would anybody believe a temporary teacher like her? In her mind, she could see the entire senior faculty looking at her strangely. Of course, Reena Singh would say she was overreacting! Ranjan too had hinted at that. Dini was an activist and believed that the woman is the best judge—but is she? Everyday life is not amenable to such simplistic assertions; it is messy, untidy, unpredictable!

Also, she was not able to get a sense of Dini. She was bright and witty and fun to be with. But somehow she managed to avoid divulging anything at all about herself. Had she ever loved a man, experienced loss and longing? Why had she chosen to adopt a baby? Shailaja tried to ask her about her life but got only copybook responses.

'I chose to be a single mother and I don't regret it,' she would reply.

Was she a lesbian?

'These women activists, they actually hate men. They are frustrated. That's why so many of them are lesbians. Lesbianism is the only kind of sex that is politically correct in their circle so they also get brownie points,' Ranjan strode into her head, displacing Dini. But Shailaja felt she understood same-sex relationships better now. There would be empathy there that would deepen, unlike a heterosexual relationship that diverged over time.

Loving a man could be heartbreaking as one got older.

'Shailaja, darling, this dress just doesn't fit anymore!'

'Please don't cry, darling. I just don't feel up to it.'

Was it completely over for them? Shailaja felt a tear run down her cheek. Would he never visit again? Even after she was being so brave and gritty in Vasant Kunj—like Scarlett O'Hara of *Gone with the Wind*, that romance film where Vivien Leigh loses Clark Gable because of her pride and arrogance and is left only with her beloved home, Tara? In spite of all the criticism she read, it still broke her heart.

She came out to her balcony for some fresh air.

'I am just going to do my evening Gongyo', said Mrs Gandhi's voice, startling her. Mrs Gandhi had been watering her plants in the gathering dusk and had seen her before she could make out who the shadowy figure was. 'Would you like to come and chant with me?' she asked.

Shailaja was about to make an excuse but her flat was beginning to oppress her.

'I'll come for some time, Mrs Gandhi,' she shrugged internally. Might as well.

Mrs Gandhi started to ply her with food as soon as she entered. 'Try khandvi—Gujarati dish, very light on stomach. I just learned to make! And green tea—very good for digestion. Must have a cup every day! I now make for Sunil every evening when he comes back from office.'

Of late, she had been talking a lot about her husband. 'You know it is important to chant from the heart. Sunil used to come back so late from office and I used to get angry. My leader told me to chant for our relationship to improve. Now, he comes back on time—mostly. If he does not come, I don't say anything; I chant if I feel angry. You must chant for what you really want. Things improve magically.'

'I am having some problems at work,' offered Shailaja diffidently.

'Oh, children giving trouble?'

'No, the students are fine; it is the principal...'

'Bosses are always giving trouble, I know. That is why I don't work. A young man at our district meeting last time narrated his experience of how much he used to hate his boss and how resolution happened. The leader had asked him to chant for the boss. He did that and you won't believe, things improved magically. He even got promotion and raise. But Sunil—he is a very good boss. Some are different! Do you want to chant for your principal?'

'No,' Shailaja replied emphatically.

'One day you will,' said Mrs Gandhi. Galvanized into action, perhaps at the prospect of a long-term goal, she spread a durri on the floor in front of the Gohonzon and brought in two large floor cushions. Shailaja noticed that the living room looked more cheerful and lived-in now. Taking down all the badly framed pictures from the wall and installing the Buddhist temple in their stead had done the interiors a world of good! Now all it needed was a good paint job.

'How much do you earn?' Mrs Gandhi asked suddenly.
Shailaja told her.
'This is very nice just to teach,' she observed. 'This principal, he can't cut your salary, can he?'
'Oh no, he can't,' Shailaja replied. 'He was insulting...'
'You should not feel insulted,' Mrs Gandhi said. 'Basically it is what we feel about things. It is up to us to make our life happy or sad. What makes you happy in your work?'
'The students,' Shailaja replied.
'So you think of all little ones you teach. Let us chant for you to be happy in your school.'
Shailaja did not bother to correct her this time and, instead, peered into the Butsudan. It looked slightly different from the time she had seen it at the enshrinement. There was the miniature silver replica of a *tulsi* plant, an incense stand, and a glass diya—all of which she had seen before. Mrs Gandhi had added a photograph in a silver frame.
'Whose photograph is this?' she asked.
'My father. The Buddhist leader suggested I add it here.'
Shailaja arranged herself against the floor cushions.
'Oh, you are flexible. Good at this age! I find it so difficult,' Mrs Gandhi remarked.
She plonked down clumsily in front of the Butsudan. Now, she had her back to Shailaja. She shuffled and brought out a little booklet and a rosary of green beads from a bright blue sequin bag that was lying on a table next to the cupboard. There was also a bell that looked like a Tibetan

singing bowl but sat on an elaborate cushion and had a mallet resting on a small stand next to it. She arranged all the objects in front of her and then ceremoniously opened the booklet.

Mrs Gandhi was quite dramatic in her recitation from the booklet. She would pause, repeat phrases and lines in a meaningful way, and then go on. Periodically, she would pick up the mallet to strike the bell that had a clear ringing sound. Shailaja peered into the booklet that Mrs Gandhi had, turning suddenly, thrust into her hands but did not attempt to recite with her. Just when her attention was beginning to wander, Mrs Gandhi paused and sounded the bell.

'Now repeat with me—Nam-myoho-renge-kyo.'

Shailaja began to chant softly with her, feeling acutely self-conscious. Life had brought her to a strange point indeed. Here she was, at seven in the evening, sitting behind a plump woman, inhaling her strong perfume, chanting words that she didn't understand. This is where her rebellion had brought her. There was a rhythm to the chanting that she liked, but they were going on endlessly. Shailaja was just beginning to get restless when Mrs Gandhi raised an imperious hand and said, 'We will do only fifteen minutes today.'

After that, there were a few minutes of silent prayer wherein Mrs Gandhi would break out into 'Nam-myoho-renge-kyo' but Shailaja didn't have to chime in.

She was again feeling weary and reduced. If Ranjan could see her now, wouldn't he burst out laughing?

'This is the trap of superstition that makes faith merely utilitarian. As though it is all about quid pro quo between the individual and cosmic powers,' she could hear Ranjan hold forth on the bastardization of religion, on the death of God in the contemporary world.

'I am feeling very tired, Mrs Gandhi. I think I will go home and rest now,' Shailaja said as Mr Gandhi entered with his branded leather briefcase and looked at her with obvious interest.

'Yes, you are looking a little unwell. You did not chant with your heart, I think. You know, Shailaja, just chant morning and evening as the leader has told me. Chant confidently for happiness. You will see the difference.'

'Yes, yes, Mrs Gandhi,' replied Shailaja, feeling very depressed instead.

What was wrong with her? Why was she submitting to such a mindless ritual? If this wasn't desperation, what was? It took her a while to shake off Mr Gandhi, who had made an entry into the living room and was asking one question after another about her 'new experience of chanting'.

She started to slowly ascend the stairs to her home.

Her mobile rang.

'Hello Shailaja,' said Ranjan's voice.

It couldn't be! She shouldn't allow herself to even think in this way. There couldn't be a connection between the chanting and Ranjan's call. She hadn't even prayed for it specifically.

'Ranjan,' she whispered. 'You're back at last?'

'I came back and got swamped again. You know what it is like when one works round the clock. Diksha has been having an even more hectic schedule.'

Diksha's work was obviously going very well.

'I need to discuss an important thing with you face to face. It is regarding teaching in DDSD and I can't...' She trailed off, feeling foolish.

'Yes, let's talk. You mean you don't want to teach anymore?' Ranjan asked.

'It is difficult to explain like this.'

'Shailaja, you know, I can't—'
'Ranjan, I know you are with Miss Strawberry—'
'What?'
'I mean I know you are with Diksha now and—' Shailaja bit her tongue.
'What did you call her?'
'Diksha.'
'No, before that… Miss Berry something.'
'There must have been some disturbance on the line. Anyway, I was saying that—that we used to discuss everything…'
'This is why I came to see you that day. We don't have to stop being civil to each other.'
'I'm sorry if I was rude then. I did apologize.'
'It is fine, Shail. I understand.'
He had called her 'Shail' again. It was like homecoming.
'Can you come to meet me?'
There was silence. Then after a while, 'Are you sure you want me to come to your flat? We can meet somewhere else,' he suggested.
'No, come home. I want to discuss things in detail.'
'Okay, I'll come over the weekend.'
In spite of herself, Shailaja found herself smiling. It was inexcusable on her part to have called his girlfriend 'Strawberry' to his face. But the name suited her perfectly; it wasn't her fault.

There was a rush of oxygen into her lungs. She hadn't realized she had been holding her breath throughout the conversation. Something had worked. She no longer felt as though the world was closing in on her. Waters had parted; he was coming to her.

Nam-myoho-renge-kyo, indeed!

October

The Unpredictable Men

At the crises centre in Nizamuddin, waiting for the basti women, Dini was reliving her meeting with RS after she had revealed her big secret to him.

'Dini, you must be thinking that I acted like a typical man,' he had said the second she reached the Munirka flat. He had travelled all day in the bus and looked rumpled and tired. There was a slight stubble on his chin.

She had stared at him silently, taking in his obvious exhaustion, admiring him for overcoming his moral dilemma. So unlike Kenny, who had dumped it all on her.

'But then I asked myself how many women in India, after finding out that they are expecting, would take such a decision. You have been very brave.'

She was not able to believe her ears. This was far beyond the forgiveness she was expecting. Besides, it wasn't true. 'RS, no! It wasn't like this—'

'Foolhardy though it might seem, you are a very courageous woman. For that I salute you,' RS was on a roll.

'I have lied to my father, my family, to you, to everyone...'

'Yes, you have. But then what else could you have done?'

It went on in this way. Dini began with protesting but

soon slipped into a game of dare. She perversely dug out every lie that she was ashamed of uttering and offered it for his review. She told him about the many adjustments, the shameful cover-ups.

'RS, my father and his sister Akka, who is like a parent to him... They are... They are very conservative. They are typical Iyer Brahmins. Akka even tried to perform a ritual of purification for Maithili. I hated that and stopped it. But they are family and I just couldn't tell them the truth about Maithili.'

'It is important that you stopped it, Dini. It's not the easiest thing to challenge one's family.'

It had gone on: her complete abasement and self-loathing, the expiation he was offering. She had no idea she was carrying so much guilt within her. But he redeemed her. The stubbornness with which he continued to adore her infused her with new hope. Dini's heart soared higher and higher. It was magical.

The balance of power had shifted between them, she thought. She had broken into pieces; he had put her together again. Their lovemaking had changed; he was more demanding. This position was new for her. Dini felt her throat dry up. An unaccustomed, almost coy smile appeared on her face.

'Didi, so deep in thought. Looks like Maithili's papa is coming!'

'Oh Jamila,' Dini started. 'Maithili doesn't need a papa. Back so early from the factory?' Dini noticed that Jamila was looking quite pale and ill.

'I couldn't go today. That doctor of yours was no good, Didi. I have been feeling so ill since then. Just couldn't go for work today.'

The abortion was months ago. After that they had met on at least four-five occasions and Jamila had looked quite healthy.

'Take me to her again, Didi. I will ask her what she did.'

Dini asked her about her symptoms, which seemed vague and probably had nothing to do with the abortion. Suddenly, Jamila burst into a peal of laughter.

'Didi, so easy to fool you, no? That operation is history now. First and last problem is this husband. Now tell me, will you get me out of prison if I kill him?'

'Oh, Jamila Behen!' Dini was laughing in spite of herself. 'I am not a lawyer.'

'But you are educated, no! You can go to the judge and tell him that I am a good woman. I saw that film, Didi. I have forgotten what it was called but there was this beautiful sardarni in England with light eyes—as beautiful as you. Her husband beat her and she poured alcohol on him and lit a match. Very nice film. I clapped and everybody was looking at me. The angrezi court lets her go free because her friend proved that it was all his fault. Look—'

Jamila was showing her a gash on her upper arm.

Dini gasped, 'Oh Jamila, what happened?'

'It happened last night, Didi. He was dead drunk as usual. I was so tired. The bus had broken down and it had taken me three hours to get back home. And then I saw that the old woman was sitting doing nothing. Told me to make methi aloo. Did not even clean the methi. I asked, "Ammi, are you planning your own nikaah? Do you have mehendi on your hands that you can't do any work in the kitchen?" So, she took the *chimta* and ran at me. Then I cooked, fed her, and was so exhausted that I couldn't eat anything myself. Kept food for that boor. Then he comes in early morning, reeking of booze, and when I ask him to stay away, throws the food on the floor. I called him a drunken idiot, so he took the kitchen knife and did this... Old woman was sitting there all the time pretending to read the namaaz.'

The scene unfolded in front of Dini's eyes as Jamila spoke. They lived in one room in the ramshackle building rented out to ten families. The two toilets and bathrooms were shared among thirty-five people. The other families must have heard the fight but nobody would interfere. Parvaiz was beating up his own wife, wasn't he?

'Jamila Behen, are you going to tolerate these beatings forever?'

'No, Didi. Only till you take me to your home and give me a place to stay.'

'You have the right to stay there.'

'And so does that drunken idiot and his good-for-nothing mother. I told them I will complain about them to the Maulvi.'

'Will he do something?'

'Ansari Bhai is a good man, Didi. Recites the namaaz five times, keeps all his rozas. But he is a man. He will ask me why I am not agreeing to produce a child for my husband.'

'Oh Jamila Behen, we can make a complaint in court, you know. There is a law called PWDVA—'

'Didi, if I go to the police, everybody in the building will turn against me.'

'No, I am not talking about the police, Jamila Behen. We can go to the protection officer. I know her, actually. She will give your complaint to the magistrate and you can get an order from court.'

'Didi, this is not England. Everybody will say I should have gone to the Maulvi if I had a complaint. If I go out of the *qaum*, then the qaum suffers, no! Jamila can die, but the community will live on.'

'Let me speak to the other women from your building.'

'You do that. Mehraj was asking where you had taken me

the other day. She was saying Didi has a special relationship with Jamila.'

'So what did you say?'

'I said yes, she does. It is matter of the heart. There is lot of love, what will you understand?'

Dini persuaded her to go to Romola Aunty to get her wound dressed. With a sinking heart, she knew that to get the women of the building to support Jamila against her husband and mother-in-law was going to be a very difficult task. She couldn't put a finger on it, but there seemed to be some hostility against Jamila. Besides, the PWDVA and its important provisions were still untried in the basti. She was planning to do a workshop on it. Of course, she would need to take permission, and there would be tiresome questions on how it related to health and well-being of the basti women, but she would handle all of that. She noticed that Jamila was still hanging around.

'Jamila Behen, you must go to Romola Aunty now. You know she leaves by seven.'

Jamila took both her hands in hers and kissed them. 'Didi, you are like an angel.'

Dini was taken aback not so much by the excess—she had encountered it time and again—but by the whiff of rose attar as Jamila came closer.

After being attacked with a knife early in the morning, Jamila had applied the only perfume she possessed to come and tell her about it.

■

On her way back, Dini wondered whether to call up Shailaja. She was feeling a little weary of the other woman's obsessiveness. Her longing for a settled home was pathetic, especially as that ex-boyfriend of hers had never offered her one! She kept coming back to it. 'Dini, don't you miss having a proper family?' she had asked last time.

Dini had at once challenged her to define 'proper'. But the conversation was still long and meandering.

'You know, I meant "proper" in the sense of usual—what you would call "normative". Even if there are a thousand problems, there is still something solid about the structure,' Shailaja said wistfully. 'And one has a social standing.'

'What is considered normative is an ideal; it hardly ever exists in reality,' Dini shot back. 'Don't you agree?'

'It does exist. If you look around, there are more families like Mrs Gandhi's than, for instance, yours. I am, of course, single, but I can recognize a normative family when I see one.' She had made singlehood sound like an affliction.

Dini gave her stock reply, 'Well, I am single too. It was my decision to be a single mom and I don't regret it.'

'Of course. But don't you want a relationship?' she had persisted.

Dini was unexpectedly irritated by the question. 'Who doesn't want a good relationship? But they are difficult to find.' She was hyper aware of her feelings for RS as she said this. But Shailaja needed to stop idealizing the man–woman relationship. She had to put it in perspective, not make it the be-all and end-all of life!

Shailaja was quite dogged. 'I was wondering whether forming a relationship is especially difficult for you as there is Maithili,' she asked.

'Having her makes it easier for me, actually.'

'How's that?'

'I'm not alone. We are a family—mother and daughter.'

'Hmm. By "normative" I meant love or marriage, a partnership, culminating in a family. Don't you think there's a kind of stability there, a pre-established order?' Shailaja persisted in asking, as though Dini didn't know all along what she was getting at.

'Oh, Shailaja. Partnership? Is this from the romance novels you teach? Real families are hardly ever reliant on romantic partnerships. What kind of partner do you think Mr Gandhi is? He doesn't share any domestic responsibilities. If anyone shares them with Mrs Gandhi, it is actually her mother-in-law. But will Mrs Gandhi ever admit that?'

'I think she does now. Are you saying a good partnership with a man is impossible? If one is heterosexual, then one would want a relationship with a man, wouldn't one? Besides, all men are not like Mr Gandhi.'

In that moment, Dini felt that she couldn't bear another conversation about eternal love and singular men! What was it with these upper-class women? Mrs Gandhi, who refused to accept that her husband was having an affair; Shailaja, who was sounding more and more like a broken Bollywood record. In stark contrast was Jamila, who held on to her plucky humour in spite of it being literally beaten out of her time and again. And there was RS's mother, who lost a beloved daughter due to patriarchy but had not lost her grit and determination. No, she, a rights activist, could not be accused of idealizing poverty and hardship. But RS had a point when he argued that at times privilege only served to enervate people.

Dini decided to postpone calling Shailaja till the next morning.

■

'Mama, Kenny called,' said Maithili happily when she reached home.

'Kenny Uncle.'

'He said I must call him by his name—not "Uncle" like a Punjabi!'

'Oh, really!'

'He said he is getting me a guitar.'

'Oh Maithili, but you are learning Bharatnatyam!'

'I could learn both, he said. Mama, please, I am big enough now.'

'We'll talk about it later.'

'Okay, I'll tell him you said yes.'

'But I haven't said yes, Maithili. You must first try it out in the evening classes nearby. Then, if you are really interested, Kenny can get you the guitar. Did he say when he was planning on coming?'

'He'll come soon. It's going to be a surprise, he said. Mama, I'll start learning now. Take me to the teacher now,' said Maithili.

'Okay,' said Dini. So Kenny was planning a visit. So soon after his last one! It had just been a couple of months—eight months actually.

'When will you take me?' Maithili was asking.

'Take you where, sweetie?'

'When are you going to take me to the guitar teacher?' yelled Maithili.

'I'll find out about a teacher tomorrow. Should we discuss your project now?'

'Why can't we go now?'

'Maithili, it is eight in the night. You have to sleep in half an hour. Let's take a look at the project on dances. What other dances are there besides Bharatnatyam?'

'No, I don't want to know,' she sulked.

'Why not? You have to submit it in a couple of days.'

'You don't listen to me.'

'I am listening. Come on, Maithili.'

'I asked Kenny if he would stay here always and teach me the guitar.'

'What did he say?'

'He said he wanted to but you won't let him stay.'

'He must not have meant it, Maithili. His home is in Shillong.'

'He said he could move to Delhi if you let him.'

'I'll speak to him and find out. But we can't have more people staying in the flat, you know.'

'Why not? There is place in my room,' Maithili demanded.

'Where will Thatha stay when he comes from Mumbai?'

'Both can stay in my room, Mama. And I will stay in yours.'

'Okay, Maithili. Now get your project. You remember, last time Miss Bhatnagar said your project on festivals of India was brilliant!'

Maithili trotted off at last to get the new project and Dini sank into the sofa with a sigh. She could have done without this latest complication. What was it with Kenny now?

Shailaja was moodily changing channels on television and half-waiting for Dini to call. 'Let's have a longer conversation about men. I'll call you after I get back from work tomorrow,' Dini had said, calling off their conversation when she felt cornered. She was such a contrarian, Shailaja thought. A poem came unwittingly to her mind: 'A Prayer for My Daughter', in which Yeats denounced Maud Gonne, the revolutionary woman who broke his heart.

> An intellectual hatred is the worst
> So let her think opinions are accursed.

> Have I not seen the loveliest woman born
> Out of the mouth of plenty's horn,
> Because of her opinionated mind
> Barter that horn and every good
> By quiet natures understood
> For an old bellows full of angry wind?

One couldn't get more opinionated than Dini. Her hatred for love and romance was old-style copybook feminism. 'Shailaja, heroines of romances are such wimps; how can you read and teach such stuff?' Or, 'Romance books are B-grade, so mindless.'

Shailaja had tried to explain patiently: 'Dini, all women who love romance—and a lot of women love romance—are not automatically "surrendered" women, who have given in to patriarchy. Besides, the romance heroines are not wimps. They are meant to be everywoman; they are the norm. In the best romances, the heroine discovers her individuality through her ability to love deeply.'

But Dini was not to be persuaded. 'How convenient that women should continue to believe that this is the only way to actualize themselves,' she shot back. 'How convenient for the men, Shailaja!'

'But surely the men you've dated were diff—I mean, you must have dated men if you are so inclined—' She had tried to argue but only managed to tie herself in knots.

'No, I'm not a lesbian,' Dini had replied impatiently. 'I don't like labels anyway.' What made her tick, Shailaja wondered. She didn't seem to need anyone except Maithili and her basti-waifs. She was like a blooming lotus in the muck of her depressing work.

But couldn't she try and look more flower-like? The top that she wore at their last meeting was pink-and-orange in its good days but had become a muddy shade of brown. If a woman pushing forty—even though she looks twenty-five—is dressed like that and has an eight-year-old kid constantly throwing tantrums around her, what would be the chances of her finding a nice man? Shailaja had seriously thought of suggesting tactfully, 'Dini, if I were you, I would throw away that top.' But she decided not to risk it.

Her doorbell rang, making her jump. How strange that Dini hadn't called to confirm her visit! Shailaja opened the wooden door and saw a tall, menacing shadow right at her doorstep. There was still the iron door with the steel netting between her and any potential murderer-rapist, but an involuntary gasp escaped her.

'Shailaja, it's me,' said Ranjan's voice. 'Why is it so dark?'

'Oh, I'm sorry, the bulb is fused. The association was going to get it changed this evening but the colony electrician is on leave,' babbled Shailaja, opening the door and letting him in. 'I wasn't expecting you till the weekend.'

'Which association?' he asked.

'The Resident Welfare Association. There is one in Defence Colony as well.' Shailaja wondered who was taking care of those mundane everyday details. Did Strawberry have the time?

'How are you?' Ranjan asked. He was disturbingly close.

'I'm fine, Ranjan,' she answered, drawing into herself even though she felt like flinging herself onto him. How could she even think like this, she scolded herself. 'How's Diksha?' she asked pointedly.

'Very well. Getting ready for her next assignment,' Ranjan replied, moving towards the sofa and releasing her from his disturbing proximity. 'I have been worried about you...'

'It's—it's a little late, don't you think,' she spluttered. She didn't want to sound blamey. But the information that the strawberry tart was having it so good in the career department had flipped a switch inside her.

'I'm sorry. It's just that I was shooting in Gurgaon and the shift packed up early. I thought I would look you up this evening itself. But I can come another day if you like,' he replied, pretending to misunderstand her.

Shailaja noticed that he had sunk deeper into the sofa; her words had not unsettled him even marginally. How dare he think she wouldn't turn him out again?

But she had called him more than once, hadn't she?

'I have been thinking about that episode with Dhar. Actually, with hindsight, it could seem quite... Grotty.'

Grotty! Ranjan had a penchant for unusual words. Now where had he picked up 'grotty' from? Was it even accurate?

'Yes, Dhar specializes in sleazy behaviour.'

'It can be very disconcerting. I am sorry I appeared to be unsympathetic.'

'I've discussed it with a couple of activists. I don't think I should take it any further,' she said.

'Yes, Shailaja. Such incidents are best forgotten. These are problems one has to put up with if one is a woman—an attractive woman at that! This is what I was trying to explain to you.'

'I thought you felt that I shouldn't have called you... I thought you were feeling put upon,' Shailaja ventured.

'Put upon? Shailaja, we were together for twelve years,' Ranjan seemed genuinely distressed.

'Twelve years eight months,' the correction slipped out before she could bite the words back.

Ranjan smiled ruefully, 'Yes, thirteen years. Beautiful thirteen years.'

'Were they...'

'We were in love and everything else was secondary. We

were young—I mean, you were really young, but I too was younger than this,' he said with the wry smile she had loved so much and patted his bald patch. 'We didn't even pay attention to our careers!'

'You feel you neglected yours too?' she asked, genuinely surprised.

'Yes, Shailaja. And both of us are finding this out to our chagrin, aren't we? Now Diksha—she's just a few years younger than you but seems to belong to another generation. She is totally committed to her profession. In a way, I am learning from her. There are always things one dislikes at work. One shouldn't allow them to retard one's growth in the profession.'

'Oh Ranjan, so preachy!' quipped Shailaja. 'Basically you are asking me to swallow the bitter pill, aren't you?'

'This is unfair, Shailaja. I wasn't even talking about you. But if the situation is so intolerable, I have a proposal.'

Shailaja looked at him questioningly.

'This is difficult to, um, put into words,' Ranjan said. 'I don't know how to say it.' He was uncharacteristically hesitant. Shailaja braced herself.

'I have no intention of insulting you by offering you money,' he went on, 'but you could think of taking a leave of absence for a couple of months. Don't worry about your expenses. I can take care of them. In fact, it would make me feel better if you accepted some money from me.'

Shailaja felt her jaw drop in surprise. This was completely unexpected.

'I don't understand,' she said.

Ranjan looked at her carefully. 'If you want to take a break from teaching, I would like to facilitate it. I realize that you might want to think about other options. You mentioned once that you were thinking of going abroad for a PhD.'

'Why do you want to do this?'
'We are friends, aren't we?'
She sighed and said, 'We are ex-lovers.'
'You mean it is all over for you?' he sounded plaintive.
'Ranjan, you were the one to call it off...'
'Yes, and I haven't heard the end of it, have I?' Ranjan said, stiffening at once. 'It takes two to make or break a relationship.'
'What do you mean, Ranjan? I did not make any trouble for you. I just walked out of the home that we had shared for twelve years and eight months with a few pieces of furniture,' Shailaja heard her voice rise. She wished there was a way of saying this without sounding tragic.
'Very heroic,' he said cuttingly.
'Yes, it was. It is heroic. Let me tell you it isn't easy.'
Ranjan's words when they came after a long pause sounded sarcastic, 'Life isn't easy for anyone. But I thought I would make it easier for you. If you have a little nest-egg, you won't feel so resent—insecure.'
'What do you mean by this? Are you saying I am acting resentful?'
Ranjan was suddenly livid, 'You've been calling me, Shail. And then there are these long silences on the phone. So much blame!'
'I have never as much said a word of blame. It is your guilty conscience!'
Ranjan started screaming, 'This is what I mean. You act like a bloody martyr. Guilt? Why should I feel any guilt? We were two consenting adults. I didn't abduct or kidnap you. If it ended for me, what could I do? Why in the devil's name should I feel bloody guilty?'
Shailaja felt tears well up in her eyes, 'Ended... You just said it wasn't over. You said we were friends...'

Ranjan was suddenly by her side. He put his arm around her, 'Hush Shail, come on. Don't be such a baby. Of course we are friends; we are much more than that. Those twelve—thirteen—years, Shail, don't you think I miss them?'

'You do? I miss you terribly,' she sobbed, snuggling up to him.

When he kissed her, it seemed logical. To walk with him into the bedroom was only natural. It had happened so many times before: she was powerless in the grooves of habit, oiled by tears and longing. She spiralled downwards.

It was only in the wee hours of the morning that Ranjan left the flat, shutting the front door quietly behind him.

Mrs Gandhi had woken up early that morning. She loved it when the heat started to abate in Delhi. She made herself a cup of tea in the silent kitchen and padded out to her little verandah to drink it in a leisurely fashion. The sun was just beginning to rise, and very soon the rays would sneak into the courtyard and her verandah. Until then, she could enjoy the coolness of the morning.

Sunil had been returning home early all of last week. Mrs Gandhi automatically thanked the Gohonzon. But he was also looking stressed and unhappy. She asked him again whether there was a problem with his bonus, but he just shook his head a little impatiently. She also overheard him talking on his mobile to that secretary. 'Reeta, that's a very big amount,' he said as though to dissuade her. The loan from Stanchart probably had not worked out. Mrs Khosla had been withdrawn and very quiet when they met last, so she was not able to crosscheck with her either. Besides, Navneeta had announced at that meeting: 'Ours is a faith-based organization. So I would request members to not talk about work or business matters with each other. Also, we must not share each other's phone numbers with anyone outside the practice! It is forbidden by the leadership and goes against the tenets of our Faith.'

It was a general announcement but Mrs Gandhi felt very guilty. How was she to have known this? But just to be sure that no harm came from her actions, she increased the time of her chanting by fifteen minutes. She was not the one to take any chances in religious matters.

Just then, she saw Shailaja's front door open and a tall figure emerge. Mrs Gandhi suppressed a gasp of surprise. As he descended the stairs, she could have a better look. Arty type! He was wearing a kurta and had a ponytail, though he was balding from the front. Who could have believed this of Shailaja? Just divorced a few months and already started an affair! She was chanting also and even then—so brazen to bring him to her flat for everyone to see! Someone could complain to her landlord; decent people with families do not like such goings-on in the vicinity. It was also the landlord's fault for renting the flat only to single women. But it could not be denied that Shailaja was proving worse than Shruti. Whatever Shruti might have done outside, Mrs Gandhi had never seen a man in her flat at an odd hour. Why had Shailaja chosen someone so old? Of course, there couldn't be much choice for a middle-aged woman—especially one who lets all her grey hair show—but still!

As Mrs Gandhi mulled over the potential this sighting could have for scandal, she heard footsteps behind her.

'Nilima, make me a cup of tea too.' It was Sunil.

Mrs Gandhi's hand shot out involuntarily and she placed her palm on his forehead, like she always did with the children if they woke up too early. 'You ill?'

'No, no,' he said, 'just a headache.'

'99 degrees,' she declared. 'You have a fever.'

'Your palm is a thermometer or what?' he asked in an amused way.

'I can tell,' she replied matter-of-fact. 'You lie down. I will make ginger tea.'

'No, I'll sit here for a while. It's nice,' he said settling down on the *mudha*.

She made the tea quickly and brought out Marie biscuits. At one time, Sunil used to enjoy dipping them in his tea.

'So peaceful!' he said, dipping the biscuit in the tea at once. 'Nobody is up yet! What were you doing on your own?'

'Just sitting. Then I saw... The upstairs lady, Shailaja, had a visitor,' Mrs Gandhi said. She was determined to share her views with her husband.

'Some man?' Sunil asked, perking up.

'Yes, came out very quietly.'

He looked at Shailaja's door as though his ghost would still be lurking there. 'Single woman—why not!'

'It is so important to get married and have a family at the right age. I worry about Neeru,' Mrs Gandhi offered.

'Why worry about Neeru? She's so young,' he said slurping the sodden biscuit and taking a sip of the hot tea.

'She's almost fifteen. I got married at twenty-two.'

'In this day and age, girls marry late. Some don't marry,' he said philosophically.

'You want Neeru to be ultra-modern?'

'What do you mean, ultra-modern? Ultra-modern type of women do not care about traditions; it's usually because they haven't been taught anything about our culture. Neeru has you and me and Mummy-ji instilling good values in her. She can never go wrong,' he said.

'Yes, girls from good families know their "limits",' agreed Mrs Gandhi. 'But they have to be taught.'

Sunil nodded and there was peaceful silence between them. The delivery boy from Safal Dairy arrived in the courtyard and started taking packets of milk to his client-flats.

Mrs Gandhi took her two litres of toned milk from him. 'Get me a packet of whole milk tomorrow,' she instructed him. 'Mummy-ji wants to make *gaajar ka halwa*. I told her carrots are still very expensive, but you know what she's like,' she said to Sunil.

'Neeru is going for Saurabh's birthday tomorrow,' Mr Gandhi said to her when she returned after putting the milk in the fridge.

'Have you told Ramprasad to keep an eye?' she asked him distractedly. Bahadur was late again. Mummy-ji would be up in no time and demand her tea.

'Yes, of course,' he replied. 'But you must also pay attention. Go and meet his mother now and then, chant with her or something. The family is good and there's no harm if you let them know that we are modern but traditional also,' he said.

Mrs Gandhi thanked the Gohonzon in her mind. She was lucky to have such a sensible husband. Mrs Batra, at the last meeting, was complaining that her husband was very naive. He had scolded her for putting 'spies' on their daughter! Mrs Gandhi decided to bring up the subject that had been on her mind for quite a few days. 'Sunil, you got your bonus and all! I am thinking we must renovate the drawing room and buy some new furniture before Diwali.'

Sunil nodded absently. The newspaper boy had just handed him the paper. He was expertly throwing the paper up to the first-, second- and third-floor flats. The newspaper roll hit Shailaja's front door with a loud report.

'Good aim,' Sunil congratulated the boy.

However, Shailaja did not come out to pick it up and the door remained firmly shut.

'Very difficult to wake her up in the morning! Rajni ki Ma has to ring the bell several times,' said Mrs Gandhi.

'Single woman—no care!' replied Mr Gandhi. 'A good and free life these women have, I always say!'

'She is chanting these days; I will tell her to offer everything to the Gohonzon—right or wrong! It will become right, ultimately,' philosophized Mrs Gandhi, but Mr Gandhi was no longer listening to her.

Soon after sending off Maithili to school with her tiffin of the hated aloo matar and paratha, Dini was in the process of checking out the headlines in the newspaper when her doorbell rang.

Peering from the magic eye, Dini did a double take. Kenny stood at her doorstep with a big suitcase and two black guitar cases.

'I wasn't expecting you,' she said, opening the door.

'I wanted this to be a surprise. For Maithili. Can I come in?'

'Oh yes, sure,' said Dini, moving aside to let him enter. 'What is it that you are carrying?'

'It's for Maithili.'

'Is it a guitar, Kenny?'

'Yes, so she told you about it?'

'She certainly did.' She had been planning to have a talk with him about Maithili's achievements in Bharatnatyam. Beginning guitar lessons would only be interference at this stage. But later—there were other pressing matters. Kenny had kept the big suitcase beside the sofa.

'You are en route to…?' she asked.

'What do you mean?'

'This suitcase is really big. Are you on way to some other place?' Usually when he visited there would be a backpack, and occasionally an overnighter.

'No, no, I'll stay for some time.'

He hadn't found it necessary to speak to her about his plans. Dini frowned.

'Oh, how long are you planning on staying?' she asked before she could stop herself.

'Dini, I want to spend time with Maithili. I am thinking I'll stay for a month or so.'

A month! Was he crazy? It would be awkward to have him staying in the flat, especially when RS was in Delhi.

'Oh, is that so?' she exclaimed

'Is it a problem?' he asked.

'Won't it be weird?'

'Why? We had decided that I could visit her whenever I liked, stay with her as long as I liked. Didn't you say so to me?'

'Yes, eight years ago. I mean up till now you've made only one- or two-day visits…'

'Dini, I'm really sorry about the past. I've been talking to Raji. She thinks I should spend more time with my daughter. She'll grow up and won't recognize me otherwise. I know I have been neglectful but I want to make amends.'

Dini felt hurt and angry with Raji. They had talked for an hour last week, and she hadn't even mentioned that she was instructing Kenny on family values.

'Kenny, you can't just walk into my flat one morning and say you want to stay here for a month.'

'Would you like me to take her to Shillong in that case?' Kenny said, being combative.

'Shillong? She goes to school here!'

'I know, and this is the reason I am here. It wasn't easy to be able to get away for a whole month,' he replied, trying to sound reasonable. 'I know you are angry—'

'I'm more surprised than angry, Kenny,' Dini shot back. 'You should have spoken to me before finalizing your programme. It isn't enough to have discussed it with Raji. Also, what about Jolene? What will your girlfriend feel about you staying here for so long?'

'It didn't work out with Jolene. We've broken up,' Kenny replied.

'Oh, is this the reason...'

This explained the presents he had got her.

'Dini, please! That is not the reason. Maithili said you told her that she has a different kind of father from other children. You said I'm a long-distance daddy and this is what she should tell her friends when they ask her,' he said accusingly.

What else could she have said! It had been difficult to answer Maithili's questions about her father. Is Kenny not my father? Why do I call him 'Uncle' then? And just when the child needed to be reminded that Mummy and Daddy were not together and gently told that another Uncle was going to play an important role in her life, the undeclared father walked in, carrying an outsized suitcase.

'I thought I was telling her the truth.'

'There are many fathers who need to stay away from their children because of their jobs.'

'This is exactly what I told her,' Dini replied.

'They are not called "Uncle".'

'They could be.'

Kenny looked stubborn. 'Well, perhaps she can have a regular daddy for a change. Anyway, I've told her to call me by name.'

'Okay fine, Kenny! I'll leave in half an hour or so,' she said. 'Maithili will be back at the usual time and you can start regular parenting right away! Of course, we'll have to work out how to tell her about the past,' she added sotto voce, and Kenny pretended to not have heard her.

She showed him into their daughter's room and shut herself in hers. It was really a bad time for Kenny to get an attack of Responsibilitis! And the devious Raji! She could have at least warned her about this crazy plan.

•

What would she say to her father, Dini asked herself.

She had told him that Maithili was very close to her Kenny Uncle: 'She thinks of him as a father figure.'

'That's all very well but she shouldn't end up thinking he's her real father. Shouldn't you tell her that she's adopted? What if she hears of it from someone else?' her father cautioned. Dini tried to explain away the situation, 'No, Appa. I am not going to tell her that she is adopted. This information can wait till she is an adult.'

'Your maid also thinks he is her father,' he frowned.

'Appa, how does it matter what people think? Kenny told me he had spoken to his girlfriend about it, and Jolene had no problems. He only visits Delhi for a couple of days anyway,' she had reassured him.

Maithili was sure to blather to her Thatha on the phone. How was she going to explain Kenny staying in her flat for a whole month? Besides, how would RS react? It had only been a few days since she had disclosed the skeleton in her cupboard to him. Just her luck that it should come dancing to their next date.

It was, of course, completely uncharacteristic of Kenny to

want to assume responsibility, Dini comforted herself. Kenny was the feckless kind. His sentimental decision to want to parent his eight-year-old daughter would probably evaporate when he realized what parenting entailed. She should just give it time. Besides, she could always make up a story explaining his long stay in her flat. She had perfected the art of throwing her family off-track.

Dini looked at her small and plain watch with some alarm. She was very late; she had an important meeting at the office. It was time to put away domesticity and get ready for office.

The country head of her NGO had sent her an email yesterday asking her to meet him. Right from the beginning, she had disliked him instinctively and knew that the feeling was mutual. More than once, he had caught her sniggering quite openly at his motivational speeches and discourses on the 'goals and targets' of their international NGO. Anyway, Nitin could not be expected to approve of somebody like her. He called her 'overly enthusiastic'—his euphemism for inappropriate. She knew that he thought her to be sentimental and opinionated. He could not be expected to understand her worldview, Dini thought as she tamed her wild hair with coconut oil. 'Arrogant prick!' she said aloud, looping a black band expertly at the end of the short plait she had braided her hair into.

In fifteen minutes, she was ready for the day: blue jeans, a new orange-and-pink kurta, and a long pink scarf. Her hair was already fluffing around like a halo around the wheat-gold of her face, set off by flashing black eyes and thick eyebrows. Should she tone down the riot of colours and replace the pink scarf with something more sober?

She couldn't find anything that matched. Let Nitin, perfectly outfitted for welfare in his greys and navy blues, be provoked, she decided.

As she was stepping out, Rani offered her a plate deferentially: 'Chee-toast, Kenny Bhaiya made for you.' He is taking this stay-home business rather too seriously, she quipped in her mind. She made herself eat one—very nice—and then said a polite goodbye to both Rani and Kenny, who had come out of Maithili's room to see what she did with his peace offering.

No point in ruffling his feathers further.

She would make that call to Shailaja on her way to office, she thought to herself. She could vent her feelings about men and their self-centredness to her heart's content. Would be good for her as well!

She called thrice but Shailaja did not pick up the phone.

■

'Hi Dini, how nice and bright you look this morning!' Nitin greeted her effusively. 'I was looking at your report. It is very comprehensive.'

'Thanks. Is it too long?' she asked.

'I thought it could be profitably edited—the life stories, for instance. There are so many. And a lot of them are, well, a little bleak…'

'Nitin, I have only put in what women actually said.'

'Of course. At Empower, one would not have it otherwise. But my worry is that after six years of work on health and education, the expectation would be for, you know, something more life-affirming in this department.'

'I am not sure that the condition in the basti is life-affirming in that sense.'

'You know, it would depend on where one looks for stories. Hygiene, for instance. We've had seven workshops. There have been many positive changes in lifestyle.'

'All case histories in my report describe how their attitudes have changed because of their participation in our project. But we also need to emphasize that this kind of change is not enough.'

'It is the tone of the report that we need to talk about, Dini. If one just considers the formal and objective aspects, there is a discrepancy between the quantitative and the qualitative. The statistics are so encouraging: the percentage of school dropouts has reduced considerably; the number of people between forty-five and sixty years of age dying of diseases has gone down dramatically. One may, in all fairness, conclude that working with women's groups and generating awareness about their rights has the potential to transform society.'

'Yes, in a limited way,' Dini tried to interrupt the glib flow.

He paid no attention and carried on, 'But on the life stories front, the women appear to be depressed. For instance, there's this wonderfully written story of the woman who retained employment in the factory after getting married. You have written it so well, but it is almost tragic—exploited by both the employer and the husband, no rightful perks provided at work, made to do all the housework in spite of the endless day at the factory. It's very realistic, of course, but somewhat defeats our purpose, you would agree. Our funders, for instance, could raise an objection regarding our methodology. They could ask us whether women are benefitting at all by the reformist thrust of our programme.'

'A question we need to ask too.'

'This would be a theoretical discussion about modernity in general. But I'm sure you agree that we don't need to stop motivating our women partners to go out into the world and claim their positions as equal citizens of the country till the issue is resolved.'

Dini had a strong urge to hurl something at his face. 'We

so that he can advise us whether our activities are in keeping with the community's faith. I don't really see the harm in this.'

'You mean seek his approval for whatever we are doing?'

'Oh please, don't be melodramatic. There is no harm in including him in the planning of activities. You do hold community meetings with the leaders present, don't you? It has been our policy to enlist the support of the elders. Besides, you must make an attempt to address the most fundamentalist section. I am surprised that a relationship has not come about till now. In fact, Ansari has even offered to have the community meetings at his place. It would be a great forum in my opinion.'

Dini had taken care to create a forum for secular people in the basti. There were a couple of school teachers, a compounder in the government hospital, the MLA who had left leanings, and then Fahim, the student at Delhi University. Ansari, on the other hand, could never be expected to take a progressive view. Besides, any proximity with him would have the effect of alienating the emerging leaders she was encouraging. Her interactions with the community were designed to isolate the regressive elements. It would be difficult, if not impossible, to explain these concerns to Nitin. For him, health and education were apolitical by definition and a leader like Ansari who had many resources was too important to be excluded from the project.

During such times, Dini felt the limitations of working for an international NGO very keenly.

That Friday afternoon, she saw in her mind a limitless desert and the promise of an oasis. How she wished she could help RS and his mother create that in far-off Rajasthan!

November

Dreams, Diamonds and Discomfort

Early in the morning, Shailaja received an email from college. The body of the email only said 'PFA' and the attachment was a scanned copy of a handwritten complaint against her by a student. The student had gone to some length to describe her teaching in rather rocky English: 'She not focus on course. She speak of things unrelated to course. She describe relationship between boyfriend and girlfriend openly. Her classes are bad influence on young people.'

The roll number of the student was not mentioned in the letter, nor was there a date. The course must be Popular Fiction, as part of which she had taught *Gone with the Wind* and talked about relationships to the great excitement of the entire class, Shailaja surmised. The complaint said exactly what Dhar had charged her with. Why had this student submitted a complaint now, she wondered. They had finished with discussions the previous week and she had given the class an assignment on the text. The letter was signed 'Ramesh'. The two boys who had enrolled for Popular Fiction had attended classes just a couple of times. But they had dropped out of the course, so their details were no longer in her register. She would have to cross-check with the college office.

It would be good to discuss the matter with Ranjan, she thought while driving to college. He was supposed to 'swing by' this evening, but she was already learning to not bank on his word. Nevertheless, Shailaja felt she was in a happier space now. Ranjan had made some bad decisions but his feelings for her were undeniable. That is all that mattered.

Buddhism had made her realize how important it was to focus on the positive aspect of things. She had gone to Mrs Gandhi's just last evening and they chanted for half an hour. She caught Mrs Gandhi looking at her curiously a couple of times. She even hinted that she was aware of something new and positive happening in her protégé's life: 'You must present your experience at the next meeting. I can say by looking at you that you're happy.'

'Now whatever it might be—right or wrong—it is good for you. You must try and make it right if it isn't,' Mrs Gandhi had continued. It crossed her mind that Mrs Gandhi might have seen Ranjan exiting her flat at an odd hour as she often lurked in her verandah, but she couldn't be bothered about what the neighbours were saying at this point in her life.

Nor was there any need to meet the principal for this silly email, Shailaja said to herself as she drew up in the college parking. Anyway, Dr Dhar no longer seemed keen to talk to her. He had not summoned her to his office after that episode. When she met him at the farewell party for a retiring colleague a couple of days ago, he had looked at her very sternly. She was unnerved; nevertheless, she had stammered a greeting—which he did not return.

The section officer in the college office looked at the complaint and yawned. 'Madam, this is routine. Any complaint we receive, we forward to concerned person.'

'But it doesn't have the roll number of the complainant!

And there is no one called Ramesh in my classes,' Shailaja said. 'I should at least know which course he is referring to.'

'Ramesh is a common name, Madam. Maybe you don't remember,' he suggested.

'No, no, the course from which it might have come has only eight students—all girls,' Shailaja said.

The SO located the email on his own computer and read through it and then brought out a file and checked—all painfully slowly!

'Madam, no course is mentioned by the student or indicated by the teacher-in-charge and the principal. You take big classes too, don't you?' he asked at last.

'Yes, of course. I have fifty-five in one general class and sixty-two in another one,' she replied.

'One of them must have written,' said the SO. We receive in complaint box here, it goes to the teacher-in-charge and the principal's office, and we forward to concerned person,' he repeated.

'But I need details of the complainant in order to reply,' she said.

'Oh Madam, hardly important! You just write a reply denying everything,' said the SO. 'From where will we get the details?'

Shailaja was not altogether satisfied with this exchange, but her Popular Fiction class was going to start in five minutes. And surely that mattered more than digging out details of silly complaints!

Her eight students had remained regular throughout the semester. She had finished evaluating the assignments on *GWTW* and she planned to discuss them that day. She was quite pleased by the responses of the students. Except spelling errors and a few grammatical howlers that were, unfortunately, part of the deep structure of Delhi English, they had done a good job. Her teaching of this course, in spite of the rude interruption by forces of convention, had been successful indeed.

∎

Shailaja looked at the eight bright faces in front of her, wondering at herself for having once thought of them as too callow for a study of romance.

The question she had given them was to discuss the characterization of Scarlett O'Hara in *GWTW*—could she be described as a feminist heroine?

'Scarlett O'Hara is a feminist icon in this romance because she learns to be completely self-reliant, Ma'am. She's different from other Southern women characters who are traditional in their thinking and whose identity is defined by their families,' said Najma defending her position.

'And Ma'am, she also doesn't care much about her children,' said Amulya, attempting to support her.

'What do you feel about her not being an ideal mother?' Shailaja asked.

'Ma'am, she puts herself first, children come later for her,' replied Najma.

'Is this then our understanding of a feminist text?' asked Shailaja. 'Are we saying that feminism is about women putting their desires above everything else?'

'No, Ma'am, children's rights are as important,' countered Krishna, who had written a marvellously nuanced answer. 'Also, Ma'am, Scarlett slaps Prissy, her black domestic. She is not a feminist symbol. She's just a... bitch...'

'But she is good with her servants and helpers, no?' countered Najma. 'She treats Mammy like a member of the family. Like we treat Rahila Aapa who stays with us. Their relationship made me think of Rahila Aapa. It's very realistic.'

Krishna shot back at once, 'She is good to Mammy and Big Sam only because they are loyal and work so hard for her. But she doesn't want Emancipation for the African Americans. She wants them to be slaves forever. Rahila Aapa can leave your employment whenever she wants; the slaves had no rights.'

'The point is that they don't leave Scarlett O'Hara's employment even after they are emancipated,' Amulya reminded her, 'so she must be treating them very well. I think Scarlett is a feminist icon and that is why Rhett Butler leaves her. Men don't like strong women.'

'I think the writer intends this as punishment for her selfishness,' said Krishna. 'The reader is supposed to conclude that women like her, who put themselves above their partners and families, achieve everything but the most important thing—the love of a man. This is the logic in the world of romance. It is not feminist at all. Feminism has an uneasy relationship with romance anyway.'

There was some sniggering at that, and Shailaja allowed a bit of back and forth. She then concluded the discussion by reading out some extracts she had selected from contemporary readings of the novel. She was confident that these students, especially the bespectacled Krishna, would fare very well in the university exams.

But wasn't true love like a gift from heaven? So what if it runs contrary to the feminist agenda at times! Shailaja was thinking after her concluding class for *GWTW*. Of course she would never say anything so sentimental and unacademic to her students. She reluctantly went into her next class, which was Business Communication and comprised sixty-two students, with about forty attending regularly. There she had to yell at the top of her voice to explain the subtleties of non-verbal communication to restless Commerce majors. And trying to relate what they were studying with everyday life cut no ice with this group that was only focussed on getting above ninety per cent marks in the university examination.

That morning, it seemed to Dini that with Kenny barging into her life a fortnight ago, everything had started to go off-kilter. There was a scene with Maithili of which he was the direct cause. Maithili's best friend, a very competitive little girl called Tarini, had accused her of trying to be special: 'Nobody calls their father by name. My mother says that you are only trying to be different and it is not according to Indian culture.'

So last evening, Maithili had wept and then proceeded on a veritable inquisition. 'But nobody calls their father by name, Mama!'

Dini had tried to explain, 'Your father and I are not married, Maithili.'

'So what? Tarini's parents are divorced and her father doesn't even live with them,' Maithili had shot back. 'She calls her father "Daddy"! I am also going to call him Kenny Papa from now. He is saying I can if you say yes.'

Dini was momentarily at a loss. She was tempted to follow her sobbing daughter to her room to try and reason with her. But she knew that if she entered the door of the room where her former boyfriend was listening to every word and where, like the Pied Piper, he enchanted her daughter with his guitar every evening, she would be walking into a downward spiral of adjustments and compromises.

Getting ready for office, Dini wondered for how long she could bear this.

Maithili had spent the entire Sunday morning helping Kenny make cheese omelettes. Dini had allowed egg to be cooked in her kitchen even though she couldn't bear the odour. But she resolved she would draw the line there: 'Kenny, no meat, please!' The shock was the ease with which Maithili took to the unfamiliar foods. She was energetically whipping egg after egg: 'Look Kenny, the white is stiff!' The stink from the kitchen made Dini gag when she ventured in for a glass of water. She wondered darkly whether genes played a role in food choices. 'I hope it is okay with you if I take Maithili for Naga food,' Kenny smirked in the evening. Still confident about Maithili's essential vegetarian conditioning, she shot back, 'Kenny, I have no problems. But I must warn you that Maithili has been discussing the need to turn vegetarian in her classes on environment.'

'Oh!' Kenny had exclaimed, his face falling. 'The good stuff in Naga cuisine isn't vegetarian.'

He had then launched into his usual spiel about animal flesh being chock-full of protein. 'Maithili is doing so many things. Surely she needs protein.'

'Kenny, several people all over the world, including me by the way, have been carrying on with busy work schedules powered only by "flowers, seeds and berries" and are none the worse for it,' she replied smugly.

But her eight-year-old daughter, the apple of her eye, again made her eat crow. From the report, gleefully supplied by Kenny, Maithili took to pork, mutton and even beef like fish to water. Kenny's wide grin bordered on being objectionable as she regarded her daughter with some alarm on being confronted with the information.

'Pork is really nice, Mama, and it is not even spicy. I ate two pieces of mutton also. Kenny says he too didn't like chicken when he was my age,' Maithili declared.

'You don't have to eat things you don't like,' she countered feebly.

'Yes, this is exactly what I said. But she just loved the meat dishes. It's all going to be very easy now, Maithili. When you come with me to Nagaland, you will be able to eat everything,' Kenny had said, smiling broadly.

It was the obvious effort that Maithili put into pleasing Kenny that was making her clench her fists. Where did daughters learn to idolize fathers in this way? She had thought she was bringing up an enlightened twenty-first-century child, but suddenly Maithili had transformed into a flirtatious little minx, fluttering her eyelashes at Kenny. He got her a strappy-lacey top and a pair of 'distressed' jeans and a Barbie stroller bag. Maithili would dress up like Little Miss Fashion Plate to go out with him. Dini feared that the next step would be cosmetics. Maithili had already tried out her kajal. Would it be lipstick now?

It was difficult to discuss her feelings with RS, and this time she did not even have the unqualified support of her Mumbai friends. Namrata couldn't see any reason for her agitation. 'It is great that Kenny is at last taking some responsibilities off your head,' she said in a distracted manner and went on to excitedly ask questions about RS. Her talk with Raji had been more complex.

'I was thinking of Maithili,' Raji said, not denying the charge that she had encouraged Kenny to reclaim his daughter.

'But Raji, you were the one who used to say that the role of the father is needlessly hyped. And then Kenny is hardly the kind of—'

'Dini, he is no better or worse than most fathers. Besides, things have changed. There were only you and Maithili in the equation earlier, and she had your complete attention. It was a complete family then. The child has been very confused recently; you've told me how she has been acting up.'

'You are being unfair. If you are referring to my relationship with RS, you know that I would never let that affect my commitment to Maithili.'

'I know. But it is only natural for your attention to be divided. Kenny is her biological father and RS isn't. RS is anyway a committed field activist. How much time would he have for a family? Besides, Kenny has been there for Maithili all through, even if it is not in the way you would have wanted. She already has a connection with him.'

She could hardly admit to anyone that it was precisely the ease with which men could take over the family that had her seething with resentment. Kenny's hyper-sentimental connection to their daughter only filled her with rage. Truth be told, a part of her would give an arm and a leg to break it. On the way to office, Dini found herself wondering whether allowing him access to her domestic space had been such a great idea after all. RS felt that she shouldn't have allowed it. 'After eight years! He has a nerve to just walk in!' he had exclaimed. 'You are not being fair to yourself, Dini!' How she wished she could close her mind to her commitment to rights—Kenny's, and now Maithili's. How she wished she could follow her heart that was taking off into uncharted territory: an idyllic space, an oasis in the desert. How she wished she could tear Maithili away from that guitar and fly her there!

■

When Dini ran into Mrs Gandhi that evening, her neglect of Shailaja and its deleterious consequences hit home. She had been rushing home from office to catch some time with Maithili before Kenny monopolized her with that guitar of his. There was a tanker parked at the colony gate, and she had to abandon her Uber and walk.

As she neared her building, she stopped short. Mrs Gandhi was sitting on the bench right opposite her staircase. She seemed to be waiting.

'Dinshee, I was waiting for you,' she said welcomingly.

'Oh Mrs Gandhi, you mustn't. My timings are erratic—uncertain,' explained Dini, trying to suppress her irritation.

'No problem. I was sitting here and chanting. And there you are. The Buddha answered my prayer.'

It was ironic how the woman considered muttering incantations publicly a perfectly natural thing to do. But then Vasant Kunj was spilling over with religious rituals. In the mornings, it was commonplace to see people getting into all kinds of ridiculous situations: Surya Namaskar, in which shapeless bodies wearing gym gear exposed bulging tummies and jiggling bottoms; tulsi worship wherein perfectly normal-looking adults ran frenetically around the small prickly plant; and of course, people with folded hands and bowed heads regularly fed dogs, cats, monkeys and cows reverentially. A few hours later, they would stone the same animals or facilitate the plunder of their natural habitats by getting the trees chopped, rued Dini in her mind.

'Dinshee, I met Maithi's papa a couple of days ago. Such a nice gentleman!' Mrs Gandhi exclaimed.

'Oh!' Dini replied.

'They were going out for dinner. Maithi is so attached, he also taking good care. I was thinking Dinshee is so lucky. Now, Mr Gandhi never takes the children out on his own. It is always, "Ask Mummy".'

'Yes,' said Dini mechanically, temporarily at a loss.

'What does he do?' asked the unstoppable woman. 'At last I have got to see him.'

'Who?'

'Maithi's papa...'

'He plays the guitar.'

'In the evening, no? What does he do for work?'

'He is a musician, Mrs Gandhi. You know, I am very tired and I have to cook,'

'Oh yes,' said Mrs Gandhi. 'How nice to only play music! I just wanted to invite you.'

Dini dreaded what she was going to say. Probably an invitation for dinner, now that her family had become 'normal'!

'I am hosting a prayer meeting this Friday before Diwali. I thought it would be nice if you come. Now that Maithi's papa is here, you must increase good karma.'

'Increase what?' Before Mrs Gandhi could launch into Buddhist philosophy, Dini hastened to add, 'I will be working late on Friday.'

'Oh, what a pity! I was thinking it would be good for you. You know the divorcee woman I told you about, she is chanting with me these days.'

Dini started guiltily. With so much happening in her life, she had been neglecting Shailaja. 'You mean Shailaja?' she asked just to make sure.

'Yes, yes, one who teaches in a school. Oh yes, you met her at the enshrinement ceremony and she was telling me you two have become friends. She has become regular with chanting. And you know something,' Mrs Gandhi paused dramatically, 'she might have already got some results.'

'What do you mean?'

'You come for the meeting and ask her yourself. But I saw this tall man who visited her twice. He was coming out of her home, once in the morning and then at midnight. I say the Buddha would take care of wrong and right...'

'Thanks, Mrs Gandhi. I will try and come for the meeting,' said Dini, instinctively cutting short her gossip. 'I will try and finish work as quickly as possible. I hope I can join in after the meeting starts?'

'Oh yes, you can't neglect work, no? This is understood. The main thing is intention. If intention is there, then no harm attaches,' pronounced Mrs Gandhi.

Dini loped up the stairs with the thought that it was just as well that chanting did not give the power of clairvoyance. If Mrs Gandhi only knew what she was thinking at the moment, she would stop looking like a cat that got the cream.

Without even ringing her own doorbell, standing on the landing, Dini dialled Shailaja's number. She could look in on her for half an hour or so once the guitar lesson started, which would prevent that music from getting on her nerves!

'I have a friend coming in for dinner. But am free till eight,' Shailaja said, a little tonelessly.

'Bhaiya and Baby have gone out for dinner,' Rani informed her as soon as she entered her home. Kenny should have let her know their programme; she wouldn't have hurried home like this. And how many times had she asked Rani to call Maithili by her name!

'Should I make something for you?' Rani was asking.

'No, don't cook anything now,' she replied. 'I am not hungry.'

'I'll keep some milk for you on the table,' said Rani. 'Bhaiya didn't want to go but Baby kept saying she wanted to have noodles at Zen Den. He told her he would make it for her here, but she's so stubborn, no! Bhaiya does everything she wants. She has started to call him Papa now.'

After Dini went up to her flat, Mrs Gandhi made her way home. What an impatient girl Dinshee was, she thought. It was difficult to ever complete a conversation with her. And did she realize how lucky she was! Chanting could teach her gratitude, but there was little chance of her becoming a Buddhist. It would be enough if she came over for the Friday meeting.

Another neighbour who had successfully resisted her attempts up till now was Mrs Jain. But she seemed to have totally withdrawn into a strict observance of Jainism. She spent long hours at the temple, fasted every other day, dressed in the simplest of clothes, and wore no jewellery. No neighbour dared to challenge her encroachments via the ever-spreading tulsi plants anymore. To Mrs Gandhi, she still seemed tortured. She had learned from one of her reliable sources that the Jains' relatives had filed a case in court challenging her possession of the flat; Mrs Jain lived alone in the flat as her children were studying elsewhere. Her husband had died ages ago, soon after the birth of their daughter, who was sixteen now. Mrs Gandhi felt that there would be no point in approaching her unless she got guidance from Navneeta about what to say to such a self-abnegating ascetic.

She was feeling very proud for being able to organize a meeting at a time when Diwali was round the corner. With Mummy-ji participating wholeheartedly in household activities, her kitchen had been overworked, producing various kinds of sweets and savouries all of last week. The entire house was dusted and cleaned, and the electrician was called to put up coloured lights in the verandah and all around the potted plants. She was quite run off her feet. But Navneeta requested her and she didn't want to refuse. 'You must serve only water or, at most, tea and biscuits, if you like,' Navneeta had said firmly. 'There is nothing to prepare, Nilima-ji. This is a discussion meeting, not a social occasion.'

Although she had nodded obediently, she knew she would definitely serve a couple of snacks with the biscuits. How could she not, especially during festival time! By the grace of Lakshmi, whose festival Diwali was, they had enough to cater many such meetings.

She needed to say 'thank you' to the Buddhist practice for so much. With her regular morning and evening chanting, her schedule had become organized for the first time in her life, Mrs Gandhi thought. With five days still to go for Diwali, all her shopping, clay diyas, candles, Lakshmi and Ganesh idols, new clothes for family and also for Rajni and Bahadur, and a big bag of firecrackers—banned by the kill-joy government due to NGO people like Dini but fortunately still easily available in black—was already done. This time she took the initiative to send hand-painted trays with packets of dry fruit to all the neighbours and Sunil's colleagues as their Diwali gifts, instead of leaving the selection to his office staff. It had cost one-and-a-half times more than last year, but Sunil hadn't grumbled at the expense. How she wished he had also taken heed of her repeated reminders about doing up the drawing room. But he left it too late and, as a result, the contractor he always engaged for repairs and renovations declined to do the work, saying he was too busy with other Diwali projects. Now it could only be done afterwards as he was their trusted man and they were both reluctant to allow unknown thieving construction workers into the home.

She entered her home and found that Neeru was hanging on to Sunil's arm, which was her way of showing affection to him since she was a child, and imploring him, 'Papa, please, please let me see what's in the box.'

'No Neeru, this belongs to Mummy-ji. If she likes, she'll show it to you,' Sunil was saying.

Sunil was back from office with Mummy-ji's jewellery. Just as well! Mummy-ji had asked her to remind Sunil to get her green box from the locker this morning but she had forgotten all about it.

'Papa, you know... You know what she's like. She never shows them to anyone,' said Neeru.

Neeru was on the mark. The old woman was neurotically possessive. Let alone be allowed to set acquisitive eyes on her jewels, neither Mrs Gandhi, nor the younger daughter-in-law, who had cleverly avoided the obligation of looking after her for ten years, knew the full contents of her locker. The only person who was privy to the treasure trove was her favourite son, Sunil, but he would always feign indifference. 'Just tell me the colour of the box or pouch you want from the locker. I am not going to open each one of them,' he would say to her impatiently. The jewels would travel to and fro in complete anonymity and, as the old woman had stopped wearing jewellery after her husband's death, lay shrouded in their cases when out of the bank.

'If you ask Dadi nicely, I'm sure she will allow you to take a look at them,' Sunil told Neeru, striding into his mother's room with the big green box.

Neeru stuck out her tongue in the general direction of Mummy-ji's room. 'As if!' she said to no one in particular.

Mrs Gandhi stopped herself from admonishing her. Listening to fellow chanters, she knew that anything regarding an adolescent's behaviour had to be broached with kid gloves, if at all. As she was going into the kitchen to see what Bahadur had done with the paneer, Mummy-ji came out bearing the green box. 'Nilima, send the servants out,' she said, being unreasonable as usual.

'Mummy-ji, Bahadur has to set the table and Rajni is with

the children in their room,' Mrs Gandhi protested. 'Why do you want them to go out?'

'Arre, make some excuse and send them out,' insisted Mummy-ji at the top of her voice. 'Sometimes listen to elders!'

Sunil was also looking at her with surprise, so obviously he had no idea either. Mrs Gandhi sighed and called out to Rajni and Bahadur, 'Sahib wants to have a salad. Both of you go to our regular vegetable shop and get some lettuce. Say salad *patta* or he will not understand. And baby corn and sprouted moong also.'

'The shop won't have these things at this time,' Rajni demurred. 'All fancy vegetables get over in the morning.'

She always pretended to be a big know-all!

'Go to the one at the other gate then. That one will definitely have something. You can also try the fellow who sits under the peepal tree. He brings fresh stuff in the evening. That's why I'm sending both of you, no? Try for green onions and cherry tomatoes also,' improvised Mrs Gandhi. 'Go fast.'

Ganesh declared that he wanted to go salad 'hunting' too. Mrs Gandhi reluctantly allowed him to go. Mummy-ji saw them off till the door and then shut the metal gate as well as the wooden door.

'What is it, Mummy-ji?' Sunil asked her affectionately. 'What secret op are you planning?'

Mummy-ji brought out a bedsheet and asked Mrs Gandhi to spread it on the dining table. She did so with alacrity; she was quite curious now. Mummy-ji sat importantly at the head of the table and asked them to take their seats too.

The four of them gasped collectively when she unveiled the jewels at last. It was an elaborate set: seven strings of pearls with three big pendants studded with rubies and diamonds arranged vertically in the centre of the necklace, and matching studs and a ring. The purple-red rubies, set amidst sparkling diamonds, were exquisite. They were big and lustrous, and their colour was like the liquid in imported bottles that Sunil sometimes got from their bootlegger. 'My father got these rubies from Burma,' the old woman told them.

Mrs Gandhi only had a faint memory of this set that was exclaimed over by many when her mother-in-law wore it years ago. It looked much grander on the bedsheet than it had on Mummy-ji.

'Can I touch them?' Teenu frisked over to her grandmother. Mummy-ji put the ring on her thumb but it was too loose.

'Give it to me. You'll drop it,' Neeru yelled and wrested it from her. She picked up the necklace. 'This is like the heroine wore in that old film *Umrao Jaan*. What does it cost, Dadi? Who is going to wear it? It is for us, isn't it? You don't wear jewellery,' she was beside herself with excitement.

Sunil shushed her, 'No, Neeru. It is Mummy-ji's. Give it back to her.'

Teenu was whining for the ring; Mummy-ji took it from Neeru and put it on her thumb.

'All this is ultimately for Ganesh's bride and the girls,' declared the old woman to the merriment of Teenu, who couldn't stop repeating 'Ganesh's bride'. 'I gave up all my desires when my husband died. Now all I want is to see Nilima wear my favourite set before I die.'

Mrs Gandhi's jaw dropped in surprise. 'I only want your blessings,' she gasped and went across to touch the old woman's feet, vaguely aware that Sunil was nodding in approval. 'You don't have to give me your jewellery.'

Mummy-ji blessed her. 'Wear it for the Diwali puja for me, Nilima. And you take a picture of her with your phone,' she said to Neeru, who wearing the necklace, was busy taking a selfie. She went on: 'I was thinking that my Nilima works night and day in the house. She plans everyone's meals; she makes green tea for my son; she gets me my medicine...'

'She's doing her duty, Mummy-ji,' Sunil said. He seemed to be quite emotional.

Mummy-ji went on, 'Who does their duty these days? Nilima is like my daughter. When she came to our home, she used to look like Neeru. Now, she too is getting on in years. She's doing more puja-path than even me. If she doesn't wear this now, when will she wear it? Neeru's wedding is still far.'

'Mummy-ji, God willing, you will live to welcome Ganesh's bride into this home,' Sunil said before disappearing into the bedroom to attend to his tinkling mobile. 'Keep the jewellery carefully, Nilima.'

With her heart singing, Mrs Gandhi recovered the jewels from Neeru and Teenu and locked them up securely in the secret safe of the steel almirah. The set was probably upward of ten lakh rupees. It would go well with her maroon sari with the broad gold border, or she could invest in a plain maroon silk sari, she thought. She already had a matching blouse. Rajni could be made to tack on the sari fall in the afternoon instead of watching TV with the children. The tailors, of course, would have no time till Diwali.

As she began to set the table for dinner, wondering when the voyagers, who had set out almost forty-five minutes earlier in search of salad, would return, Sunil came into the dining area. 'Nilima, you've no idea how much happiness you've given me by winning Mummy-ji's affection. It is family that is most important,' he said thickly and went back into the bedroom.

Shailaja felt conflicted after Dini called up to say that she would drop by for a while in the evening. No, it wasn't because of Ranjan. He would reach only after nine—if he came at all. It was because of all the lies she had been living. She tried to tell herself that her affair was nobody's business. There was no reason to confide everything to Dini, especially as she was so strong-headed.

Mrs Gandhi definitely thought so. 'Dinshee thinks she knows everything about relationships. Then why isn't her husband with her? She's so sharp-tongued; which man would like?' If Shailaja told her that she had resumed her affair with Ranjan, Dini would at once start talking about 'male privilege' and 'gender entitlement'. She would manage to suggest that Shailaja was surrendering her autonomy by going back to him. It was no use to try and explain to her how different he was from the general run of men. But hiding things didn't come easily to Shailaja. She hated the fact that she wouldn't be able to talk uninhibitedly. There were other ways of empowerment besides Dini's impassioned prescriptions, and why should she not try them out first, she had been saying to herself. But last time when she went directly to Mrs Gandhi after visiting Dini, she had felt disloyal. It was ironic that at Mrs Gandhi's enshrinement she had become friends with someone who was so dead-set against the practice.

It occurred to Shailaja that Dini appeared quite distracted these days. She momentarily had the idea that there might be something new happening in her friend's life as well. There were two men she had met at different times at Dini's. One appeared to be from the Northeast. Maithili, who would usually interrupt their conversation with her prattle, was engaged in a raucous game of indoor Frisbee with him and ignored both her mother and Shailaja Aunty completely. 'Kenny,' Dini introduced him economically and later added, 'Maithili is very close to him. He lives in Shillong.' He looked like a college student. Was he related to Maithili? What was his relationship with Dini, Shailaja wondered. But he looked too schoolboyish to be Dini's boyfriend. Then there was a very dark man, who seemed to be more of a possibility. Dini had introduced him using her usual shorthand: 'RS, works with a tribe that was classified as "criminal" during colonial times. He's creating employment opportunities and awareness among them.' Dini looked more animated around him than she ever did around anyone. But then, she could hardly be having an affair with an NGO worker from a village in Rajasthan!

The bell pealed in record time after her phone call, and there was Dini at her doorstep in her signature mismatched and indifferently ironed attire. She looked somewhat tired and vulnerable. On an impulse, Shailaja hugged her and regretted it immediately when Dini stiffened.

'Hi Shailaja, how are things with you? I just ran into Mrs Gandhi and she invited me for her Buddhist meeting on Friday. Are you planning on going?' she asked, making towards the only cushion-less chair in the room and sitting down in her usual upright manner. Her tone was matter of fact—too matter of fact, thought Shailaja.

'Yes, I think so. I have been chanting with her now and then,' said Shailaja making a clean breast of it abruptly. 'Will you have some tea or something?' she asked quickly.

'Nimbu-paani, if it's not inconvenient,' Dini replied in a formal tone.

Just then the bell pealed again and Rajni ki Ma walked in. Shailaja asked her to make the nimbu-paani, 'Make two glasses. Put salt and sugar in both and don't put ice in one.'

'Didi, tell me what to make for your dinner also. The

other house has a Diwali card-party tonight, and I have to make three–four dishes still. I will make everything quickly,' she declared. 'Hello Dini Didi, you have come back early this evening?'

Dini nodded and smiled back at her.

Shailaja hadn't thought about dinner yet. 'Just make a vegetable and dal,' she said to her. 'I think there is some *gobhi* in the fridge. Make that and dal-palak. You make that so well. Don't put too much red chilli in either. And four rotis and some rice please.'

'Is Bhaiya coming?' Rajni ki Ma asked. Shailaja had taken pains to explain to her how Ranjan liked his food—low on spice and fat, lightly done—and also his allergy to peanut oil. Rajni ki Ma had at once remarked on his advanced age. 'Much easier to cook for a younger person like you,' she had quipped.

'Yes, he might have dinner,' Shailaja replied and turned back to Dini, who was looking at her closely.

'Ranjan is coming this evening. I mean, probably coming. I wanted to tell you we're back together,' she blurted out.

There was silence between them.

'The starlet didn't last very long,' Dini observed at last.

'Oh no,' Shailaja replied. 'It's not like that. I had called him after that incident with the principal...'

Dini didn't say anything.

'He came and we talked about it. He was so concerned... And then I realized he still means a lot to me,' Shailaja continued.

'What did he say about the harassment incident? He must be feeling guilty for having put you through such a thing,' Dini said.

'What are you saying? He wasn't even there...'

'I don't mean that literally, of course. But the principal

referred to your boyfriend. Men like your principal think of a woman with a boyfriend as easy game. Ranjan must have realized how much harder things have become for you after the break-up.'

Shailaja was quiet.

'So, is Ranjan helping you fight this?' Dini asked.

'Fight what? It was probably a misunderstanding on the principal's part. I've decided to let it be. Discussing it with Ranjan has cleared my head. Besides, he is with Diksha for now,' she admitted falteringly. 'So he doesn't owe me anything. He offered monetary help, though. He said that if I wanted to resign, he would—'

'Are you resigning, Shailaja?' Dini asked at once.

'No Dini, why would I? I love teaching. That incident was... not very significant. And then nothing has happened after that,' Shailaja replied.

'What about Diksha? Would she be fine with him visiting you, having dinner with you?' Dini asked.

'I don't have a clue,' Shailaja replied at once. How full of questions Dini was! 'Anyway, why should I care? She didn't consult me when she started an affair with Ranjan.'

Rajni ki Ma came in with the nimbu-paani.

'Very refreshing! Thank you, Renu-ji,' said Dini.

Shailaja stared. Rajni ki Ma had actually divulged her real name to Dini.

Dini was talking to Rajni ki Ma with a tender smile. 'I keep meeting Rajni. She comes with Teenu to the park, so I know she's fine, working hard for Mrs Gandhi. How's your younger daughter?'

It made her a little jealous to watch the easy familiarity between the two. Rajni ki Ma seemed to hero-worship Dini. She was telling her proudly about the big tips 'madams' gave her younger daughter, Mahima, at the beauty parlour where she worked, and then went on to criticize the meanness of Gandhis' Diwali gift to Rajni: 'Such a cheap sari! I told Rajni to give it to her sister-in-law!'

'How do you know so much about her family?' Shailaja asked Dini as soon as Rajni ki Ma's back was turned.

'Mahima had got involved with a driver. He was married. So both Rajni and her mother had come to me for advice.'

'What happened?' Shailaja asked in spite of herself.

'I went with the three of them to talk to him,' Dini replied. 'He went back on everything he had promised Mahima. Said she had misunderstood his intentions. I arranged an abortion for her—she's such a lovely girl, just nineteen at that time—and gave her an introduction to this NGO that does livelihood training. She seems to be doing well now!'

'Dini, you see so many of such cases, such betrayals,' Shailaja observed.

'Yes, I do. And there's a pattern to them,' Dini replied.

'I was wondering whether it is making you cynical about men—all men... About relationships in general,' Shailaja offered tentatively.

'Maybe,' Dini replied, calmly. 'Or makes me see them for what they are, perhaps? Male privilege doesn't operate only in the lower classes, you know. I must go now. Your boyfriend must be arriving any minute,' she added without smiling.

■

At 9.30 p.m., Shailaja ate the bland dinner that Rajni ki Ma had prepared. There was no sign of Ranjan, no message, no call. He could have at least let her know that he would be late, she thought. It hadn't been pleasant to spend the entire evening straining her ears for the sound of his footsteps on the stairs.

Shailaja chanted for five minutes; she found it difficult to concentrate in the evening. It went much better if she was doing it with Mrs Gandhi. She then changed into her new nightgown. She had recently spent a couple of hours trying to shop judiciously from the lingerie section of Marks & Spencer. It was bursting at the seams with Diwali shoppers, and she had almost despaired of finding anything suitable. But then this one, fortunately marked down forty per cent, had caught her eye. It had black and white stripes and just a hint of black lace—severe but sexy! She had kept it for a special evening with Ranjan.

Almost an hour later, she was jolted out of her favourite Anita Brookner novel, *Look at Me*, that she was reading for the third time. Was that her doorbell? It rang again, unmistakably. It was almost eleven-thirty, and she had given up on Ranjan coming over. Shailaja jumped out of bed and went to open the door.

'Oh darling, you look scrumptious,' Ranjan said, his hand exploring the contours of her body as soon as she closed the door.

She got a whiff of purple grapes, fermented in vaults thousands of miles away.

'You've had dinner... and wine?' she accused him.

'Still hungry,' he replied. 'You're not supposed to look like this at midnight.'

The courting that she missed so much; the comfort of escaping from complexities; the surrender to the voluptuous moment! It was only by one or so that she could steel herself to have the talk with him that she had been planning subconsciously since Dini's visit.

'Ranjan, are you happy?' she asked.

'No, I want more,' he replied sleepily.

'Please,' she said, sitting up in bed. 'I want to know about your new life.'

'My life is the old life,' he replied, opening his eyes at last. 'You're the new independent woman. Tell me about you first. How's that bête noire of yours, that principal?'

'He's been very silent,' she said.

'Good,' Ranjan said, attempting to pull her down again. 'Let the beast sleep.'

'No, there's something I want to show you,' Shailaja said. She accessed the student's complaint mailed to her by the college on her phone and gave it to Ranjan. He groaned at having to sit up and wear his glasses to read it.

'Terrible,' he said. 'Shailaja, is this the kind of English you teach your students? No wonder your principal is miffed.'

'Ranjan, please! Do you think this could be serious?'

'I can't imagine anybody taking this seriously, not even the esteemed Dr Dhar. He has only forwarded it to you, I notice, not asked for an explanation,' he chuckled.

'He did look at me in a stern way at the farewell.'

'There is no pleasing you, you know. Last time weren't you complaining that he looked at you too fondly?'

The heady feeling of having him by her side, his hand on her thigh like in the beginning of their relationship, were once again working to drive her apprehensions away.

'Really!'

'But tell me, did you really tell the students about your boyfriend?'

'Yes, I did. I told them what it felt like to have someone you love go away,' she said with a catch in her voice. 'I explained heartbreak to them.'

'So, when will you tell them about his return?' Ranjan asked drawing her to him.

'After you tell me about your new life,' she replied at once.

Ranjan released her and sat up. 'You are asking about Diksha, aren't you? I won't lie to you, Shail. On the one hand, it is exhilarating to be with someone so youthful, but on the other hand, she inhabits a world that is considerably different from ours,' he said softly. 'Her friends are a completely different set, very different from ours—mine. Their parties, for instance, last forever, and at times I feel completely exhausted—mentally, I mean. And then I want to come home to you.'

Shailaja reached out to kiss him. This was enough. Her heart was singing. He was more comfortable with her. He would come back. It was obvious that it was just a matter of time. They could live here instead of paying the ridiculously high rent in Defence Colony. They would be the rare live-in couple in Vasant Kunj. Would Mrs Gandhi suggest that they get married?

She slept deeply that night and had no idea when Ranjan abandoned her bed.

◈

November

Double Trouble

Teaching was almost over for the semester, and Shailaja was feeling thankful that she would at last get some time for herself. She was exhausted. It seemed to her that in the last fortnight she had been either teaching extra classes or waiting for Ranjan. It had taken Dini to point the latter out to her.

'It's not much different from what it was earlier, Shailaja. You are on your own even now,' she argued in her usual cussed manner. Shailaja tried to explain that she needed that relationship with Ranjan, even though their meetings were occasional.

'A couple of secret assignations! How can you even call it a relationship? His relationship is with Diksha, isn't it?' Dini was contrary.

'Are you saying nothing secret qualifies as a relationship?'

Dini seemed at a loss for words momentarily. So uncharacteristic was it for her to not come back with an answer immediately that Shailaja found her mind going to the rumour that Mrs Gandhi had mongered to her recently—'Some women are born lucky, not like you and me. Now look at Dinshee. Maithili's papa is back. I was telling her that if she chants even a little, there's no saying the extent to which the benefits would go. But does she listen!'

At that time, she had paid scant attention as she was accustomed to Mrs Gandhi's patently inaccurate constructions about other women's lives. For instance, she had told her that Mrs Jain had taken *sanyas* from the world, so disheartened was she by a court case her relatives had filed against her, whereas Shailaja knew for a fact that she was negotiating the sale of her flat and planning to join her daughter in Mumbai. She had overheard Mrs Jain talking on the phone when she went to her flat to request her yet again to shift the tulsi plant with all its little hooks and spears from the landing. Regarding Dini, Shailaja made a feeble attempt to set the record straight: 'Oh, Kenny is not Maithili's father. He's her distant relative from Nagaland. Maithili is adopted!'

'Arre, he is her father. Maithili calls him Kenny Papa; I myself heard with my own ears! What adopted? She is Dinshee's daughter... Look at their hair—like each other's!' Mrs Gandhi insisted.

It would be just like Dini to give Kenny a red-carpet welcome in her home and encourage Maithili to call him Papa to inculcate Northeastern values in her, without worrying about what this would look like to an outsider. Shailaja, too, was suspicious in the beginning. But they were so disparate. No, it couldn't be!

Dini was coming for dinner to her place this weekend. Rajni ki Ma was going to make her *gatte ka saag*, 'famous all over Vasant Kunj,' she had bragged, and fiery hot *lehsun ki chutney* that none of the memsahibs could even put on their tongues, she had cautioned. Accepting the challenge, they were also going to get rotis made with the millet flour that Dini had procured from Rajasthan through her mysterious contacts. *Bajre ki roti* is what goes best with lehsun ki chutney, apparently! Surprisingly, Dini had taken the initiative to make this programme. Why was she seeking her out time and again these days, Shailaja asked herself as she drove to college.

'I suppose Ranjan won't risk joining us for dinner,' Dini had put in casually. She would always make him sound conniving.

As she parked her car, Shailaja resolved to not discuss Ranjan with Dini ever again.

The staffroom was quite empty. There was a small group of temporary teachers in the corner. Most of them had joined after her. A few older permanent teachers sat with newspapers in front of them. She couldn't see anybody from her own department. 'Have you got your exam duties?' she asked the temporary teachers. Her status was the same as theirs, though she was so much older.

'Yes, Shailaja, there was an email from college,' one of them answered.

Shailaja wondered why she hadn't received an email. She decided to go up to the office to get her duty chart.

She met the peon at the door of the staffroom.

'Madam, I was looking for you,' he said.

Shailaja signed and took the letter he handed her. It was not the usual way of sending the duty chart. But then Dhar had been bureaucratizing the college more and more.

There wasn't very much to do, so she decided to get some books from the library. She liked the college library. It was cool and well-stacked. It would be a much better place than the staffroom to spend the next hour or so before the department meeting, she decided.

As she walked into the library, she felt that the library assistant at the counter for issuing out books wanted to say something to her. Shailaja liked to chat with him. He seemed to have a genuine interest in literature. Last time, he had asked her about *Gone with the Wind*.

He was startled that a 'filmi novel' like this one had found its way into the English Literature syllabus. She had tried to explain the concept of popular fiction and he asked her many questions: 'But Madam, it is not like Shakespeare, is it?' She felt that his receptivity to her explanation was far more than that of her own department colleagues.

'Madam, had Literature course been like this in my time, I would have also done a BA honours in English,' he said with some longing.

But today he seemed withdrawn and formal.

Shailaja smiled at him anyway. 'I am going to issue some more popular fiction to enjoy while the exams are taking place,' she remarked.

He fidgeted with the pen lying on the counter, visibly uncomfortable.

'Is all well?' she asked him.

'Madam, I am not sure that you can issue books. I will have to ask the librarian,' he replied hesitantly.

'Why, what happened? I am not aware of any notice saying we can't issue books.' Shailaja wondered what Dhar had been up to now.

'Madam, haven't you got the letter?'

'Which letter?'

The assistant looked more troubled by the minute. 'Madam, the letter from the principal...'

'Yes,' Shailaja replied, surprised that the library should know about the student's complaint.

'Madam, only the teachers of the college can issue books,' the assistant said, turning a dark red.

'But I—' Shailaja suddenly remembered the duty chart. She hadn't opened the envelope; was it the duty chart or something else?

She brought out the letter, her hands trembling. It was a

notice of termination. Her service was terminated with effect from today—Friday the 22nd! After ten years of teaching, she had indeed been thrown out of her job, with no reasons specified!

Yes, knees do buckle, Shailaja discovered as she suddenly found herself sitting on the bench intended for bags at the entrance of the library. The assistant looked at her anxiously from his high perch behind the counter.

'I hadn't seen the letter,' she said unnecessarily to him as he turned an even darker red. Drawing in a deep breath with some effort, she got up from the bench and started to walk away.

'Madam, my cousin is SO in Kalindi College. He was saying that the principal is quite nice there.'

In spite of her distraction, Shailaja was touched. He was trying to help her find another job. But there would be the exam season soon, and then the winter break. This was not the time principals hired teachers, no matter how nice they were! And very few jobs came up in January–May, or the 'even' semester, as it was called.

Dhar hadn't specified reasons in the letter but she could easily guess what they would be. He had constructed a whole case against her: the summons during the mid-semester break that she had ignored and the student's complaint. Dereliction of duty and then moral turpitude! She had not submitted explanations in writing for either, had she? Where had her mind been? What had she been thinking? Her bank passbook danced in front of her eyes as she drove back. She only had a couple of thousands, but then she never had more than that in her account. She had bumbled along in DDSD for the last ten years with the confidence that this job was hers for the asking—that she would be made permanent whenever the university chose to hold interviews in her college.

Sachin and Anita, active members of the Delhi University Teachers' Association, or DUTA as it was known, used to ensure that temporary lecturers like her were re-appointed every year. But then these two no longer had the clout. Besides, Shailaja knew that Anita would say that she should have acted against the principal earlier. In fact, subsequently, much like Dini, she too had seemed very disappointed by her decision to not lodge a complaint against Dhar. But nobody could have predicted that the man would be vengeful enough to take away her job. This was a really bad time, and she was almost without money. She had paid advance rent for six months for her flat; her meagre savings were completely wiped out. For the first time in her life, at the age of thirty-six, she was facing a real financial crisis.

She went home and tried Ranjan's number. The phone rang and rang.

Ten minutes after Dini got into office that Friday morning, Nitin summoned her to his chamber.

'Is it true that you took Parvaiz's wife to the gynaecologist and got her an abortion without taking her family into confidence?' he asked without fanfare.

This was not Nitin's urbane style at all. She noted that his fair and vacuous face had beads of sweat standing on it.

'Nitin, how is this even relevant?' Dini replied, stalling for time.

'You'll have to leave it to me to decide what is relevant in this case, Dini,' he lashed out, his face clenching like a fist.

'May I know what case we are discussing here?' she hit back in reflex.

'I paid a visit to the basti and took feedback from the community—'

Dini found herself livid. 'This is totally unacceptable. I should have been informed beforehand.'

'I am sorry, but this procedure cannot be followed if there is a complaint against the concerned programme officer. In this case, there was a written complaint that I forwarded to you.'

'But I replied to it, didn't I?'

'I am not sure that challenging the validity of the complaint can be considered an adequate reply. I was hoping you would explain what exactly happened.'

'I have no problem in telling you what happened—in fact, what is happening as we waste time in our offices. Jamila is being beaten up by her husband and mother-in-law. She is being brutalized on a regular basis. This is what is happening, and we are doing nothing to stop it. She is made to work in the factory and then at home. It is like slave labour. Is it so difficult to understand why she doesn't want to have a baby under these circumstances?'

'Dini, three women have testified in front of the Maulvi that you two would close the door of the office. They said they saw you hugging each other.'

'Nitin... This is...'

'Of course, I know. It can't be true. I can't imagine you starting a relationship with the lady in question,' he said, relaxing a little. But there was a leer on his face; she wanted to hit him.

'I don't know what you mean,' Dini said, challenging him.

'The lady in question claims that she loves you and wants to live with you,' he said, looking at her squarely in the face.

'You spoke to Jamila?'

'Look, I was called by the Maulvi. I know you have a bee in your bonnet about him, so I went to meet him by myself.

He had called all the women there,' Nitin was looking deeply worried again.

'This is a breach of protocol. I have been working in the basti for six years. How can you conduct an inquiry without informing me?'

'I informed you of the complaint. I want you to address the issues. I want a reply in writing.'

'A reply to what, Nitin?'

'I want to know whether you are responsible for Jamila's abortion. Did you help her in any way to have an abortion? If yes, what made you go against the stated policy of Empower?'

'Is there a policy against helping women who are being beaten up by their husbands?'

'Dini, you are there as the health and education officer and, as we have discussed before many times, this project pertains to health and education alone.'

'My work involves listening to women and documenting their experiences.'

'You are not supposed to interfere in family and community issues.'

'Am I supposed to walk away when there is a crisis?'

'I have said this before. This is not a place for bleeding-heart sentimentalism. We have goals and targets and those are important. We have created women's groups to bring about progressive changes in the family. We are doing development in accordance with a particular philosophy...'

'During this process, we can't suspend the fundamental rights of women citizens of India. Mercifully, these are guaranteed by the Constitution.'

'You are accused by the community of having a sexual relationship with her.'

'By the Maulvi and his henchmen! They are not the community.'

'I want a written reply,' replied Nitin, sternly.

Although she was trembling in anger, it did cross Dini's mind that Nitin did not look smug for having cornered her.

■

'Just resign,' RS said in the evening. She had gone directly to his guest house after work. With Kenny stationed in her flat, she had unaccustomed freedom to plan her outings these days. 'You have so many doubts about this job anyway. This confirms my thesis that these international agencies are quite incapable of bringing about any real change. They are neo-colonial...'

Dini was sorely tempted to ask him to explain this remark further. At any other time, she would have found his use of the academic term 'neo-colonial' delicious. It would be a riproaring exercise to cast the neurotically political correct NGO, Empower, as a newfangled colonizer of a developing country at a meeting with Nitin. He would probably sue her for defamation. But she had other more pressing concerns. 'I'll have to get another job, RS. I can't just resign. I have responsibilities,' she said

'Dini, this could be an opportunity to think of the future.'

With great effort Dini bit back the query at the tip of her tongue. At such a moment it would be hazardous to ask what he meant.

RS, however, kept going on. 'The present state of affairs is not workable. We can't continue to live more than 750 km away from each other, meeting once a fortnight. I hate this.'

'You could move to Delhi,' she said, knowing she was being disingenuous. RS was part of the management of his NGO, and they had sent him to New York for the training programme in that capacity. It was not just a job that he could resign from. But then, she couldn't resign from being mother either, could she?

'I am in the middle of my project. I need at least three years to make the youth somewhat self-sufficient. I am hoping their success will motivate others. I'll be able to get away for fairly long periods after that,' he was explaining patiently.

'And Maithili goes to school here in Delhi. It would not be fair to drag her away from an environment that she loves. Besides, where would she go to school in Banswara?' Dini knew she had to persist with this line of argument. It was the only one to which RS would be somewhat amenable. Besides, everything she was saying was completely true.

RS was starting to look rather crushed. 'Yes, you have a point. But we could take up a place in the city. There are good missionary schools there, you know. St. Paul's is there.'

'What would be the point of shifting from Delhi in that case? We would still have two households. Besides, RS, missionary schools are oppressive. Maithili is used to a free and open environment. You know, in her school teachers are supposed to work with each child individually. There are just twenty-five students in a class. Regular schools are like factories with sixty children to a class and a harassed teacher who has to somehow manage the show,' Dini said, feeling uncomfortably elitist.

'I am all for alternate schooling, but she would also have the two of us as guardians. Surely together we can provide an enlightened educational environment. Of course, by the time she is ready for college and university, we will be able to shift our work to a metropolis. Besides, 60–70 km of distance is an improvement on 750 km, isn't it? We could divide up the childcare days. I could work from home at least twice–thrice a week. Anyway, I need to keep time for office work. Reporting and organization of data are getting neglected with my present schedule.'

Dini's heart melted with tenderness. How generous was he!

He was offering to surrender his time in the field to babysit Maithili. How was she to tell him that there was little chance of Maithili accepting him as her guardian? Her days were full of Kenny Papa these days. She was soaking up his way of life, his conventional value system.

'Dini, I need somebody like you to work with the women,' RS stated suddenly. 'I have been concentrating on the young men mainly but real development will begin when women start to talk about their rights. A lot of them are engaged in prostitution. The men act as pimps. This is encouraged by the community. They are being exploited.'

'Let me think about this, please.'

'You could make a real difference. The government officers only use a moralistic discourse and are not above taking advantage of them in every way possible. This fourteen-year-old girl is pregnant and believes that the block development officer is going to marry her. You would be able to make the women see the situation for what it is. You could teach them to be self-protective. This is not what anyone else can do,' he pleaded. But then as though making an effort to check his enthusiasm, he added, 'Of course you must take your time. But you must also allow yourself to look ahead. It seems to me you are not looking at the future.'

Dini was surprised; it sounded like criticism.

'What do you mean?' she asked.

'I mean that you have to think of yourself as well. You can't limit all future plans just because—'

'Just because I am a mother? But I *am* a mother, RS. And it is precisely because I am thinking ahead that I am so tentative.'

'If only you could hear yourself. You are playing the self-sacrificing Bollywood mom.'

'You mean I should abandon my daughter without a second

thought just because… just because you are offering to marry me?'

'This is bloody unfair,' he lashed out.

'It sounds like that to me,' she said stubbornly in spite of herself.

'Well, how does this sound? "I am thirty-seven but I am not going to start the work of my calling. I will also not marry the man who loves me. The reason is weighty and significant. My eight-year-old daughter would not want to change her school."'

'Is it because I am not falling in line with your plans for the future that you are calling me middle-aged and stubborn?'

'What do you mean? I haven't called you middle-aged…'

'I mean the typical male expectation from the partner. I must abandon my life and become a part of yours because the clock is ticking for me.'

'Dini, you are being patently unfair. You are twisting everything I am saying. This is not a gender issue. I am thinking of what you want to do. All of us, men and women, need to go ahead and do what we want, and time is finite, after all,' RS said.

'You are being unfair, too, by not even trying to understand. Maithili is no longer a baby. She has clear ideas about where she wants to be, what she wants to do. I can't ignore her wishes and desires.'

RS heard her out patiently and responded, 'I don't know as much as you do about bringing up children, but are eight-year-olds the best judge of their requirements? After all, parents with transferrable jobs also bring up children, don't they?'

'I never question your priorities. Why are you so critical of mine?'

'I am not being critical of you. I am trying to understand. Besides, I can't bear this.'

'RS, Maithili is headstrong. But I have brought her up in peculiar circumstances—so many lies, cover-ups!' Dini gulped. 'The present situation is so difficult for me, with Kenny claiming her as his. But this is the way it has turned out.'

RS looked uncharacteristically crestfallen. 'I love you for the way you have brought up Maithili. She is so confident, so fearless. I told my mother that you are teaching your daughter dance and music, and she was so excited. But she also said she can teach dance to Maithili too and why should you waste good money paying strangers to do so. I showed her a picture of the two of you and she said Maithili is like a doll...' He paused and then said in a rush, 'I hate the idea of Kenny being in the same flat, in the next room from you...'

It was the first time he was admitting that Kenny's proximity to her affected him to this extent. She hugged RS tightly. It was becoming a habit with her to weep on his clean shirt and leave kajal stains all over. 'Take off your shirt,' she said to RS.

'Dini,' he exclaimed and raised his brows exaggeratedly.

'Oh, don't be silly! I just want to hug you and cry,' she replied, smiling in spite of her tears. Where was she going with all this?

Was there a way to rewind life—do it all over again, very differently this time?

November

Unravelling

Monday dawned and Dini was still uncertain about how to frame her reply to Nitin's allegations. She had started from home earlier than usual to escape Kenny's breakfast-making and reached office before anyone else. She sat at her desk and stared at the screen. The previous evening, she had finally made an unscheduled visit to the basti to meet the women but was only able to speak to a very subdued Jamila. The woman told her about Nitin's visit and the charges made against both of them at the public meeting held at the Maulvi's. It sounded like a veritable witch-hunt. With insinuations about her immoral relations with Dini, Jamila's husband and mother-in-law had managed to get the community up in arms against both of them.

'Didi, I denied it all. I said I never went to the doctor either with you or with anybody else. They told me to swear on the Quran; I did that too.'

'Oh Jamila Behen,' Dini sighed, knowing how much it meant to Jamila to be truthful and fearless. Besides, she also knew that Jamila's protestations would be of no avail. Nitin had already made up his mind to withdraw Dini from the project and give in to the Maulvi's demands. Jamila was but the scapegoat.

'Didi, Allah knows that you did it all for me. I cannot let any harm come your way.'

Dini was touched. It was Jamila, not her, who was completely at the mercy of the community.

'Remember this always. Jamila loves you,' Jamila said. Her emotions seemed to be at a feverish pitch. Her eyes were swimming; there were red spots on her cheeks.

'We will face this together. We must explain the situation to the other women, especially to Rasoola and Kaneez. If they saw us embracing, they have to understand there was nothing wrong in it.'

'Rasoola and Kaneez won't come, Didi. Don't waste time waiting for them.'

'How do you know they won't come? Rahima and Ghazala came, didn't they? I spoke to them, explained everything. They said they would support what is right and fair.'

'Oh, my innocent Didi! You think they or anybody else will take a stand against the Maulvi publicly? Rahima and Ghazala will do what their husbands tell them. Nobody cares for what is right and fair in this world.'

'Why? You do and I do too,' asserted Dini. 'You are going against your husband and the Maulvi!'

'Didi, there's only you and me then...'

An unaccustomed silence descended between them. Jamila was holding tightly onto Dini's hand and pressing it repeatedly to her heart. The thought that she might be suicidal crossed Dini's mind and she nervously began asking her many questions about her work in the factory. How could she convey to this tortured soul that there was a future beyond the present situation? But Jamila answered in a straightforward manner, detailing the leave due to her and the amount of money in her PF account. Dini felt reassured as her tone was quite matter-of-fact. No, Jamila was too sensible to harm herself. She would win ultimately. She would have to if there was any fairness in the world. Yet, when the wiry woman, old before her time, squared her shoulders and got up to leave, a lump rose in her throat.

'Shabbakhair,' she exclaimed spontaneously to Jamila's retreating back as though flowery good wishes for the night could fend off real-life problems.

Jamila looked back, her face breaking into an impish smile. 'You have learnt it well, Didi. Shabbakhair. A pity you couldn't be mine forever!'

Dini had sat in the community room long after Jamila left. As she had prophesied, nobody else came to meet her.

She began writing her reply to Nitin with the image of Jamila's face, as she had looked while bidding goodbye, on her mind. She decided to address the communication to the head office in Geneva. 'Dear Ms Astrid Engvig,' she wrote. She clicked on the home site of the NGO and found a photograph of the director. The face framed by blonde hair was kind. Words started to flow immediately. Dini described her visits to the basti, her meeting with Jamila, the pathetic work conditions in the factory, Jamila's daily routine, the sexual demands by her alcoholic husband, the beatings...

> I admit I went beyond the scope of my work to provide assistance to this courageous woman and am tendering an apology and my resignation.
>
> However, I am writing to you to request re-envisioning the role of Empower in the basti. If with all the monetary and human resources at our command, we find ourselves unable to encourage the genuine desire for freedom and dignity on the part of a woman like Jamila, we are acting contrary to our stated objective of empowering women.

She paused, wondering whether she was overstating her case, but this was her only hope. She finished writing the email and sent it off before she could change her mind. She looked around the office. It looked cold and clinical.

■

Dini walked back home slowly. She had got out of her Uber at the colony gate. Dropping by at RS's had only made her feel more conflicted, and she wanted some more time to think. RS had been emphatic that her time was up with Empower and that she should not expect her letter to make any tangible difference to the situation: 'Don't waste time on them, Dini. Now that you have proof of the sham work they do, it is time to explore other options than these high-profile NGOs.'

Of course she had already realized that by appealing to the director of the NGO, she was requesting support from those she opposed ideologically. Astrid Engvig was one of the leaders of the international, hyper-articulate clique that Nitin and most of her other deracinated colleagues had aspirations of joining. These were also the people who were sucking the development sector dry of resources with their obscenely large pay packets. Right from the beginning, Dini had defined the mode of her work in opposition to theirs. She was proud of her connect with the ground. But now, it was clear to her that her distance from the ground was considerable. RS was the grassroots activist; she wasn't. Of course, he would have picked up the tell-tale signs of unrest in the community: the remarks of women—that she was partial to Jamila, for instance.

'Didn't you realize that the women were talking about both of you behind your back?' RS had asked. Dini's mind had not gone there at all. She often wondered whether there was a sexual element in Jamila's 'love' for her but never thought of it as a big deal. She never referred to it or encouraged Jamila in any way, but didn't censure her for it either. To have 'discouraged' Jamila out of respect for the views of the community, as the fork-tongued Nitin had opined, would have snuffed out a significant mode of rebellion that Jamila was using. She couldn't have abandoned her faith in the immense scope of women's sexuality, nor her genuine respect for Jamila's pluckiness, she told herself. She couldn't have handled this in any other way. No, her relationship with Jamila was above reproach. This is what she had indicated in her letter to Engvig.

But a disquieting thought was rearing its head in her mind. Wasn't there an eerie similarity between RS's radical views about development and Nitin's glib equivocations? RS, too, put the community above the individual rebellious woman. 'We have to get cues about development from the community, not from theory, concept notes and targets and goals!' he would often say. 'We can't aim to foist an alien value system on them.' But what if a lone woman wants to break out of the constricting community norms? Are we with her or against her? Dini challenged him in her mind. Besides, she wondered, what did he actually feel about Jamila's romantic feelings towards her? 'Are you sure Jamila is a lesbian, Dini?' he had enquired, as though it were an aberration.

She had to concede that her high-profile international NGO, though fundamentally flawed, was the only place that had the potential to provide her the space for radical ideas. It could not be denied that her work, however theoretical, had sustained and nourished a rebellious woman. RS was never going to understand or appreciate this.

Dini shook her head vigorously to banish confusing thoughts. She too squared her shoulders and walked on. Shailaja had been calling her all weekend. She would look in on Maithili and then subject herself to the tales of love and romance that the other woman was sure to inflict on her.

■

Dini walked into her home, hoping the over-enthusiastic father would be out. Kenny had told her that he had bagged an offer for two musical gigs in Delhi. He had startled her by placing a wad of notes on the table yesterday: 'I must do my bit towards Maithili.' Apparently, he was making money off music for the first time in his life. Dini felt unreasonably angry. Kenny had blundered into their lives and sneaked into Maithili's affections. Now with her job situation becoming unstable, she needed his help more than ever.

Kenny was in the dining space, stirring sugar in a glass of milk. 'I tried to call you several times,' he said in an accusing manner.

Dini started. She had put the phone on silent while drafting her reply and then, as was happening increasingly, forgotten to unmute it. She brought the phone out from her bag.

There were several missed calls. Kenny's accounted for ten out of them; Shailaja had called twice.

'I was in a meeting and had put my phone on silent, but this is the time I return usually,' she replied. 'Why were you calling me?' she enquired.

'Maithili's down with fever. It has come down now. I gave her a paracetamol and sponged her. Your office said you had left for home. Where was this meeting?'

Not bothering to reply, Dini rushed into her daughter's room. Maithili was asleep and Rani was sitting at the bedside.

'Baby has high fever, you are so late,' Rani said, equally accusing.

'You can leave now, Rani. Anyway, her f—father was home,' she replied briskly.

Kenny had come into the room and was standing right behind her. After Rani left, he said to her, 'I can see how difficult it must have been for you...'

Dini felt tears pricking her eyes. She turned away. She felt his hand on her shoulder. Pulling herself together, she directed a quizzical look at him.

'Dini, can't we begin again?' said Kenny, looking ridiculously young and vulnerable.

'I don't know what you mean, Kenny.'

'Is it so difficult to understand?'

'After so long?'

'I'm sorry. I was chasing a mirage. I wanted to be free, feel free all the time. I realize I was wrong. If one has children, one has to be there for them. I have been selfish—'

'Kenny, please don't... I can't...'

'Can't what?'

'Can't talk about starting anything now.'

His face fell. 'Is there somebody else?' he asked.

'Kenny, I have never asked you such a question. What gives you the right?'

'Maithili was ill, and we couldn't get in touch with you for over four hours.'

'You have been inaccessible for eight years!'

Dini realized she was shouting. Maithili had woken up.

'Oh, how are you, sweetie?'

'Mumma, don't scold Kenny Papa. He sponged me and brought down my fever,' said Maithili.

'Of course, honey. How are you feeling now?'

'What were you saying to him?'

'Are you hungry, sweetie? Should I make tomato soup for you?'

'Yes, make tomato soup. But don't put *lauki*, only tomato... Kenny Papa, you stay here...'

Dini felt crushed as she came out of the room. How had things managed to fall into such a conventional pattern merely by the entry of a man into the domestic scene? This could be any middle-class household where the wife-mother returning home guiltily after an extramarital rendezvous tried her best to make amends to her children. Dini put the boiled tomatoes in the blender and ran it angrily.

It took three days and six phone calls for Shailaja to get Ranjan to visit her. On Monday, late in the evening, at last her doorbell rang and her saviour presented himself. As she threw herself into his arms, she noticed with half a mind that he was looking frazzled.

'Why didn't you tell me about it?' asked Ranjan again, a little sharply.

Shailaja had waited for him with a longing so deep and desperate that she felt she would lose her sanity. With the desire for her former life throbbing painfully, she even imagined herself storming into the Defence Colony barsati, walking into the familiar bedroom that had turned into hostile territory and dragging Ranjan away from the solid teak wood bed that she had bought second-hand from Amar Colony—a real steal! She had not been able to chant for the last three days. Rajni ki Ma had come and hung around in the house like an apparition and then left. The unfinished scenario with Ranjan that she had imagined played in her mind while she told herself again and again that he was coming to see her on Monday evening and there were only 47, 38, 20, 5 hours, 4 hours, 3 hours, 2 hours 30 minutes to deliverance...

Here she was in her Vasant Kunj bedroom, in Ranjan's arms at last, tears streaming down her face, and he was asking her a strange question: why didn't you tell me about it?

She tried to burrow into his chest. She didn't have to answer the strange question, didn't have to pay attention to his suddenly shrinking, withdrawing body, didn't need to wonder why his voice was squeaking with anxiety and irritation. In his arms, she could hold her fear and humiliation at bay.

But he was asking her again as to why she hadn't told him about it earlier.

'You got the letter on Friday. I can't believe you didn't tell me, Shailaja. You called so many times.'

'But what would you have done, Ranjan? I was in shock. I just didn't want to tell you on the phone. I wanted to be able to hold you.'

He stroked her back a little absent-mindedly. 'This is real bad news. It will travel all over the university.'

'I just don't know what to do, Ranjan,' she sobbed.

'You should have gone and met him immediately. This is what I would have told you to do.'

She started with surprise, 'Met whom?'

'Dhar, of course. Don't you think you must talk to him?'

'No, I don't want to. I have nothing to say to him.'

'Really! Is this a lovers' quarrel? He is the principal. You need to confront him. Tell him it is too sudden and you should have had notice. You could apologize for what happened in class. Tell him it was a misunderstanding—'

'Ranjan, that would be like begging!'

'I don't know what else you can do.'

'I have the option of raising a stink. I did call up Anita

and Sachin, the DUTA activists in college, and they told me such things were happening to temporary teachers all over the university. They said they would speak to the DUTA president…'

'These guys obviously have their own issues with the administration.'

'Yes, the university authorities have become very oppressive,' Shailaja said.

'But tell me, did they believe you when you told them about Dhar?'

'What do you mean?'

'Did they believe you when you told them that Dhar had made a pass at you?'

'Of course they did. I didn't tell them the whole story. But Anita was very angry at his behaviour.'

'Then why didn't they do anything about it up till now?'

'Anita asked me to lodge a complaint with the committee against sexual harassment. She told me how to do it and explained the procedure,' Shailaja said.

'Is that all?'

'She also warned me that the complaint might not go anywhere. She told me that the committee in our college is nominated by Dhar…'

'So, she was also discouraging you at the same time. Look, it seems to me she doesn't, um, see eye to eye…'

'I am not a teachers' union worker like her and I'm not a political activist. But beyond that… I can't understand what you are getting at.'

'It seems to me that your activist friends aren't quite convinced by your story, Shailaja.'

Shailaja sat up in bed. 'Of course they believe me. But why…'

Ranjan was shaking his head in a disbelieving manner.

'The narrative doesn't hang together. If they believe you and they hate Dhar as you say, they would have done much more.'

'But what can they do when things are so bad in the university?' When Ranjan didn't reply, she asked tremulously, 'Ranjan, tell me something, Do you believe what I told you?'

Ranjan took his time formulating an answer, 'It seems to me... Well... You know you could have misread the whole thing. It could just have been true that the students found your lectures a little too explicit...'

'Are you blaming me for the way I teach?'

'No, of course not, Shail.'

'Then what are you saying?'

'See, you have been very anxious, you've been having self-esteem issues and it is perfectly understandable that—'

'Perfectly understandable that I concocted a sexual harassment issue to make myself appear more interesting?' Shailaja asked softly. Of course, she would wake up and realize it was a bad dream.

'These things aren't ever at a conscious level. All that I'm saying is that one needs to be very careful in professional spaces—'

'And you feel Anita and Sachin also saw it like this?'

'I am wondering whether talking to them was a good idea in the first place. They might have said something publicly to put Dhar on his guard, especially if he didn't intend to make a pass.'

'Didn't intend to make a pass? But Ranjan, he did. He made a pass alright.'

'I am trying to present another likely scenario here. It is possible that he was issuing you a well-intentioned warning about how students were processing your lectures.'

'Are you telling me I am delusional?'

'I didn't say that. I said you have been exceptionally anxious and depressed.'

'And that would make me imagine things?'

'No, no, Shailaja... I am not suggesting that you're making up what happened. But the conclusions you are drawing may not be very accurate. Dhar doesn't speak English very well. He may have been trying to explain things in a paternalistic manner. But you feel wronged so easily; you feel everybody is out to take advantage...'

'Is this what you think of me?'

'One can't go on playing victim. You have cast yourself as a permanent victim. Also, we can't tell ourselves that the world owes us something in return. I mean, why talk about your personal life in class? It's not a clinic for therapy.'

'If this is what you feel about me, why have you been coming to see me?'

'Shail, I care for you. I've been able to make a new life for myself but you—'

'But I what?'

'I hate to see you like this. I blame myself.'

This is what he told himself. He came to make her feel better about herself. He was giving himself to her in charity.

'I think I hate you.' Shailaja was amazed that she said it.

'Oh really?'

'Yes, please leave.'

Shailaja couldn't believe she had asked him to leave. But this is what she heard her voice say.

'There you go again. Don't be silly. I—'

'Please leave, Ranjan.'

'Don't do anything you'll regret later.'

'I hate you and I want you to leave,' she said coldly.

'Okay, if this is how you feel,' he replied, cold as ice too.

She watched him as he pulled his clothes on. For the first time she noticed his sagging belly. No wonder he wore kurtas more and more.

'You need help, you know. If I were you, I would take myself to a qualified therapist,' he said through gritted teeth.

She got up well after he had left to lock up her front door. This was her space—her space that she had to guard. She would hold on, not let people gatecrash; not let people drive her away. She would hold on...

∎

Had she slept at all? When Ranjan left, it was dark, but now the windows in her bedroom were bright and the bell was ringing insistently.

'I have been at the door for half an hour,' complained Rajni ki Ma. 'I was afraid you had fainted or something... And here you are, hale and hearty. It seems you are taking another day off from college. How many days do they allow you? Nice job it is!' she continued to mutter.

'I have lost my job,' said Shailaja.

'Oh yes, you can afford to joke about these things. But you should be careful. If you take so many holidays, they will throw you out. You mark my words,' she replied.

'I am not joking. Here is the letter,' Shailaja insisted, a part of her wondering why it was important to share this information with her employee.

'Oh Ma, as if I can read angrezi,' exclaimed Rajni ki Ma, looking at her curiously.

'Don't worry. I can pay your salary this month. I will have to think after that.'

'It is not good to joke about these things. You know, Lord Ganesh descends on one's tongue while one is joking about such things and then... And then they come true.'

'I am not joking, Rajni ki Ma,' Shailaja tried again.

Rajni ki Ma shrugged and began her work in the kitchen. Shailaja kept sitting in the living room, her mind empty of all thoughts. The phone jingled and she picked it up without even glancing at the screen.

'Hello Shailaja,' said Dini's voice. 'Where have you been? I called so many times. About our weekend programme, I'm so sorry—'

'It's fine,' Shailaja interrupted. The last time they spoke was a week, an age, ago—the dinner plan made then seemed to belong to a previous birth.

'Please don't be angry. I need to explain...'

Shailaja listened with half her mind, vaguely wondering why Dini was sounding so unlike her usual self.

'I am having a terribly complicated time both at work and at home... I am going to be out of my job soon,' said Dini.

Shailaja blinked in surprise. Was she hearing herself speak?

'And then, you know, Kenny, whom you met. He has been at my flat for more than a month and it's so... He is Maithili's father.'

'Oh Dini, I don't know what to say,' Shailaja managed at last.

'Yes, my situation is complicated but I didn't want you to think that I am avoiding you or—'

'I am actually out of a job.'

'What, you resigned?'

'No, I got a letter of termination... I got it on Friday.'

'But how can they—' Dini asked.

'Yes, it seems like a bolt from the blue but actually it was expected. I think nobody believed me when I told them about Dhar...'

'Don't be silly. I believed you. So did Anita in your college.

I spoke to her actually. I know her through a trade unionist. I was going to tell you.'

'But your job...' Shailaja felt hysterical laughter bubble up. 'How is it that you of all people are in danger of losing your job?'

'It is a long story. Are you all right, though? Did you tell your... Ranjan about it?'

Why that pregnant pause before Ranjan's name? Shailaja saw red. How dare Dini?

'Did you tell Maithili's father?' she spat.

'Shailaja, really,' expostulated Dini. 'What would Kenny know about my kind of work? And listen, it seems to me that you are blaming me for not listening to you when you had that episode with Dhar. Such things happen all the time. I had asked you to lodge a complaint and so did Anita; she told me that you were categorical about not wanting DUTA to interfere.'

'Dini, you've had the time to talk about me behind my back but no time to meet me...'

'Yes, I am busy. I have a life, you know—a daughter, responsibilities...'

'Yes, I know how important all this is. I am the one who has nothing! I have no real relationships! Neither have I adopted a daughter, nor do I have an ex-husband! All that I have is an ex-boyfriend, somebody who by definition doesn't count, on whom I have no right, on whom I should have no right...'

Shailaja realized she was screaming. But Dini had no bloody right to disapprove of her relationship with Ranjan. They had lived together for thirteen years, and Dini... She was this champion of women's rights, wasn't she? Besides, had she been paying attention, she would have known what Dhar was going to do.

'You disapprove of me, don't you? You think this is what

women like me deserve! And you set yourself up as this women's libber—' yelled Shailaja.

'Don't be silly! Why would I disapprove of you?'

'You are just a prudish Iyer. That's who you are. You disapprove of women like me who have had sex outside marriage. Or sex at all. Even your daughter is adopted.'

Shailaja felt a hand firmly rubbing her back. Rajni ki Ma had stationed herself right next to her.

'Didi, Shailaja Didi… Shailaja…' she was saying. She hardly ever called her by her name.

'Shailaja Didi, drink this water.'

The voice at the other end of the phone line was also repeating her name, 'Shailaja, Shailaja? Hello? Are you there?'

No, she wasn't there. Not there for anyone.

'Listen, we need to talk about this. It's not like this…'

Of course it was like this. All wrong. There was no difference between Dini and Ranjan. Dini was wrong; it wasn't about being a man or a woman, rich or poor. There were only those who had everything, like Strawberry, and those who didn't; people who cared and people who were cared for. Dini should have been on her side. But she was on the other side, with those who disapproved of her.

Rajni ki Ma took the phone away from her. 'Didi, you have the water. I am making some tea for you.'

Shailaja felt herself being led firmly to the bedroom.

Rajni ki Ma was the only one who was there for her. But she would have to go soon. She worked in three more houses. And she had no money anymore to pay her.

'Rajni ki Ma, you go. It is late,' she said.

'You don't worry about me. I will go after some time.'

Rajni ki Ma helped her get into bed.

The phone was ringing insistently somewhere in the house.

'The phone...' whispered Shailaja.

'I'll get it later,' replied Rajni ki Ma. 'You have tea and lie down.'

The tea was warm and sweet. Shailaja dropped back into bed exhausted.

Dini felt very restless after her talk with Shailaja. She had sounded so disturbed; it was as though she was having a breakdown. But then, wasn't this only to be expected after the series of self-destructive choices she had made? At first she had let the principal get away with making a pass at her, and then gone running back to her exploitative ex-boyfriend. The principal was a bully who had predictably become bolder when she failed to confront him.

And that Ranjan! What was he but a spineless guy who fed off his women emotionally? This kind of sleazy liaison was just the black hole that women like Shailaja were destined to fall into. All in the name of love. Dini pulled herself short. Women like Shailaja? Was she doing exactly what she blamed patriarchy for—slotting women into types? Shailaja was vulnerable and looking for advice and friends. As an activist, she should have tried harder to make her see things from a different perspective, talked with her more.

But then how dare Shailaja call her prudish! It was laughable that she should think of her as an old stick in the mud. Was it because Dini had refused to wear the sleeveless kurta she had got for her? Of course, Shailaja had no way of knowing about her iconoclastic personal life. Dini shook her head impatiently. With Maithili's fever down to normal, the fruit of her iconoclasm was tucking into fried eggs for breakfast with Kenny Papa to get 'fighting fit' quickly.

Dini concluded she couldn't afford to be critical of Shailaja. Her own love life had come to a crossroads. She extended the image in her mind. RS was beckoning from the low road.

'I have too much baggage,' Dini muttered to herself, seeing in her mind Maithili's new pink Barbie stroller-bag, rolling precariously on dung-splattered village paths.

Of course, there would soon be a reply from her NGO—if not from Engvig, then from somebody else—accepting her resignation. She would need to look for a similar job to be able to pay the rent. Dini felt herself recoil. She wasn't prepared to deal with another Empower, another Nitin.

Besides, RS would blame her for being a coward, for not daring to respond to her life's calling. He would feel that she had copped out to the bourgeois value system. Well, he wouldn't be wrong. She had capitulated, hadn't she? To that dashed pink Barbie stroller-bag, to her daughter's exclusive school, to her father's Brahminical values?

RS and she would continue to meet but his heart would withdraw from her inch by inch. Gradually the frequency of their meetings would become less—from a fortnight to a month, two months, six months. She would have to teach herself to not wait for her lover and get used to the gaping hole, the permanent void in her heart. For there could be no other like this union, she was certain of this. Dini regarded the sinking in her chest as if from a distance. This is what Shailaja must have experienced when Ranjan started to see someone else.

The smell of eggs was creeping into the bedroom. Dini decided to get out of the flat, go and meet Shailaja, reason with her, make her realize that losing a job and a boyfriend doesn't necessarily signal the end. These were accidents that strong women faced squarely. You don't suddenly move bag and baggage to a village that you could hardly locate on India's map, for instance. You don't give up everything you have learned at the university and an established international NGO. Not even when your heart suddenly takes to behaving like a giddy teenager's...

■

Rajni ki Ma opened the door for Dini. 'Good you came, Didi. Shailaja Didi has fainted,' she said.

Dini rushed into the bedroom, alarmed. Shailaja seemed to be asleep.

'Shailaja, Shailaja,' Dini called. 'You are sleeping with your mouth open.'

Shailaja opened her eyes, muttered something incomprehensible and turned over.

'No, Renu-ji, it is fine. She is asleep,' she exclaimed in sheer relief.

'It is not fine, Dini Didi,' proclaimed Rajni ki Ma. 'I have to tell you. It's very bad. You please call her parents or sister, brother. Somebody has to take care of her.'

'Renu-ji, both of us can take care of her together, can't we? Anyway, I don't have her parents' number.'

'Didi, I have to work. And so do you...'

'Yes, of course. But it will be fine. Let me see—she is sleeping now and you may go. I am on leave today; I can sit here till she wakes up.'

Rajni ki Ma muttered something about coming back in the evening.

Dini stationed herself at Shailaja's bedside wondering what she had gotten into.

■

'So, do you want to kill yourself?' Dini asked conversationally as Shailaja sipped the strong instant coffee, the only kind Dini was able to find in Shailaja's kitchen.

'Dini, really!' Shailaja replied, propped up on two pillows, looking wan and drawn.

'You are refusing to get out of bed; you have hardly eaten anything the last two days. You can't last very long like this,' Dini replied in a matter-of-fact tone. 'I give you about 48 hours more.'

'You can go. I will be fine...' Shailaja whispered as tears plonked into her coffee.

'You are not very convincing somehow,' said Dini.

An inadvertent giggle spiked through Shailaja's tears.

'Shailaja, Renu-ji wants me to call your parents.'

'Please don't, Dini. Please. It is not going to... I don't want them to see me like this.'

Dini grabbed the opportunity. 'You'll have to hurry up and get well then. Otherwise it will be difficult. I took leave yesterday and came back early from office today; Rajni ki Ma has been sleeping here at night...'

'Dini, I don't know how to thank both of you,' Shailaja muttered.

'You could get out of that bed. Then give me some lunch.'

Shailaja looked a little confused but finished her coffee. Dini heaved a sigh of relief. A couple of times in the last two days, she had panicked thinking that Shailaja would dehydrate with all the tears she was shedding.

Suddenly, Shailaja said with real fear in her voice, 'But Dini, what should I do now?'

'We are going for lunch,' Dini replied soothingly.

'You know what I mean!' Her voice was rising. 'I don't know how I'll manage.'

'What is the immediate concern, Shailaja?' Dini asked.

'I don't have any money.'

'You will get your salary for this month?'

'Yes, but that's all I have...'

'Come on, there's a whole month to plan after that!'

'The rent every month and petrol... The car is due for service...'

'Shailaja, it is not so bleak. Really! We can plan together. I too have to.'

'You told me you were going to resign. Oh my God, I am so sorry, Dini. You said on phone... But you went to work...'

'It is true that I might have to resign from my job. I have a reply from the headquarters and an offer... Also, Maithili's father is here at this moment in my flat and I—I am not sure... I don't know what to do with him—them...'

'Oh Dini,' Shailaja exclaimed. She sat up in bed. 'But if you have adopted her legally and all papers are complete, he can't take her away, can he?'

Dini realized that Shailaja was under the impression that Kenny, the biological father, had returned to take his daughter away from the adoptive mother. She had completely misunderstood the nature of the problem.

She was reaching out for Dini's hand. 'I am so sorry I screamed at you.'

'Don't keep apologizing, Shailaja. I know how tough it has been for you,' Dini replied carefully.

Shailaja got out of bed slowly. Dini waited for her to stand on her feet.

'Should we go to Sagar Ratna for a dosa? I want to tell you more about Maithili.'

Shailaja nodded a little uncertainly. 'I am not so... Okay, let's go,' she said.

■

It seemed they had been talking to each other for months and years, and something unfamiliar, something unexpected was happening to both of them.

Dini had confided the story of her affair with Kenny and Maithili's birth to RS not so long ago. But this was different. Faced with Shailaja's open-mouthed admiration, Dini felt a warm glow, an affirmation. 'Is it the singular lack of frisson that leads to this level of comfort with a woman,' she wondered.

Shailaja, on her part, was wrenched from her own debilitating hysteria by the sheer surprise she was experiencing. Dini, the NGO madam, the no-nonsense Iyer woman with coconut oil in her hair, who refused to wear a sleeveless kurta! It seemed incredible that nine years ago she had gone off with a man purely out of 'desire'. And then refused to marry him after discovering she was expecting his baby! Would she have dared to have Ranjan's baby out of wedlock?

When Dini began to hesitantly narrate the lies she had told her family, Shailaja frowned and asked, 'But how do you know your father will not accept your baby?'

'I know my father's limitations. Besides, most families are the same. Your family didn't accept your decision to live with Ranjan, did they?' she replied.

'Dini,' Shailaja began slowly, 'at times I think I gave up on them too easily.'

'I thought they made their disapproval very evident. You told me about an email your sister wrote to you. It sounded nasty.'

'Yes, Naina is a bureaucrat and expresses herself rather categorically. But I feel I should have taken their sensibilities into account. Besides, the irony is that they were right...'

'Right? You mean because Ranjan started an affair with this starlet?' Dini asked.

'Yes, I believe that the major part of their concern was me;

it wasn't only what people would say. They were going by what is the norm. Men betray women, especially if the man is like him and the woman like me.'

'What is this about "man like him, woman like me"?' Dini asked at once.

'I mean—I mean,' Shailaja gulped and Dini panicked that the waterworks would begin again, but she carried on without breaking down. 'I mean that he was already a well-known filmmaker when we started; he is rich and sophisticated...'

'He was also fifteen years older, whose film won an award, no doubt, but the funding for his next venture is yet to materialize,' Dini interjected cruelly.

Shailaja was quiet.

'If we talk in purely conventional terms, you were—are—fifteen years younger, attractive: a definite asset,' Dini continued.

'My parents must have known that the gap would narrow. Time keeps a different pace for men and women,' Shailaja replied.

'This is a very patriarchal notion of time,' Dini shot back.

'But don't you think it is the reality in our patriarchal society? I mean, don't give me a textbook answer. Isn't life for older men much easier? Doesn't an older man just seem more...' Shailaja paused to find the right word.

'Sexual? Yes, we are socialized to regard older men as interesting and experienced and older women as being on the shelf.' Dini suddenly noticed that Shailaja's hair was looking different. Before she could stop herself, the question was out, 'Shailaja, have you dyed your hair?'

'Yes, just last week,' she whispered. 'It was getting very grey in front so I went to the beauty parlour...'

'Okay,' Dini said, with some effort holding her tongue that was twisting maliciously. 'We were talking about families...'

'I always thought that you had managed that exceptionally well. Your father sounded proud of you. I was jealous!' Shailaja said.

Dini fell silent. The past tense was a giveaway. Shailaja was judging her. But what she said next was deeply empathetic: 'Dini, I suppose you couldn't have told him about the baby at that time as your mother had just passed away; he wouldn't have been able to take it then. But things are different now…'

Dini shook her head. Her eyes were brimming. This was the limit. She was supposed to be counselling Shailaja.

Shailaja reached out a hand to caress her cheek, 'I'm sorry. I am no one to judge you. Look at my life!'

Dini spoke with some difficulty, 'I'm sorry to have been so critical of you. I should have tried to understand better.'

'No, no. I feel I have done something very wrong. Ranjan was cheating on Diksha. It is adultery, or kind of… I shouldn't have…' Shailaja replied, shaking her head sadly.

'You can end it now,' Dini said.

Shailaja gave a bitter laugh, 'I don't need to. He has gone away. He is not going to come back anyway.'

'What makes you so sure?'

'I was cruel to him, Dini…'

'He knows you have lost your job, that you are short of money. Won't he come back to check on you?'

Shailaja shook her head, 'I just know he won't. Why should he anyway?'

Dini was angry. 'What do you mean? Are you saying that your present situation has nothing to do with him? This is a very strange notion of responsibility, especially because two minutes ago you said you feel responsible for him cheating.'

Shailaja was quiet.

Dini went on, 'You spent so many years with him.'

'I wanted to,' Shailaja replied.

'He too wanted it, Shailaja. You could have used those years for personal advancement, gone abroad to do a PhD, for instance! You told me you had started corresponding with a professor in Berkeley.'

'Yes, but I didn't follow it up. Ranjan didn't stop me from applying.'

'No, but he didn't warn you either that after thirteen years you would have to fend for yourself. Incidentally, why don't you have any savings? What was the financial arrangement while you were together?'

'The normal arrangement! We used to split costs.'

'Of course. But in what proportion were you splitting costs?'

'Half and half.'

'You were paying half of the actual expenditure? But Shailaja, you were just starting your career at that time. He's years older. Besides, he has so much more than you.'

'I don't think it was exactly half. He used to pay the rent and the petrol bills as well and I took care of the electricity and water bills, etc. But at times my salary wouldn't be enough, so I would ask him...'

'Shailaja, were you spending your entire salary on the home?'

'It isn't—wasn't—that much,' admitted Shailaja.

'And you think this was a normal—fair—arrangement? For you to have nothing left at the end of the month?' Dini was kicking herself for not having asked these questions earlier.

'It is so difficult to come up with a fair arrangement. You are an activist, so...' Shailaja replied.

'So everything I say is suspect? Why do you distrust activism so much?'

'Because feminist activists don't take men's feelings or situation into account. Ranjan too loves—loved me. He was quite generous while we were together. Besides, I told you, didn't I? He came here to offer me financial assistance.'

Dini was quiet for a while. 'I am glad he has a conscience and is ready to make it up to you.'

'I won't take that money.'

'Why?'

'I'm not a beggar. I wouldn't want to lose my self-respect.'

'Why would taking money that he owes you amount to begging?' Dini asked patiently.

Shailaja laughed suddenly. 'Dini, you are a fine one to preach about financial rights. You assumed all responsibility for Maithili—financial, emotional, everything. How do you explain that?'

'I chose to have the baby.'

'Kenny wanted the baby too, didn't he? You told me that he had religious scruples and was very relieved that both of you were not committing the mortal sin of abortion.'

'He had no money of his own, and I didn't want his family money. Now that he has started making some, he will definitely contribute. It'll be necessary for him to do so,' sighed Dini.

'Well, what about child rearing? He seems ready enough to do that as well. You could get yourself more of an outside life.'

Dini wondered whether RS and Shailaja had a telepathic connection, especially as what she said next could be him speaking.

'Dini, you live like a nun. I thought you had never had a relationship,' said Shailaja. 'You can look for another partner, you know. Or you could start with Kenny again, I mean, if you've forgiven him for not being there for you all these years,' she added.

■

Dini wondered what to say. She felt a strange desire to confide some more in this woman who, a while ago, had been so prostrated with grief that she could barely get out of bed. She desperately wanted a friend. Namrata and Raji were no longer on the same wavelength as her. Namrata couldn't see the problem in following RS to the village. 'Just try it out, Dini. Don't get married, by all means. Kenny is anyway ready to take over looking after Maithili.' Raji had been tight-lipped and her disapproval seemed to transmit with an added edge on the phone: 'You must do what you consider best—for Maithili and for yourself.'

'I—I am seeing someone,' Dini said to Shailaja.

'Oh my God, who? When? You are always working or you're with Maithili...'

Dini fidgeted with her scarf. This was more difficult than talking about Maithili. 'He is an activist. He works in a village in Rajasthan.'

'Oh, you mean RS. I met him once, remember? Are you in love with him?'

'Don't be silly.'

'My God! Dini, your face is red... Are you blushing?'

'You are being very, very silly. It's not like that,' Dini said.

'You mean you're not... You mean it is not sexual?'

'Uff, what kind of a question is this? We are adults.'

'Are you in love with him?' Shailaja asked again.

'I don't like this word—"love". I am suspicious of such sentimental... tosh.'

'And I've been going on about Ranjan. Did you think all that was tosh?'

'Shailaja, please, I know you are a very loyal and committed person—'

'But tosh? Really, I had no idea that this was what you thought of me,' Shailaja complained.

'Do you think it is fair to turn things around in this manner? We were talking about me. RS and me! Please!'

'What did you say is his full name?' Shailaja asked.

'Radhey Shyam.'

For some reason, both of them burst out laughing.

'Although your face resembles this tomato when you take his name,' said Shailaja picking up a slice of tomato from the salad, 'we will begin with rejecting any possibility of love between the two of you.'

Dini was feeling quite unlike herself. It was as though they had changed places. But Shailaja's face looked animated in a way it hadn't in ages. She didn't want to lose the opportunity to make her regain control.

'We have been seeing each other for almost six months and we're very compatible... But it is difficult,' Dini disclosed.

'Why, what is the problem?'

'Maithili...' Dini whispered.

'But isn't she too young to have an opinion on this?' Shailaja seemed genuinely surprised.

'No, Maithili doesn't know... RS wants—RS feels that it would be a good idea for me to shift base to the village in Banswara where he works. He is doing some amazing work and feels that I could begin working with the women there...'

'So, is he proposing a partnership?'

'Yes, he is proposing marriage,' whispered Dini, 'but I can't marry him or anyone. I have responsibilities as a mother.'

Shailaja seemed to understand as she was nodding. She suddenly said, 'I'm so jealous. I would give anything to have a lover like RS.'

Dini couldn't contradict her, but nor could she agree.

'He is waiting for you to make up your mind. He

understands your constraints,' Shailaja whispered with longing.

'Not quite,' put in Dini.

To Shailaja's questioning look, she replied, 'It is not as though he understands completely. He can't. We inhabit very different worlds. He can't appreciate my concerns fully. His family is... His mother has never been to the city, you know.'

Shailaja was looking at her spellbound. 'And you say it is not love that draws you to each other!'

'We believe in the same things. I think that is more important,' Dini asserted.

'In that case, there should be no dilemma regarding the village,' Shailaja said perversely. Her cheeks had regained colour, Dini noticed. 'Oh Dini. It would be so incredibly romantic to go away with him.'

'Shailaja, have you been to a village in Rajasthan? Life is *incredibly* difficult there.'

'But you are not the type to run away from tough situations.'

'I didn't think you would be so excited about RS and me,' Dini observed.

'Why not?'

'RS is not your kind of romantic hero, is he?'

'No, I don't think so. But he is your kind alright, Dini. You admire his work.'

'Yes, I do. But I can't do what he does.'

'It is social work, isn't it? It's trying to make things better for people who are suffering.'

'Uff, it is not so simple.'

'It can't be too complex either. After all, you came from Mumbai and did some pretty good work in a Delhi basti, didn't you? What's to stop you from learning about Rajasthan? You go there and do what you do best, which is empower women and have a roaring affair while you're at it,' Shailaja said, smiling a little.

'Really,' said Dini, laughing in spite of herself. 'Trust you to imagine a post-feminist romance in a Rajasthan village. But you didn't tell me what I should do with Maithili. Abandon her? Or make her study in a school that she would hate?'

Shailaja caught hold of her hand, 'Oh, I'm sorry. I got carried away. I didn't mean to be insensitive.'

Dini pressed her hand. 'No, you're not being insensitive.'

'But you can work out an arrangement with Kenny. You know, some sort of time-sharing…'

'Oh, I don't think… But I am feeling much better after telling you about it,' Dini whispered again. 'I am really feeling better.'

While this life-changing conversation was taking place between the two residents of top floors, it was just a usual pre-winter afternoon in the Gandhis' ground-floor flat.

Mr Gandhi was at office, Mummy-ji was taking a nap after lunch, Neeru and Teenu were at school, and Ganesh and Rajni were watching TV and eating potato chips. Mrs Gandhi was sitting in her newly renovated living room, ruminating. Diwali puja had gone off exceptionally well. They had invited Sunil's brother's family and, for the first time after years of hostility, the entire family sang the *aarti* together. Mummy-ji had wept and embraced both her daughters-in-law several times. The younger daughter-in-law hardly took her eyes off the ruby-and-diamond set that adorned Mrs Gandhi's neck and ears but did not dare say a word. Mummy-ji had been categorical about the virtues of her older *bahu* and she knew she was routed!

Mrs Gandhi felt that a new way of life had begun for her this Diwali. A woman's life begins afresh with marriage, her mother used to say. When the bride throws rice over her shoulder on leaving the parental home, she leaves behind her childhood and youth and begins a new phase of life. She wished she could tell her mother how well she had done after being reborn yet again in Buddhism. Unfortunately, her mother had passed on years ago when her daughter was still inept and unhappy. 'But she must be watching over you; she must be so proud of you,' the Buddhist fraternity had reassured her.

With a shudder, Mrs Gandhi thought of her wedding anniversary just six months ago and the mix-up around that paltry gold set and that ring with not even a one-carat diamond. She had been foolish enough to go to Dini and weep about her problems. How miserable she had felt! Besides, what would Dini know of such things? Maithi's Papa was visiting so often these days but was the family ever together? Dini avoided even looking at that Ken-ny. And this was after he had been caring enough to take Maithi out to dinner. Why did she marry him and have a baby then? How many times she had asked Dini to chant, but did she listen!

She, on the other hand, had overcome such a big challenge in her own marriage. For all practical purposes, she presided over an ideal Indian home now. That slut Reeta! May she be happy and content with her lot, Mrs Gandhi prayed automatically. She had been chanting for months for her enemy's happiness and she knew how important it was to offer Buddhist support to even the worst foe. It pays rich dividends. 'Tell her I am chanting for her; she will receive benefits. Best thing would be that she joins the practice too,' she had told Sunil. He appeared to listen; he even nodded. Little by little, Sunil started to divulge to her sympathetic ears as to how the slut wormed her way into his care and concern. Hard-luck story after story! He was much too soft-hearted, she told him, and it was inevitable that unscrupulous women would take advantage of him. She also assured him that it wasn't his business to find the funds Reeta needed. He didn't have to feel guilty if her loan from Stanchart failed to come through. Sunil would look visibly calmer after such conversations.

All marriages go through ups and downs, they had discussed at the Buddhist meeting. Victory lay in overcoming the bad period. Mrs Gandhi's next milestone was a family holiday—their very first!

'Of course you can go for a family holiday. Just chant for it. Do fifteen hours,' Navneeta had said, specifying the duration for which she must chant. 'Nothing is impossible. When you chant, you will find ways. The best way to reach your goal will appear.'

And magically, one after another, obstacles melted away. The key to this particular victory was her older daughter, with whom her relationship had improved steadily since the enshrinement.

She had already sold the idea of the family holiday to Neeru beforehand: 'We can celebrate New Year in Shimla with a family holiday. We can have a bonfire. It will be cold enough for you to wear your new Benetton coat. There might even be snow.' As she expected, Neeru went after Sunil over the pasta-and-pizza dinner they were having in the mall: 'Let's go to Shimla, Papa. Everybody in my class is going out for New Year. We never go anywhere'

'But what about Mummy-ji?' Sunil countered with a frown. 'She can't travel to Shimla with us in the cold.' Mrs Gandhi was ready with reassurance on this delicate matter: 'I have already planned the arrangements. We'll be away for just four nights, five days. Rajni will stay the night and Bahadur will come early in the morning. There will be somebody in the house all day for Mummy-ji. Neeru wants to go so much. Let's go, no!'

'But how can Mummy-ji be all alone on New Year? She will feel very left out,' Sunil objected rather belligerently. But she had prepared herself for this as well. She knew that to achieve anything, it had to be imagined fully. 'I have discussed the programme with her and she says we should go. In fact, she says she will go to your brother's place for the New Year; his wife has been begging her to spend some time with them. We will do a special Christmas celebration with Mummy-ji, Sunil. Mummy-ji can invite all her neighbourhood friends for a jagraata on Christmas Eve. Old ladies have nothing to do then as their children and families are busy with Western celebrations.'

'And we can speak to Dadi on WhatsApp on New Year, on Chacha's phone. Rajni also has WhatsApp, so you can talk to Dadi throughout the holiday if you want,' Neeru had added for good measure.

Poison was changing into medicine in front of her eyes. Mrs Gandhi resolved to share her big victory at the next big meeting which was going to be at Mrs Khosla's farmhouse. Such a lovely, big bungalow and right next to Vasant Kunj! Her only concern was how to narrate so much in the five minutes she would get to speak.

Her reverie was interrupted by the sight of two women, hand in hand, walking past the window she had got reopened during the renovation—Shailaja's idea and a very good one at that! She was out in a trice. The duo was indeed Shailaja and Dini. She hadn't met Shailaja in over a fortnight. When had these two become such close friends, Mrs Gandhi wondered.

'Hello, hello, how are both of you?' she asked. Then in the same breath noticing Shailaja's pallor, she couldn't help asking, 'You are looking a little unwell, Shailaja. Is it your time of the month again?'

'Hello, Mrs Gandhi, how are you?' Dini greeted her. 'Shailaja has been feeling out of sorts. We went out for lunch and just came back.'

'Very good idea,' replied Mrs Gandhi. 'Women should go out to enjoy themselves at least once a week. I have also joined another kitty party. We who stay at home must also let hair down, no?'

For some reason, this made Shailaja snort in merriment.

'I was thinking of coming to chant with you in the evening, Nilima-ji,' she said.

'Oh yes, you didn't come for the last meeting at my place. We will chant for good health, good fortune. You will feel better.'

'I have lost my job,' Shailaja replied.

'My God! When did this happen?'

'Last week.'

'Why didn't you call me right away? We would have chanted together and not lost so much time.'

Dini interrupted with a frown, 'Shailaja! Do you really think you can get another job by chanting?'

'No,' replied Shailaja. 'Of course,' said Mrs Gandhi at the same time.

For some reason, this made Dini laugh. Both girls were in a good mood, thought Mrs Gandhi. Shailaja had the tall man coming to see her, so obviously she was happy in spite of losing her job. Rajni had whispered that her mother said he came in a big car, but of course she couldn't ask which make the car was. She didn't want to encourage gossiping among the servants. But as far as she knew, Dini had nothing to celebrate.

'Chanting won't get me a job, but it will make me stronger,' Shailaja said, looking at Dini.

Dini actually touched Shailaja lightly on her shoulder and said, 'I approve of you getting stronger.'

Mrs Gandhi had never seen Dini act so affectionately. But wasn't Shailaja more her friend, her fellow chanter?

'Shailaja, Mummy-ji has made that *kaanji* that you liked so much. Come in and have some,' she urged, trying to reclaim her friend. 'It will also help your tummy.'

'What is kaanji?' Dini asked.

These Madrasis! They live in North India all their lives and never learn anything, Mrs Gandhi complained to herself.

'A drink made with black carrots and beetroot. It is fermented in the sun for two–three days. It becomes a lovely red colour and is pungent with mustard when it is ready,' Shailaja was explaining. 'Traditionally, it's made during Holi but nowadays, as black carrots are available all year, people make it whenever they like.'

'Yes, Mummy-ji was also saying this is not the time, but I made her do it. It tastes good now also. See for yourself. We can also chant together,' hazarded Mrs Gandhi. 'The issue of job has to do with your money karma and a lot of chanting might be required before we get results.'

Surprisingly, Dini did not refuse outright, and just gave her one of her piercing looks.

Mrs Gandhi took them into her drawing room with some ceremony and stood by for their response. Sunil had sanctioned much more money for the renovation than she dared to hope, so after taking down the wallpaper, she chose the most expensive paint job from the ones Shailaja had suggested.

The drawing room walls were now lime green with three painted panels of leaves and foliage.

'It looks like a forest,' Dini exclaimed.

Shailaja too was smiling. 'I had no idea it was done already—lots of leaves! The green is very soothing.' Shailaja had suggested one narrow panel for the room but that seemed too sketchy to Mrs Gandhi.

'Vasant Kunj is so green so I thought I must make my house match,' Mrs Gandhi said.

'Mrs Gandhi, they cut so many trees in the park right in front of your flat this time. You should have stopped them,' snapped Dini, as if on cue.

'Oh Dinshee, how could I stop them?' replied Mrs Gandhi, regretting her unthinking reference to the trees of Vasant Kunj. 'Mrs Khanna had called the association workers specially to cut that silk-cotton tree. The cotton pods give allergy to her son.'

Before Dini could start off on how it was against the law, Mrs Gandhi made her escape to the kitchen. Everybody said Dini didn't know where to draw the line. Mrs Malhotra was complaining to her that the association was being held to ransom by these NGO-type women who loved trees more than human beings: 'Once they start talking about the environment, only the Almighty can stop them. Such hypocrites! They talk as though trees are their relatives who we are murdering!'

As usual, Mummy-ji was pottering about in the kitchen.

'Should I fry some pakoras for your friends? Last time, they ate so many,' she asked.

'Oh no, Mummy-ji, they are just returning from lunch.'

'You can also go,' said the old woman magnanimously. 'There is no work during the day.'

Shailaja could have asked her to join them, especially as she had met Dini at her place for the first time, thought Mrs Gandhi as she took out her new serving tray from the cupboard and called out for Rajni.

'Rajni has gone to buy more potato chips,' Ganesh answered.

Of course Rajni had kept the tray away without cleaning the brown stains left by tea cups. Now she had to wash it. Grumbling, she poured out the kaanji in cut-glass tumblers, taking care to provide tiny forks for the pickled vegetables. She also looked high and low for paper napkins. Bahadur had tucked them deep inside the lowest drawer. Servants were more trouble than help, she complained as Mummy-ji nodded vigorously. These days she agreed with everything: 'In our time, we employed only one servant to clean the house and wash the utensils and we knew where everything was.' When Mrs Gandhi frowned, she added hastily, 'But then there were so many women in the house to do the work. You alone can't do everything and I am old!'

As Mrs Gandhi approached the drawing room, she heard her friends talking to each other. Their voices were so soft and intimate that she inadvertently started to eavesdrop.

'—before I ask him for money, I am going to chant about it,' Shailaja was saying.

'Okay, chant by all means if you like,' Dini replied.

'Dini, I know you are not a believer, but it would really help if you too chant about RS and Kenny.'

'Shailaja please, I think I can work things out myself without resorting to an ancient Japanese prayer. And I don't have to decide between RS and Kenny. It is over with Kenny; we only share Maithili now. My relationship is with RS!' Dini replied.

Mrs Gandhi drew her breath in sharply. So, Dinshee was having an extramarital affair. What about her family, her poor daughter? She always knew that this one was up to no good! But then her Buddhist training kicked in. It was not fair to blame only her; the fault is never on one side totally. Though Kenny was nice, he was hardly husband material, he was 'Chinese-looking' and played the guitar all the time! Dini was, after all, from a good South Indian Brahmin family. Her parents must have been devastated when she married him. But she is so stubborn; what could they have done? Girls realize that they should have listened to their parents only when it is too late. Hope this RS is from a decent family.

'It's good that you have such clarity,' Shailaja was saying.

'It's important to move on. You have to move on too. Closure is required with Ranjan now. You must have that conversation about the money he owes you. He has to give it to you even if he doesn't see it your way.'

Dini should have been sounding anxious and afraid. But she seemed to be instructing Shailaja in her usual know-all manner, Mrs Gandhi thought.

'Not sure what you mean, Dini. He had offered me money, though we didn't discuss amounts. But if he decides not to give it now, I can't force it out of him.'

'Shailaja, you can ask for it legally too. You lived together for thirteen years,' Dini said emphatically.

Oh my God! Was the tall man Shailaja's ex-husband? Of course she must take money from him. Dini was suggesting the sensible thing, for once. He was coming and staying nights too.

'But we weren't married! Maintenance can be claimed only if the woman is or was married to the guy,' Shailaja protested.

Mrs Gandhi could not believe her ears. Shailaja had been living with him without marriage. These girls! One worse than the other! This changed things completely. Of course he wouldn't give her a single paisa. Why would he? It was her fault to go and live with him without marriage. And now she was calling him at night. But how sneaky of Shailaja to not tell her what she had been up to.

'I am not suggesting that you file a court case right away. But you must know your rights. You were paying electricity and water bills. Those must be cheque payments. They will establish you were living together. There is a provision under PWDVA—'

'The domestic violence act? But it wasn't violence... I just told you.'

'It is cruelty to leave you with no money to call your own after thirteen years,' Dini asserted. 'But have a talk with him first. You may be right... He might be decent enough to compensate you willingly for all that you put into the relationship.'

Ha, no chance! thought Mrs Gandhi to herself. Why should he give money to a woman he didn't even marry? These girls knew nothing about the real world. It was difficult enough to make legitimate husbands spend money. Even Sunil had given her the money for renovations only because the children insisted. 'Papa, I'm ashamed to call my friends home,' Neeru had declared. 'Saurabh's mother was looking all around. She must have noticed that the wallpaper was torn.'

The conversation in her living room seemed to falter. After a while, Dini said, 'Hey, I must head home. I have to go and see what Maithili is up to. Let's go in and call Mrs Gandhi.'

Mrs Gandhi made her entrance with the tray.

'Kaanji, everyone,' she said cheerily.

As she handed the glasses around, her heart filled up with compassion. Poor, poor girls! Both were in for big trouble and they didn't even realize it.

'It's so pretty,' Dini said, holding out her glass with the deep red juice to the light.

The light was making Dini's skin glow. Why did these Madrasis put so much oil in their hair? She could look so much better with a visit to the beauty parlour. Wasn't Shailaja looking much younger with her hair dye! It is important to look young for the men. But Shailaja would only make more mistakes if she relied on Dini's crazy advice. If only these girls would include her in their lunch dates, she would tell them about the ways of the world and lead them to the path of happiness with Buddhism.

Mrs Gandhi suddenly had a vision of all three of them spending an afternoon together. At that moment, she wanted it more than anything else. They could have lunch and then go shopping. She would buy them some pretty clothes as New Year gifts. Kalpana Boutique was having a sale and they had such bright, pretty salwar-kameez sets. Not too expensive either!

'Day after is the Zadankai meeting and sharing of experiences. It is in one of the farmhouses nearby. You two come as my guests and listen to how Buddhism changes lives. I will speak for the first time in such a big meeting,' she said to them, expecting a flat refusal from Dini.

'Congratulations,' both of them said together.

'I would love to come for it, Nilima-ji,' continued Shailaja and then she turned to Dini and asked her outright. 'Will you come with me, please?'

'Really! How can you go on with this after...' Dini replied, in an irritated tone.

'Dini, we met at a Buddhist meeting. Please. I need you to be with me all the way.'

It seemed that Dini was about to refuse again, but then she thought the better of it. 'I'll come to ensure that you chant for the right thing,' she said with a little smile.

Mrs Gandhi felt a stab of envy, but she turned her attention at once to the Gohonzon to get rid of that negativity. One more potential chanter! This was another big victory for her. She resolved that she would chant for both of them. She would not give up on Dini even though she was so irritating. There must be a lot of good in this prickly character, a great deal of incipient Buddhahood.

2024, Now

It is evening and I feel that I have spent a good part of my life just writing and revising. I want a happy ending, especially as this was my stab at writing an autobiographical novel.

Of course, there is a view that all novels are autobiographical. All of them, even if one chooses to write about the man on the moon or a rabbit? But wait, for this novel I did not spring so far from myself. I am an older woman who has been called 'Aunty' by people of various ages for many years now. This novel has been brewing since the shock of that first hailing.

So, which character did I appoint as my 37–38-year-old mouthpiece, one may well ask. Shailaja, Mrs Gandhi or Dini? The answer is not altogether straightforward; there is a twist right at the beginning of my tale.

When I, a single woman of a particular age—too old to be in the conventional marriage scene, too young to be past marriage—moved into a top-floor flat in Vasant Kunj, the neighbours asked me the usual questions: 'Husband? Single? Children?' I could have answered in various ways. In the beginning, I wore my sad and taciturn mask: 'Yes, I was—am still married. No, my husband will not be staying with me. Yes, I have two sons... I am hoping they will stay with me.'

At once I earned a rejuvenating cup of tea from the ground-floor lady. She served it with Marie biscuits. She said, 'Start chanting "Nam-myoho-renge-kyo". You will get miraculous results. Happiness will come.' First frame.

In my husband's home, I was the scarlet woman, a cheating wife; in Vasant Kunj, I had transformed into a wronged woman and found sympathy. However, by the time I climbed the two flights of stairs to my flat and dialled up my friend at whose place I had hidden the children—from my husband who was refusing the divorce—I was feeling victorious. When my boyfriend came that night, we celebrated with wine and music and tandoori chicken takeaway from the Central Market. We did a little dance. I was exhilarated by the new me. I remember gasping between giggles to him, 'Had I told Mrs X that I have walked out on my husband and will be living in sin here with my boyfriend, do you think she would have made me that cup of tea?' We doubled up laughing. I was acting with abandon. I felt free, like a bird. Second frame.

The next day, I got my two sons from my friend's place and they, at once, saw the bars that I had not paid attention to up till then. *Why can't we play cricket downstairs? The neighbours never used to object at Papa's place... And you said the aunty at number 1276 is nice.* My sons were 11 and 13 then, old enough to recognize power play. Their mother had walked out of an upper-middle-class family home—of her own free will, Your Honour. She has broken her home; she cannot expect everything else to remain the same. She can't have her cake and eat it too, Your Honour. I was ridden with guilt and then I was indignant. I resolved to change the way people thought; I wanted to change the way my world behaved with women who transgressed. Third frame.

All these frames capture a different 'me'.

Of course, we are different people at different times. 'All the world's a stage,' the great bard Shakespeare had famously said. 'And all the men and women merely players; One man in his time plays many parts, His acts being seven ages.' But what did Shakespeare know about living in Vasant Kunj flats—about women who congregate in the step-well at the first hiss of the water tap? He didn't know that women in such situations do not have the scope to play one character after another sequentially. We play many parts *simultaneously*. We have to, in order to survive Vasant Kunj.

So, I have written about the women I have played, the women I brush past daily, whose voices I mimic to dissemble mine. Slowly it became unclear to me which voice was essentially mine. Vasant Kunj has reconstituted an essential me with all the women living close—too close—to each other: Shailaja, a woman alone; Mrs Gandhi, a quintessential housewife of Vasant Kunj; and Dini, who is the desire to change the world.

Writing is therapy and writing this autobiographical novel has been rewarding in that sense. My life has never appeared in a clearer single frame to me than it has now, when Shailaja, Dini and Mrs Gandhi are transitioning to their next acts. They have learned to play each other. Shailaja and Dini have become interchangeable. Shailaja is enjoying a single, independent existence in the US, and Dini is experiencing love and domesticity between Delhi and Rajasthan. And my quintessential housewife, Mrs Gandhi, is chanting herself out of drudgery into desire.

It is the desire for the other woman that brings me into focus, though momently.

And the future reveals itself.

A Saturday, Two Years after the November Unravelling

※

Dini got down at the Delhi Cantt Railway Station at five in the morning. She liked taking this train, even though it meant walking almost a kilometre to catch the Uber. The narrow road to the station would be chock-full of taxis and cars waiting to pick up passengers, and as usual, she had told the Uber driver to wait at the turning.

She slung her backpack and prepared herself for the brisk walk. She was looking forward greatly to her weekend with Maithili.

Two years ago, when she got an international grant to develop women's groups in the villages of Banswara—thanks to a recommendation by Astrid Engvig, the director of Empower—Dini was plunged into anxiety about her daughter. Maithili had refused to leave her school to study in Rajasthan, and Kenny was ferociously insistent on his right to have 'equal' time with her while opposing her plan to shift base. 'What do you mean by you are thinking of shifting to Rajasthan with Maithili! She doesn't even want to go. What if I take her to Shillong instead?' he had threatened.

It was actually Shailaja who passionately advocated 'time-share' to her with the naivety and enthusiasm of a non-parent. Dini suspected it was more to further the narrative of 'true love' she had spun around RS than from the perspective of childcare. However, that turned out to be the only possible arrangement and, surprisingly enough, it was working.

Not only did the competition with Kenny that had been driving her mad melt away, Maithili also became more tractable with just one of them in charge at a time. Moreover, her Brahminical father had taken to spending long periods in Delhi and even made friends with Kenny after learning the truth about Maithili's parentage. Kenny and he now played chess with each other.

Of course she had to put up with his 'forgiveness'. 'You made a mistake but you've suffered enough,' he would say, for some reason making her eyes well up every time. He was also waiting for her to 'forgive' Kenny and begin 'family life' at long last. It didn't bother her, but RS, who hadn't given up on asking her to marry him and make their relationship public, would protest occasionally. However, Dini steadfastly refused to tell her father about him. Her primary focus at this point was to gradually ease Maithili into an alternate lifestyle. She had taken her to Banswara three times. Last time, Maithili had done her class project on their village tourism programme and spent a lot of time discussing the practises of the village community with 'RS Uncle'. Unlike RS, Dini did not feel that these fledgling developments needed to be exposed to public scrutiny.

Dini had noticed that Maithili made it a point to not mention RS to either Kenny or her grandfather. That was good, Dini decided, signalling to the driver of her Uber that had just swung into view. It meant that Maithili was growing up and understood different kinds of lives. Her next goal was to have her spend the entire winter vacation in Banswara and get her to bond with RS's mother.

Dini was excited at the prospect of an evening with her Vasant Kunj friends. Shailaja, who was arriving from the US this afternoon, would be staying overnight at her flat and would catch the flight to Kanpur the next morning. She had got admission in the PhD programme at the Gender and Women's Studies Department of the University of Minnesota last year and was coming back to spend some time with her parents. They would have the flat to themselves as Kenny was away for a gig in Goa. That was a stroke of luck as technically this was his time with Maithili.

'Please invite Mrs Gandhi as well for dinner. I really want to meet her too,' Shailaja had requested. Mrs Gandhi was being a darling in keeping Maithili supplied with home-made cakes and other goodies. So Dini had invited her too, though she knew she would have to answer a million questions about her domestic arrangements. But there was an almost indulgent smile on her face as she thought of Mrs Gandhi.

Mrs Gandhi had successfully rebuffed her efforts at any feminist transformation. Whenever they had met, basically as a support group for Shailaja after her breakdown, Dini had felt obligated to point out the need for her to be more assertive: 'Mrs Gandhi, why can't you tell Mr Gandhi that you want to go for the office retreat with him? Why should you always go through your children or your mother-in-law?'

'But it's happening, no? That's more important! I chanted for it and it's happening. It's my victory,' she would reply stubbornly. Dini worried as to whether Mrs Gandhi thought anything rationally anymore. Her mind was always in a whirl of Buddhist activity. She talked continuously about Buddhist meetings and mysterious goals and targets. But undoubtedly she had become a more pleasant person. She was less judgemental.

'You mean Ken-ny and you will do half-half of Maithi!' she had exclaimed disapprovingly when she found out that Dini was leaving for Rajasthan, and Dini had groaned to herself fearing the kind of things she would say to Maithili in her absence. But a couple of months later, when Dini returned to Delhi for her time with her daughter, she seemed to have revised her opinion about the unconventional family arrangement. 'I met your father in the park and he was saying you are doing very important work. He said he's proud of you. If parents accept, then everything is fine,' she had declared to Dini. 'This half–half is also fine. I will chant for your family.'

Dini thought naughtily of what she would say if she told her about RS this time. Should she challenge the extent of Mrs Gandhi's faith by asking her to include her Dalit lover in her chanting?

In the taxi on the way to Vasant Kunj, Dini planned the dinner menu. It was the first time after Shailaja left that the three of them would be getting together like this. It called for celebration. She decided to attempt a tiramisu, Maithili's favourite dessert these days. She hadn't made tiramisu before, but the recipe seemed simple enough! And Rani could do a couple of their signature Palakkad dishes. Shailaja loved the *thoran* and sambhar Rani made, and Mrs Gandhi, too, liked 'South Indian'. She was bound to bring along a dish or two with her anyway. Shailaja was going to pick up wine from duty-free; she had promised. It would be quite a party.

Dini marvelled at how far Shailaja had come since her meltdown. She bit the bullet and committed herself to a life in academia. It seemed she was doing fairly well.

It hadn't been easy to convince her to ask for maintenance from Ranjan in order to be able to secure her future. Not that he made it any easier. He refused to answer her calls, and Shailaja despaired until Dini paid him a 'friendly' visit with a lawyer from an NGO that facilitated out-of-court settlement for divorcing couples.

'We weren't married, so there's no question of alimony,' Ranjan declared at once. 'You can talk to my lawyer.'

Dini had come prepared for this. 'Ranjan, I don't know how the legal process works,' she replied. 'But as legal points come up in such discussions, I brought Sheetal along. Her NGO has the top lawyers in the city on their roll.'

'Dinitia, you're with Empower, aren't you? I have heard of you from Shailaja. You can't threaten me like this,' he continued superciliously. 'I don't owe her anything. I offered her some money, but that was purely a sympathetic gesture. I know she's in a bad place, and I would have given some money to help her out. I might still do so, but she has to understand she has no claims, legal or otherwise. You people who make so much about ethics and morality should explain it to her, not abet her in extortion.'

'I won't be handling her court case, Ranjan. Empower doesn't do this,' Dini replied, trying to control her temper. What a chauvinist he was! 'I am here as her friend and an activist. We compute alimony in terms of what the woman invested in the partnership, not only the money but the hours of work too. This is the fairly straightforward ethic we subscribe to. I can mediate if you like. Shailaja is not asking for very much. But I must warn you that I'm reaching a mind-boggling figure when I do the math for thirteen years.'

Sheetal piped up, as if on cue: 'Or I can talk to your lawyer if you like, sir. The point about marriage can be settled in court.

We have photographs of both of you across a period of ten years. We have proof of the water and electricity bills she paid for your Defence Colony residence. We also have your interviews where you admit to a relationship that you say is "much deeper than a marriage". One of your recent interviews refers to the funding you've managed to get from an international producer for your next film. It's enough for us to get a good interim maintenance. The court is bound to be sympathetic to her as she has lost her job. You are anyway a known name...'

'Talk of double standards,' he had spluttered.

However, after that initial bluster, he did shell out enough for Shailaja to manage to stay on in her flat during the time it took to make her applications. He had even come to say goodbye to her at the airport. That surprised Dini and she felt a little worried when she saw Shailaja's face crumple while hugging him. Just as well that she went so far away, Dini thought. She badly needed closure on this one. She could compliment herself on facilitating it for her.

The comfortingly ugly Vasant Kunj buildings swung into view. Cutting short her reverie, Dini rushed up the stairs after paying the driver. It was still very early. She had to ring the bell several times to get Rani, who had been staying over, to come sleepily to the door. And she waited for a full half an hour before Maithili woke up and threw herself bodily on her. 'Mama-mama-mama! Why didn't you wake me up as soon as you came in! You wasted so much time,' she complained, and Dini felt some unaccustomed wetness in her eyes.

■

Dini thought her alcohol- and egg-free tiramisu looked scrumptious. Her sponge fingers ('They are called lady fingers in America,' Maithili informed her) had come out really well, and the rest of the recipe was a breeze. She had debated with herself whether to borrow some Grand Mariner from Kenny's bar and then desisted. Maithili was a child, after all. It was bad enough that they would be drinking wine in front of her.

'Mama, can I take a bite?' Maithili asked coming into the kitchen. She had been in and out throughout.

'I've made a small dish all for you. It's in the fridge,' Dini said, ruffling her hair. Maithili's ringlets needed doing. 'Wash your hair and I'll style it before dinner,' she said.

'Momma, I miss you,' Maithili said while nuzzling her.

'Will you come to Banswara this winter?' Dini asked.

'I miss you here,' Maithili replied.

'Then who will do the women groups' programmes? And all those children...' Dini said. 'I'll come in September anyway.'

'Is RS uncle your boyfriend?' she asked.

'Yes,' Dini replied.

Maithili took out the tiramisu from the fridge and started eating it quietly. 'Kenny Papa has a girlfriend too,' she said after a while.

'I know. It's okay, isn't it?' Dini asked her, her heart in her mouth.

'It's okay but not perfect, Mama,' her newly grown-up daughter replied. 'Mama, your tiramisu doesn't have that smell like the one Kenny Papa gets from the Taj. But it's really, really nice!'

'It's perfect actually,' she added in response to Dini's questioning look.

■

Shailaja had stopped dyeing her hair. But it was now coloured in different shades of pastels. She was smiling widely as Dini threw the door open.

'You look so... exotic,' Dini said to her.

'And you look... just as cussed,' Shailaja replied.

They hugged. Dini thought that Shailaja looked at peace with herself.

Her flight had been delayed but she was full of beans. She entered into an animated conversation with Maithili about American universities and her research on popular fiction. Just as she went in to freshen up, Mrs Gandhi arrived, followed by Rajni bearing a big tray covered with a tablecloth. She was smiling widely.

'I made Shailaja's favourite mutton-mince koftas. Where is she? And Mummy-ji has sent some kheer and rasgulle for Maithili and you,' she said to Dini. 'It is allowed to get non-veg in your home, no? You don't have Brahmin kitchen anymore, do you?' she asked excitedly.

Shailaja re-entered the living room and hugged Mrs Gandhi. 'How are you, Nilima-ji? I've missed all this so much. Don't worry about the non-veg. Dini is making *laal maas* in Rajasthan these days,' she added naughtily.

Dini kicked herself for having sent her pictures of RS's birthday party. WhatsApp makes one divulge too much, she was thinking.

'Shailaja, you played Holi on the flight or what?' Mrs Gandhi asked, genuinely surprised by her appearance.

Dini and Shailaja both burst out laughing at that. Shailaja went up and hugged Mrs Gandhi. 'I am teaching the foreigners Indian customs and values,' she said.

'Good, good,' said Mrs Gandhi. 'Indian values are the best in the world.'

'But not the Indian rupee,' interjected Dini.

'Let's drink to the sinking rupee,' Shailaja said, 'while I get paid in dollars!'

'You get paid for studying?' Mrs Gandhi asked. 'Sunil was saying this college-university job is best option for wo—'

'I teach too,' Shailaja replied, pouring wine in three stem glasses. 'I work very hard, Mrs Gandhi. As hard as they do in offices.'

'Oh these are drinks, no?' exclaimed Mrs Gandhi. 'I don't take.'

'Fermented grape juice,' said Dini, feeling wicked.

'Fermented—like kaanji? No alcohol is added?' Mrs Gandhi crosschecked. 'But wine is alcohol, isn't it?'

'No alcohol is *added*. The grapes are kept in huge barrels to ferment—' Shailaja was trying to explain wine-making, but Dini cut in, 'You try it and see. This wine is from France.'

'It's a Carménère from Bordeaux,' said Shailaja. 'My favourite. It's kind of rare. I was lucky to smuggle in three bottles from duty-free.'

Mrs Gandhi took a tiny sip. 'Like grape juice only,' she said, 'A little sour—fermented, no! Must be very little alcohol. Mummy-ji will say I have become too forward,' she added with another excited giggle.

'Who do you make laal maas for?' she asked, suddenly turning to Dini. 'I too have recipe.'

'For RS Uncle—and me, when I am with them,' Maithili replied. She had come into the living room to help herself to the koftas.

'Oh, RS!' exclaimed Mrs Gandhi. 'He is in Rajasthan! So that's why...'

From where had she got to know about RS? The flummoxed Dini decided to take the conversation elsewhere before Mrs Gandhi could dig further.

'Have you made a lot of friends, Shailaja?' she asked turning to her.

'Yes, a few! A couple of people in the department... And my flatmate is really nice. He's from Guyana,' Shailaja said.

'Guyana is in Africa?' Mrs Gandhi asked.

'No,' Maithili replied. 'It's in South America, Aunty.'

'Yes, but my flatmate is Afro-Guyanese,' said Shailaja.

'You living with "negro" man?' the shocked Mrs Gandhi asked.

'Aunty, you are not supposed to say that word,' Maithili said.

'Oh, what? "Negro"? Very black man, then. Same thing, no? Neeru also always telling me not to say this that. But is it safe?' she asked Shailaja. 'What will your parents say?'

'Oh Nilima-ji, he's not my boyfriend; he's become a very good friend, though. He's very sweet and helpful. Isn't everyone equal in Buddhism: black–white, Hindu–Muslim?' Shailaja explained gently to her.

She must be such a good teacher, Dini thought. Mrs Gandhi, she noticed, was turning out to be quite a drinker. She had finished her third glass before they could make it to their second. Two spots of red were standing on her cheeks and she seemed quite merry.

'Of course all are equal in Buddhism. But you must look for a good NRI, doctor or engineer, there in America and get married once for all! They make so much money there. Good you are chanting regularly, that will help,' she was saying to Shailaja. 'It is good opportunity.'

'No Nilima-ji, I'm chanting to fall in love with a really nice man—black, brown or yellow, poor or rich, I don't care,' replied Shailaja, grinning. 'Love makes all the difference, doesn't it, Dini?'

'You girls!' exclaimed Mrs Gandhi. 'Love-shove is not for us at our age.'

'There's no age for love, Nilima-ji,' Shailaja protested. 'Love sets one free of all such considerations.'

'Mama, why didn't you invite Jamila Aunty and Chhoti Didi for dinner?' Maithili asked suddenly. 'They are also in love with each other. Chhoti is Hindu,' she informed Shailaja. 'They are both gay.'

'I'm meeting them tomorrow. You want to come?' Dini asked her. She loved the way Maithili had taken to the idea of Chhoti and Jamila.

'Dini, Jamila is the woman from Nizamuddin basti, right? Where is she now?' Shailaja asked.

'In Noida. She's taken a place of her own there. She's now with this lovely girl Chhoti,' Dini said. 'Some neighbours are troubling them. I am going to put them in touch with an NGO so that they can find some support.' She was in fact quite worried about them.

'This rampant prejudice against the LGBTQ+ community is shameful,' Shailaja observed. 'I think we need more progressive legislation. I mean just repealing Article 377 is not enough. It's just the beginning of the discourse on rights for the community.'

'India is traditional, ji,' said Mrs Gandhi, who was following the conversation closely. 'Now you girls are ultra-modern. No harm in that! But 99 per cent people will not accept this kind of relationship—'

'In fact, Mrs Gandhi, in our village, we have two women living together. The opposition to them doesn't come from older people, only from some young men who have got themselves some education in the city,' Dini replied firmly.

'You girls turn everything topsy-turvy,' Mrs Gandhi said in a good-natured way. 'According to you, villages are ultra-modern and educated people like us in the cities are backward... Whatever it is, family is most important. Mother, father and children. One generation and then the next. That can't change, no? This is the way life goes forward.'

'You have all that, mother father, grandmother and children, in your home. So do you think your life is ideal—the best life—of the three of us?' Dini shot back. She hadn't meant to be aggressive but she'd had a lot of wine too.

'Dini, really!' Shailaja protested softly. 'This is not—'

But Mrs Gandhi had already started to reply, 'No, no, Dinshee. No one is better or worse. The Buddha is equal in all three of us. Three of us have... You know... We call it karmic connection in Buddhism. I come to you and you come to me, whether we like or not! This evening, Sunil had invited friends. I told him no, I go to Dinshee. Shailaja is here after so many months and we have to chant together. Maithi missing Mama always. I chanted and you came, and Shailaja and I get to meet. All karma! I told him, let Mummy-ji manage and I will make koftas before I go. He was saying this and that but I said I have to go.'

'Can't believe this... Wonderful, Nilima-ji,' both Shailaja and Dini spoke together excitedly. Mrs Gandhi looked confused.

'We have to drink to your rebellion,' Dini said.

'What rebellion-shebellion? I don't do anything like that. I do my Buddhist duty. Everyone in the home is chanting now, except Sunil. Everyone understands. He will chant too, I'm sure,' said Mrs Gandhi, gulping down her fifth glass of wine. 'This is making me feel very warm inside. Grape juice should be cooling, no?'

'You're the best, Nilima-ji,' Shailaja said.

'We really have to drink to this,' Dini repeated.

'Just one more glass and then Shailaja and I will chant. Dinshee, Maithi and you also sit with us,' said Mrs Gandhi, being assertive with a vengeance! 'I can't take too much of this juice, give only half glass. I'm not ultra-modern like both of you!' she said to Shailaja.

༺∞༻

Acknowledgements

This book has been long in the making and has made and remade a lot for me in the process. A whole lot needs to be acknowledged. Beginning at the beginning, my writer group discussants in Delhi: Manju Kapur, Janet Chawla, Lyndee Prickitt, Mala Bali, Charty Dugdale, Sonam Wangmo, Deepti Priya, Gopika Nath, Noor Anand, Seema Kohli, Megan Stack, Amy Kazmin and the late Sujatha Mathai. Wonderful women, amazing hosts, inspirations! They are the major reason I was able to keep chugging away at *Aunties*.

I wrote a large part of the book during the fall of 2017 while on a Fulbright-Nehru teaching fellowship at the Interdisciplinary Center for the Study of Global Change (ICGC), University of Minnesota, Minneapolis. My sincere thanks goes to Adam Grotsky and the Delhi Fulbright office for the opportunity to see Vasant Kunj from a distance. Warm thanks also to colleagues, students and others at Minneapolis; and to Uppinder Mehan and others at Moravian University in Bethlehem, Pennsylvania, for their generative questions following my readings of what was then work-in-progress.

Manju Kapur has been the voice of sound sense in my ears right from the time I wrote my first novel. For this one, too, her suggestions were invaluable throughout. It is not easy to find the words to thank her, especially as she would insist on the mot juste!

My endeavours to get it right were also aided by some unusually generous people, who not only gave patient answers to many random questions but also instantaneous feedback on situations, paragraphs and images that I would suddenly oppress them with: Priya Mirza, Vibha Iyer, Udyotna Kumar, Udit Khurana, Shraddha Aditya Vir Singh, Mukul Marwah, Poonam Bagai, Aditya Gautam and Partho Datta. It would have been no fun without you.

I owe a big thanks to Nidhi Dalmia and Manju for their sound advice that led me to Rupa Publications. Thanks also to Kruttika Vijay at Ira Law who facilitated this journey to publication with the greatest care and competence, making it an experience I will cherish forever. I am still touching wood that Dibakar Ghosh, charming and ever affable, even after a twelve-hour working day, is my commissioning editor. It has been a delight to work with him, and especially exhilarating to interact virtually with the creative and insightful editor, Smita Mathur. Warm thanks also to Padma Pegu for her meticulous copyediting, done against an unrealistic deadline. I have indeed been unusually fortunate.

Of course, none of the above would have been possible without Kanishka Gupta, my agent who remade so much for me with his characteristic verve! The lucky star who rose for me on the darkest night. Thanks for believing in *Aunties*, Kan, and for rekindling hope.

To conclude with my constant that makes me 'me': Sanjay Kumar and I started our second lives together in Vasant Kunj twenty-two years ago with my two sons. The centre firmly holds!